Encountering Our Freedom

By

Jamal R. Laidley

EXT Space.

Imagine flying through space and you see many Suns, planets, and stars of all shape and sized. Then you go through a black hole rapidly and end up to a green medium size planet inside a solar system with 8 other planets. Then you go through another black hole and you see another galaxy that looks like Earth but by the time your eyes focuses, you take off again into another black hole and end up in another galaxy but this time you enter a purple planet that seems to have buildings and other intelligent life forms but as soon as you start to see what they look like , you take off and head into another black hole. Then you travel through Space

Narrator

Look up into the clear night sky, What do you see? A plethora of stars actually billions of them. Each star represents a sun just like ours. Each Sun, has planets and moons just like ours. But why, do we as humans think we are the only ones alive in this vast ever increasing universe. Maybe its fear, fear of the unknown that make us think that we are the only ones out here. Or maybe, it's something more sinister. A plan of somewhat. A plan, so perfect, it made humans think that they were the only ones in the universe. Little do they know that they are among millions of intelligent beings. The only reason why, we humans think this, is out of fear. Fear of what and by whom? There is something special about humans but it's not that they are the only ones in the universe. It's because they possess a special power. This power would free the universe from enslavement. It's something so powerful and inspirational, that their jailers too scared to let free. They imprison them on this planet. It's their will power, the will to be free and explore the unknown. A special quality, that few in the universe possess and something that their jailers tried to eradicate centuries ago but we don't remember it, it's like it was erased. Well this is the story of why and how it happen.

EXT Space a massive size ships traveling fast through space comes into focus. The ship rapidly slows down and enters a solar system. It's our solar system but centuries in the past.

Enter command center of High Command Mothers Ship.

These are race of humanoid beings whose main purpose is to follow High Command orders and conquer the universe. The Commander of the ship an aged humanoid who's fought many battles for High Command for many cycles. No one but him and High Commands, main scientist Dr. Elisa has ever put eyes on the true leaders of High Command. High Command consist of three males humanoids. Whose only origin is that they were created by a being called the Master. High Command cannot remember exactly who Master is but they think that he created them to conquer the universe. In order to conquer the universe they created a clone army that would follow their orders without thinking. High Command knew that they needed a being that would lead their army across the universe while they stay safely at their home planet. They then created the Commander.

He is on his way to battle a race of aliens, The Orion's, which they conquered and enslaved many cycles ago but do to a failed experiment by Dr. Elisa, they overthrow their captures and now they have commenced war against High Command to ensure their freedom. The Commander is under orders either to subdue The Orion's or eradicate them. The Commander conditioned for war would love to just destroy them but he has to follow his orders or else. After many battles the Commander request High Command give him soldiers with intelligence. Reluctantly they created enhanced soldiers, called the Elites, and placed them under the Commander. With these enhanced Elites and basic soldiers, the Commander, went about conquering the universe.   His Mother Ship is a massive one whose wings extend into a half moon shape. The command center sticks out in the middle of the massive wings with a long haul , stretching to the middle of the sharp tips of the wings.

Commander:

Why did the FTL DRIVE stop?

Captain:

Our AI system detected an unexplored solar system and invoked an exploration scan

Commander:

What does this have to do with our mission? I have no time for this

Captain:

AI system disclosed that there are two planets in this system, that they are the perfect place to establish a hub for our interstellar missions, especially since we can no longer have access to Orion's hub. They have all the resources we need to refuel and restock for travel

Pilot 1:

Commander I can initialize mission override and take control of the ship. But I need your override code

Captain:

AI already notified High Command and orders returned that we explore this galaxy

Commander:

If High command orders us to explore then we must explore. Captains get your team of elites and take a research team to find out why AI wants us to explore

Captain:

Commander, AI also detected that there are primitive life forms on the blue planet and they have the mental capacity to learn

Commander:

I'm Tired of these primitive life forms across the universe. Do you know how many of them I've encountered in my cycles? I progressed some, wiped out a few, and watched others genocide themselves once we intervene

Captain:

Orders from High Command, Commander

Commander:

What is it?

Captain:

High Command wants us to intervene with a selected amount and build a base on the red planet and progress them

Commander:

Again!

Commander:

I hope High Command knows what they are doing. The last time we did something like this it backfired and we end up closing off a whole galaxy from travel

Captain:

these primitives don't seem to be like the ones we met on that Septus galaxy

Commander:

Captain the Orion mission needs my attention. Take your team and Research Two ship to the red planet and begin the process. I will continue on with my mission. Your one of the best and now I am promoting you to head of this mission here. This should only take someone like you 25 cycles to complete the mission. Don't let what happen to your brother, happen to you. He was a good soldier. I never can understand why he made those decisions that cost him his existence. Make sure whatever he succumbed too doesn't affect you too. I have no problem doing this same thing I did to Victor to you

Captain:

your orders will be followed

Int. Quarters of the elites and researchers. This is the Captain's selected group of soldiers. They were created with the ability to fight strategically and use their intelligence to win battles. They've spent many cycles together, fought many battles, and conquered many worlds. All they know is to follow High Commands orders and win by all means necessary. They are an experiment though. No other soldiers expect the Command and the Captain have the abilities as they do. High Command knows not to let too many of their soldiers be intelligent because they might overthrow them.

LT:

ATTENTION CAP present

Everyone stands up to salute the Caption

Cap:

Okay men

SGT:

Cap why did we stop

Captain:

Gear up. We have a mission

LT:

again, I thought we were heading back to the Orion for a little fun with them bastards.

SGT:

DO I get to get my gun off

Captain:

I SAID Gear UP DAMNIT. We don't ask questions once orders are given from High Command

LT:

I thought the reason why you recruited us for this elite team was because we asked questions. We were breed differently remember.

SGT:

yeah if you wanted the regular, you shouldn't have enhanced us

Captain:

Keep talking and not gearing up and I will have the lot of you regressed and wiped

LT:

Really Cap! Wipe. I thought that was only used that on the primitives

SGT:

AI system won't allow you to use that on us. His computations are the law out here away from High Command. AI knows that we are too valuable to the mission

Captain:

AI can always be override by the Commander. He's not afraid to do it. He's done it before, REMEMBER

LT:

I tried not to Cap. We all miss him

Captain:

too much yapping and not enough moving. We depart now. Oh yeah, there are primitives on one of the planets. Our orders are to capture, transport them to the red planet, and progress them. They will help us build a base on the red planet for resource. Once they complete their purpose, we'll regress and wipe them

LT:

SO it's just like all the other …

SGT:

typical mission. I still haven't heard about me getting my gun off. I just got this upgrade suit

Captain:

don't worry; we're still having problems in Orion. If we wrap this up quickly enough we can still get there and have some fun

SGT:

great. I'm surprised AI would take us out of the main mission for this. Why didn't he just send the regulars in?

Andi:

yeah why take us off Orion's mission for this! They don't need us here!

Captain:

it's the Commanders choice

LT:

looks like he's worried about how we're going to act after Septus.

Captain:

let's not worry about Septus. Let's get this mission done and show them that we're not affected b y that. Now roll out damnit

TROOPS:

YES SIR!

INT: Captain and he's team aboard Research Two spaceship. Heading to red planet

Captain:

LT did the environmental land

LT:

yes

Captain:

was the material teleported.

LT:

already done SIR. Took care of that as soon as we released from
MS

Captain

MS this is Research Two, we are heading towards the red planet
to conduct this first phase of our mission.

MS:

Safe travels Captain see you in 25 cycles

Captain:

yes MS and save some of those Gentras for us. This is going to
be an easy one might only take us 10 cycles

Captain:

let's get on with this mission. I'm getting tired already from
being here

Navigator:

Yes Captain

INT Research Two Ship. Hovering over blue planet. It's a beautiful planet full of blue water and green lands, mesmerizing to the Aliens.

Captain:

well, at least this planet looks better that home. Too bad we might have to destroy such a beautiful place. Let's get down there troops and carry out our mission.

LT:

Captain AI marked four locations on the planet where we could find viable candidates for progression.

Captain:

Okay LT. That means we we'll split on in four teams. LT, SGT, SI, and Don, take a landing ships and your teams to capture viable candidates. Each of you will take 100 candidates a ship. Remember, this is the first time we've encountered these primitives so we're not too sure how this will react to the serum.

LT:

hopefully its not like Orion, they are still a problem even after 200 cycles.

Captain:

We'll worry about Orion, after we finish this mission. Now that the micros are working on the base on the red planet we needs there's primitives to finish the other part. I just received a comm, from the MS and we lost our base in Orion, so we need this one here. Remember I don't need an Orion on my record

SGT:

these primitives look weak from what AI reports says.

Captain:

remember you didn't see the full report. These primitives have an off charted capacity. If we don't do the experiment right they could be worse than Orion. Another thing. High Command is sending in Elisa to conduct the program. He will arrive in 2 quarter cycles.

LT:

was that a wise call Captain, all reports point to him starting the Orion thing pushing the research to the limits. He overrides AI restrictions to see what he could discover with them.

Captain:

we have no real proof on that matter. For some strange reason AI never recorded the events that unfolded to make Orion happen

LT:

well if the Orion's and these primitives get together we're going to have a problem. Not even an army of Elites will be able to handle them

Captain:

LT sounds like you already predicting our failed mission

LT:

No Captain but with Elisa here anything can happen.

Captain:

let me worry about that, that's part. Your mission is to grab candidates and bring them back to the ship. Go and carry out your mission

Troops:

Yes Cap!

INT of Captains quarters of research Two

Captain:

Elisa it was you that made Orion happen. Victor told me he was going to stop you. He told me that day he was going to go to your lab after our communication and put an end to your experiments.

Cut too:

(Victor plane being destroyed by the Commander Mother Ship)

Then he ends up attacking the Commander and High Command. Victor I don't know what happen to you after we communicated but I will find out, when Elisa gets here. Even if I have to torture him to find out I will. You took something from me Elisa and I want my revenge. Its blood for blood here and I promise you Elisa your blood will be spilled for VICOTR. You might have brainwashed him, I'm not sure. I do know that, but shit won't work on me I won't allow it. You and your fucking experiments COST ME. High Command and AI may turn their heads when it comes to you and your research but I won't not this time. As soon as I get my chance I will find out what you DID and get my revenge

INT. Red Planet base. 8 cycles from the time The Captain left the mother ship. The beings from the blue planet are progressing rapidly. The ones recruited to build the base, with the help of the micros have almost completed the new hub. Some of them are interacting with the basics and some of the elites. They have formed friendships with each other. This is the first time it has ever happen. Elisa a natural observer, notices this and now wants to experiment on the possibilities of what can become of this friendship.

Captain:

Elisa what's taking so long with the primitives? We've been here for eight cycles, why are we not ready to leave. I planned on leaving in 10 cycles.

Elisa:

well captain you military types are always in a rush, you should know better not to rush

Captain:

don't talk to me about Military types Elisa, you know nothing about military types

Elisa:

you know nothing about what's really going on in this universe but your brother did, (with a smile on his face)

Captain:

DON'T YOU EVER MENTION him around me again or else ELISA. I don't care WHAT...

LT:

Captain, Can I talk to you outside

Captain:

what is it LT

LT:

outside Cap

Captain and LT walk outside of Elisa lab. Captain is angry and wants to hurt Elisa. Lt knows this so he's works on calming Cap down.

Captain:

WHAT IS IT LT?

LT:

Cap, you got to calm down. Elisa has too much power with High Command and the Commander. Whatever he says they do. I know you want to know what happen to Victor, Trust me Cap we all do but now isn't the time. Get yourself together before they think you were infected with the same thing that Victor was and they wipe you Cap. I cant lose you too, Cap

Captain:

your right LT, that's why we work so well as a team. I will get my answer before this mission is through

LT:

I will help you find out Cap, I need answers too. Remember we are the first ones that they allow to think on their own for the most part. We are always being watched. Especially after what Victor did

Captain:

I knew Victor and so did you. He would never attack the Commander. It's not in his programming. Elisa must have done something to make him attack High Command. I had a comm. With him right before he attacked. He told me he knew Elisa was up to something that if High Command found out they would eradicate him

LT:

Cap, why didn't you say something to High Command then

Captain:

I couldn't like you said we are an experiment and Elisa owns
High Command. Without proof we can't do anything.

LT:

Don't worry Cap we'll find proof, hey an accident might happen
in his lab you never know/ HE's always doing something
irregular in there. It might just cost him his existence.

INT Elisa Lab where he conducts the primitive experiments.
Enter Corin and Elisa. Elisa the top scientist for high command
looks out at the Red planet. Outside the window the wind
blows red dust across the vast mountains in the horizon. Elisa
looks worried but he doesn't say anything to Corin. After 8
cycles, he's found no new data to help him on his plan. Corin
his only trusted assistant goes through the data collected on the
primitives.

Elisa:

(at the desks holding a vile and a syringe in a lab coat)

Corin, what are the results on the blood test we did,

(as he looks to Corin)

Corin:

(at a massive screen moving things around on the screen with
her hands)

Lab results show that these life forms capabilities that far exceed the Orion's'

Elisa:

exactly what I thought. This is why I am here I knew we would finally find the race that the prophet talked about those thousands of cycles ago.

Corin:

Elisa this is getting very dangerous. The last time we did this, a war started and is still going on! They will eradicate us if we continue to do this..

Elisa:

This is what was prophesize about. We cannot stop now. If we stop High Command will win. They will destroy everything. There will be no freedom in the universe only terror of High Command. We must do this. The Orion experiment was a success. We placed a new enemy that High Command has to fight. They are too distracted, with the war to pay attention to us. I knew the Orion's, capabilities weren't enough to stop High Command but it would be enough to make High Command fight them. Those dictators can't leave any beings alone who might have the potential of beating them.

Corin:

ok Elisa, I am with you but you know that Captain thinks you did something to his brother. He blames you. We have to do something about that soon

Elisa:

Victor was a good person.

(Elisa looks out the window again, Flashback of Victor enraged from hearing High Command plan for the universe. His emotions are uncontrollable now. See Elisa trying to calm him down and tell him his plan but Victors too enraged. He yells at the Elisa and tells him there isn't enough time for that, we must act now. Victor tells Elisa goodbye and good luck. He runs out of the lab towards the carrier bay.)

Cut to:

Victor planes blasted by the Mother Ship.

Corin:

Elisa ... Elisa...

Elisa:

oh, I never thought he would react the way he did after learning the real truth about High Command plans.

(He turns away from the mirror and look towards Corin but we cannot let his death be for nothing)

Corin:

We should tell him the truth

Elisa:

WHO?

Corin:

The Captain

Elisa:

that's too dangerous, you saw how his brother acted. I can't afford the same incidence to happen again. We are too close in finding our answers.

Corin:

This is strange

Elisa:

what is it?

Corin:

The computer just ran a complete scan of these primitives and it shows that their genetic code is similar to us. It's 100% exactly match.

Elisa:

what do you mean exact match, let me see this data

Corin:

I'm sending it over to your screen now

Elisa:

it can't be…

Corin:

the computer ran the test twice

Elisa:

(off to the side, so Corin can't hear him)

What am I going to do now. If they are a complete match to them, How could they exist? Where did they come from? I thought they were created by the Master. Did he create two beings exactly the same but why separate us from each other. These primitives don't have the war gene like us. They just exist in little communities across this blue planet. What now? What am I going to do?

Corin:

Elisa what did you say?

Elisa:

nothing Corin

Corin:

Don't lie to me Elisa, not now. Not after these new findings, what do they mean Elisa?

Elisa:

I don't know what to think or do. I don't know what they mean Corin, I'm lost. I have to go for a walk and think

(Elisa walks out of his lab with a perplex look on his face)

EXT Red Planet

After many cycles on the Red Planet, many of the Enhanced humans and the aliens started to interact with each other. Some started physical relationships with each other.

LT:

I'm not suppose to be doing this with you

Shelia:

Why

LT:

I am a soldier and I must focus on my mission. Plus interacting with your kind is strictly forbidden. If we get caught we both can be wiped

Shelia:

Wipe, what's that...

LT:

It's what my kind does to other races that we encounter once we finish with them. We come to their planet and take whatever we want. Sometimes we use the planet for strategic purposes. If we don't need them we wipe them. Which means we either take away their memory of us or we destroy them

Shelia:

why would you do something like that

LT:

it is what we are programmed to do. It's all I've known since I was created

Shelia:

Created weren't you born like me

LT:

No they created me in the lab. They wanted the ultimate soldier, with all the technological advances of our culture and with the ability to think without AI system orders. It was an experiment

Shelia:

are all of you created

LT:

yes

Shelia:

starts to sit closer to LT,

LT:

I feel so lost right now

Shelia:

Don't be, we will find a way to figure it all out

LT:

Are you sure

Shelia:

I have a good feeling about this...

(Cuts away after Shelia kissing LT)

INT Hallway heading towards the Mess Hall. Elisa is walking towards the mess hall while thinking to himself. He seems lost. He's not paying any attention to anyone but his thoughts. He's confusion about the new information discovered, written all over his face.

Elisa:

exact match 100% but different in so many ways. There don't seek war which is the exact opposite of us. they are not as advance as us but they have the same mental capacity as us. How, how does this happen? We all thought it was the Master who created the Overlords and then they created us, but something is wrong. I don't understand this at all.

(Elisa continues to walk into the eating area, As he walks he continues to think about this new information. He looks over to everyone eating and talking, He notices all of the primitives and humanoids getting along, The Elites, the basics, and the primitives are all there eating. They are not primitives, they are us. Inspiration sets in. As Elisa glazes over the crowd a slight smile comes to his face. A light bulb goes off in his head. An idea is forming and now he must act on it.)

Elisa:

We call them primitives but we are the primitive ones. They've found a way to coexist without war but all we know is war. This is some sick experiment. It must be. Is this what the Master plan? Did he create the two races to see which one would survive. I have to find a way for them to survive, even if it cost my existence. But how do I conceal this data from High Command. If they find out they will order the immediate eradication of them. I need to get down to the blue planet as soon as possible but that damn Captain won't let me do it. It's too dangerous to fill him in. I don't know if I can trust him or not. Look at what happen when Victor found out. DAMNIT.

(Elisa leaves the mess hall and heads back to his lab in a hurry)

INT Command Center:

James:

Captain, orders in from High Command. Emergency priority one.

Captain:

send the message to my quarters now James

James:

yes Captain.

(Captain gets up and leaves the command post towards his quarters)

James:

Emergency priority one, I wonder what's so important.

JR:

Not sure but its probably not good, If Captain is taking the orders in his quarters away from us then it's serious

Jake:

I heard it's getting bad in Orion

JR:

Don't let the Captain hear you say that. I heard he was sent here because his brother attacked the commanders ship in Septus. They don't trust him and his men, on the battlefield

James:

they are the elite squad. Unbeatable in so many battles. I wondered why they were here on this basic mission

INT Hallway

Captain:

Priority one orders. Damn it's getting bad in Orion then. I should... be out there with my men. Instead I'm here, on this damn planet. I can barely step outside for more than an hour because of the thin atmosphere here. I have the guy who caused the death of my brother here and I can't do anything about it. It's time for me to get my revenge and answers. I prefer both but I will settle for just revenge.

(Enter LT who's running towards the Captain, with a look of dread in his face)

LT:

Captain, Can I talk to you?

Captain:

what is it LT

LT:

in private Cap

Captain:

I'm heading towards my quarters, to get my priority one orders from high command. Join me

LT:

PPPP Priority one Cap, maybe it can wait

Captain:

no time but now LT. you seem to have something important on your mind. You are my best soldier and comrade. Let's hear what I can do to relieve that look.

LT:

ok Cap

They both continue to walk towards the Captain's Quarters

INT Elisa ReGen Lab other side of the base

Elisa:

Now that we know we share the same biology. We can create hybrids that will be unstoppable. High Command will not be able to beat them. They will have our technology and their untapped potential. These hybrids could control things with their minds, have superior strength and many more undiscovered capabilities. We need about 5 more cycles to really tap into their potential. I need time to research our code and find ways to expand their capabilities.

Corin:

then we are going to need the Captains help. He controls what happens on this mission in regards to the military. He is one of the progressive soldiers that we gave the ability to think on their own. Plus some of his closest men seems to be attached to these enhanced ones.

Elisa:

Let me think about it. We do have to be careful now. If we tell the wrong person our whole plan is destroyed and the future is lost. I do need to get to that blue planet

Corin:

We need him Elisa, the risk outweighs the danger. We are running out of time.

(Corin heads to the back room of the lab to look over some new data collected.)

Elisa:

There must be a way to speed up this process.... Things are happening to slow. Orion might not last as long as I initially thought. They are holding strong but they need help. I need for these humans to get in the fight but even they aren't strong enough to win. The ideal plan would be a hybrid of my race and the enhanced humans. I need a way to figure out how. If I could only get on the blue planet and enhanced the the ones there but how...

(In rushes Corin with a look of shock and despair)

Corin:

ELISA ELISA we've had a break through, we've had a breakthrough

(Elisa still contemplating what he should do next at first doesn't even hear Corin entering or calling out to him)

Corin:

Elisa can you hear me are you OKAY!

Elisa:

hum what

Corin:

Wake up Elisa, we have a breakthrough

INT Captain's Quarter LT and Cap, hear the news from High Command

AI SYSTEM:

Video Message Priority One Verify your Identity

Captain:

This is Captain William Russell of the Vendasine Progrssive Regiment Space Quitrent Unit

AI System:

Identity verified. You have another in this room that does not have the necessary authorization to hear this message.

Captain:

This is my second in command LT Vincent Thorn, I authorize him

AI:

Authorization for LT received and approved by Captain William Russell

AI:

Message as followed:

HIgh Command:

(a dark and fierce voice proceeds)

Captain Russell, our battle in the Orion section is lasting longer than expected both sides are taking on heavy losses. We need you to send a regiment of reserve basics to the Orion Section. The Commander will be waiting for them in a private location.

They will receive their orders when they get near Orion. You will not send any of the progressed units. They are not needed.

AI:

END OF MESSAGE Captain

AI:

I have selected the proper regiment needed for this task and sent them their orders. They will leave red Planet base in a tenth of a cycle, Captain

Captain:

They don't need the progressive unit. They only want the basics why

(his thoughts in his head as he does not tell his LT them)

LT:

why are we held back Captain

Captain:

that does not matter, we have orders and we do not question our orders

LT:

I know that Cap, but that's when they call us in. When the basics are losing we win. What do they think a group of basics can do when they have a whole battalion over there losing. We are the best of the best but they are placing us on the sidelines. What did we do?

Captain:

It's because of Victor. Victor is the reason why the Commander left us here those cycles ago and Victor is the reason why we remain here.

LT:

but that we one situation! We done so much more for high command than any basics. Only we can win the war without so many loses.

Captain:

they don't care about loses. Especially basics, they will just create more and send them to battle. This is a message from High Command that they don't need us and that we are a liability. If we make any noise about this command they will just eradicate us and move on. Every decision that High Command makes is a precise calculations. Especially with that damn AI

INT: Mother ship in the Orion galaxy. High Command communicating with the Commander

HC:

what's the progress of the situation over there

Commander:

it's going to take more cycles than expected to complete our mission

HC:

we need this completed as soon as possible, we have the rest of the universe to destroy

Commander:

you've taken away my best soldiers from me and now want me to complete a war with only basics

HC:

They were a bad batch. They think they are the only ones. We will not need them after they complete their mission on the red planet, especially if this Orion situation continues

Commander:

does that mean we are going to eradicate them

HC:

yes, we tried a water down version of us with them and the outcome is uncontrollable

Commander:

what about Elisa

HC:

we can create another one, if needed

Commander:

how long do I have before we deem Orion unnecessary

HC:

we will leave that up to you. Our spies on the red planet report that Elisa is conducting some unregulated experiments with the primitives that might show some interesting results. We may need him to continue it until we can replicate it on our own. So you have some cycles to finish this

Commander:

what experiments? Why wasn't I informed of this

HC:

no need to worry. Elisa thinks he's doing his experiments unmonitored but the AI is always watching and reporting back to us

Commander:

can we trust him anymore. He might be the reason this Orion thing happen. We just don't have any proof of it

HC:

We have no time for uncertainties only definite. We do know that these primitives show remarkable aptitude potential that resembles our own. They might have some distant relations with us. This information requires that Elisa continue his research for the time being. These primitives shows sign of far greater potential then we have ever encountered

Commander:

with all the problems we are having with Orion, does it make sense to conduct such dangerous experiments? They might turn on us like Orion. With the data you've provided, they could be what the prophecy predicted. We might have encountered our demised. We should just eradicate them now

HC:

AI recommends Elisa continues his research and we agree with AI. You just worry about gaining back Orion. If you can not do that then we need the red planet. We don't want to cut off another section of the universe. So take care of Orion and we will handle Elisa and those primitives

AI:

Video link end

Commander:

that damn AI is ruining things. First it takes away my best soldier and now it wants us to continue research into a race that might be our demise. If it was up to me I would destroy them and move on. That's what I recommend when we first encountered these damn Orionions now look at us. I'm losing good men and time. I don't care if they can be recreated. These men have experience. The recreated don't. they just have conditioning. Let me keep my thoughts to myself before AI or high command deems me unnecessary.

INT High Command Headquarters on the other side of the galaxy on a barren planet. High Command consist of three

Overlords, who are aged humanoids. They want complete power over the universe. They care about nothing but destruction and will do anything for it to happen. No one knows where they came from or why they want destruction so much. They were cloned a long time ago by a being called the Master. The three Overlords stand around a roundtable across from each other. They are viewing the data from the war in the Orion galaxy.

Overlord 1:

what do you think about this commander

Overlord 2:

he fits his purpose for now

Overlord 3:

he follows commands to the letter. That's what he is conditioned for so I say we keep him around for now. When he expires we have backups ready to go

Overlord 1 & 2:

agreed

Overlord 1:

now what about this new race of primitives? Are they the ones who will bring about our demise?

Overlord 2:

Nothing in this universe can bring about our demise. We control this universe and will never lose that. Plus the AI says we must continue this research

Overlord 3:

brothers do you think that we rely on this AI computer too much.

Overlord 2:

I see no reason to not continue to rely on it. It's proven its functionality

Overlord 1:

I agree

Overlord 2:

So we will allow Elisa to continue his research then.

Overlord 1:

make sure AI keeps an eye on him and reports back if anything changes. We don't need a repeat of Orion

Overlord 2:

it won't happen again. If the situation in Orion continues we will invoke the Wipe Protocol and leave that section

Overlord 1:

that means we need the base on the Red Planet and those primitives or humans I want to call them to continue our plans

Overlord 2:

we don't need any of them the Orion's or these damn humans. We should just destroy them all. ALL the UNIVERSE NEEDS IS US!

Overlord 3:

calm down brothers. Our plan is working soon we will reign over this entire universe. Once we do we will come back and destroy Orion and anyone else that doesn't follow our rules

INT Red Planet Base, Dr. Elisa lab. Enter Elisa, Corin, and Shelia

Shelia:

what is happening to me Corin

Corin:

I'm running test now. The results are coming.

Elisa:

what is the holdup Corin

Corin:

It's taking longer than expected. I have to hide our research from the AI monitoring system. They increased security protocols since the Orion mishap. This is the first time something like this has happen with our race.

Shelia:

I don't feel too good Corin

Corin:

(shocked at the results)

Elisa, please come here and look at this

Elisa:

What is it

Corin:

just come here please

Elisa:

FINE

Corin:

you should be worried about this

Elisa:

WHY, this is what I've always wanted. Look at these results.
These numbers are off the charts

Corin:

I'M worried Elisa. How are we going to hide this

Elisa:

we will figure this out one way or another

Shelia:

faints

Corin:

Elisa quick hurry

(looks at Shelia)

Elisa:

oh no not now

Corin and Elisa rush over to Shelia. She has fainted on the ground. Elisa and Corin pick her up and place her on the bed. They connect a tube to her arm and run a full body scan.

(Corin hooks up the scanner to Shelia and they wait to see what the results.)

INT Captain Quarter. Enter Captain and LT. LT is worried about something. He just doesn't know how to tell Cap what's on his mInd.

LT:

I have something to tell you Cap

CAP:

what is it LT, Your never shy, what's bothering you, LT

LT:

I've messed up Cap. I don't know what to do. Something strange has happen to me since we arrived on this planet.

Cap:

Stop beating around the system, and come out and tell me what is going on soldier

LT:

I've met someone Cap and she's a primitive. She has me feeling different when I am around her. I know I'm not suppose to be feeling like this. I've tired to fight it but I can't. Now she is sick and I don't know why. She's down at Elisa's lab and they won't let me in or tell me what's going on. What should I do Cap please tell me, help me out

Cap:

you've really screwed up soldier. How am I going to fix this? What am I going to do to clean this up? You've made a real mess here. You tell me this now at this time when we have a war going on that they won't let me join. I have the person responsible for Victor's death here and I can't do anything about it and now this. You know we are not allowed to mix with primitives. If High Command finds out they will order you and her eradication.

LT:

I'm sorry Cap but please help me please

Cap:

calm down soldier, you may be my LT but you are also my friend. Let's go down to Elisa Lab and see what's going on with this primitive

LT:

her name is Shelia

Cap:

listen soldier it's those damn emotions that got you in this situation right now but in respect I will call her Shelia

INT Elisa Lab. Enter Sheba on the table lying down. Elisa and Corin are working on their computers

Shelia:

where am I? what happen to me?

Corin:

you went unconscious, Shelia but you will be alright for the most part

Shelia:

what do you mean for the most part?

Elisa:

There is a life form growing inside of you

Shelia:

what, What do you mean?

Corin:

you have a hybrid growing inside you?

Shelia:

A hybrid! Please someone tell me what's going on

Elisa:

you have a mix between your primitive race and one of us growing inside of you. It's the first of it's kind. We have to monitor this.

Corin:

We have to hide this....

(Knock Knock)

INT Outside of Elisa's Lab

Cap:

why won't this door open. AI Emergency override, open this DOOR now

AI:

you don't have the necessary authorization to open this door

Cap:

I have full authorization for everything in this base

AI:

You don't have permission to open this door Captain

Cap:

give me your light weapon

LT:

Cap are you sure

Cap:

give it to me now

LT:

okay Cap

Cap:

Elisa open this door right now or I will shoot it open

Corin:

Elisa what are we going to do now?

Elisa:

Don't worry it's locked only you and me can open it

Corin:

it's the Captain ELISA

Elisa:

now is not the time, what am I going to do

INT Hallway outside of Elisa Lab

Cap:

OPEN THIS fracken door now or I will use force, ELISA

LT:

Cap, I think you may need to calm down. AI is watching us

Cap:

I don't give a frack about the DAMN AI

Corin:

We are all going to die

Elisa:

(with a look of despair)

open the door Corin

Corin:

no not now im not going to do it I don't want to die

Elisa:

that is an order, do it NOW

Corin:

No

Elisa:

fine I will do it myself

Cap:

I am counting to a fifth cycle then....

Lab Door Opens and LT rushes in. He sees Shelia and runs
towards her. He gives her a hug and kiss and ask her if she is
okay and tells her that he was worried. The Cap walks up to
Elisa, with a look of rage in his eyes

Cap:

why am I locked out of this lab?

Elisa:

only Corin and I are authorized to be here

Cap:

I've come to set this primitive free from your crazy lab research

Elisa:

I'm not doing anything to harm this woman. Your LT has done
enough.

Cap:

what do you mean?

Corin:

it's time Elisa

Cap:

time for what, what in the stars is going on here, DAMNIT I require a response ASAP

Corin:

time to tell him the whole truth

Elisa:

(Reluctantly)

Captain maybe you want to sit down. I didn't want to tell you this because of how your brother reacted when he found out. I didn't want the same thing to happen but now you and your LT has forced my hand. I'm still not convince that you are ready

Cap:

what do you mean about Victor, What happen to Victor what did you do to him?

Elisa:

I told Victor exactly what I am about to tell you. Maybe you should take a sit

Cap:

I'll STAND

Elisa:

Suit yourself

As Elisa tells the Captain and LT, the real plans of the Overlords and why they need this red planet. Then you see flashbacks of what really happen to Victor. You see Elisa telling him about what he is doing on Orion. How in order to stop High Command plans on destroying the whole universe and only keeping a few planets around. Also they plan on destroying the progressed unit of elites which includes him and his brother. They felt that it might be a good idea to have soldiers to think in battle and have the freedom to make decisions in life. Then after creating the elites they felt it was too dangerous to have them around too long. Elites might try to overthrow them. They plan on using the elites for a few cycles and then eradicate them. Once Victor heard the real plan of High Command the look in his face change from anger towards Elisa to rage aimed at High Command.

As Elisa continues, Cap sits down confused by Elisa story.

Then Victor grabs Elisa by his shoulders and tells him we must stop this. Elisa tells Victor that he is enhancing the Orionions to a level far beyond protocols. He needed them to develop to be an enemy against High Command. An enemy this dangerous will force High Command to attack them with all their strength. Victor being a soldier first wanted to attack High Command now. Elisa tells him he's not ready for an attack now. Only 50%

of the Orionions were progressed at that time and the next 50% wouldn't be done for at least a quarter cycle. Elisa tells Victor that he needs more time to do it right. He had to conduct his experiments under the radar of High Command and AI. Victor is pissed he tells Elisa good luck and runs out of the lab. He runs toward the flight deck of his fighter jet and boards his plane. Victor takes off. The commander is requesting Victor to stand down and report to his quarters. Victor doesn't acknowledge the Commander and keeps flying.

Then the Commander tells the gunner to aim at Victor's ship and fire. Victor dodges a few shots and fires back. Victor's plane isn't strong enough to damage the Mother ship and finally you see a shot hitting Victor's ship and he is gone.

INT Elisa Lab. Elisa, Captain, Corin, LT and Shelia are all sitting in a circle in pain and worried about their future. LT and Shelia look at each other. Tears start to form around Shelia's eyes. LT moves closer and holds her hands. The Captain stands there with a blank look on his face. Elisa and Corin look at each other. Elisa then tells the group that they discovered that the beings on the blue planet are an exact match in genetic code to them. Elisa has no answers on how this happen but he tells them that if High Command finds out then they will destroy everything. Everyone who knows this information and the planets. So now we have to figure out a way of hiding it.

LT:

(as he hold Shelia hands tightly)

What are we going to do now

Elisa:

I'm not done there is something else

Cap:

what is it?

Elisa:

a new life form is growing in Shelia. It is the first of its kind and it is the answer we've been waiting for, the only problem is we must hide it from AI and High Command.

LT:

A life form?

Elisa:

it's part yours

LT:

What?

Cap:

what kind of unrestricted experiments are you conducting here ELISA. What am I going to do now? How is that even possible? Our race can only be created.

Elisa:

that's why I said it's the first time this has even happen and I had nothing to do with it. It was your LT and Shelia. I did not interfere at all. This was my plan, it was what I was trying to do on Orion but after thousands of tries it just would not work. I therefore had to find another way. I increased the Orion's ability to fight by giving them superior combat genes. I was not sure how the experiment would come out but it seems to be working

Cap:

working alright a little too good. They are giving the Commander trouble. I just had to send them a regiment of reserve basics to help the war

Elisa:

good

Cap:

besides all that, what are we going to do now. We can't hide her from AI. She can't stay in this lab forever.

Elisa:

we must come up with a plan

Cap:

I have one. We will send her to the blue planet with the rest of them

LT:

CAP NO, PLEASE

Cap:

sorry LT but it's the only way

Elisa:

we need to figure out a way to make more of these hybrids.
They are the key to finally defeating those Overlords and setting
the universe free

Cap:

that's your job, scientist, not mine. I have to figure out a way
to get her out of here.

INT Overlord base

AI:

incoming message

Overlord 1:

transmit analysis

AI:

analysis of primitives DNA reveals that they show identical
coding. Relationships cannot be determine at this moment

Overlord 2:

what does that mean, IDENTICAL

AI:

they are maybe descendants but I need additional data to make a decision

Overlord 3:

how could this be true. We were create eons ago by the ONE

Overlord 2:

AI check your data something is wrong

AI:

my data is correct additional data needs to be collected in order to make a decision. AI recommends that Dr. Elisa continues his research but focuses on this new data

Overlord1:

agree we should let Elisa continues his research on these humans as you call them brother but if the data reveals they are related to us we must destroy them

Overlord 3:

we've almost conquer the whole universe and now we come across relatives by accident. How could this be?

AI:

Their origin in unknown

Overlord 1:

i need some answers

Overlord 3:

get Elisa on the link

Overlord 2:

hold on that command AI

Overlord 3:

why

Overlord 2:

if AI found this, why didn't Elisa and if he did why didn't he report it

overlord 1:

he is right

Overlord 2:

AI what is Elisa doing

AI:

I do not have complete access to Elisa research

Overlord 1:

remember he's not one of us we gave him permission to conduct his work without us involve

Overlord 3:

he comes from one of the other primitive planets that we
conquer eons ago.

Overlord 2:

we must make sure he's not up to something now

Overlord 1:

calm down brother. He's been with us too long. Anything we
ask him he does even when we asked him to eradicate his own
people

Overlord 2:

true, I don't want anything to backfire on us. We are too close
to completion

Overlord 1:

stay calm nothing in this universe can stop us not even a distant
ancestor

Overlord 2:

well establish comm. With Elisa now AI

AI:

as you requested

Enter INT of Elisa Lab. Corin and Elisa are studying the genetic
code of the hybrid inside Shelia to see how they can mass
produce hybrids

AI:

comm. Requested from High Command Comm requested from
High Command

Corin:

Elisa its High Command, they know they know

Elisa:

calm down, don't show it on your face or they will know. They
don't know anything they have no access to my research. If
they did we would be eradicated already. AI open comm.
Channel with High Command

AI:

opening comm. Channel

Elisa:

My Lords what can I do for you

Overlord 2:

AI has report that these humans on that blue planet show signs
they are related to my race

Elisa:

I saw that data

Overlord 2:

why did you not report that

Elisa:

I wanted to further research this my Lord. I did not want to disturb you with every detail, only information pertaining to our mission

Overlord 3:

we find this very important and require further details

Elisa:

That would require me to go to the blue planet and conduct other experiments there. I need to collect more samples on the planet in order to figure out these humans origin

Overlord 2:

you have our permission to do just that. You have 3 cycles to conduct this alternative research but we want the current one to continue also. Can you handle that on your own or do we need to send in an additional team to you

Elisa:

I am fully capable of doing both my Lords

Overlord 1:

we expect no less from you

AI:

end of Comm

INT Overlord base

Overlord 2:

it seems like he is up to something

Overlord 3:

that's always how Elisa seems.

Overlord 2:

we should send in some spies

Overlord 1:

we don't need to yet. WE have enough going on in the Orion galaxy. Let us focus on that for now. The fact that they may or may not be descendants isn't enough to send additional resources to that planet when we plan on destroying it anyways once we win back Orion. We don't need two bases in the sector

INT Elisa lab on the Red Planet

Corin:

they are getting closer

Elisa:

don't worry, I allowed the AI to see that data. I knew it would report it to High Command. I knew they would want me to further my research, now I have the permission I needed to go to the blue planet but I only have 3 cycles. That's not enough

Corin:

why didn't you tell me

Elisa:

I couldn't

Corin:

one day you will fill me in on what's going on in that head of yours

Elisa:

when it's all over I promise I will, now contact the Captain we have a mission to conduct

Corin:

yes Elisa

Corin gets on the comm. and sends a message to the Captain.

Captain:

tell Elisa to meet me in my quarters

Corin:

yes, Captain.

Beat

Corin:

Elisa, the Captain said to meet him in his quarters

Elisa:

on my way

INT Captain's Quarters with Elisa and the Captain

Captain:

you know a few cycles ago I wanted to kill you, Now we're allies plotting the demise of the Lords. I swore an oath to follow and protect them, until I move on from this existence. Now look at me. My friend turned into my enemy and my enemy turned into my friend. How about a drink

Elise:

funny how things work in this crazy universe. I'm happy we are friends instead of enemies Captain. Yes I will have a drink

Captain pours Elisa and himself a drink. They sit and contemplate on how to win against High Command.

Cap:

me too.

The Captain and Elisa touch glasses.

Cap:

Now what did you want to talk about?

Elisa:

I found a way for us to get to the Blue Planet without High Command watching us

Cap:

What is it?

Elisa:

I leaked to Ai, that the primitives or humans as High Command calls them. Are somehow related to your race. Now they want me to research this further. Now you will receive orders to prepare a mission to go to the blue planet and assemble a team of basics, elites, and researchers to help me with my research. I have 3 cycles to complete it

Cap:

hum, continue

Elisa:

don't show too much happiness Cap

Cap:

I'm not, I'm a soldier, I'm here to figure out all angles to make sure nothing backfires, First everyone on this base still thinks that I hate you and blame you for Victors death. That means we must keep up that façade. Now I have to find soldiers that I personally trust. To go on this mission

Elisa:

who in your group of elites, do you really trust

Cap:

not all of them would follow me over High Command. Their conditioning is deep in the genes

Elisa:

what if I could do something about that

Cap:

I'm listening

Elisa:

I've developed a serum from the DNA of the hybrid to activate free thinking. I developed it for your race to free them from the conditioning of the Over Lords. It's still in an experimental form though.. I have not tested it yet. There's no way to know, how your race will react to it. Unless you give me some of your basics to test it on. They will follow your orders. All we have to tell them is that it is an immunization for them while they are on the blue planet.

Cap:

how dangerous is it?

Elisa:

I have no way of knowing Cap, sorry

Cap:

let me think about it. We don't need another Victor or Orion situation right now. I will find a few good soldiers maybe from my yellow regiment. How many do you need?

Elisa:

I need about five of your elites and at least a hundred of basics.

Cap:

you don't ask for a little huh. Let me see what I can do

Cap:

(The Captain reaches over to his comm. Device.)

AI summon my elites to the flight deck

AI:

message sent Captain

INT Flight Deck. Enter SGT, LT, Will, Tarbin, Neno, SI, Oska, Artis, Vincent and Andi. These elites handpicked by the Captain are his most trusted. They were directly under Victor's command and would follow him to nonexistence

Andi:

why are we here? first they won't let us have any fun in Orion. Now we're summon to the flight deck

SGT:

it better be so we can shoot something at least

Tarbin:

all you guys do is complain and shoot things

SGT:

that's why they created me to do, unless you have something else for me to do Tarbin

Tarbin:

you wish

SGT:

doesn't hurt to ask

LT:

will you two shut up this is important

SGT:

what's up with you LT, you haven't been yourself lately. I mean you've been off lately

LT:

I'M FINE. Just get ready for the Cap and stop playing around like basics

WILL:

will all of you shut up, I'm trying to read

Neno:

I like that you always are reading but what are you always reading

Artis:

at least he reads. More than I can say about you SGT

SGT:

keep talking rookie, I am still your Sergeant. I'll have you on guard duty in that awful red dust out there

AI:

Elites you are summon to Elisa regen lab

SGT:

this is bullshit, I'm no basic! Don't have me report to one place and then to another. I'm no basic. Plus I'm not comfortable going to Elisa Lab, at all

Tarbin:

oh I thought you were this rugged elite soldier. I thought nothing fears you

SGT:

when high Command gives someone complete control and doesn't monitor them then I have to worry about that. Even the Commander has AI watching every move he does

Oska:

it is a little unnerving

INT Elisa regen Lab. Enter Cap, Elisa, and Corin

Elisa:

I hope you know what you are doing

Cap:

you've left me with no choice we are running out of time and these are the only ones I trust to handle the situation

Elisa:

but…

Cap:

let's hope your serum works Elisa

Elisa:

I hope so

(Door opens to Elisa Lab the elites walk in)

LT:

Cap your soldier are here as reported

Cap:

Thank you LT, ad ease elites

SGT:

Cap what's this secrecy all about

CAP:

SGT what I am about to tell you can never leave this room and never talked about unless in a secure area. By secure I mean without monitoring of the AI. There are only a few areas in this base where that is possible. Now each of you have a choice as of right now. You can leave this room right now and no one will ever judge you. Or you can stay here and listen to what I am about to tell you. I have to warn you. Once you hear what I am about to tell you there is no turning back. You will risk eradication or being wiped by High Command. This is some real shit. This information lead to Victors nonexistence.

SGT:

I thought Victor died because of HIM

(as he looked over to Elisa)

Cap:

that's what we all thought SGT but I know now the real reason

Oska:

Victor was like a brother to me. I want to know the truth

Cap:

he was close to us all. Now who's in? If you don't want anything to do with this I understand but step out of the room NOW.

SGT:

this sounds like its going to be fun, I'm in

Neno:

Cap I'm with you until the end of times I made a promise...

Artis:

I took an oath to protect High Command and follow them without opposition but Victor was a friend and I have so few of those. Truthfully the only friends I have for the most part are in this room now. I have no one else. So if you guys go ahead and get yourself killed I will have no one else, so I'm in

(Oska looks at Tarbin they both shake their heads)

Tarbin and Oska:

We're IN Cap, We owe it to Victor

Will:

do you really have to ask, fine IM in now can I get back to my book

Andi:

They won't let me fight in Orion well then at least I'll be able to fight with my elites. Who has time to live forever

Vincent:

(Vincent a older and wiser elite stands up)

Cap you know I was in charge of this unit. We won many battles while I was in charge and I was a dedicated soldier. I remember the day Victor was created and place in my unit. Following High Command every order. I destroyed entire worlds at their will. I owe that soldier, he saved my life once and I couldn't save him that day but if you're giving me a second chance to honor him then, I'm IN

Cap:

Vincent I wasn't even going to ask you but I'm happy you me will follow me. We have much to do with little time to do it. We have to win. This may very well be our last chance too!

SI:

I'm with Vincent

Cap:

good, Elisa now fill them in from the beginning

Elisa:

OK this is High Commands mission for the universe and you

While Elisa voice over, images of events in the pass that lead them to where they are now and the Overlords go on the screen

Elisa goes over High Command. Plan to conquer the universe and destroy anything that they deem unnecessary. They want to go back to any planet that gave them any type of resistance and destroy them. How they plan on eradicating the Elites because they are a watered down version of themselves. They figured that, one day they might try to fight against them. They also plan on destroying any intelligent life in the universe. They know that if any race is intelligent as their own, one day they will be able to fight them. Now the discovery of the humans, peaked their interests. They want to know how these humans are the related to the Overlords. They always thought that they were created by the master and they were one of a kind. The Overlords now want Elisa to research their existence and how they ended up on this blue planet. That's their orders but that's not what they are going to do. Elisa tells them about the hybrid life form growing inside of Shelia and that its part LT's genes. They go over the fact that this life form is smarter, stronger, and resilient, then any other life form they have ever encountered. This life form will be able to defeat the Overlords and stop their reign over the universe. Their real mission is protecting it by all means.

Vincent

(stands up.)

I have something to say. (The group turns around and looks at Vincent)

I didn't want to say this but now I can, there is another one.

Elisa:

What do you mean another one?

Vincent:

I am in the same ship as LT, I have a little one too coming

Elisa:

this changes things. Why didn't you come to me?

Vincent:

I'm a soldier first and I know what can happen if this information comes out. Therefore, I made a decision to hide it

Cap:

Well then, I guess we have two little life forms and their mothers to protect from High Command. Anyone else have any more surprises

(The Captain looks around the lab at his troops, Corin, and Elisa. No one says anything.)

Vincent:

Now you see why I didn't say anything. I'm here on this red planet hearing that they want to destroy me because I am a failed experiment. Someone who was loyal to them. I never knew why they ordered me to do the things I did. I just did them. I came here to carry out another mission and that was my plan but now they want me gone. I will destroy them before they get a chance to end my existence or the life form inside Angie

Cap:

ok troops this is the plan. We are going to take Shelia and Angie fledglings to the blue planet. Our orders, is to establish a secret base on the blue planet and conduct our research there. That's is exactly what we are going to do. We have to find out if there is a quicker way to mass produce these hybrids like High Command does with us or do we have to wait. If we have to wait then, this is going to be a long battle. We will have to find other ways. I'm commanded to send a regiment of basics down there too. The Dr. developed an experimental serum from the genes of the hybrid to release our race from the control of High Command conditioning. I want you to help him recruit a hundred basics from the yellow regiment and send them to get the injection before they head down to the blue planet. If the serum works I will have everyone on this planet and my ship injected with it.

Neno:

how are we going to control all of these basic thinking freely? There is no way of telling how they will react to these new abilities.

Andi:

Neno's right Cap

Cap:

you have a point but we are running out of time. We have no choice

Oska:

how long does your serum take to work?

Elisa:

I've only done the experiment via computer. This will be the first time I will be able to run it live

SGT:

WHAT are you kidding me!

Elisa:

I have no sense of humor

Andi:

you guys have lost your mind.

SI:

hey I'm still in, I'm dead if it works or if it doesn't. So let's go for it

Tarbin:

I agree

Neno:

well then since you put it that way it really doesn't matter. If it works we will have an army to fight with us. If not then we will have another army to fight

Elisa:

While you are on the blue planet, you will also recruit more humans to progress.

SGT:

that's just great more of them. Anything else Cap?

Cap:

(as he looks sternly at him)

DO you have something to say SGT?

SGT:

Yeah let's say we recruit more humans and progress them right?

Cap:

yes

SGT:

then we enhance everyone else

Cap:

yes, get to it SGT

SGT:

there's one big problem I see

Cap:

I don't have time, just say it NOW

SGT:

How many cycles is it going to take for these hybrids and
enhanced to be battle ready? From what I see these hybrids are

going to take many cycles to grow and there's no telling what the effect on everyone else. This EXPERIMENTAL serum will be or how long it's going to TAKE! WE CAN'T WIN. I'm a warrior but a warrior knows when he's times up and it seems like our time is up CAP

Neno:

You're not as dumb as you look

SGT:

stop playing around don't you see it, WE... CAN'T WIN NO WAY NO HOW! WHY BOTHER

Cap:

BECAUSE WE CAN and WE HAVE TOO! We are all soldiers in this room damnit. We never give up no way no how! Andi what were our odds on Zekos

Andi:

IMPOSSIBLE CAP

Cap:

AND WE WON... Neno, what happen in Acros

Neno:

WE WON CAP

Cap:

LT, what happen in RIOS? WHAT WERE OUR ODDS?

LT:

we weren't suppose to make it out CAP

CAP:

AND WE DID

beat

I COULD go over so many more missions, battles, and wars where our odds were next to none and we made it. YOU SEE SGT, despite what the odds are we don't run and hide like some Achilles! We stand our ground and fight no matter what we DON'T GIVE UP! THAT's WHAT makes us ELITES the fact that we stand when everyone else sits, we rush in, when everyone else runs out! WE Accomplish the impossible, when everyone else throws in the gush.

(As he looks at SGT)

CAP:

SO don't tell me to give up we can't win. If you feel that way strap yourself with an E9 and walk out of this base right now. I rather you do it to yourself. I will not give you the honor of doing it myself SGT! SO WHAT'S ITS GOING TO BE SGT? Will you kill yourself?

Tarbin:

I'll do it for you Cap

Cap:

stand down Tarbin, Or will you fight with me, SGT? I prefer the latter myself

(SGT looks around at everyone's face. They are all waiting for his response. SGT takes a deep breath and looks at the Captain)

Cap:

do you need some time

SGT:

NO CAPTAIN. I Sergeant Loca Ester will stand by my CAPTAIN and his men until I reach nonexistence. I apologize to everyone here sometimes I speak without thinking

Elisa:

no your right we have a lot to do but let's not lose our faith

Neno:

I have a question?

Elisa:

what is it Neno?

Neno:

If our race and these humans are related. How are we created in a Lab and these humans seem to be breed to create without labs

Elisa:

that's one thing I want to study on the blue planet. Maybe you can help me out with that. You seem too smart to be a soldier. Given you are an elites but there's something more to you then that.

Neno:

Thank you Doc. Also why are they so different from us?

Elisa:

your species doesn't show affection possess the ability to procreate. Your conditioned to fight. That's one of the differences between the humans and you. They have no conditioning. It seems like their purpose is pure. To live.

LT:

to live

Elisa:

after monitoring them for some time now they don't seem to want fight unless its necessary. Most of them only fight when they have too. You destroy everything in your path. Maybe this was a experiment by the Master. He might have created both races. One conditioned for destruction and one for Life. That's why the hybrids are so strong, they have both sides. This is why we must leave them on the blue planet away from High Command conditioning. This way they can learn from the humans.

Cap:

they need a balance Elisa. If they only know peace how are they going to defeat High Command

SGT:

you guys sound like you don't need us anymore just the Hybrids

Tarbin:

wow SGT, are you starting up again

Andi:

I'm ashamed to say this but I'm with SGT on this one. We're the elite. We've taken on entire planets and won. So say we can't beat those old things on that horrible planet

Cap:

I appreciate the fight in you men. Hope is not lost, I'm your Captain. It's my job to think of every angle so there are no surprises

LT:

it's time Cap

Cap:

ok men grab your gear and I'll assemble the research team and the basics to go with you. Remember you have three cycles to make some progress. DISSMISSED

Cap looks at Elisa

Cap;

I hope your right

Elisa:

I've massed produced the progression serum. I will inject it to as many primitive humans as I can and let's hope it works. You know I think Overlord 2 is onto us. I know it.

Cap:

if we can't do it maybe the future ones will. I will buy you as much time as I can. I'll get LT to grab a hundred of the yellow basics to go with you. Let's hope Overlords 2 isn't onto us or this won't work

Elisa:

let me worry about the Overlords, just keep the Commander off me and I'll do my part with the Overlords

INT blue planet base. It's a base inside of a mountain. The outside of the mountain is a yellow sand ridden land. The wind blows the yellow sand across the land. No one can see the base from above. Not even High Command knows exactly where the base is. The sand blocks the AI on Research Two, from reporting to High Command the location of the base. The massive base location is perfect for Elisa and the Elites to recruit humans and progress them.

INT Elisa Lab Enter Elisa and Corbin. 1 cycle after leaving Red Planet base

Corbin:

The Captain's plan is working but we don't have enough time.
I've seen signs that the basics are starting to thinking on their
own and a majority of them have interacted with the humans.

Elisa:

It's a gift and a curse

Corbin:

I can't hide this from AI and High Command much longer. Soon
they will find out and I have no clue on how to explain this. If
High Command finds out they will destroy everything. This
hybrids are too powerful for them to control. I need the
Captain to come down here now. Corin setup a secure link with
the Captain and tell him we need to talk in person

Corin:

yes Doctor

INT Elites in the mess hall sitting at their table with most of the
basics and humans around them

Andi:

A whole cycle has passed and I don't see us getting to any
position to win

SGT:

I have to agree with Andi, we're fuck

Tarbin:

oh SGT,I thought you'll never give up

SGT:

when it comes to you, I won't

Tarbin:

well this is about...

LT:

will the two of you act accordingly, we have a mission to do.

(LT leaves to go see Shelia and Tarbin walks over to a basic)

SGT:

what is this mission again. All I see is the Doc ...

Vincent:

Shut up! We are not in a secure location. Your loose lips will cause us to fail and I'm not going to fail. If you make me think that you are a liability to this mission. I will not hesitate to get rid of you. GET IT.

Vincent slams his tray on the table then picks it up and walks away

Neno:

if you guys would just open your eyes and see what's going on, you will see the light

SGT:

see what...

Neno:

Look the basics and the humans are cohabitating with each other in massive numbers. They soon will have small hybrids and some are starting to show. The Captain's plan is working. It's our mission to protect this. We must not allow High Command or AI to find out about this. Now stop complaining about progress and see progress happening in front of your eyes.

SGT:

must be the books, that open your eyes so much. If you didn't say anything I would not even noticed

Neno:

your stuck on being a soldier. One day, there will be no need for soldiers than what will you do?

SGT:

there is always a battle to be fought

Neno:

look at Vincent even he found out that there's more to this universe. One day you will too. Even Oska has found a friend. Look at her, she's happy

SGT:

all I've known is war, but being here and opening my eyes to the universe and this blue planet I can see that there is more. I just don't know if I'm ready...

Neno:

your never know until you try just be open

SGT:

you're a good person Neno, how did you get like this

Neno:

it was Victor. He came to me right after I was created. He asked me if I was ready. All I could say was yes. He gave me a book to read and I read it. Then when I brought it back to him he said good. He asked me many questions and I answer them. Then he told me I was different. He took me under his wing and showed me the universe through his eyes. Every time I would finish a book he would give me another one. We fought a lot of battles together. I learned from him. He came to me when he found out about Elisa and High Command and asked me to do him a favor...

SGT:

what, what he came to you what did he ask you?

Neno:

he asked me to finish his mission and only tell people you can trust

SGT:

so you already knew

Neno:

yes, but I didn't know who I could trust

SGT:

Thank you

Neno:

for what

SGT:

I've earned your trust and that means a lot...

Neno:

I will do anything to complete Victor's mission even falling into nonexistence

SGT:

I will be with you until the end Neno

Neno looks at SGT, gets up and gives him a head nod, then walks aways into a dark hallway. SGT sits there looking around at everything going on in the mess hall. His eyes lock on Tarbin who's talking to a basic but notices SGT looking at her. A smile slowly starts to form on her face. SGT puts he's head down showing embarrassment but then looks up again at Tarbin with a smile on his face too. Tarbin finishes her conversation with the

basic and starts to walk into the same hallway as Neno. SGT
gets up and rushes to the same hallway after Tarbin

Continue into the INT Hallway Tarbin walking down toward her
room

SGT:

Tarbin, Tarbin hold up

Tarbin:

(with an attitude)

what is it SGT

SGT:

you know talking to Neno, made me realize that I was wrong
with the way I talked to you and my behavior towards you

Tarbin:

wow not what I was expecting to hear from you, right now

SGT:

Let me finish. I know that there is more out there in the
universe and I know how important this mission is to our future.
I just want to say I am sorry and I hope that one day, we can
leave my old ways in the past

Tarbin:

we'll see

SGT:

(with a smile)

Thank you Tarbin.

(Walks away with a smile)

Tarbin:

(stands in the middle of the hallway with a smile on her face looking up to the roof. She's not sure how she's feeling but it's a good feeling. In comes Oska, walking towards her.)

Oska:

what are you looking at and what is that weird smile on your face

Tarbin:

I'm not sure, SGT...

Oska:

oh my, what did he do this time? What did he say?

Tarbin:

no it wasn't the same SGT...

Oska:

what do you mean, not the same

Tarbin:

something changed with him, I can't explain it

Oska:

it must be this planet. It seems to have an effect on us

Tarbin:

can you explain it to me

Oska:

(with a smile)

I wish I could

They walk off together.

INT Elisa lab. Enter Elisa and Corbin

Corbin:

we're going to die aren't we Elisa

Elisa:

don't lose hope yet

Corbin:

we only have a cycle left before we have to report to High Command. What are we going to do? We don't have enough time, ELISA

(Elisa walks over to Corin and puts his hand on her shoulder.)

Elisa:

I know it looks bleak for us but we have created something here that works. We're going to fight until the end to make sure our work here continues. We might have to invoke our last resort plan but it's still too soon to even think about that. Lets wait until we talk to the Captain and see what we can do. Now lets go meet our Captain. He should be arriving soon.

INT Command center of research Two the Captains ship

Pilot:

Captain Sir

Cap:

what is it

Pilot:

AI has notified me that Dr. Elisa sent you a priority one message from the blue planet

Cap:

I have no time for Elisa. High Command just informed me, that the Commander needs an additional regiment of basic in Orion. I have no time for him and his crazy experiments

Pilot:

I understand Captain but this message is marked important

Cap:

I will take it in my quarters.

Pilot:

I will send it now

(Exit Captain from command center)

Pilot:

looks like the Captain still doesn't like the Doc

Marshall:

would you. He does these crazy experiments that no one has access too. No telling what he's doing on that planet. Probably setting it up for destruction

Pilot:

We have no comm. With the troops down there at all. I wonder what they are doing

Marshall:

it's not our business to find out what's going on. We are only allowed to know our duties on this red planet

Pilot:

you think the Captain will allow me to join the group that's going to Orion?

Marshall:

I don't know. That's the Captain decision. Now pay attention to your duties and stop asking so much questions or I will report you

Pilot:

yes sir

INT Hallway. Enter Captain

Cap:

I wonder what Elisa has to say to me. I hope it's good news. What am I going to do about the basic issue. We only have two regiments of basic left on this ship. The other, is on the blue planet with Elisa. I hope my plan with them works. It should.

For some strange reason everyone who interact with those humans, change. I can't let High Command know, if they do they will surely destroy this whole sector. Why, why do these humans have so much power over us. I need to know. Knowing will help me defeat High Command.

(Doors to Cap's quarters open. He enters and sits in front of his monitor)

Monitor:

Welcome Captain. You have a priority one message from Elisa. Please verify authorization

Captain places his hand on the Screen

Monitor:

Authorization received and verified as Captain William Russell.
Secure message

Dear Captain, This is Corin. Elisa needs to see you in person to talk about the progress of our mission. How soon can you come down here?

End of Message

Cap:

Damn, now I have to come down to that planet. Let me get the basics on their way to Orion then I will. Monitor send a reply back. I will come as soon as I can. Set priority one encryption.

Monitor:

yes Captain. Message sent

Cap:

Monitor hail the command center

Monitor:

Captain to Command center

Marshall:

yes Captain

Captain:

Order the members of the yellow regiment on the blue planet to transport ship back to my ship. Also, tell the rest of yellow regiment here to prepare for transport to the Commander's ship. . As soon as the troops from the blue planet reach here they will depart together.

Once they get here have all of them meet me on the flight deck Tell green regiment that they need to gear up to come with me to the blue planet. After yellow regiment ships out I will head to the blue planet.

Marshall:

yes Captain, your orders will be followed

Cap:

tell the Ruthledge he's up to fly this mission to meet the Commander. He better not disappoint me.

Pilot:

No Captain I won't. I will make you proud

Marshall:

yes Captain

Cap:

Captain out

Captain takes a sit on his bed holding his head. The mission is starting to take a toll on him. He doesn't know if he can beat High Command. He start to question his plan. He knows he can't show how's he's feeling to his troops. He's tried to hide it but he's on the brink of breaking. He then looks over to an image of Victor and is rejuvenated. I promise you brother I will not fail you! I will continue, where you left off. Even if, it cost me my existence. This is going to be a bloody war. Victor hopefully my backup plan works.

INT Flight Deck. Yellow regiment ready for transport

Cap:

I stand here looking at an unstoppable force. This is your moment to prove that. This is the time where you will stand up to those Orion's and destroy them. They think they can beat us. No one in the universe can. So go and show them how powerful you really are. We've lost a lot of men to this battle but that means nothing to us. We were created to fight. Not to care about whether we will see existence again. Our purpose in this universe is to follow high Command. That's the oath we took. When we were created. So go out there and fulfill your oath. Show High Command that you will not stop until the universe is under their control. No time to second guess yourself, Just do it. Just FIGHT AND WIN TROOPS MAKE ME PROUD TO HAVE WORKED YOU. NOW LOAD up into the transport ship and CONQUOR ORION

TROOPS:

YES CAPTAIN!

Yellow Regimen runs into the transport while the Captain stands there watching. He sees the ship take off and pauses while it leaves he's ship.

Cap:

ok Blue, we are heading down to the planet. I know you want to go with yellow to assist the Commander with those damn Orion's but our mission here isn't done and is as important as the Orion one. There is no doubt in my mind that we will see war soon. This blue planet is full of wonders so indulge in them as you can because soon we will fight. You will receive your orders once we reach the planet from your commanding officer. So GEAR and LOAD up, it's going to be an experience of a lifetime!

The troops board the ship. The Captain turns to the Marshal

Cap:

make sure you take care of everything on this planet while I am gone. I shouldn't be gone more than a quarter of a cycle. If anything goes wrong, contact me immediately. You understand that soldier

Marshal:

yes Captain. Don't worry I will take care of everything here while you are gone

Cap:

make sure. The base is almost done. By the time I get back make sure it is completed. I want to give High Command good news. They hear enough bad from the whole Orion Fiasco. I don't want to give them bad news over here too they might just wipe us all and start over. It's not the first time they've done that.

Marshal:

you orders will be followed to the letter CAPTAIN, as he salutes him.

The Captain salutes him back and heads inside the ship. The door closes and the ships takes off from the Red planet. To the basic inside they are heading to the blue planet, their thought are to carry out High Commands orders but the Captain thoughts is Coup d'état. The basics don't know that they are all part of his plan. The immunization that they received before leaving was an updated form of Elisa serum. It will speed up the process of freeing them.

EXT. the outside of the base which is in the desert.

The blue planet base is inside of a mountain. It's winter time in the desert. The brisk cold breeze hits up against the entrance walls of the base. The security guards outside of the base have their full body armor on while they stand guard. Soon the Captain will come to visit. The serum running through their body has taken effect. Almost all of the soldiers at the base know the true reason why they are on this planet and can't wait to see their Captain.

They've waited for almost three cycles to see him and thank him for free their minds. Some due to finally having freedom to make a choice left the base to live on the blue planet. Due to the Elisa wanting to maintain control of the base, he allowed them to leave. The Captain doesn't know this information but he soon will. No one knows how he will react to it. Many of the deserters, deserted because they have children with the humans and in fear of their death, they left. The tension level increases every day. Everyone knows High Command wants to hear results of Elisa research. Everyone wants to know what Elisa is going to do. There's a sense of relief with them, due to news that the Captain is on his way. Everyone awaits his arrive and to hear his plan. They love their new life here on the blue planet and will do anything to remain. They hate the suppressive force of High Command, and they are willing to die to protect this new freedom acquired on this planet. Unknown to everyone on the blue planet, there's a small fraction who hate being freed and wish they never knew what was really going on. They know High Command won't take them back once they find out that they now posses the ability to think on their own. Therefore, they remain quiet for now.

INT Transport ship heading towards the Blue Planet.

The Captain stays in his room thinking about what to do next. He knows a battle is approaching. It's a battle for the survival of the universe. He struggles with being a leader. He knows that it's an impossible mission but he knows he can't give up. There's too much on the line. He knows he has to remain strong especially in front of his troops. Time is running out and he still doesn't have a plan on how to defeat the Commander. There is no way of convincing the Commander to switch sides. He has spies on the Commander ship, whose sends him coded updates on the Orion mission. The Commander taken heavy loses but the Orion's are losing. They don't have enough manpower to defeat the Commander but the Commander needs reinforcements. The closest reinforcements would be the Captain's Elites but the Commander under orders not to use them. High Command is creating another army but its going to take at least ten cycles for them to be ready. He doesn't have

10 cycles. The Commander would use the wipe and close off that quadrant from travel. Once he does that he will head towards the Captain and the red planet base. No one but High Command and the Commander knows if he will wipe or continues to fight until the reinforcements come. A situation like this would cause anyone to crumble. Not the Captain, not him, he knows what's at cost if he does. He knows that if they lose to High Command then that's it. The universe will be enslaved by High Command forever. HE won't allow it. Since the Commander taken heavy loses the battle with him would be even but if he waits until his reinforcements come they have no chance on beating the full fledge force of High Commands army. No one is that powerful or at least no one they have ever encountered. He weighs his options as the transport ship thrust through space heading to the majestic beauty of the blue planet. As background of space. The blue, green, orange, brown, white, and grey colors emulating from the planet with space in the background would have even the hardest emotionless creature take a second look but the basic undergoing a transformation due to the serum are in awe. A sense of calmness takes over the ship, as it approaches. They have no clue of the life changing situation they're embarking on. This blue planet is the completely opposite of their home planet. Where mesmerizing colors shoot out from this planet only darkness comes from theirs.

Their planet is a dark place where no life can exists above ground. Everything on their planet is clone from the food to the soldiers. They know nothing about nature and the natural process of growth. If they only knew what was approaching them. the basics look on they see the wonderful blue beauty of the blue planet with it's sun radiating the dark

INT Command center of the transport ship

Pilot:

AI notify the Captain that the ship is about to land

Pilot 2:

WOW

Pilot 1:

Wow What?

Pilot 2:

Nothing, I didn't mean to say anything

Pilot 1:

Are you ok? Did you get your immunization shot before we left?

Pilot 2:

yes I am FINE! Disregard anything I said

Pilot 1:

OK

AI:

Notifying the Captain now

AI system sends a message to the Captain comm. Device. The Captains comm. Devices starts to bleep, a sharp and piercing noise, four times, while on his desk.

Captain half asleep sitting by his desk reaches for his comm.
Device

Cap:

(in a distraught manner)

YES

AI:

The ship is about to land and the pilot would like you to come to
the command center

Cap:

notify the pilot that I am on my way. Captain out

AI:

Captain is on his way Pilot

Pilot 1:

confirm AI

EXT Blue planet base

Its almost spring time on the blue planet. The desert warms up.
Animals roam around outside the base of the mountain. This is
the first time the aliens ever seen such animals. Some are as big
as their ships while others are smaller than their eyes. Amaze
by the animals sometimes you might just find then looking at
them in awe. Some animals soar across the sky like their ships
while other prowl throughout the ground.

EXT. Bay Doors of the mountain base. Enter two guards who wait outside of the main entrance awaiting the Captain and the troops to arrive.

Smith:

here's Captain's ship

Gek:

finally the heat is unbearable outside. At least the Red Planet was cooler during the day. Why couldn't we choose a base in a cooler area?

Smith:

when get a chance why don't you just ask the Captain or Elisa why they chose a base here

Gek:

no way! Have you noticed the look on Elisa face lately? He looks crazier than ever. I'm not asking him anything he might just inject me again. This time with something I really don't want.

Smith:

hush the ship is almost here open the bay doors

Gek:

there opening now

Smith:

FINALLY

As the Bay doors to the base opens, The massive amount of aliens and humans await him exiting the ship. There's something strange though all the men in the base are armed. The ship lands. First the members of the Blue Regiment come out and stand in attention waiting for the Captain to come out. As soon as the Captain comes out, Elisa walks towards him. The Captain gives Elisa a head nod. Elisa turns around and signals the Elites. When the Captain walks pass all of the Blue Regiment members, the Elites rush in fully armed and tell them to put their hands up. A look of shock goes over all of them. They look to the Captain for orders. The Captain turns around and signals them to stand down and follow the Elites commands. Once all of Blue Regiment stands down, the Captain walks over to them

Cap:

I have to apologize to you men. You came down here on orders of High Command to conduct a mission. Unfortunately, that's not what we are doing down here. Men I am here to tell you that High Command doesn't need you anymore. Due to the information that Dr. Elisa discovered, we all are liabilities. Once the data we found on this planet is sent to High Command, they will eradicate all of us and destroy this section of the universe. They can not let this information get out. The beings on this planet are US. High Command called them primitives but they are not. They have the ability to create life without the lab. Dr. Elisa and I, have maintain comm. silence with High Command to hide this information but we can no longer. Once they find out our findings they will send the Commander here to destroy us. I will not force you to fight by my side like High Command! You all have a CHOICE! But I warn you to CHOOSE WISELY! You can remain here and fight by my side or walk out those bay doors and watch the battle. Now if we don't win, the Commander will come down to this planet and destroy EVERYTHING. Once my men stand down you will have to make a choice

The Captain looks to his elites and signals them with a head nod. The Elites lower their weapons and take a step back. The bay doors open.

Cap:

now Choose

Everyone of the Blue Regiments puts their hands down and look at each other. They then look to other members inside of the base that they know and haven't spoken to in almost three cycles. Confusion sets in

SGT:

COME ON WE DON'T HAVE TIME FOR INDECISION

Cap:

(looks at SGT with anger)

STAND DOWN SGT, NOW. THEY HAVE THE SAME CHOICE AS YOU DID SOLDIER

At that moment a few members of the Blue Regiment walk over to base camp members and shake hands. Then about 5 members start to walk towards the bay door. As they walk, Vincent steps forward and speaks

Vincent:

I cannot tell you what to do soldiers but if you walk out remember you can always walk back in. It's your choice to find a reason to fight. Everyone here in this base has, I hope you will soon!

(Then one of the five, an officer turns around and looks at Vincent then he looks at the Captain)

Jack:

why should we stay and fight? You talk about choice but I don't see any choice, here. We are all going to die because of this damn mission. What's the point, why should we stay and fight with these damn primitives, for a planet that's not ours?

(Once he says that Dr. Elisa walks to the front of crowd on the right side of Cap)

Elisa:

There's more to High Command then you know and there's more to the mission then your Captain told you

Cap:

Are you sure you want to get in to all of that now

Elisa:

they deserve to know the complete truth! No More Secrets I'm tired of them now

Cap:

ok as he puts his head down and shacks it. He looks at The troops and turns to Elisa and tells him to tell them the whole story.

Elisa:

this is the whole story

As Elisa tells everyone in the bay high Commands plan and what he and Corin discovered the rest of Blue Regiment look at each other with disgust. Then fear sets in. They know that it is an impossible mission. How could they defeat the Commander? Even if they did what's going to stop High Command from sending out another army after them. They are scared

Elisa finishes telling the group the whole story and a bleak silence covers the room. Out of nowhere a young basic walks out of the Blue Regiment and turns to them.

Bran:

Why are we still here talking about this. I agree with Jack there's no choice to make!

Jack:

EXACTLY

Bran:

No Jack your right about there's no choice but you are wrong for walking out of here. We must stay here and fight. We have no choice, if we let High Command win here, then the future of the universe is gone. We are soldiers but now we get to fight for a JUST CAUSE. Captain hopefully I don't just speak for myself but we are here to assist you in this matter. If we don't we're all eradicated, at least we can die honorably.

(He turns to look at Jack)

Bran:

(as he reaches his hand out for Jack)

what do you say JACK

Jack:

I'm no Elite nor am I a grunt. I am a officer, I can't allow you to go into battle without me. Ok Bran

(as he shakes his hand)

let's do it.

(Jack walks towards the Captain.)

Cap

(as he salutes him)

I ,Jack Sves, would like to report for duty. How can I help you?

Cap:

ad ease Jack, glad to have you aboard. You're needed.

(Jack then looks over the rest of Blue Regiment standing in the middle of the bay)

Jack:

why are you still standing there? Did you come to stand around or get to work and prepare for the battle of our life time!

(The rest of Blue Regiment look at each other and nod their heads. They then proceed to look at Jack with a smile and give him a nod too. Each member simultaneously salutes the Captain)

Blue Regiment:

Captain, Blue Regiment here for Duty!

At that moment everyone smiles and rejoices. The tension, that was building up for all those cycles seem to release and a new found tenacity takes it place. They look up to the stars and a feel unstoppable.

Cap:

Well troops im not going to say this is going to be an easy battle but if we all do our parts WE CAN WIN

(That night everyone at the base rejoice and partied together. The humans, Elites, and basics all had fun with each other. They all reconnected with each other and talked about how beautiful it was on this planet and how happy they are there. Almost everyone attended the festivities but the Captain and Elisa, whom held a meeting in Elisa Lab away from everyone else. Only Corin and LT were there.)

INT Elisa Lab in the Mountain Base

Cap:

give me an update and don't leave anything out Elisa

Elisa:

should I start with the good or the bad

Cap:

give me the bad first

Elisa:

OK, We don't have enough time. I am still working on progressing the hybrids. This natural process makes it harder to manipulate then our cloning process. Even if I was to clone them I don't have the necessary equipment to do it. All I could do is play with the genes and have a natural creation.

It takes at least 18 cycles for a hybrid to grow. We have only 23 of them on base now. There are more out there on the planet

Cap:

(with a look of being lost)

what do you mean more out there on the planet.

Elisa:

I was going to get to that next. In order to maintain order on this base I had to let some of our troops leave.

Cap:

(holding his head)

how many left?

Elisa:

about a 50 of them. Some left due to their relationships with
the humans and others left because of their new found
freedom. They said they were tired of fighting.

Cap:

don't they know that if they don't fight it will be all over

Elisa:

they said they wanted to live free even for just a little time. Plus
you took a hundred of the troops and sent them to the
Commander

Cap:

(scratches his head)

OK not bad Elisa, I had to send them to the Commander

(as he places his hand on his face)

LT what are the odds of getting them back?

LT:

I don't know Cap, they are scattered all over this planet now.
DO we need them?

Cap:

we need EVERYONE. Knowing the Commander like I do he will come with everything available to him and that means we have to do the same

LT:

you don't make things easy do you?

Cap:

One day we might see easy, LT. Ok Elisa, fill me in on the rest of the information

Elisa:

Well with the Blue Regiment and the humans here we have a formable force to fight the Commander. The humans have one weakness is that they have no combat training. Your Elites started to train them these past few cycles but its not enough. They are no way near the Commander army

Cap:

what else?

Elisa:

Corin tracked back our genes and the human genes and found that someone manipulated a few genes to make you draw toward war and destruction. The human's war gene is turned off for now but....

Cap;

don't stop now but what?

Elisa:

The hybrids are a problem

Cap:

what now?... what problem?

Elisa:

some of them war gene is turned on and some are off but they all share a higher intelligence then both of our species. They have an untapped potential that I am only starting to discover.

Cap:

so some will fight and other won't

Elisa:

no that's the strange thing. They have the ability to turn it on and off at will it seems but they are too young for me to fully understand it. I don't have the necessary equipment to speed up the process. Corin is working on developing the same machine as High Command but it's taking longer than expected. We are using items here on the base to create it.

Cap:

anything I can do to help

Elisa:

no this planet has plenty of resources to use but you might have to send down a shipment of micros

Cap:

done! What else?

Elisa:

well we introduced the serum in the fluids on the Red Planet base. They should be reacting to it by now. As soon as you get back to the base, you will have more soldiers. You know the soldier...

Cap:

I know, let's move on. They will serve their purpose soon enough. Anything else?

Elisa:

Any suggestions on what I should tell High Command or should I just send them the data?

Cap:

that's your decision? As soon as they receive the data they will send the Commander here to destroy us all

Elisa:

well then I guess it doesn't matter what I send

Cap:

I give us about a full cycles after you send the information
before High Command sends him. Then it's going to take him
about a half cycle before he gets here.

LT:

That means we have a cycle and a half to prepare for war.

Cap:

yes LT. Now next task is to round up as much our soldiers who
left and get them in the FIGHT

LT:

How am I going to do that?

Cap:

you'll figure it out LT, I know you will. Elisa I need help with the
defense on the Red Planet. The Commander will go there first.
What can you do for me?

Elisa:

I'm more a genetic scientist but Corin knows a lot on weapons.
Corin...

Corin:

Yes, Elisa

Elisa:

the Captain needs your help with the defenses of the Red Planet base and his ship. You should go with him and help

Corin:

My work is here with you. I don't want to leave, not now

Elisa:

we all have to make sacrifices in time of war. Plus you're needed more there, then here

Corin:

who's going to help you with the Research

Elisa:

don't worry about that. The Captain needs to utilize your expertise.

Corin:

FINE

(Corin walks out of the lab with a look of frustration on her face)

Cap:

you should talk to her and tell her how you really feel

Elisa:

what do you mean?

Cap:

it seems like someone didn't need the serum to develop
feelings

Elisa:

I have no time for that. The universe is in danger

Cap:

ok Elisa but I hope your not blind to what's going on in front of
you. We all have choices to make, make sure you don't regret
that one. On that not I'm heading out. I head back at dark. We
make our report in a cylum, let's discuss it before

Elisa:

agree

(The Captain stands up and nods his head to Elisa, then
proceeds out of the Lab with the LT following him.)

INT Hallway of mountain base.

LT:

Cap

Cap:

yes LT

LT:

do you think we can reach out to the Orion's for help?

Cap:

hum, I see where your going with this LT. The only issues is that
how do we get to Orion without being detected by the
Commander. It's a nonexistence mission but it might be worth
it. Let's head to my quarters and fill me in on your plan

LT:

yes Cap

Little did the Captain know but this idea just popped into the LT
mind and he just said it. As they walk to through the hallway the
LT, contemplates on his plan. They arrive at Cap's quarters.

Cap:

what's your hesitation, LT

(As they walk into the room)

INT Captains Quarters

LT:

well Sir, I really don't have a plan on how to do it. I just thought
of it. I didn't even expect you to consider it.

Cap:

Never underestimate your ideas follow them. They will guide
you in your darkest hour. When the sun rises, summon the
Elites to my quarters, I'll have a plan by then. Now go spend
time with that little friend of yours

(Lt gets up and walks towards the door. He turns around and looks at the Captain)

LT:

did we make the right decision?

Cap:

we made the only decision we could make at that moment. If we had to do it over again, I'm sure we would have done the same thing. No see her and ease your mind our work had only begun

LT:

yes Cap.

LT walks out of the Captain's quarters and heads towards his own. When he gets there Shelia and their son is sleeping by on the bed together. The LT takes off his coat and shoes. He proceeds to kiss his son on his forehead and then Shelia. He lays on the other side of his son and falls asleep

INT Captain's Quarters Night

Cap:

that LT is going to be a great soldier. He has good intuition. The only way to get a ship pass the Commander is to cloak it. Then the next issue is how to we get the Orion to fight with us. Is the enemy of my enemy a friend or an enemy? It's worth the risk.

As the Captain finishes the drink he poured he falls asleep at his desk.

INT Elisa Lab Night

Elisa:

I NEED ANSWERS

Elisa starts to trash his lab. Throwing vials and dishes. He takes he stool and throws it right at window looking at out at the desert. He then falls to his knees in grief. He repeats what am I going to do, What am I going to do? What am I going to do? Over and over. He then yells out HELP! AS he screams help, the doors to the lab open and in walks Corin

Corin:

ELISA WHAT'S GOING ON HERE!

Elisa:

(cries out)

leave me, leave me I'm trouble, as he remains on his knees

Corin:

rushes over to him and gives him a hung

Elisa:

I'm NO GOOD< I'm NO GOOD

Corin:

Stop Elisa, your great

Elisa:

no I'm not. I've killed my whole race in fear of High Command. I try to tell myself that they were better off dead then be slaves to High Command. That's just me justifying my wrongful act. I took the Orion's, a peaceful race and turned them into a war ridden race. Just to create an enemy for High Command. It's my fault Victor's dead. SO much destruction in these hands. I'm a scientist, I'm suppose to create but all I do is destroy. You should stay away from me! I'll end up destroying you

Corin:

You did what you had to do. I know you Elisa, after all these cycles together, you're a good being. You and to do what you did. If you didn't the universe would be under high Command control already

Elisa:

I'm so sorry for how I treat you Corin, I really am. I'M LOST, I don't know what to do anymore

Corin:

You're not lost, your too strong of a being. I know you will be able to figure out. I believe in you Elisa.

Elisa:

your too good for me Corin

They both remain on the ground Elisa and Corin stand in front of each other. Tears run down his face. Corin takes a cloth out of her pocket and wipes the tears from Elisa eyes. They remain there for a moment looking at each other. As they look into each other eyes, they unknowingly get closer and closer, until they kiss. It's a beautiful kiss but as soon as the moment is over then both quickly stand up and brush themselves off and Elisa puts his glasses on. Corin gives Elisa his drink

Elisa:

Thank you

Corin:

sure

Together they clean up on up the lab. A few moments they glance over at each other and smile. As soon as the lab is clean, Corin leaves with a small smile on her face. As she leaves Elisa, looks at her glowing. she looks back to see Elisa smiling at her. The automatic door to the lab closes as they look at each other

INT Captain's Quarters Morning

The Captain wakes up to an empty glass and an impression of the desk on his face. He heads to sink to clean up his face. As he washes his face there's two knocks on the door

(Knock Knock)

Cap:

hold on

AS he finishes washing his face he takes a cloth to wipe off the water. As he wipes off his face he walks to his door. He pushes the button to open the door and in walks his Elites all of them

SGT:

rough night Cap?

Cap:

listen, I brought you down here to talk about a secret mission. I'm won't lie to you. You might not make it back from this one. Not only will you have to elude the Commander but also the Orion's who don't know that you are coming.

Andi:

what's the mission Cap

Cap:

I need someone to go to Orion and ask for help

Andi:

HELP, they're not going to help us plus HOW?...How are we going to get there undetected? Then How are we going to get the Orion's to help. IT'S IMPOSSIBLE!

The Captain door opens and in walks Corin, Dr. Coaxe, and Elisa. They carry a small disk with them.

Cap:

that is why I asked Elisa and Corin to come to this meeting

Elisa:

before I left Orion, I bonded with their leaders. They agreed to keep in comm. With me in order to maintain our relationships.

Even though I didn't want to do what I did to them but they asked for it and are grateful for it

Neno:

asked for what?

Elisa:

they asked me to change them into a more warrior race. They knew I mapped their genetic code. They knew I could change them and help them fight high Command. At first I was reluctant to do it because they were such a peaceful race whom only wanted tranquility. I didn't want to take that away from them

SGT:

but you did anyways, huh

Tarbin:

Stop SGT let him finish

SGT:

Sorry Elisa, please continue

Elisa:

We developed sub-space way of communicating with each other. The only issue is that we have to be at least an parcel away from each other. We are just out of reach but if you take the ship Coaxe developed here, you will be able to get there and back. This disk is the way we communicate with each other and you need our authorization code. If you don't use the code, they will know, I'm compromised and respond with force.

Cap:

Dr. Coaxe can we see the ship

Coaxe:

of course it's my prize possession. My greatest invention yet. Please follow me

The groups look at each other with confusion. Dr. Coaxe is a strange looking being with a hump and a single eye. He has two legs and a tail that he sometimes uses to help balance himself when he uses his feet and hands at the same time. He manipulated his genetic code to look this way because it helps him create things. Most don't ever talk to him due to his strange look. The group, continues down the hallway and enter a hidden elevator that no one but Elisa and Corin knew about. It's the elevator to Dr. Coaxe lab. As they enter the elevator an uncomfortable look appears on the face of the Elites. This is the first time anyone but Elisa and Corin been in Coaxe lab so a smile is on his face. As the exits the elevator into a dark ominous room, the smile on Dr. Coaxe changes to laughter

Dr. Coaxe:

don't worry everyone nothing is going to happen to you here. I've never had outsiders visit my lab before hold on I know there's a light somewhere.

Elisa:

Light on

As soon as Elisa completes his command the lights to the lab turn on. The place is a mess with parts and all types of other materials all over the place

Dr. Coaxe:

Oh yes I forgot about that command, you see I no longer need light to see. Follow me to the ship

The group look at each other and shake their heads but follow Dr. Coaxe to another room quite larger than his lab.

Dr. Coaxe:

lights on

The room lights up and you see the most beautiful crafted ship ever. A dark grey ship with a cockpit in the front and wide wings attached to the haul. The door to the ship, adjacent to the wing. Its about 25 feet long with a round shape wing sticking out of the back part. The group looks on in awe. They never expected to see something like this from a fellow looking as strange as Dr. Coaxe but it's a work of art

Dr: Coaxe:

now you see it's a beauty isn't it? It took me almost three cycles to finish it.

Neno:

you were down here the whole time? How? How did you eat?
How did you clean... oh forget that

Dr. Coaxe:

you see this new body I developed doesn't need typical
nutrients as yours. I've developed it so I would only need to eat
every cycle or so and I create my own food. You know, its
better when you do it yourself

Cap:

ok fine, but what do we have here? Give me the layout

Dr. Coaxe:

yes yes, well this ship can do 1.5 FTL speed and can cloak.

Andi:

no way this ship can do that! I mean it looks great but damn no
way!

Dr. Coaxe:

ah my young warrior, you doubt it, Maybe if we had time I
would show you what it can really do.

Cap:

ok, I'm not going to order any of you to do this mission but I do
need someone to step up

SGT:

I'll do it Cap

Cap:

do you know what I am asking of you, SGT

SGT:

yeah, you want me to fly to Orion, speak to them about us joining forces, and then come back with an army to destroy the Commander. Then we going to take the fight to High Command

Vincent:

you make it sound so easy

SGT:

(with a serious look on his face)

hey Vincent, I know what type of mission it's going to be

Vincent:

I know you do

Tarbin:

I'll go with him Cap

Oska:

WHAT

Tarbin:

I'm your best pilot and you need someone to watch over SGT, to keep him inline.

SGT:

no Tarbin, its too dangerous

Tarbin:

Cap, any objections

Cap:

NO

SGT:

Cap you can't let her do this

Cap:

it's her call, SGT

Dr. Coaxe:

well I have to train you two to fly this ship, it doesn't fly like any other.

Cap:

GREAT, you two stay here with Dr. Coaxe and learn how to fly this thing and the rest of us will head back up.

(As the rest of the group heads towards the elevator, Tarbin and SGT look at each other, then the group leaving. Dr Coaxe wraps his tail around SGT and an arm around Tarbin, he smiles)

Dr. Coaxe:

I'm so happy you guys are going to be down here with me

(Tarbin and SGT disguised by Dr. Coaxe just look up in the air and shake their heads. Dr. Coaxe walks them to a monitor and has them sit down. He then puts an helmets on the two of them)

Tarbin:

WAIT, WHATS THIS?

SGT:

HOLD ON DOC, what you are trying to do to us?

Dr. Coaxe:

well my ship doesn't fly the conventional way, as the ships you are use too. It taps into your mind and makes a connection, allowing your thoughts to fly the ship. Since thte two of you will be flying the computer must assess your compatibility, in order to determine if you two can actually carry out this mission. Now sit still this might hurt a bit

SGT:

wait what

Dr. Coaxe:

ACTIVATE

Tarbin & SGT:

NO WAIT STOP, THE EXPERIMENT

Computer:

Assessment complete, 100% compatibility

Dr. Coaxe:

GREAT, your perfect for this ship.

SGT gets up takes the helmet off and runs over to Dr. Coaxe and raises his hand in an attempt to hit him.

Tarbin:

Stand down SGT

SGT:

WHAT was that, you crazy Doc?

Dr. Coaxe:

it read your mind and thoughts to see if you posses the ability to fly the craft under any condition. Especially, during fear. As soon as you guys simultaneously, repeated the same command, the test ended. It was a positive result

Tarbin:

(as she removes a electric tack from her hand)

you could have said something Doc.

Dr. Coaxe:

then you would know what I am testing.

SGT:

ok doc what's next? And you better not plug me in to anything else!

Dr. Coaxe:

well, now it's time to plug you into the simulator

Tarbin:

What simulator

Dr. Coaxe:

what you thought I would have you fly my prize without practice. For the next few sun rises you will be down here until sunsets practicing.

(Their training takes 6 Earth days. While training Tarbin and SGT relationships improves greatly with the encouragement of Dr. Coaxe. In order to optimally, fly the ship they must be in sync. They start as soon as the sun rises and stop as the sun set. It was a draining training. These soldier are use to using their hands and feet to fly the ship but with this ship everything changed. They were mentally exhausted every day. They had to imagine the plane taking off before the plane could take off and if one second they thought of something else the plane would crash. After day four, they started to get the hang of it and started to have fun with the simulator. It amazed, Dr. Coaxe on how fast they were learning how to fly his ship. He liked these Elites, By the third day, Elisa and the Captain developed a plan on how these two would get to Orion without notice. It was dangerous but the only way)

INT Elite training room inside mountain base. Morning after the third day of training. The Captain is leaving for the Red Planet

SGT:

you want us to do WHAT?

Elisa:

with the cloaking ability of the ship, you they won't be able to detect you.

SGT:

and if they do I will have a hundred laser shooting at me. We're good but not that good flying this ship. Come on Cap, There's must be a better way

Cap:

(The Captain, looks at SGT, puts his hand on his shoulder)

Nothing, while you were training, we were up here going through many scenarios, and this is the best one.

Tarbin:

OK Cap, when do we leave

SGT:

When do we leave, you've lost it

(Tarbin hits SGT in the head harshly)

SGT:

what the....

Tarbin:

ARE YOU IN OR OUT, I'll go by myself

SGT:

NO way I'm going to let you go by yourself. I just had to get it off my chest. This is madness and you all know it

Cap:

well what else are we going to do?

SGT:

are you sure your commlink works anymore

Elisa:

the last time I used it was when I left Orion

SGT:

WHAT, that was fifty cycles ago. COME on Cap

SGT looks around the room but no one in the room feels sorry for him .

SGT:

Fine, I'll do it but I'm not going to be happy doing it

Cap:

now that you got that off... Can we move on? Let's get these ready for their mission. Dr. Coaxe, how long for the ship to be flight ready?

Dr. Coaxe:

it's ready now Captain

Cap:

Great, How long for them to be done with their training?

Dr. Coaxe:

two more sun sets

Cap:

fine at the end of the second sunset, you have a go ahead, understood?

Tarbin & SGT:

(AS they salute the Captain)

Yes Cap

Cap:

Well you two, This may or may not be the last time we see each other. By the time you get back, the battle will be on. Safe Travels

Tarbin & SGT:

Same to you Cap

Cap:

Corin, are you ready?

Corin:

yes

The Captain and Corin turn around to leave. As they walk out the door heading to the Captain's transport ship Corin turns around and runs back to Elisa and kisses him. Elisa shocked stands there at first and then kisses Corin back. As she turns around, they hold hands. As she continues through the door the hands start to separate with their fingers being the last to release from touching.

Andi:

Well then Doc, looks like you guys were doing more than just some research here, huh

Elisa:

don't you have something to do soldier or maybe you want to help me with this experiment, I'm working on

Andi:

OH no doc, I have some work to do. See you later!

Andi and the rest of the Elites walk out of Elisa lab. After they leave, Elisa sits down and looks out of his window into the desert as a big bird with massive wings fly over a tree. Seeing this puts a smile on Elisa face. He misses Corin but never really told her how he felt. He regrets it. He remains in his sit and continues to look out at the sky, while the Captain's ship exits the atmosphere. He knows that He may never see Corin again. The impeding battle confirms it.

INT Hanger bay of the mountain base.

As the Captain and Corin board the transport ship, Corin stops and looks back. This maybe the last time she will ever see her Elisa.

Cap:

He's a lucky man

Corin:

Who?

Cap:

the one your missing

Corin:

I don't miss anyone

Cap:

(with a small grind on his face)

If you say so

The bay doors of the transport ship closes and the two go to sit down in the Captain's Cabin, to discuss the defenses of the red planet and the Captain's ship hovering over it.

Cap: .

So what's your plan?

Corin:

I think we can use the same technology on Research Two shields and use it on the Red Planet base.

Cap:

Do we have enough time?

Corin:

I don't know but it's worth a try

Cap:

ok, whatever you need, just tell me

Corin:

let me go and run my calculations. After that I will tell you what
I need

Corin gets up and walks out of the Captain's Quarters. As she
walks out the Captain pours himself a drink and sits down by
the window, looking at the Blue planet get smaller as they
proceed closer to the Red Planet and Research Two.

INT High Command Base

Overlord 2:

what about the Commander

Overlord 1:

hail him now AI

AI system sends a request. The Commander deep in battle and
frustrated by the heavy loses taken by the war in Orion doesn't
want to return the comm.. to High Command

INT Commander's Mother Ship. A massive ship the size of a
small moon. The command center stick out on top of the ship.
It's rectangular shape with massive wings , eclipse most of the
Orion's moons. The ship after many cycles of battling the
Orion's, is damaged. The Commander doesn't want to stop
fighting but the ships technicians warn him that they cannot
continue fighting and may have to retreat the battle zone and
repair the ship before continuing fighting. They are deep in
battle when they receive the request from High Command

Comm Tech:

Commander

Commander:

what is it?

Comm Tech:

I received a priority one request from High Commander. They request a cycle with you in private

Commander:

in the middle of this... I have no time to discuss anything with them

Comm Tech:

I sent that in reply but they sent a message for you to make time NOW

Commander:

(with a disguise voice)

FINE, I will head to my quarters. Tell them I am on my way to talk, Damnit. Major, take control of the helm until I get back

Major:

yes Commander

The commander walks out of the control center frustrated by High Command, wanting to talk to him while he's battling the Orion's. He never thought he would be here this long. No one knew the Orion's would battle as hard as they are right now. Most troops left on the ship are exhausted from the nonstop fighting. They would welcome a retreat but they know they that they will never retreat.

INT dark hallway due to damage from battle. Sparks go off everywhere.

As the Commander walks to his quarters he contemplates on the report he will give High Command. Everything that could go wrong has. His massive ship needs repairs. He's lost hundreds of regiments and the only ones left are the Captain's Basics. He knows that High Command will eradicate him for far less. He's worried about his future for the first time since his existence.

Commander:

well this is it. Who knew these primitives had so much fight in them. I thought this would go like the others but not them. Their will to survive is strong like no other. I have to commend them. They destroyed my main gun so I have no way of just eradicating the whole planet. The only thing I have left is my wipe gun. I may have to use it and retreat. This ship needs heavy repairs, it's going to take a whole cycle to fix it.

As the Commander continues to think to himself, he enters his quarters

INT. Commanders Quarters

Commander:

AI, activate comm. Link with High Command

AI:

Activating link now, Commander

INT High Command control Center

AI:

Overlords, I have a comm. Link with the Commander

Overlord 2:

FINALLY

Overlord 3:

Commander what do you have to report?

Commander:

heavy losses in manpower and the ship. I need to retreat for at least a cycle to make sufficient repairs in order to continue this war

Overlord 2:

not what we want to hear, at least not from you COMMANDER

Commander:

not what... I wanted to report back to you SIR

Overlord 2:

What about the planet beam

Commander:

that is damage beyond repair in a battle with the Orion's. A ship crashed into it loaded with explosives. WE underestimated these primitives RESOLVE. They are defiant to the end.

Overlord 1:

what do you recommend AI

AI:

analyzing data... AI recommends, The Commander use plant erase

Overlord 3:

plant erase....

Overlord 1:

Commander, what about the planet?

Commander:

the planet needs extensive reconstruction. Most of their above ground structures are destroyed. We were unable to inflict enough damage to affect the bases below ground

Overlord 2:

Do we need to replace you?

Commander:

Masters, you've taken away my strongest warriors, best pilots and left me with only basics, to fight a formable enemy

Overlord 2:

are you saying you can't win, Commander!

Commander:

NO SIR

(while rubbing his head. A rush, of moisture appear on his head. The Commander is sweating),

I CAN WIN. I will not lose to these Orion's

Overlord 1:

we need to counsel, Commander. Wait for our decision

AI:

Commander link to High Command disconnected

The Commander sits in his seat and looks up at the ceiling. He still sweats. He has no clue on the way his masters will decide. Never has he been on the other end of the Overlords decision. Will they eradicate him or allow him to continue in their service.

INT High Command control center

Overlord 2:

that Commander is useless, we don't need him anymore

Overlord 1:

no brother we do. Our new army still needs four cycles to complete the growth process

Overlord 2:

Can't we speed up the process

Overlord !:

No... we still need him

Overlord 3:

you are correct

Overlord 2:

fine so he stays, for now but we need to do something about these Orion's

Overlord 2 & 1:

agreed

Overlord 1:

give him a cycle to repair the ship, if he cannot do it in a cycle then we'll order him to wipe the area

Overlord 2:

He should only need a half of a cycle... that's all we are going to give him

Overlord 3:

why haven't we heard from Elisa or the Captain?

Overlord 1:

their reports are over due

Overlord 2:

something's wrong, AI hail Elisa Now

AI:

yes

As the AI system sends a message to Elisa

INT Research Two ship Command Center

LT:

Cap, Cap

Cap:

what is it LT, is anything wrong down there?

LT:

I was able to recruit about 80% of the men who deserted. The rest could not be found

Cap:

good job Lt, anything else

LT:

with Dr. Coaxe help, we were able to train the humans and the basics how to fly. Dr. Elisa and Coaxe reprogrammed the micros to materials from the planet and begin construction on ships for them to fly

Cap:

good, what is Elisa up to now

LT:

ever since he reprogrammed the micros, he's stayed in his lab and will not let anyone in

Cap:

fine, keep up the good work and keep me posted on the ships

LT:

yes Cap

Cap:

James establish a commlink with Elisa and send it to my quarters

James:

yes Cap

Captain gets up and walks out of the Command Center and heads towards his quarters, he worries about Elisa and his troops. He is a wise and perspicacious man but he knows the chances of winning the battle approaching is bleak. He knows he cannot give up not now too many lives are at risk if he does. The burden of his position weights down on him. Cap has no clue what Elisa is doing on the blue planet but he knows he needs him at his best in order to win. The sinister plan of High Command needs all the good left in the universe to stop them and Elisa is the key to figuring out how to do it.

INT Cap Quarters.

Cap walks over to his commlink and hails the Command Center

Cap:

James did you reached Elisa yet

James:

No Cap still working on reaching him

Cap:

well keep trying and keep me posted. Elisa I hope you're working on something good

(Cap lays down on his bed looking up at the ceiling)

INT Elisa lab Blue Planet

AI system:

Dr. Elisa High Command requesting your audience now

Elisa sitting in front of a monitor. He's breaking down a genetic code of someone. He is surprise by the information that he finds

AI:

Elisa your audience is requested from High Command

Elisa:

(as he rubs sweat from his head)

huh... what

AI:

I have a commlink with High Command

Elisa terrified from what AI just told him doesn't answer at first. He sits in his chair lost. This is the moment he knew was coming but all the preparation he did before didn't prepare him for this moment. He wipes more sweat from his face and walks over to his commlink

Elisa:

AI put High Command through

AI:

establishing link now

INT Control Center of High Command.

AI:

Overlords I have established comm. With Dr. Elisa

Overlord 2:

FINALLY put him through

Overlord 3:

Elisa, ... what do you have to report to us

Elisa:

(nervousness starts to set in)

Masters...

Overlord 2:

you're not one to fumble around come out and tells us your findings now, slave

Elisa:

(as he wipes his head again),

My data... shows that these beings are...

(Elisa puts head down he's nervousness is quickly picked up by Overlord 2)

Overlord 2:

why are you so nervous slave?.... What aren't you telling your MASTERS

Elisa forms a fist and then pounds it on his desk. The frustration of being a slave for High Command for some many years, the destruction of his home planet, and the many lives lost due to his service, finally reached his boiling point. He breaks

Elisa:

YOU KNOW WHAT, I'M TIRED OF YOU THREE. THESE humans are the same as you are but better. They are a fledging species but one day they will be more powerful than you. I've made sure of that. IS THAT WHAT YOU WANTED TO HEAR?

Overlord 2:

SLAVE who do you think you are defying? I will make sure your
nonexistence be a painful one

Elisa:

(in a disgusting and angry voice)

Being in your service was painful enough there is nothing you
can do to me to make that pain go away. I've followed your
orders for far too long. Too long have I lived in fear, no
more...NO MORE... I will not live in fear anymore, my behavior
may cost me my existence but your IDEALOGY, will cost you,
yours.

Overlord 2:

SLAVE, I will send my whole armada to your section to destroy
you and those humans

Elisa:

I don't care, there's nothing you can do to me now

Elisa ridden with anger disconnects the link between him and
High Command. He quickly gets up from the commlink and runs
over to his computer. There was a virus program he's been
working on since Corin left, in his computer database, awaiting
him to initialize it. As he gets to the computer, he then proceeds
to load up the program. The sweat comes down from his face
faster than ever. He is anxious and nervous, as he looks at the
word execute blinking on and off on the screen. He's not too
sure what to do. He misses Corin, she's always helped him with

the major decisions but she's on the Red Planet and he doesn't have time to setup a link to her. If he is going to use the virus, he has to do it now. Elisa, takes his glasses off and looks up at the ceiling. He proceeds to close his eyes and press the button. At that instant the lights in the whole mountain base flickers on and off. The power required to process the virus is enormous. Sucking energy from everything in the base to power it. The virus passes through the AI system instantaneously, and infects it. The AI system in an attempt to fight the virus goes through a reboot. The whole base losses power and shuts down. No one in the base but Elisa, knows what's going on. Everyone panics, thinking it's an attack by the Commander.

INT Command Center of Blue Planet Base

LT:

what just happen?

DiDO:

I'm not sure LT, we just lost complete power and it seems like the AI system is down

LT:

get Elisa on the link NOW

Dido:

I can't LT our comm. Units are also down

LT:

well what's working, it this an attack

Dido:

I have no answers for you

LT:

well soldier get them and I mean now. We might be under attack and I have no eyes out there...

Dido:

I'm trying SIR,

LT:

FINE, kano, Andi, and SI, grab your gear and head to the top of the mountain through the shaft

Andi:

ARE you Serious, that shaft... no one goes up that thing. Plus it's going to take hours

LT:

WE need answers... go up there and get them. While you head there, I'm heading to Elisa lab

Andi:

How are you going to get there, this whole base is down

LT:

there's a passageway through D block, I can still access.

Andi:

OK men you heard LT, let's go to the mountain top

(While Andi and the other men leave the command center, LT
pauses for a minute thinking about his son and Shelia.)

LT:

If I don't make it, I will make sure you two do. Dido, get this
place back in order. I want answers by the time I get back

Dido:

yes LT

(LT leaves the command Center and walks down the hallway
towards a hatch which leads to a tunnel. He first starts out
walking but as his thoughts turn towards his son and Shelia he
picks up speed and starts to run to the hatch.)

INT High Command control Center

Overlord 2:

AI reestablish comm. Now with that vile slave Elisa

AI:

I no longer have the ability to communicate with Dr. Elisa

Overlord 2:

what do you mean?

AI:

there seems to be a solar flare in the area and we are cut off
from that sector until it passes

Overlord 3:

where is the Captain?

AI: locating Captain... Before the flare, the last know location of
the Captain was aboard Research two in orbit over Red Planet
base

Overlord 1:

can we establish a comm. Link with him?

AI:

No master, I am completely cut off

Overlord 2:

that little primitive, I want him destroyed now.

Overlord 1:

calm down brother, we will handle this situation

Overlord 2:

I WILL NOT CALM down. DID you hear what he said about those
damn primitives....

Overlord 3:

if what he said is right we will handle it, calm down

Overlord 2:

Clearly you two don't seem to be as concern as you should be.
He is intelligent enough to do something to prevent us from
conquering the universe

Overlord 1:

how could one being stop the ALMIGHTY THREE OVERLORDS,
no one in the universe can stop us

Overlord 3:

true brother, but we must not be too over confident

Overlord 2:

I said many cycles ago we should just destroy them all. Now our
army, sustain heavy damages in Orion and the new one still
needs more cycles to grow. We must destroy these humans
now. If it's true we are related. Then Elisa found something on
that planet that we should be concerned with

Overlord 1:

I think not. They are too regressed to be any concern to us

Overlord 2:

they might not be a concern but Elisa...

Overlord 3:

well then, what are we going to do now

Overlord 2:

I say we send the Commander to wipe out the whole sector

Overlord 3:

what about the Captain and the basics

Overlord 2:

If he cannot control Elisa, than clearly the Captain usefulness expired. Destroy them all

Overlord 3:

AI, have you establish the link yet

AI:

I am working on it, the flare seems to have damaged the links to that sector

Overlord 2:

IT's Elisa, he's done something

Overlord 1:

He may be intelligent but not even Elisa, can cause a solar flare

Overlord 3:

AI, have you figured out the issue?

AI:

NO Sir, I no longer have access to that area

Overlord 3:

we have a problem. AI, how many of our soldiers, are in that sector?

AI:

We have three regiments left in that sector

Overlord 2:

We can afford to lose that number, especially with our new army still growing

Overlord 1:

it's going to take time to get the Commander out there. His ship is still damage

Overlord 2:

I don't want to hear any excuses, I want him out there ASAP

Overlord 3:

we have to give him time to repair his ship

Overlord 2:

No we don't, it's not the Orion's he's fighting. He's fighting those rejects

Overlord 1:

Those rejects conquer worlds for us

Overlord 2:

not without the Commander. They are nothing without him.
Send him now

Overlord 3:

Fine brother… but I hope your right

Overlord 1: I

still feel that we should wait and not make a hastily decision

Overlord 2:

If the Commander can't regain control of that situation with
these primitives, then his usefulness is expired, too. That would
be the second task in a row that he's failed us.

Overlord 3:

OK, AI establish a link with the Commander and send this
message…

AI:

establishing a link now

INT Commander's Mother Ship control Center

Comm tech:

Commander…. Commander

Commander:

what is it pilot?

Comm. Tech:

orders in from High Command Sir

Commander:

well give them now

Comm Tech:

The orders are as follows:

We want you to head back to the sector Elisa is in. We want him to find Elisa and destroy the base on the Red planet and leave no beings alive. We want, the complete and otter destruction of that sector including our soldiers. Anyone and everyone must be destroyed. Don't fail us again

Commander:

Are they serious?

Comm Tech:

that's the end of the message

Commander:

Tech I'm heading to my quarters. Send a message to high Command requesting an audience for further data on this new mission

Comm Tech:

Yes Commander

The Commander, struggles from getting up from his seat due to the news of his new mission, is perplexed. He needs some clarification. This is the first time his orders require him to destroy members of his own team without a reason. The message from High Command just tells him to go there and destroy everything. He usually follows high Command, orders without hesitation but this time it's different. These soldiers over there had proven themselves to him. He's bother by his orders. He continues down the hallway of his battered ship. They've retreated to the outskirts of the Orion's galaxy, while they repair as much of the ship as possible. The commander knows his ship is in no condition to go and battle Elisa, especially if the Elites and the Captain are on the other side of the battle. He also knows he cannot tell High Command no. He's failed in the war against the Orion's. They will send him into nonexistence if he says no or that he needs more time to repair the ship. Most system functionality are below minimal requirement. He's worried but he's a soldier and worry won't help him at all, so he continues he's track through the dark and gloomy ship to speak to him command.

INT Dr. Coaxe Ship heading towards the Orion Planet

SGT:

I'm starting to think this might not be a good idea

Tarbin:

Why?

SGT:

we have yet to acquire comm. With the Orion's and now we seem to have lost comm. With Elisa and the Captain.

Tarbin:

I'm reading a solar flare in that area. It must have knocked out the comm. System in that sector

SGT:

I hope so, if not and let's say it was an attack then we are too late and this mission is worthless

Tarbin:

why are you so skeptical

SGT:

(with a smile on his face)

I'm just being real. I will have to say, if I'm going to die at least I'll die fighting with you

Tarbin looks at SGT and smiles back. Then the computer on the screen beeps three times. The are getting closer to the point where they can establish comm. With the Orion's.

SGT:

what's that beeping sound

Tarbin:

not sure let me check... looks like we are getting closer to our first stop

SGT:

I hope they are willing and able to help us

Tarbin:

let's keep our fingers cross

SGT:

well let's see if we can get a little more out of this ship and get there faster. What do you say?

Tarbin:

ok fine, but we have to be careful, we are also getting closer to the Commander, from what I can see on this ion screen

SGT:

THE COMMANDER, out here why?

Tarbin:

I am not sure but if I am reading this right then that's his ship signature signal

SGT:

(nervously)

this is not good, let's not speed up. We have no chance against him and his ship

Tarbin:

so you have learned something these past few cycles

SGT:

you know I am a sergeant

Tarbin:

(with a cute smile)

I thought they may have made a mistake when that happens

SGT:

One cycle, One Cycle I swear

Tarbin:

you swear what?

SGT:

nothing...but one day you will

INT Research two control center

James:

Cap, that solar flare hit out our commlink. We cannot communicate with Either planet bases

Cap:

can you fix it

James:

I think so, but the funny thing is that I didn't feel a solar flare or can trace one back to this sun.

Cap:

What are you saying James

James:

I don't know Captain. One minute the ion screen is blank then the next we just experienced a flare but only our Communication systems were effected

Cap:

(holding his head with his left hand)

I need some answers James. How long do you think before we can reestablish communications with the bases. I need to talk to Elisa now,

James:

I don't know Cap but Kisko and I won't stop working on it until we get it

Cap:

can you get a reading on SGT and Tarbin

James:

my long range tracking system is also out. It seems like every system which the AI is involved in is out

Cap:

all systems

James:

yes Cap

Cap:

this isn't a coincidence, then. I know who might have something to do with this

The Captain proceeds to get up and walk out of the Control Center. He's heading to his quarters. Once he gets there he starts to look for something

INT Captain's Quarters

Cap:

where is it? Where did I put it? It's been some cycles since I had to use it but I know its here somewhere

(The Captain looks everywhere in his closet, under his bed, in-between the cracks on the wall, and then he remembers. He walks over to the wall on the far right side of his room. He knees down and places his hand on the floor and rotates it counterclockwise for a full cycle. A low tone hum is heard and the floor rises up in an upright position where the Captain hand was. A light beams up and a device hovers in the air.)

Cap:

here you are... let's see if this thing still works.

(The captain turns on the device and it starts to glow from red to orange to blue then beeps.)

Cap:

Elisa, Elisa can you hear me?

INT Elisa Lab on the Blue Planet

(Elisa still distraught from his conversation with High Command and him implementing his virus into the AI system doesn't hear the secret comm. Device that he created for the Captain and him to speak in secrecy while on separate bases. He developed a device that uses a frequency that only birds on his home planet used.)

Cap:

Elisa, Elisa can you hear me...Elisa

(Finally Elisa slowly snaps into now and hears the comm. Device going off. He looks at it first with confusion. First he snaps back into the time he lived on his home planet before High Command came. Then he remembers how the Overlords, forced him to destroy his home planet or they would enslaved everyone and kill his family. This turns his confusion state of mind to pure rage. He reaches for the device)

Elisa:

WHO IS THIS? WHAT DO YOU WANT? I AM NO COWARD! I WILL HAVE MY REVENGE!

Cap:

Elisa,

it's me Cap calm down. What's going on down there? We've lost all communication throughout this whole sector and I've lost long distance communication with SGT and Tarbin... Elisa do you hear me?

(Elisa still dazed and remembering only wanting revenge doesn't respond to Cap at first. Then after a moment he realizes that it's the Captain trying to speak him not the Overlords)

Elisa:

Cap...Cap is that you, Cap?

Cap:

yes man it's me. Are you okay what's going on over there?

Elisa:

I'm sorry Cap, I really am...

Cap:

what do you mean? What did you do?

Elisa:

I just started the WAR…

(Caps perplex thoughts increases as he waits for Elisa to explain to him what's going on and what he did?)

(Cap sits down and holds his head while shaking it. He's lost. He wants to be angry at Elisa but he knows Elisa is under extreme pressure and he just wants to help. He scratches his head)

Cap:

Elisa, what's going on? What do you mean, you started the War?

Elisa:

I did Cap, I started it and now they are coming

Cap:

ok you're not making any sense…

(Cap gets up and leaves to head back to the Command Center. Once he enters, he looks at the pilot)

Cap:

how fast can you get me to that planet?

Pilot:

Cap... the planet... I'm barely keeping this ship in orbit over this planet. Until I am able to reestablish my gyro and navigation system, We're not going anywhere

Cap:

does... teleportation work?

James:

Surprising, Cap that's one of the systems that still 100%

Cap:

get me down to the Red Planet, now. Get me to Corin's Lab

James:

Cap are you sure you want to leave the ship now

Cap:

I have no choice, She's the only one that can get Elisa to make some sense again. He's losing it and I can't have that right now. I need him

James:

I understand Cap, but....

Cap:

No buts just do it. I'm heading to the teleportation room. Make sure you got the coordinates right and beam me down there

James:

It will be ready for you Cap

(The Captain hastily walks out of the control center to the teleportation room. As he slowly walks the lights start to come back on due to the backup system. He passes, through each corridor and entering a new hallway, the lights turn on. A look of determination seeps in and his pace picks up. He enters the Teleportation room)

INT Teleportation Room

Cap:

James are the coordinates ready

James:

yes Cap

Cap:

Well proceed

(The lights on the machine turn on. A mist of green, purple, blue, red, yellow, and grey, engulfs the Captain and in an instance he disappears)

Back at Research Two Control Center

James:

I hope Cap knows what he is doing

Pilot:

when has he been wrong

James:

it's not about being wrong, it's about surviving and winning....

INT RED Planet Base Teleportation room

Tele Tech:

I have an incoming from Research two

Tech 2:

well put it through

(As soon as the tech presses the acceptance button, the small colorful mist surrounds the pad on the machine and the Captain appears)

Cap:

Where's Corin?

(The techs look at him with confusion)

Cap:

Soldiers Where is Corin

In walks Marshal, who hasn't seen the Captain since he left for the blue planet some cycles ago

Marshal:

I hope you're here, with some god news. My whole base is down Captain

Cap:

it's good to see you old friend, Where is Corin?

Marshal:

she's in her lab

Cap:

let's talk while we hurry to her lab Marshal

Marshal:

What's going on Cap

Cap:

We have a battle coming our way and looks like soon

Marshal:

How soon

Cap:

that's why I need Corin, I think Elisa did something but I can't reach him. He's out of it. Corin is the only person who can help

Marshal:

That damn foul, I knew that doctor would be the end of us all

Cap:

bare with him Marshal, he's under extreme pressure

Marshal:

Pressure that's when I do my best

Cap:

Remember he's not one of us nor is he a soldier. Now let's get to Corin lab now

(They continue to walk towards Corin Lab. The Captain warns Marshal of the upcoming battle and tells him to get his troops ready. When they reach the Corin's lab doors the Cap turns to Marshal)

Cap:

I'll take it from here Marshal. Get your troops ready. I have a bad idea that they will attack this base first. Get all the nonessentials, ready for transport. I only want battle ready personnel here.

Marshal:

We've lost 80% of power. I need at least 50% to do all that

Cap:

do what you can. I will get the power back online

Marshal:

Ok Cap

(Marshal turns around and walks away. The cap enters Corin's labs to see Corin working on her computer frantically.)

INT Corin's Lab

Cap:

Corin, what's going on?

Corin:

He did it, He really did it

Cap:

did what?

Corin:

he introduced a learning virus into the AI system. It is the complete opposite of the AI system in every way. Right now they are fighting each other and Elisa's winning.

Cap:

that's Great but we've lost everything

Corin:

oh, I working on that. Just a few more calculations and programming and it will be all back to normal but with a new AI system. One that we control

Cap:

what about Elisa?

Corin:

one second I'm typing in this last command and there… done.

(As soon as she does that the base seems to awaken and you hear all the machines turn on. A loud noise hums throughout the base. Corin looks at the Captain)

Corin:

Now, what are you saying about Elisa?...

Cap:

He's nonresponsive

Corin:

oh no this is trouble…

Cap:

what is it?

Corin:

looks like the Commander ship is heading our way

Cap:

ALREADY… Ok pack up and get to the Hanger your coming with me

Corin:

why?... I thought I was needed here. I've got the shields working

Cap:

Perfect, can you run the system up on my ship

Corin:

yeah with this new AI system I can

Cap:

pack up we have to go now

Corin:

What about Elisa?

Cap:

here take this and talk to him, he really needs you

Corin:

while I pack

Cap:

I'll be back soon. By the time I get back, you better be ready to leave.

(The Captain walks out of the lab running towards Marshal in the hanger bay.)

INT Hanger

Cap:

Marshal, Marshal what's the update

Marshal:

we just got the power back online. I don't know what you did but good job.

Cap:

no time for that, I need updates

Marshal:

well we're about 20% in gathering up the nonmilitary personnel. By sun fall, we should be almost done.

Cap:

great keep at it. Looks like the battle is coming to us soon

Marshal:

HOW SOON

Cap:

As soon as I know, you will. Get my transport ready, I'm heading back to my ship with Corin.

Marshal:

anything else you want me to do SIR

Cap:

not the time...

(Cap grabs his comm. Device and calls for Corin)

Cap:

Corin, Corin how long before we get communication back online

Corin:

I'm working on it. How many things do you want me to do at the moment, talk to Elisa, get the communication back up, and pack

Cap:

You can do it, I'm heading back to you now

INT Corin's Lab

Corin holds the special commlink device Elisa made for the Captain.

Corin:

Elisa…. Elisa… Elisa…

No reply

Corin:

Elisa… It's Corin, I'm here.. pickup the device…

(Elisa laying on the ground almost paralyzed from terror of the upcoming war doesn't respond to Corin. The device lays on the ground next to him. You hear Corin voice first starting off low but as she continues to talk, her volume increases. Still Elisa doesn't respond to her. Corin keeps trying, then tears start to form in her eyes. She needs him but its more than that she loves him.)

Corin:

Elisa answer me I need you, please don't abandon me

(as the tears flows from her eyes)

...Please Elisa, talk to me

Elisa still on the ground can hear Corin crying. It does something to him. A feeling overcomes him. It's the same feeling that he felt when they kissed but more intense. He starts to slowly move his body. First his legs, then his arms, and finally he sits up. He starts to look for the comm. Device and notices it on the ground next to him

Elisa:

Corin... Corin is that you? Is it really you, Corin?

(Corin tears of pain start to change to tears of joy now that she can hear Elisa voice. It soothes her.)

Corin:

Yes Elisa it's me, It's Me Elisa

Elisa:

I messed up Corin, I messed the whole thing up. I FAILED you and everyone here

Corin:

No Elisa, No you didn't fail

Elisa:

it's ok to tell me the truth, I failed, it's over now

Corin:

get up Elisa and look at your monitors, It worked you crazy being, it worked, you did it

Elisa:

what do you mean?

Corin:

get up from the ground and walk over to the monitors, I'm sending you the new data now

Elisa:

How do you know I'm on the ground

Corin:

(with a smile on her face and wiping the tears from her face)

I know you Elisa

(Elisa starting to feel better because of Corin starts to get up from the ground. He rises slowly to his feet and walks over to the monitor)

Corin:

do you see it

Elisa:

I can't believe it

Corin:

YOU DID IT ELISA, you created a whole new AI system more powerful than High Command

Elisa:

WOW... wait do you see this

Corin:

yes looks like they are going to pull out of Orion and head towards here

(In walks the Captain.)

Cap:

Are you ready

Corin:

I have Elisa on the commlink

Cap:

great I knew you could do it but we have to GO NOW

Corin:

what about Elisa

Cap:

you will see him soon, now grab your stuff the transport is
ready. Tell him you will see him soon

Corin:

I will

Cap:

I need you two together for what I have plan, now grab your
stuff and let's go... NOW

(Corin grabs a smaller monitor and heads out of the lab in back
of the Captain. As they head towards the hanger, military
personnel run by them in all directions. They prepare for
upcoming war.)

Corin:

High Command, sent orders to the Commander to wipe out this
whole sector

Cap:

I know. It's standard procedure when something like this
happens

Corin:

Something like what?

Cap:

I figured Elisa, shared with them, that the humans are them but have the capability to be much stronger that them. Also, High Command knows about the hybrids too. How much did I get correct so far?

Corin:

Everything, How did you Know?

Cap:

I didn't become Captain for my looks. Did you say the shield works

Corin:

If they used the LDB, more than once then shields won't hold

Cap:

That will give me the time I need to do what I have to do

Corin:

what do you mean?

Cap:

I'll fill you and Elisa in once we get to my ship. Can you Track SGT and Tarkin now

Corin:

yes, they are almost at the comm. Point

Cap:

good

The Captain and Corin walk into the hanger. All the nonmilitary personnel are there loading into ships. Some ships are heading to Research Two and some to the blue planet.. Everyone is running around. The Captain is the only one who seems to be calm. He walks over to Marshall

INT Hanger

Marshall:

Well Cap, it's an honor to fight by your side all these cycles

Cap:

Remember if you can get out in time then….

Marshall:

I'll fight to the end Cap, I will not abandon this base

Cap:

remember the Blue Planet is there

Marshal:

that's only if we succeed with your plan. Everyone here is ready

Cap:

ok Marshal, it's an honor old friend, see you on the other side

The Cap tips he's head to Marshal and Marshal does the same thing. Marshall turns around to talk to one of his soldiers and the Captain boards the ship with Corin behind him.

Corin:

so what's your plan?

Cap:

you will soon know

EXT Space Dr. Cozxe ship under cloak flying through space to the Comm point on the Navigation system

SGT:

Well we here, You should do it

Tarbin:

Why

SGT:

I'll just mess up...I'm not good at talking

Tarbin:

(Tarbin with a smile on her face looks at SGT)

You're doing fine talking to me this whole time

SGT:

but your different...

Tarbin:

different how?

SGT:

we have a mission to do, We'll talk about this later

Tarbin:

You're so smooth, fine

SGT:

make the comm. Link

(Tarkin looks at SGT out of the corner of her eye. She grabs the device that Dr. Elisa gave them and types in the code that he gave them)

Tarbin:

Hello, is anyone there

SGT:

do you think it worked?

Suddenly, A Darth Vader type voice answers. It's Crakos, Elisa main contact to the hierarchy on Orion. Crakos a massive, built man but very intelligent is Orion's go to man. He has a strong voice in their government. It was him who suggested that they allow Elisa to experiment on them and give them the ability to fight High Command. They rose up from slaves to warriors faster than they could ever had without Elisa.

Crakos:

Hello, Elisa is that you

SGT and Tarbin look at each other with confusion. Then Tarbin picks up the device again

Tarbin:

no this is Tarbin. Dr. Elisa sent us here to ask for your help

Crakos:

Who are you? And where is Elisa? Is he ok?

Tarbin:

my name is Tarbin and I have another with me name SGT, where we soldiers whom fought for High Command. Now we fight against them

Crakos:

hmm seems like Elisa is up to his old tricks again. How is he?

Tarbin:

He's....

SGT:

look at the monitor, we're receiving a message from the Cap

Crakos:

you never answered,... is everything ok

Tarbin:

YES, we just received a message from our Captain. Elisa is fine

Crakos:

well why did he sent you

Tarbin:

we want to talk to your leaders. Elisa sent us to make a request

Crakos:

well, I may be able to set up something but we are already
fighting a battle over here. It might not be safe to come this
way

Tarbin:

We'll risk it

Crakos:

fine I'll send you the coordinates to our Cyssero base. A friend
of Elisa is a friend of mine

Tarbin:

(in excitement)

great thank you

Tarbin turns to SGT and kisses him with excitement. They first
look at each other then pauses. Neither is sure what to do next.
Unknowing to them, one of the Commander recon ship pops up

on their radar. They have no time to look further into the kiss they must react

SGT:

what's that noise

Tarbin:

looks like we have a visitor

SGT:

well, is the cloak on

Tarbin:

it's on, now the real test is if it works

SGT:

they must have tracked us when we communicated with Crakos

Tarbin:

Can't be, Elisa said he used it plenty of times before

SGT:

things change maybe they figured it out, Maybe this is a trap

Tarbin:

well how about you stop yapping and lets figure it what to do

SGT:

let's attack

Tarbin:

if we attack then they will definitely know we're here

SGT:

so what do you suggest

Tarbin:

that we do nothing, just coast in space until it passes by or until it detects us

SGT:

well what if it detects us

Tarbin:

then we destroy it

As the two sit nervously in the cockpit of the ship the recon ship gets closer and closer. Then tension increases as the ship moves closer on the radar. Tarbin, slowly turns to her right and grabs her helmet. She places it on her head and looks at the navigation map inside of the helmet. She notices that the ship will directly hit their ship. Tarbin slowly, by thinking activates the thrusters on the left side of the ship to move it out of the way. SGT looks out of the cockpit window for the incoming ship. He is very anxious now. He knows that if this recon ship sees them then there is no way they can reach Orion without the Commander detecting their ship. Tarbin knows this as well but she hides her nervousness from SGT. The ship gets closer, its small ship with a large circle rotating around its tail end. The haul only stretches out about nine feet from the rotating circle.

Tarbin and SGT stay still and turn off anything that might give off energy and reveal their position to the recon ship. As the ship approaches they can now see it with their eyes. Tarbin grabs SGT hand and they look at each other while the ship passes them, no more than five feet away from the top of their ship. They rejoice, the recon ship doesn't detect they are there.

Tarbin:

Let's follow it

SGT:

let's not push it, let's continue on our mission

Tarbin:

but we can gather recon information. Since we're this close why not

SGT:

because we might have remain undetected to a little old recon ship but I don't want to test our chances with the Commanders ship

Tarbin:

fine, lets continue on but a real soldier would do both

SGT:

don't do that

Tarbin:

don't do what?

SGT:

don't try to get me to follow that ship by saying a real soldier
would

Tarbin looks at him with a grin

SGT:

Fine but we are not getting as close as we did with the recon
ship

INT Research two Control Center

(The Captain walks in with Corin. He looks at James and the
pilot, gives them a head nod and proceeds to sit down.)

Cap:

Corin sit down by the communication computer.

James:

are we going somewhere Cap

Cap:

yes bring us within the teleportation distance to the blue planet.
Corin and I are heading down there for a meeting

James:

is everything OK Cap

Cap:

men war is coming which isn't new we've known it was coming
but now we know when. As we speak the Commander is
gearing up to head towards this sector and destroy it.

(James and the Pilot look at each other, then turn to look back
at the Captain)

Cap:

Now if we can proceed, or do you have any more questions

James:

No Sir

Cap:

great get me within distance pilot

Pilot:

Yes Cap

Cap:

Corin any data from those two

Corin:

they sent a message that they made contact with Elisa man and
now they are heading towards Orion

Cap:

great, keep me posted

The pilot starts to type in the proper location in the Nav computer. When he's done he looks to the Captain

Pilot:

Cap the location is calculated

Cap:

Proceed

Research Two starts to power up and move. It slowly turns to the right and as soon as it faces the blue planet it disappears rapidly only leave a slight hologram of itself in space. Now it reappears right above the blue planet

Pilot:

Sucha beautiful place

Cap:

it is, and it's our job to protect it and it's inhabitants ... James take control of the helm, We're heading to the teleportation room

The Captain gets up and looks at Corin, whose typing into her monitor something. The Captain focus on his mission doesn't ask her what she is doing.

Cap:

are you ready ?

Corin:

yes

They proceed to leave the Command Center. Corin takes a min and looks outside at space and then she looks at everything in the center. She has a slight feeling that this maybe the last time she'll be in space or onboard Research Two. Then a smile comes to her face, she realizes that she is going to see Elisa which makes her happy. The two leave and head towards the teleportation room.

INT High Command Control Center

AI:

Master, The Commander requesting an audience

Overlord 2:

Useless, what does he want

Overlord 3:

let's hear what he has to say. We owe him that

Overlord 1:

agree

Overlord 2:

WE OWE HIM, he owes us for his existence

Overlord 3:

put the Commander through, AI

AI:

yes Master

The Commander just finished walking to his quarters. As soon as he enters, he commlink goes off making a loud beeping sounds. The Commander fumbles with it and then grabs it

Commander:

what is it

Major:

Ai just sent a message wanting to establish comm. With you and High command.

Commander:

link it to my chambers system. I will have my discussion with them here

Major:

yes Commander

INT Command Center

You see the Major typing in the code at his place transferring the link to the Commander's Chambers

Comm Tech:

the message is encrypted

Major:

As it should be, whatever discussed between High Command
and The Commander is nothing for us to know.

Comm Tech:

yes sir

INT Commander's Chambers

(Commander weary from the battles in Orion and the pressure
from the Overlords walks over to his desk. His commlink goes
off.)

Major:

Commander Ai, established a link to High Command

Commander:

Put it through Major

(The Commander falls to his chair and turns on his monitor
awaiting the link from High Command)

Overlord 2:

What is it slave

Commander:

Master, you want me to leave the battle here and head over to the Captain

Overlord 2:

Are you questioning your orders

Commander:

No Sir, but I thought the Captain was carrying out his mission according to your orders

Overlord 1:

He did. Ai revealed to us new information and we must act now and why are you slave asking US questions?

Commander:

Sorry Sir. TO be clear Sir, you want me to go there and destroy everything, Even our Troops?

Overlord 2:

Again, I think you are questioning your orders

Commander:

(scared by the way Overlord 2 talks to him)

again Masters, I just wanted to know why, I could use them here, that's all

Overlord 2:

you need not know why. You need to just do as you are
ordered. Also, Before you leave that sector, fire the wipe beam
or did you let that get destroyed too

Commander:

No Sir it still works but we can still win this battle

(Overlord 3 looks to Overlord 2 with shock)

Overlord 3:

Are you sure you want to do this Brother

Overlord 2:

We have no choice this war far exceeded our expectation and
we must move on.

Overlord 1:

I agree

Overlord 3:

So we just wipe...

Overlord 2:

we don't need this sector yet, when the time is right we will
come back and take IT, like we always do

The Commander confused from the silence by the Overlords
checks to see if he is still connected to them

Commander:

Masters are you still there

Overlord 2:

anything else you would like to discuss or can we get back to
more important matters

Commander:

(nervous)

No master, that's all

Overlord 2:

you have your orders carry them out or else

As soon as he says that the link cuts off. The commander leans
back into his chair. The years of service to High Command takes
a toll on his mind. The fear of losing his existence is the only
reason why he continues. He thinks about Victor. He places his
head down, while putting his right hand on his head. He shakes
it, while rubbing his forehead.

Commander:

I actually respected what you did, If only I had the courage to
do what you did Victor. You died an honorable death my
Friend...

(He picks up his commlink with his left hand and presses the
button)

Commander:

Major... this is the Commander

Major:

yes sir

Commander:

Prepare the ship for departure

Major:

ARE we retreating Sir

Commander:

No we are going to pay the Captain and Elisa a visit

Major:

should I pull back Everything

Commander:

yes we are going to need everything we have left for this
mission my comrade

Major:

I will get on it Sir

EXT Space Near The Commander's Mother Ship orbiting a moon on the farthest planet in the Orion's galaxy

(Dr. Coaxe ship spies on the Mother Ship. Tarbin and SGT notices that the ship sustained heavy damage but they see that micros, tiny robots work on fixing it. There's some basics orbiting around the ship in spacesuits working on the ship too)

SGT:

wow looks like the reports of the battle here was right

Tarbin:

yeah looks like those Orion's put up a fight like no other

SGT:

yeah I've never seen the Mother Ship with this much damage...

Tarbin:

Let's not take it as a victory yet, seems like they will have it up and running soon again

SGT:

true, well lets continue on to our primary mission

Tarbin:

Let's

(Dr. Coaxe ship continue on to the location that Crakos gave them. As they pass through space they see many ships destroyed, some ships were the Orion's and some the

Commander. Never have they seen so much wreckage before. The debris stretches across the whole area. They come across a wide green planet, with three moons. Once they pass the final moon, the almost run into the rest of the Commander's armada. They stop the ship)

SGT:

What are we going to do? We can't just pass them

Tarbin:

AI is there another way around them

AI:

Yes but you must uncloak and then activate the jump computer

SGT:

I KNEW this was a bad decision... AI how much time will it take for the jump

AI:

approximately 20 sec

SGT:

20 SECS

Tarbin:

We can do this, we are a team

SGT:

How?

Tarbin:

Place you helmet on and activate the weapons system. With the help of the AI I will get the ship to jump just outside of the planet where their Cyssero base is

(SGT puts his helmet on and looks over to Tarbin)

SGT:

I knew what this mission was going to be when I signed up so let's do it

(Tarbin smiles at SGT moves closer to him and kisses his helmet. She then leans back to her position and puts her helmet on)

Tarbin:

AI deactivate cloaking and activate jump sequence

AI:

Cloak deactivating and jump sequence activating

As the cloak system deactivates, it appears right in front of a High Command fighter. The pilot of the fighter was looking down at his leg but looks up to see a ship. He is shocked but by the time he reaches for his weapons, SGT fires a blue laser beam that goes right through the ship causes it to explode. Other ships notices the ship and the explosion and turn to face SGT and Tarbin

SGT:

you better hurry, THEY'VE NOTICED US

SGT continues to shoot at the fighters. Some move out of the way and get in attacking position. While others too slow to react are blown up. SGT activates the ships flying controls, as he thinks to go to the right it goes to the right, he thinks up it goes up. He dodges the red lasers of his enemies and their pulse missiles . He does a complete 360 to dodge a pulse missile which ends up hitting a larger ship and causing a massive explosion. This explosion gets the attention of the Mother Ship

INT Commander Mother Ship Control Center

Recon Tech:

Major we have a problem

Major:

what is it

Recon Tech:

Seems like we have an unknown ship fighting in the middle of our armada

Major:

One ship against our armada

Recon Tech:

yes

Major:

order our ships to retreat back to the Ship, We are leaving this awful sector anyways

Recon Tech:

yes sir

INT Dr. Coaxe Ship

SGT:

I am unstoppable... You can't stop an elite

Tarbin:

done

(The ship disappears right before the armada received the order to retreat. The ship reappears in orbit of a beautiful blue planet. As they enter the planet's atmosphere you see gigantic mountain ranges and enormous trees. The ship flies over them to a large body of water. They see the larger Cyssero base in view. The base received heavy damage. The once large skyscrapers are now only rumble. They continue on towards a large hangar door. They stop hovering over the base in front of the doors)

SGT:

Well we're here, contact Crakos

Tarbin:

something's wrong, that was too easy

SGT:

TOO easy, did you see me out there

Tarbin:

that's what I mean, we would never allow an enemy to leave
once they engaged us

SGT:

we're elites, how many times have our enemies retreated...

Tarbin:

I have a bad feeling

The hanger doors open outwards allowing the ship in. As they
fly in, they see many ships. Most of them undergoing extensive
repairs, while others seem unfixable. An Orion guide them to
an area to land the ship.

SGT:

they can't help us. Look at this place

Tarbin:

Looks like The Commanders not the only one who sustain heavy
damages in this war.

SGT:

if he only knew...

Tarbin:

good thing that he doesn't

They land the ship and look at each other. They know the situation is bleak over here. Tarbin gets on the commlink

SGT:

what are you doing

Tarbin:

I'm contacting the Captain he needs to know what we found here

SGT:

let's hold up on that and gather more Intel before we...

Tarbin:

Fine

The two walk out of the ship. Crakos awaits them at the bottom.

Crakos:

My friends glad you made it.

(Tarbin and SGT look at each other as they walk down the steps. They have to look up at this massive alien, Crakos. He hugs the two of them and brings them into the air. As he drops them, he proceeds to walk in a direction that leads out of the hanger)

Crakos:

Well you didn't fly here for nothing, come on everyone's expecting you

(As they walk through the hanger, some aliens look at them with anger and others surprised to see two of high Commands Elites in their hanger and not trying to enslave them.)

Crakos:

don't worry about them, they know that you are with Elisa. They don't blame you

Tarbin:

Seems like you've taken heavy damages

Crakos:

it's war but thanks to the gods, we're given a break

Tarbin:

WHAT break

Crakos:

the past quarter cycle neither us nor them have fought

Tarbin:

so you mean... they just stopped

Crakos:

yes... then right after speaking with you they pulled back all their ships. Even now, our long range sensors can only pick up the Mother Ship

Tarbin:

OH.....NO

SGT:

what

Crakos:

What's wrong

Tarbin:

I knew something was wrong. Think about it SGT

SGT:

think about what

Tarbin:

what's standard procedure for wiping

SGT:

NO....NO... Crakos... we must leave now.. tell your people to leave... NOW

Crakos:

don't worry this base is too deep underground we are safe here

SGT:

No we're not, not safe from that...

Crakos:

from What

Tarbin:

The Commander has a weapon inside the Mother Ship, that's hits the central cortex of our brains and wipes their memories

SGT:

we got to get back to the ship maybe we can stop them

Tarbin:

there's no stopping it,... trust I know

SGT:

listen to me

(as he grabs her by both arms. He looks into her face and smiles)

I know we got off to a bad start but I know you. You're not one to give up so don't do it now. Let's at least try

(Tarbin looks up at SGT and smiles. She leans over and kisses him…. Then a loud humming sounds rattles the whole building and Everyone fails to the ground)

INT Mother Ship control Center

In walks the Commander, he then sits down in his chair and turns the chair to face the Major.

Commander:

Major is the device ready

Major:

(reluctantly)

Yes Commander

Commander:

well…

The commander looks through the shield window of the control desk into space. Anger takes over him, then disgust. He turns back to the Major

Commander:

Do it

(The Major presses the button and a grey beam fires out of the Mother Ship. The beam spans across what seems to be the whole galaxy like a shooting star.)

(As the beam travels a look of despair comes across the Commanders face. He regrets what he just did. As he sits there he realized that he regrets everything that he has done under the service of High command. He hates himself)

Commander:

Major is it done

Major:

yes Commander

Commander:

Are we ready to depart

Major:

almost. Also we had one fighter jump in the middle of our armada and fought for about 25 seconds then jumped out.

Commander:

that doesn't matter now. We have a new mission.

Major;

Calculations are done Commander

Commander:

Well let's get on with it

INT. Captain's Chambers onboard Research Two

(The Captain received a secure message from The Commander's Ship)

Captain:

No...No...NO those wretched beings.... The whole Sector.... Damn. Ai hail Elisa

AI:

locating Dr. Elisa, this may take a few moments... Dr. Elisa located. Would you like to communicate?

Cap:

yes put him through

(Elisa on blue planet in his lab with Corin working on a new weapon)

Corin:

we have an incoming communication with Cap

Elisa:

put him through... Cap

Cap:

Elisa....

Corin can't hear what the two are talking about but she can see the grief on Elisa face. The grief turned to anger and Elisa tells Cap bye

Corin:

what was that about?

Elisa:

we have a quarter cycle to finish this

Corin:

Are we going to really use this

Elisa:

the Cap seems to think so

Corin:

but that means...

Elisa:

that's his decision

Corin:

... Well ...OK... what did you talk about

Elisa:

They wiped the Orion's and we think Tarbin and SGT were there too

Corin:

OH.... NO...

Elisa:

well doesn't look like we going to get any help from the Orion's anytime soon. It's all up to us now

Corin:

We can do it..

Elisa:

the only good news is that... High Command rushed, The Commander and his ship is in need of heavy repairs

Corin:

well our chances increased

(Elisa still sadden over the news of the Orion's and the mission doesn't respond to Corin. He first looks at his monitor and tries to finish a calculation but gets frustrated and throws his glass towards the left wall of his lab almost hitting a vile with a blue colored sample on top of a lab table. He grabs his head and screams IT ALL ENDS! Corin at first shocked from hearing the glass shattered against the wall, quickly snaps to and rushes over to Elisa and places her hand on his shoulders)

Corin:

it will be ok... they are still alive

Elisa:

if it wasn't for me, this wouldn't have happen

Corin:

if it wasn't for you.... They would still be slaves...

Elisa:

I know... I know

INT Research Two Orbiting above the blue Planet in Space

Cap:

James can you establish a Link between us and the two bases

James:

I'm sure I can get something going

Cap:

I want to broadcast to everyone

James:

Give me a few...

(Cap looks around the control deck of his ship. He sits down and looks to James)

Cap:

ready James

James:

Yes Cap but each base will receive a time delay

Cap

how much of a delay

James:

not too much

Cap:

fine set it up

James:

it's ready

Cap:

to the united forces in this section. I your Captain want to give you an update of our situation. A half of cycle ago, I felt we might need some backup against the Commander. I sent a small group to Orion's galaxy with the Help of Dr. Elisa. I just learned that this mission failed. The Commander under the orders by High Command, wiped that whole sector. Fortunately, for us, the Orion's fought a great war. They damaged the mother ship in such a way the Commander had to retreat for repairs. During these repairs, High Command, felt that The Commander should come here and destroy us. Well they underestimated the Orion's and they've underestimated us as well. He's on his way here in a battered ship with battered weapons and exhausted men. This will be their downfall and why we shall win. High Command thinks they are untouchable. We are going to give them a reason to fear us and this sector by destroying the Commander. We have a quarter cycle until he gets here. So prepare yourself and if there is anything you want to do, do it because this will be a battle to the end.

(While The Captain gives his speech, you seen a montage of planets, the bases, and the faces of the everyone on both bases and ships, while they hear the Captain. LT and Shelia spending time with their son. Then Neno, reads a book in his chambers. Andi and Si are working out. Oska looking at a hologram of Tarbin and crying. Vincent with his twins playing. Marshall looking out of a window at a red dust cloud spinning around rapidly next a tree. Then Elisa and Corin working in the lab and smiling at each other. SGT on the ground with Tarbin on top of him next to Crakos. You see Dr. Coaxe ship in the Orion's Hanger and a screen is on. The screen shows a hologram of the human's galaxy and a red dot on the image of the blue planet with the words "Return Home". Dr. Coaxe inside his lab walks into a chamber and injects himself with a bluish green substance and walks over to his bed. He lays down and falls asleep. Return back to the Control Deck of Research two, James and the Pilot look at each other with a smile)

INT. Research Two Control Deck

(Cap after finishing speaking looks at James)

Cap:

ok James...I'm done

James:

cutting off link now

Cap:

Men prepare for war.

James & Pilot:

Yes Cap

INT Commander's Mother Ship Control Center

(While the ship is moving through the darkness of space, some
of the interior repairs are ongoing. The still need exterior
repairs. The commander enters the control center to see about
ten of his basics working on the damages. There's sparks flying
all over the place. The workers have dark gum all over their
body and clothes. Commander still frustrated about on taking a
mission with his ship so battered just walks in and looks at the
Major)

Commander:

how much longer Major

Major:

we have less than a quarter cycle left. The ship is slow due to all
the damage

Commander:

Can we get any more speed out of this thing

Major:

any faster Commander and the ship will fall apart

Commander:

what about weapons, what's the status on them

Major:

we still have the wipe beam, some exterior laser towers are operational, and we have about a third of fighters left

Commander:

what about the main gun

Major:

the light destroyer... Well Commander due to heavy damage to its cooling system, which we can't fix on the interior... we can only use it about once..

Commander:

one time?

Major:

any more than once, then it will overheat and blow up the ship

Commander:

hmm... changes my strategy.. What about shields

Major:

do we need shields?

Commander:

Major we are going up against our toughest soldiers and I think they know we're coming

Major:

they know

Commander:

I'm no fool Major, some of the men on this ship are loyal to him

Major:

but we're taught to follow orders

Commander:

if I told you right now to get on your knees and pull your laser out and shoot yourself, Would you do it?

Major:

YES Commander

Commander:

Well they wouldn't especially that Captain. These men we're condition to fight to the end and follow their own way. Oh yes, Major we have a battle waiting for us and it's not one I see us winning.

Major:

then why

Commander:

like you said we follow orders. I don't know why they want me
to destroy this sector and our fellow men but I know I can't
argue with High Command

Major:

so what do we do

Commander:

we fight...

INT Captain's Chambers on Research Two still Hovering over The
Blue Planet

Cap:

If I was you, with a battered ship, the first thing I would do is
take out the military base. Therefore, If I position this ship right
here, I should be able to counterattack. .. AI get the Marshal on
the link

AI:

Yes Captain establishing link with Marshal

(Marshal is running around the Hanger of the Red base. More
soldiers in the background moving plane parts around. Some
are loading the weapons up on the ships. Marshal enters the
elevator heading up to the Command Center when he's hailed
by Cap.)

Marshal:

Yeah

Captain:

I need you to evac, the base as soon as possible

Marshal:

No way Cap, we're not leaving until it's over or we're dead

Cap:

he's coming to you first

Marshal:

yeah I know. But before he can shoot that cannon, I'll be able to fire at least a shot at him

Cap:

A shot isn't going to be enough

Marshal:

that's when your plan comes into play. I've evac everyone that wanted to leave. The rest are here for the battle

Cap:

are the ships ready

Marshal:

almost ready to lift off...we're loading the weapons in now

Cap:

As soon as they are ready, have them meet up with me on my ship

Marshal:

Ok,

Cap:

Cap out... Ai hail LT

AI:

establishing link with LT

LT is leaving his quarters. He was just spending some time with his family. He approaches the door, then his comm. Device goes off. The baby makes a noise and Shelia looks up to see Lt leaving.

LT:

(quietly as the door closes)

Yes, Cap

Cap:

did I catch you at a bad time?

LT:

no, what is it

Cap:

I need you to send all available ships and pilot to my location

LT:

That means me too

Cap:

Maybe you should stay

LT:

I'm one of your best I'm not sitting this one out

Cap:

Well it's your decision, I need everyone now. The day we've prepare for is now

LT:

IS HE HERE

Cap:

He will be, also evac the base and I mean everyone

LT:

Will do

Cap:

Cap out

INT Cap Chambers

Cap remains sitting at his desk with a drink of some kind in his hand. He looks at a hologram picture of him and Victor. Rises the glass towards the image

Cap:

All the pieces are in motion Vic. Wish you could be here I hope I have better luck than you did against him

(As the Captain and his troops prepare of the upcoming battle the Commander ship travels through space towards them. They are ready.)

INT Mother Ship control Center

Major:

(as he turns away from his monitor and looks at the Commander)

We are almost there

Commander:

good, Make sure we are in firing distance to the base on the red planet

Major:

We will enter the galaxy momentary

EXT Red Planet Hanger

(Marshal, the humans, and basics load up into the ships.
Marshal puts his helmet on and closes the cockpit of his ship.
He activates the commlink on his heads up display_

Marshal:

okay men, the day is here. You all have your coordinates. Blue
Team… Ready

Blue Team:

Ready

Marshal:

Green team… Ready?

Green Team:

Ready

Marshal:

Black Team… Ready?

Black Team:

Ready

Marshal:

ok lift off

(The three squadrons take off in every directions. They are
about 40 planes soaring through the sky of the red planet

heading towards the Captain's ship. As soon as they enter
space the Mother Ship appears)

INT Mother Ship Command Center

Major:

Commander, we here but it seems like they are about 40 ships
leaving the planet

Commander:

(with a small grin on his face)

I thought you well

Major:

what was that Commander

Commander:

get this ship in firing distance

Major:

we are about 5 minutes away

Commander:

good

INT Research Two command Center

James:

The Mother ship is here Cap and its heading towards the red planet

Cap:

what about our fighters

James:

they just left the base and are entering space now

Cap:

order then to separate into their squadrons and attack the Mother Ship

James:

yes Cap... Marshal this is James

Marshal:

yes

James:

the Mother Ship is here, Cap wants you to engage

Marshal:

Yeah I figured that

EXT Space right above the red planet

Marshal:

ok green squad I want you to head towards the right side of the ship. Blue the left and Black I want you to head towards the Cap and give him all the protection that he needs

INT Mother Ship Command Center

Major:

We have about thirty wing fighters heading towards us

Commander:

How many fighters do we have left

Major:

we have about 100

Commander:

send them all out to attack the fighters

Marshal:

yes Commander...

(Major gets on the Commlink)

Major:

Battle stations... Battle Stations. All pilots to their fighters... All gunners to their station

(Hallway after Hallway troops on the Commanders ship run around. Due to the damage of the ship sparks fly everywhere as they run through the hallways. Enter the large hanger of the mother ship. Fighters after fighters fly out into space and head towards the Marshal and his planes)

EXT Space

Marshal:

ok here they come Green and Blue team engage

Blue One:

there's at least a hundred of them

Marshal:

They should have brought more....Fire at will men

(As Marshal and his lighter and faster fighters engaged the bigger and war battered ships of High Command. The black team head towards Research Two and LT still on Earth evacuating everyone from the base)

INT Mountain Base Earth Hanger

LT looks at Oska, Vincent, Si, Andi and Neno

LT:

I have nothing to say

Vincent:

There's no need to say anything. We're all thinking the same
thing. Let's just get out there and do what we do

(Each member looks at each other with a look of determination,
they've never experienced before. This was the first time they
we're fighting because they choose too. They smile at each
other and turn around towards their ships. Lt enters his ship
and activates a hologram of his family)

LT:

I do this for YOU and for MY Captain

(They take off. The lights turn off inside the base and the
hanger door closes. Each Elites flies their own way into space.
Vincent first flies over the ocean and then heads straight up.
Andi and SI flies circles around each other making figure eights,
laughing all the way up into space. Neno flies over the desert as
the lions and Elephants look at the plane and roar. Oska looks
at a hologram of her and Tarbin with a sad look on her face she
heads straight up to space.)

INT Research Two Control Center

James:

Cap, black team is heading our way there seems to be about 30
fighters heading our way from the Mother Ship

Cap:

Tell Black team to turn around engaged the fighters

James:

Black Team Black Team... Your Orders are to turn around and engage the enemy

Black team Leader:

Understood... Well you heard that men, let's have us some fun

INT Mother Ship Command Center

Commander:

how much time left?

Major:

we have about 4 minutes left

Commander:

what about the Captain's ship

Major:

right now it's stationary near the blue Planet

Commander:

that doesn't sound like him hmm...

Major:

I sent a squadron to attack

Commander:

(as he scratches his right arm)

Hmm

INT Command Center of Research Two

Cap:

Where's Elisa and Corin

James:

in the engine room

Cap:

hail them

James:

there online sir

Cap:

Are we ready Doctors?

Elisa:

in about three minutes

Cap:

keep me posted

EXT Space

Marshal:

blue three take that gun out, it's killing us out here

Blue Three:

trying Sir but I got two on my back

Marshal:

anyone close to Blue Three

Green six:

I'm almost there Blue three

(Blue three tries to out maneuver the two fighters behind him. A laser shot grazes his right wing)

Blue three:

that was a close one. Green Six I'm a goner if you don't get here soon

Green Six:

right behind you Blue Three

(Green Six comes from the top and blasts one of the fighters. The ship blows up and Green Six ships passes through the smoke)

Green Six:

one down, one more to go. Ok Blue three...I need you to bank right in two seconds

Blue three:

count it

Green Six:

Now

(Blue Three banks right which gives Green Six the line of sight he needs to blast the fighter. Green Six blows up the fighter with a laser beam but as soon as he yells)

Green Six:

YEAH Blue Three.....NOOOOO>>>>>

(Bomb Green Six was blown up by a phaser gun on the Mother Ship.)

Marshal:

I need someone to take out those Guns ASAP, Their killing us out here

Blue Two:

we're running out of men and time Marshal. There's too many of them

Marshal:

no time to give up now. We didn't come here to lose

INT Research two command Center

Cap:

LT what's your ETA

LT:

Cap we will be there in seconds

Cap:

get here fast they need you guys out there

(As soon as Cap says that Oska flying as fast as her ship can go wisp by Research Two heading towards Marshal and the fight)

Cap:

who that... Oska?

James:

yes sir

Cap:

Go Get 'EM

LT:

We're here Cap, where do you need us

Cap:

follow Oska, we're doing bad out there

(The battle near the Red planet worsen. Many of the Rebels ship destroyed due to the fight. Marshal has them fall back and regroup to form new squadrons. As they regroup, The Mother Ship opens up its main blaster opening)

Marshal:

Red Base is it Ready

Toca:

Yes

Marshal:

FIRE

(A blue beam fires out of the red base. It soars through the atmosphere of the planet and enters space. Travels right pass Marshal and his regroup fighters and hits the Mother Ship right in it's tail.)

Marshal:

Damnit

The rear of the Mother Ship explodes but the main gun opening continues to open)

INT Mother Ship Control Center

(The beam, from the base damages the ship. It's engines are still burning and on the Control deck, pieces of the ship starts to explode and electrical fires surges throughout the ship)

Commander:

Put OUT THAT FIRE…

(Tech gets up and runs towards a grayish plastic bottle about three inches in size. He opens it and sprays in towards the electrical fire)

Commander:

Give me an update

Major:

(Our engines are down, cooling system is at 25%, electrical fires are going off throughout the ship, and it seems like that blast took out the power to most of our exterior weapon towers)

Commander:

is the main blaster available

Major:

yes but it's dangerous, we could lose the ship

Commander:

FIRE

Major:

YES SIR… FIRE MAIN BLASTER

Marshal:

Get out of there Toca, Now

Toca:

too late Mar….

(The Mother Ship fires it's main blaster and the radiating red beam heads in the direction of the red planet base. It hits the base and all you see is smoke, explosions, fires, and pieces of the base flying in the air. Moments later when they smoke clears. Marshal looks at his monitor and sees the damage. It's like the base was never there. Where the base was, is now a deep crater.)

Marshal:

It's not over yet…

(Oska fighter appears and simultaneously shoots down two fighters with her laser beam)

Blue Seven:

WOW

Marshal:

that's Oska for you…Ok men, I'm not going to let her get all the fun

(As the Marshal and his men head towards Oska fighting a hanger door on the Mother Ship opens.)

INT Mother Ship Command Center

Commander:

Major take the rest of the fighters and finish this

Major:

yes Sir

(Major and five of his men head out of the Control Center)

EXT Space

Marshal:

Well it's only 6 of us versus twenty of them

LT:

Don't forget us

(In flies LT and the Rest of the Elites. They line up each of their ships and wait)

LT:

Well looks like this might be the end

Vincent:

wouldn't have it any other way, brother

Andi:

let's go for it

(They proceed towards the rest of High Command fighters. Then out of nowhere five more ships fly out of the hanger and head towards the Elites)

Major:

Traitors... why don't you just Die as ordered

SI:

He's delusional...

Vincent:

don't underestimate him....

(As Vincent talks a beam comes from the Major ships and blows up two of the rebels ships)

Major:

that's all you got...I thought I was fighting Elites

Oska:

He's mine

LT:

OK...

Marshal:

The rest, our duty

INT Research Two Command Center

Elisa:

we're ready in here

Cap:

Good Activate it

(Research two starts to radiate a bright gold color. Then disappears from orbit of the blue planet. It then appears next to the red planet and immediately fires on the Mother Ship with a bright green blast and two light torpedoes all the Mother Ship and explosions goes off in the area the torpedoes and the laser blast hit.)

INT Mother Ship Control Center

(The impact of the weapons cause the Commander to fall from his seat and hit the ground. He shakes his head and puts his left hand on a new deep wound bleeding from his forehead because of shrapnel. He sits back down and smiles)

Commander:

I was waiting for you to show your face....I thought you well, my friend

Tehc:

Commander... our shields are down

Commander

Fire what we got Now

Tehc:

ok

INT Research Two

Cap:

great job Elisa... Elisa... Are you There?

James:

No response from the Engine room, I'm reading high
temperatures down there

Cap:

No... NO... James, I'll be back

(Cap gets up and rushes out of the control center. Running
through the ship an explosion goes off and the Captain is
thrown into a wall and then the ground. He lays there for a
second, then grabs his commlink.)

Cap:

James what was that?

James:

Cap we just got hit by the Mother ship... Our shield are down to
thirty percent

Cap:

How about weapons

James:

We're running low Sir

Cap:

Fire another torpedo but this time at the wing

James:

Yes Sir

(Cap gets up and continues to run towards the engine room. His Commlink goes off again)

James:

Cap...

Cap:

what

James:

If I don't vent the engine room it's going to blow

Cap:

hold on I'm almost there

(Cap finally gets to the engine room and what he feared is what happen. Elisa and Corin are dead and there's a blazing fire going off in there. The Ai won't allow him to open the door)

Cap:

AI OPEN THIS DOOR

AI:

Sorry, opening the door will risk the ship. I recommend that you
vent this room

Cap:

NO open the Door!

AI:

Sorry... I am venting the room now.

(A large grey blast door closes off the engine room to the Cap
eyesight. Then a bay door opens up next on the exterior of the
ship. The fire shoots out of the room as well as the bodies of
Corin and Elisa. The Cap breaks down and lays by the door of
the room. He pounds the door with his hand and a tear comes
out of his eye.)

EXT Space

(The Battle rages on in space. The Major and Oska engaged
each other. The Major get behind Oska. Oska turns to the right,
the Major does too. As Oska turns to the left so does the Major.
Sweat forms on Oska face. She has never faced anyone as good
as the Major. He shoots and hits one of the small engines on
Oska ship. Oska starts to tremble in fear. She looks behind her
and sees the Major right behind her laughing)

LT:

Oska are you ok

Oska:

I'll be fine

(Oska and the Major battle leads them too far away from help. Oska is by herself.)

Major:

don't worry Oska, I'll make it quick or I might take my time with you traitor, HA

(Oska ships takes another hit this time on the other side of her ship. She's losing power... Her ship stops)

Oska:

LT thank you for everything

LT:

Oska... Oska...

Oska:

no need... I've los....

(The major fires on Oska ship immediately blowing it up)

Major:

She's not even a...

(Out of nowhere Neno fires on the Major ships blowing it up)

Neno:

That's for Oska, you Bastard

Neno turns around and proceeds towards the Mother Ship

INT Research Two outside of the Engine room

James:

Cap... Cap

Cap:

James

James:

Cap it's bad we're out of weapons and we're losing power.

Cap:

I'm on my way

(The Captain gets up with rage in his eyes. Runs to the
Command Center. He passes many of his men dying on the
ground. The battle cost him a lot. Most of the crew is dead due
to explosions or fires.)

Mother Ship Command Center

Tehc:

Commander we lost Major

Commander:

how about the ship can it fly

Tehc:

no

Commander:

what about the wipe

Tehc:

still available but If we use it...

Commander:

What, What is it?

Tehc:

The ship will explode

Commander:

I already knew I wasn't going to make it out of this alive.
Activate the wipe

INT Research Two Control Center

(The Captain walks it and sits down)

Cap:

James let's finish this

James:

Cap we have a problem... The Mother Ship

Cap:

what about it

James:

looks like they are going to use the wipe Sir

Cap:

Tell everyone to retreat

James:

Doesn't matter Cap...By the looks of it, if they use it then the whole sector will be wipe

Cap:

What about the fighters

James:

there's no way for them to escape

Cap:

James aim this Ship towards the Mother Ship

James:

WHAT...

Cap:

We're going to plot a course towards the center of the Mother Ship and crash into it

James:

That will kill us Cap

Cap:

we have no choice... You can escape into one of the pods... I won't judge you

James:

No Cap, I'm here until the end. Plus you can't fly this thing by yourself

Cap:

well it's been a honor James

INT Mother Ship Command Center:

Tehc:

Commander... Research Two is heading right for us

Commander:

the IRONY... How much time until the wipe is ready

Tehc:

It's going to be close

(AS the Commander and Tehc wait for the wipe to fully power up. The Captain and James hastily heads towards the Mother Ship hoping to stop them.)

INT Research Two Control Center

Cap:

What about our fighters?

James:

Sorry Cap, they completed their mission but they gave up their existence

Cap:

OK

(Research two continues on it's kamikaze mission. They pass the wreckage of the fighters fight. They pass LT's, Neno's, Andi's, Si's, and Vincent's ships some of them completely destroyed while others with big blast holes in them.)

Cap:

They passed honorably

Cap:

well James it's our turn

James:

I'm Ready

INT Mother Ship Command Center

Commander:

is it ready

Tehc:

yes but it's too late

Commander:

FIRE

(The Mother Ship fires the wipe beam. It was aimed towards the blue planet but due to the extensive damage to the ship the bean spread across the whole universe. As soon as the beam fired Research Two collided with the Mother Ship. A massive explosion like a sun going supernova goes off, destroying anything close to it.)

INT High Command Planet Overlord's control Center

Overlord 2:

well then...

Overlord 1:

He wiped the sector

Overlord 2:

do we leave them or send our army

Overlord 2:

Send them

Overlord 1:

no need at least not now. If they ever try to leave that sector then and only then. We have more galaxies to conquer.

Overlord 2:

agreed

Overlord 1:

we will send a monitor to oversee their progress. AI send out a satellite

AI:

yes, Master... Satellite sent

Overlord 2:

good. Now how long for our new army to finish growing

AI:

less than a cycle.. The new Commander is ready now.

Overlord 1:

Bring him in

(The new commander is an exact clone of the Commander. He walks in and salutes the Overlords. He takes the Oath)

Encountering Our Freedom Chapter Two

EXT Global Federation Beta base

Voice Over Loud speaker:

T Minus twenty four hours until Launch

As the VO speaks, image a wide angle view of the massive base with 8 large space ships. Many Techs are outside working on the ships and beyond the ships you see a big crowd of onlookers behind fences camped out. You zoom into reporters and camera men covering the launch. One reporter is broadcasting live.

Connie Hall:

This is Connie Hall broadcasting live from the space launch base. In about 24 hours, 8 massive space ships will leave in order to find other planets for humans to live once the Earth finally dies in a hundred years or find resources to help heal our planet. I hope I speak for everyone here and all over the world, and say hopes are high that we will find the necessary resources to heal our planet, our home.

Camera Man

What the hell is that. LOOK OUT

Then a small orbiting satellite glides over the base and starts to hover over it. A beam of light shoots out and starts to scan the base.

(Screams from the crowd)

Oh MY God take Cover! Run for your lives! It's Aliens they've come for us RUN!

Tech

What the hell is that?

Soldier

What is that beam of light

Soldier 2

Don't know! Should I shoot it?

Tech 3

Do something, aren't you a soldier

Tech 2

Is it one of ours?

Soldier 2

I've never seen anything like that before

Tech 1

What do we...

Tech 2

Run for IT, who knows what that light is It might give us cancer

INT Command Center of Global Federation Beta Base

General Gethros

Lt. Jackson.... Please tell me you know what that thing is

Lt. Jackson

No Sir... but we have a comm. from the Alpha

General Gethros

What is it?

General Walker

General shoot that THING DOWN NOW

General Gethros

Lt. you heard the man someone take that thing out

LT. Jackson

Yes SIR...(Jackson gets up and walks towards another computer)
Taking AIM SIR

(Jackson starts to press onto a screen. While he's pressing a
laser gun pops out of the base main tower)

General Gethros

DO IT

(Jackson shoots a laser beam and the satellites turns to ashes)

General Gethros

SOMEONE get the bases PR and psych reps out there now... I
need damage control on this situation ASAP... Block all
communications within a fifty mile vicinity. Walker you still
there?

Walker…. Walker…

Lt. Jackson get him back on the line now!

Lt. Jackson

I can't get a reply from Alpha

Gethros

We're they attacked

Lt. Jackson

No Sir….Hold on wait something strange just happen…

Gethros

What Soldier this isn't time for suspense

Lt. Jackson

Looks like Walkers on beta base now and heading towards the training simulator

Gethros

That son of a bitch has no right…

(As he sits back in his seat, with a look of anger on his face)

He thinks he can do whatever he wants now, huh?

Lt. Jackson

What do you mean Sir

Gethros

(In a whisper)

Nothing… Nothing… Get the Captains to the War room Lt.

(places his hand on his head and shakes it)

Shit he was right, it's all true

INT Space Beta Base Command Center

Lt Jackson:

(Over the loud Speaker)

All Captains must report to the ready room now, All Captains must report to the ready room now

INT Space Training Room

(A team of astronauts are working out in their thermo space suits in zero gravity. Another team is doing combat training in 10 times gravity environment. In walks a mysterious older man in a trench coat)

Walker:

Tech turn off simulator now

Tech:

But they are in the middle of their training. The Captain said not to disturb them, no matter what

Walker:

Do you know who I am soldier?

Tech:

NO I don't

(Walker proceeds to reach into his inside pocket of his coat and takes out a badge. As soon as the Tech reads the badge, He stands up and salutes Walker)

Tech:

Sorry Sir, I didn't know

Walker:

Stand down soldier and turn off the AI system

(The tech proceeds to turn off the AI environment)

Captain James:

Tech, didn't I order you not to turn off the AI until I told you too

Tech:

I am under different orders Sir

Captain James:

Who's

Walker:

Mine

Capt. James:

MINE, MINE WHO...... HELLO.... TECH who's orders are you under?

Tech

(Looks up to Walker for permission to answer the Captain. Walker gives him a no head nod. Cap James, frustrated that no one is answering him and the fact that his training session with his team was cut short, starts to take off his space suit.)

Cap James:

Men stay here I will be right back.

(Cap James proceeds to walk towards the control room. His men look at him confused and start to take off their suits. Most of them were exhausted from this impromptu six hour training sessions, were glad that someone stopped the Captain)

INT Training Room Control Session

Cap James:

Tech now who's this me character, that interrupted my session damnit

(Walker who's back was to the Captain when he walked in turns around with a smile on his face)

Walker:

Is that a way to greet an old friend?

Captain James:

(With a Big Smile on his face)

General, Sir, as he salutes him. Then he proceeds to hug him

Walker:

OK, OK put me down.

James:

Sorry General

(The two look at each other and then James smile leaves his face as he looks at Walker)

James:

Hold on if you're here then there is a problem. Are they scrapping the mission? Are you taking over the mission? What's going on here General?

Walker:

Hold on son, you're asking a lot of questions all at one time. Were you inside the simulator all day?

James

Yeah I was getting in some last minute training before launch tomorrow. Why what Happen?

Walker

Let's go for a walk

James:

This doesn't look like good news. Tech tell my men, that they are on break for now but stay close

Tech:

Yes, Sir

(As the tech grabs his comm. device and speaks)

Looks like Someone in there has God on their side. You guys get a break

Chin:

Who was that?

Tech

That was General Walker

Blackburn:

General Walker, oh this is serious

Christian

Who's General Walker?

Blackburn:

You don't know who General Walker is? Enlighten her Sam

Sam

General Walker is the man they call in to carry out all black ops
missions in the world. When you hear of a dictator killed, head
of a cartel murdered, a clan dissent government overthrown out
of the blue, it was him. Rumors had it that they asked him to
run this mission to space and he turned them down.

Blackburn:

That's how Captain James got the promotion because he was
Walkers number one and Walker told them to give it to him.
But if he's here then something is wrong

Jay

You're just trying to scare us. We don't scare easy old man as
he slaps Brace high Five

Brace:

Yeah old man we're the best of the best. They recruited us
from all over the world for this mission

Blackburn:

Yeah, you're the best of the best! I'm not convinced about that
yet

Jay:

Oh don't worry old man when he get to space and trouble
comes we'll be the ones who stay calm and do what we have to
do

Brace:

Have you even been out to space before?

Blackburn

(with a grin on his face)

Kids I've done missions that won't be unclassified until I'm dead for at least a hundred years. You don't really know why I am here but trust me as this mission continues you will

LT. Daniel

You guys can stay here a bicker like a bunch of retired old ladies but I'm going to have a shower and get a drink. It looks like something is brewing behind the scenes and I have to be in the right sense of mind to handle the information

(LT takes the part of his suit that he took off and proceeds to walk towards the locker room. Blackburn and the rest of the team follow behind him)

INT Captain James Chambers

Cap James

Well are you going to fill me in or just leave me in suspense?

Walker:

Well son, take a sit

James:

I rather stand

Walker

Suit yourself, Can I get a drink?

James:

Wow, I thought you gave that up

Walker:

I did

(James reaches into his cabinet and takes out a bottle of whiskey and pours the two of them a drink)

Walker:

Thank you

James:

OK General, enough spill it

Walker:

Son I prepared you for any situation within this world. I wish I had more time to prepare you for this...

James:

You're talking in riddles Sir

Walker:

Shake his head

James

This... What?

(Walker proceeds to reach into his pocket and take out a small rod shape device and raises it towards his face.)

Walker

Ready

(The two of them turn in a mist and disappear)

INT Alpha Base inside a mountain in the jungles of Africa

(and Walker reappear. James is amazed a blank look on his face which turns to scare)

James

Cough, cough, cough...

(Falls to his knees)

WHAT the FUCK was THAT

(looks around)

WHERE THE FUCK AM I?

Walker

Remember you are still a soldier and I am your superior

James

Sorry SIR but what the...

270

(As James stops talking, he looks up to see a massive being walking towards him. James reaching for his weapon realizing that he doesn't have it on him starts to look for his knife. Again he doesn't have it. Then the being starts to talk)

Dr. Coaxe

Welcome back Walker

James:

What the HELL is going on here?

Dr. Coaxe

Is this the one? Hum. Does he know who he really is?

Walker

No not yet, I was just about to fill him in

James:

I am right here, stop talking like I am not in the room, who the hell are you? (As he looks at Dr. Coaxe)

Dr. Coaxe

(He presents his tail to James. James confused shacks it)

My name is Dr. Coaxe

Walker

James this is Dr. Coaxe. You are now at our Alpha base. Let me give you a tour and fill you in on what we do here

(James, Walker, and Dr. Coaxe proceeds to tour the base.)

Walker:

Well James while I was on my first black ops missions in this continent.

James:

Excuse me Sir, where are we exactly?

Walker

We are in a secret base in Africa, we call it Alpha. I found this location about 30 years ago. A rebel leader running away from me ran up the mountain and I chased after him. We both reached the top at the same time. He reached for his gun first and shot, while my back was against the wall. It missed. He had a look of shock on his face, me reacting to him missing I pulled my gun out and shot him. I didn't know, that the look he gave me meant that he was giving up because of what he saw.

James:

What did he see? Sir

Walker

It seems like the bullet awoke the dormant AI system that runs the base. During that process, the base cloaking device shut down due to the power drain. Later I found out that it did quite more than that.

Dr. Coaxe

That shouldn't have happen... It was more than just the bullet. I think that the two of you activated the AI. I theorize that when you place more hybrids together their abilities increase. That's why your unit is so special

Walker

Let's hold up on that one Doc

James

What are you talking about what about my unit?

Walker

(Sigh)

fine... your unit was an experiment

James

An experiment?

Walker

The higher ups wanted to know the true capabilities of the...

James

Hold up my unit's an experiment and what the hell do you mean?

Dr. Coaxe

they had to see if my hypothesis was correct and looking at your mission success rate, I was right

James

I signed up for the military to serve and protect my nation. Not to be some fucking experiment. And WHO"S experiment was in and what the hell is a hybrid

Walker

Come on Jim, Deep down you already knew something was different with certain members of your team. Members that seem to do things far beyond human capabilities. After reading some of your reports even you seem to be able to do things that normal humans no matter what training they receive couldn't do!

James

What are you saying General? Do you mean you gave me missions that if I was a normal soldier, I would have died?

Walker

Sorry Soldier but it's why I recruited you for my unit and it's why you were able to survive thus far

James

This is not what I signed up for!

Walker

We are not the ones in charge soldier. We are soldier we get orders and we follow them. That's it. Don't think I was happy about the missions they gave us. I lost a lot of men these past few decades. If it wasn't for these alien genes I would look older than I do.

Dr. Coaxe

Oh yeah it does slow down your aging process, allows you to heal faster, and you are immune to certain diseases that regular humans are vulnerable too

James

Great so were some type of super soldier human

Walker

Yes and if the world found out they would not react in the nicest way towards our kind. That's why only certain world leaders knew about this base and the real history of world. We could not let everyone know but in less than a week the whole world will.

James

So now what? Huh? How did you get into this base anyways?

Walker

I tried to open the doors

James

How

Walker

I used my gun and then explosives but nothing worked.

James

So how did you get in?

Walker

I'm getting to that. Unbeknownst to me you see, the AI system now on, began the process of awakening Dr. Coaxe and all of the systems of this base. Even it's defenses.

Dr. Coaxe

Yeah it was a security procedure. The first thing I did before I placed myself into hibernation was put that protocol in. I program it to activate once my people returned. It was suppose to protect the planet.

James

Ok so what happen next?

Walker

A beam of light shot out of the top part of the bay doors and scanned my body. The doors open and a voice said welcome hybrid Walker

Dr. Coaxe

Another security procedure of the AI system. That I did not program in. For some reason maybe it was rush in programming the system. Or it was the AI system learning on its own or a failsafe it's creator put in

Walker

Wait... let me continue.... So I entered the base. The voice continued to give me directions to follow

James

Follow

Walker

Yes, follow. So I followed the voice. It lead me to a chamber where I saw something sleeping. The voice was counting down to the reversal of the hibernation process. Me out of bullets, no comm. device to reach the outside world, and completely lost just stood there and waited in awe

James

Waited for what Sir

Walker

My death. You see James this was before, I met you and all the rumors of me started. I was green just like you were when we first met. I didn't know what was waking up or how to handle it

James

Hold up what did the voice mean welcome hybrid Walker

Walker

I'm getting to that. Well as I waited for this creature to thaw out. An image appeared before me

James

An image?

Walker

Yes an image

Dr. Coaxe

Failsafe of the base

James

Seems like this base has a lot of secrets

Dr. Coaxe

More than you know

Walker

Well the image started to talk to me.

(James stops walking and looks up to the ceiling. Then looks to Dr. Coaxe and Walker)

James

What do you mean started to talk

Walker

Well it talked to me. It was a hologram. James. While awakening the AI system seems not only activating the system but it also hacked it to every server around the world and gathered all the information it needed, to catch up. It knew who I was as soon as it scanned me.

James

So it knows who everyone in the world is?

Dr Coaxe

Not just our world but anywhere High Command been since the beginning

James

High Command...

Walker

Pay attention this shit is about to get real. Open your eyes son; does Dr. Coaxe look like he's from this planet? Does this base look like any type of base you'll ever been on? We teleported here. Have you ever teleported before? This isn't some CERN experiment. How do you think we were able to build space ships that can go faster than light in such a short period of time? Son we just started our space program less that 60 years ago. Now we have the capabilities to travel to galaxies far beyond what out telescopes can see. We have maps of the universe son, where do you think we got maps from. Never during your trainings did you ask yourself how?

James

No Sir

Walker

Well all that came from this base, the AI system here, Dr. Coaxe, and the alien visitors to this planet

(James perplexed just stands there and starts to take everything in)

Walker

Don't stop walking now son there's more

(The three men continue to walk into a room. First they are scanned by a beam of light.)

AI

Identity accepted, Welcome hybrids Walker, James and Dr. Coaxe

James

What is this room about?

Walker

You want answers huh, I'm going to let you get them the same way I did. Take a seat soldier and put this helmet on

James

Is this dangerous?

Walker

Just take a seat and put the helmet on. This computer is only compatible with aliens and others who share their genetic code

(As soon as Walker says that he puts the helmet on James and gives the Doctor the go ahead head nod)

James

Wait what.

AI

Information downloading into cerebellum

Dr. Coaxe

Will he survive the download?

Walker

I did plus he has to we need him now more than ever. Especially, since they are on their way. How are the upgrades to the base going?

Dr. Coaxe

Don't worry we will be fully operational before they get here. Plus we do have a backup; his cousin Rick also has the genes.

Walker

How much time do we have?

Dr. Coaxe

If they continue on their course, they will be here in seven days
or so

Walker

Can we launch tomorrow? Are the rest of the hybrids ready?

Dr. Coaxe

No we have to do some of the members of his team whom we
kept chained. I can't wait to see what happens when we awake
them ALL

Walker

Well what's taking so long?

Dr. Coaxe

There on their way here now

Walker

Good. I wish we had more time. Did the AI locate anymore
Hybrids?

(James sitting in the chair shakes as you sees the helmet light up
and flashing lights by his eyes)

Dr. Coaxe

We are more prepared then we were the last time. Yes but these new ones are too young

Walker

That doesn't matter anymore... I have an unknown enemy coming towards me with intent to destroy a whole planet out of fear of what we could do to the universe... Plus we don't have any Intel on their new capabilities. That scout came out of nowhere. We're going to need everyone! Plus I have a feeling they don't want us on this planet anymore

Dr. Coaxe

It's not just fear... They saw what happen in the past. This time they are going to bring a strong enough force to destroy everything. That satellite was a scout. Our AI did detect it and since our AI been dormant since the first battle, they don't know that our AI is still linked to their. We know what they know and they don't know we know. Do you really want to use teenagers? I wouldn't want you guys on this planet either. No one really knows what you guys can do.

Walker

Let's pray it can detect more than just that scout. When that Mother Ship comes! It doesn't matter whether they are teenagers or not we need them. Begin the recruitment process on them too. I need to find them and protect them. We're going to need them soon.

INT Global Federation Space Base Commissary

Rick

(as he eats a piece of chicken and stuff some noodles in his face)

So did you hear our Captain is off base?

Mike

Can you not talk with food in your mouth?

Rick

What I'm hungry

Mike

You're always hungry

Melissa

I did hear that Cap off base

Jay

How could he leave the base right before launch

John

I feel there's something going on that we don't know about

Rick

Like what?

John

Not sure but if Walker came here and then Cap disappears. Something isn't right. Like that thing that just appeared over the base.

Jay

Here you go Skywalker, is there an unbalance in the force too man

John

Keep joking but tell me when my instincts were ever wrong? Plus did you hear that bullshit about it being some training op?

Brace

Yeah, I heard they used the bases laser system to destroy some flying globe or something

Scar

I'm not one to feed into his instincts but he's right when he gets a feeling I tend to listen because he's usually right. Plus that wasn't a training op. If it was we wouldn't have been in the simulator

Chin

Then what was it? An attack

Scar

Right after that, the General order all Captains to the ready room and now the base is on Yellow Alert. What I'm trying to figure out is who would attack us. This mission involves every country all over the world. I think this is the first time our planet's been so calm. I mean no one's fighting. Every nationality, religion, culture, you name it is working together on this space mission. I think this is the first time since the beginning of time that there's actually peace on Earth.

Jason

If we use our past as a baseline the only time enemies unite is to fight a greater enemy. The enemy of my enemy is a friend.

Rich

Don't feed into his bullshit too Scar come on man you're the big man fearless a natural born killer and you're telling me that you believe this instinct shit too? You probably believe in Aliens too

(Blackburn taking a drink while Rich continues to speak. He then spits out some of his drink after Rich says Aliens)

Scar

All I'm saying is that John might be right again cause there something wrong going on and they're not telling us anything. I mean they have the world's best of the best here and they are going to send us into space. Who's going to stay here and protect our countries?

John

Maybe that's what we're doing?

Scar

So you think they are sending us into space to protect the
planet?

John

It doesn't make a lot of sense once you say it but sometimes the
truth sounds like a fairy tale and what they tell us is really fiction

Jason

Well then that doesn't make sense? That we are going to fight
out in space but against whom? It's a bit too Sci-fi for me

Chin

Well if you think about it, everyday they find more and more
planets that could sustain life and every star in the sky is
actually a sun. There's billions of stars. I would be a fool to
think that we're the only life in this universe.

Rich

Shit while we're at it lets start to believe in mutants and super
heroes too... On another note who's that over by the cakes?

Phillip

Her name is Lt. Isis but don't even think about it. She might
look good but she's a high ranking intelligence officer, which
means she's dangerous. For what I've heard, she's a Psych girl.
You don't want to let her get into your head

John

A psych officer? What's that?

Chin

They get into your head man that's all I know. In Basic my Sergeant told me to be careful around them. They know how to predict shit

(Blackburn quite seems spaced out to the group)

Brace

You ok over there old man? Thought I might had to give you CPR, now you just look lost

Jay

Damn and we're going into space with you

Blackburn

(Looks at Jay and Brace)

I'm not sure you two are ready for what about to happen

Jay

Man we trained for years to go into space

Brace

Yeah it's no biggie

Blackburn

So you really think it's only space you were training for….

(Blackburn gets up and shakes his head at the two of them.)

you will soon find out what this mission is really about..

(As he turns around and walks away)

Brace

What the fuck is that old man talking about?

Jay

Man forget him

Rich

Will you two shut up for once I want to know more about this Lt. Isis?

Brace

Then go talk to her and stop day dreaming about her

Rich

I will…

(Rich gets up from the table and goes over to Isis)

John

I think Blackburn knows something… I'll going to go talk to him

Jay

Man fuck him. That old man doesn't know shit

Brace

You really think he knows something John

John

I DO...

(John gets up and starts to walk towards Blackburn)

Scar

Gets up quickly... Hold up John I'm coming with you

Jay

ARE you two SERIOUS.... You really think that old man knows something that we don't

Brace

Jay....

Jay

WHAT

Brace

I'm going with them

Jay

You too What the fuck... Fine let's all go and see what the old man knows. And when we find out he doesn't know shit then... Y'all owe me. I think I you will be doing my laundry duty for a month (as Jay turns around he sees the group leaving the Commissary.) Hey hold up I'm coming wait for me

Brace

Hurry up damnit

(Jay runs after the group)

EXT Hallway outside of the Commissary Enter John, Scar, Jay, Brace, Philip, Rick, Christian, Melissa, Blackburn, Chin, Sam, Dreke, and Jason

John

Blackburn... Blackburn... hold up wait

Blackburn

What's on your mind soldier?

John

We want to know what you know

Blackburn

I'm not sure you're ready for that... Especially frick and frak over there. Plus you guys don't have the clearance for that

Jay

I know you're not talking about us old man

John

Jay stand down and shut up for now

Jay

WHAT

Brace

Jay listen for once

Rick

Don't mind him Blackburn he's ready I know he is

Blackburn

Rick are you sure?

Rick

Yeah…. Let me call it in and get the clearance for them

(Rick goes into his pocket and pulls out an ear lobe size device and puts it in his ear)

This is Rick to Lt. Daniel

Rick

Lt. Daniel permission for transport members of the team to Alpha location

Blackburn

What he say?

Rick

He said go to a secure location for transport... Turn on your comm... Device Blackburn

(Blackburn takes his right hand and places his finger onto the outside of his ear and presses down)

Blackburn

Activated

Jay

What the hell is going on Blackburn?

Blackburn

Your cousin seems to think that you're ready to know the truth... Now let's go or are you scared

Jay

(In a non-convincing tone)

I'm not scared

Rick

Don't worry cousin. It's time you find out a secret that...

Blackburn

No time for that let's go. We only have a small window to
teleport. WAIT where's Rich?

Rick

We left him talking to that psych officer

Blackburn

We can't leave without him. Someone call him on his comm.
and tell him to meet us at my quarters

Jay

(Reaches into his pocket and takes out a small comm. device)

Rich... Rich...Rich... It's Jay we have a mission lover boy

INT Commissary

Rich

Still in the commissary talking to Lt. Isis pretends not to hear the
message)

Isis

You should get that soldier

(with a smile on her face)

Rich

I really don't want too... We were just started to get to know
each other

Isis

Trust me we will have another time to get to know each other better. Plus it's important that you answer

Rich

(Goes into his pocket and pulls out his comm. device)

WHAT is it?

Jay

Met us at Blackburn's quarters. We have a mission

Rich

What mission?

Jay

No time for questions just meet us ASAP. We're under orders

Rich

FINE,

(as he looks to Isis...)

Hey when I get back you want to do lunch or even dinner

Isis

Let's start out with lunch...Soldier Boy

(with a glow in her eyes and a smile)

Rich

(Takes Isis hands and kisses it)

Bye Luv...

(Turns around and runs away)

High Command Mother Ship Command Center

Jensen

Commander....

(Commander spins his chair around to face Jensen with a look of frustration on his face)

Commander

What is it?

Jensen

They seem to have detected our scout and destroyed it Sir

Commander

There's no way they could have detected our scout it was cloaked.

Jensen

It seems it uncloaked Sir

Commander

No matter. What Intel did it gather anyways?

Jensen

Seems they have some space ships gearing up to launch into space

Commander

Any readout on the ships?

Jensen

The scout wasn't able to complete a scan. We just know they have the capabilities to enter space and travel to other galaxies

Commander

No weapons readout?

Jensen

No Sir

(The Commander sits back into his seat and thinks to himself)

Commander

I wonder if they know we are coming. Hmmn should I report back to High Command and request more support. My predecessor failed against these puny things. He lost his existence to them but how? I don't care if they share the same genes as us. There's no way they could have defeated me. I will not make the same mistake as he did. I will destroy them

(with a smirk on his face).

Those ships can't stand up to the power of this mother ship. After I destroy these things, I will head over to the Orion sector and finish what he started. It's clean up duty time. All the past mistakes he made I will fix them. Then High Command will give me whatever I want

Jensen

Commander... Commander

Commander

WHAT Jensen

Jensen

We seem to be blocked out of the humans sector now...

Commander

What do you mean... blocked out

Jensen

I've lost the ability to scan the sector with long range satellite. It's like the satellite is gone Sir

Commander

It can't be! Do they have the technology to detect our satellites and destroy them? Something is wrong they couldn't have just progressed this far since we found out they were going into space. Someone must be helping them but who? Who could be so foolish to help them? From the data collected from that battle everyone was either killed or wiped. No one could have lived that long since that last battle without our technology to sustain them. Maybe it's just malfunctioning. It has been a long time since we left that satellite there. Jensen don't worry about that. There is nothing that can stop us from defeating these humans. Are our soldiers ready?

Jensen

I've started the rejuvenation process

Commander

Good. Make sure you turn their battle senses all the way up. We are going to destroy everything

Jensen

Yes Sir. Do you want me to keep the restrictor on them?

Commander

NO I want them fully aware and ready for carnage. This is revenge and when you're out for revenge you don't hold back. We will make them and those fucking Orion's, an example of what will happen if you ever go against High Command

Nicklous

Sir we've never sent the soldiers out without a restrictor before. During the experiment they had to evoke the self destruction program because they won't stop fighting. They started to attack everyone once the mission was done... You're the commander Sir but are you sure you want to do this?

Commander

Did I give an order...? I want them to kill everyone and everything. I'm not leaving anything living in this sector once I leave

(The Commander gets up and starts to walk towards the door. As he gets to the door, the door opens and the Commander turns around.)

Commander

Don't ever forget that you are replaceable. When I give an order that's that. This isn't a democracy. I am in charge here. Remember if we fail we die anyways

(The Commander continues to walk out of the doors)

Nicklous

This is bad very bad. I've never seen the Commander behave like this. He's usually calculated sometimes too much calculated. This mission seems different. You we're here when he received the orders from the Overlords, he had a look of rage in his face! Like it was him that lost that battle.

Mack

Let's not talk about this. We have our orders and we better follow them or it will be us that self-destruct. I rather it be someone else then me. ...

Jensen

Yes Sir. I'm already beginning the program process

Mack

Brembo our target is the third one from the sun let's stop at between the fifth and sixth planet to ensure the safety of the ship

Brembo

Yes Captain

Mack

It's in all of our benefits to allow the Overlords and the Commander to get their revenge

INT Blackburn's quarters

(KNOCK KNOCK)

Blackburn

Open the door

(Jay walks towards the door and opens it... Rich walks in)

Rich

So what's the big deal for ya'll to interrupt me? We don't really have a mission huh?

Blackburn

(Takes his finger and presses his ear)

We're ready LT

Rich

Ready for what...

(The group turns into mist and disappears)

INT Command Center of Global Federation Beta Base

Soldier

General... we have an unauthorized teleportation to the Alpha base

General Gethros

Who teleported?

Soldier

Looks like it's most of Captain James team

General Gethros

Damnit Walker we don't need to tell the world what's going on... They should have never gave him carte blanch   I don't care if he is who he is

Soldier

General do you want to me to contact Alpha base

General Gethros

No, no need it won't change anything. How is the implementation of the AI system going Corporal?

Corporal Smith

Working on it General. Seems like we're about 60% done.
Another hour we should be finish and ready to go

General Gethros

We have almost a week until they get here. According to that
thing at that base, they're not coming here to talk

Corporal Smith

What about the civilians outside the base and the rest of the
world. The shields aren't powerful enough to protect the whole
planet are they?

General Gethros

Not my business. I'm here to make sure this base is ready for
war. The world leaders feel that the masses aren't ready to
know that we are going to be attack by aliens. They feel they
would panic and riot

Corporal Smith

What about our families Sir? My wife and kids?

General Gethros

I have no clue soldier. I can't worry about that now I have a
mission to complete... Hopefully they survive and we win. If we
lose... we all die! So it really doesn't matter. Don't think that
you are the only one with a family. We all signed up for this.
Now Contact the Space Station Lt.

Lt. Jackson

Yes Sir... Space Station this is the Command Center come thru

INT International Space Station

Denise

Major Aduor. We have a comm. from the Command Center

Major Adour

Damnit what does he want now... I have enough problems with this space station. I really don't want to talk to him

Denise

Do you want me to tell him you're busy?

Major Adour

No put him through.... General how can I help you?

General Gethros

Anything to report Major

Major Adour

Not since the last time we spoke General. This space station is too old to handle the task we need it to do

General Gethros

Are you saying you can't complete your mission? Cause the scientists down here seem to think that the space station is the best facility to handle the system. Should I call the President and tell him that we can't carry out his orders?

Major Adour

All I'm saying General is that I need to be working on my mission instead of being on this comm. device. As soon as I have anything new to report I will contact you. Major out

Lt. Jackson

We just lost comm. General

General Gestro

That damn Major he better complete his mission

INT International Space Station

Major Adour

That damn General is always on my ass. Johnson what's the status of that upload and repair

Johnson

Man when you asked me to go to space with you, I never thought that I would be in this Smithsonian relic.

Major Adour

Hey man we're in space right

Johnson

You knew that if you told me that I would be in this piece of shit I would have said no

Major Adour

Are you sure about that Buddy... When I came to you, you just
lost everything in the divorce. You had no job, no woman, and
depress. Now look at you

Johnson

Oh yeah, I'm in a smelly piece of shit awaiting an alien attack
and on the front line of it all... Thanx Major, I feel so much
better about my situation now!

Major Adour

You'll have time to bitch at me after the mission

Johnson

Really are you sure about that? Cause I'm trying to figure out if
you're delusional or on drugs!

Major Adour

I'm still your ranking officer

Johnson

Don't pull rank on me now! You STARTED this shit...

Major Adour

Did you even answer my question? How far are you?

Johnson

I'm about 50% done but we might have a power issue

Major Adour

Power issue

Johnson

Yeah, the brilliant person who decided to pick a 30 year old space station to be the hub for a global comm. system clearly didn't take into account the power needed to run it. We're going to have life support issue and a whole mess of other things once we turn this thing on. How do they think we are going to stay here during the battle?

Major Adour

They don't. As soon as you finish we're teleporting to the ship

Johnson

Teleport…Ship… what are you talking about?

Major Adour

OH… did I forget to tell you…

Johnson

You sneaky son of a… Well come on tell me

Major Adour

We're leaving once you complete this upload; we join up with the fleet cloaked on the other side of the planet

Johnson

We have a cloaked fleet…There seems to be a lot of information
you left out about this mission

Major Adour

I just receive permission to tell you everything. Now hurry up so
we can get out of here. Intel suggests that since this space
station is so old the aliens won't bother investigating it. It is the
perfect disguise for our comm. system or at least that was what
the brass at Alpha Base suggested. So get to it!

Johnson

(While He Salutes)

YES SIR!

INT Global Federation Command Center

Lt. Jackson

General Gethros, I'm receiving a comm. from Alpha Base

General Gethros

Put it through

General Walker

Gethros are you there

General Gethros

I'm here but I hear you were on my base, why didn't you inform
me of your presence

General Walker

No time for that…. I need an update on the containment of the enemy fly over information

General Gethros

We have our best soldiers working on it. We told the civilian witnesses that it was a training op. We notified all our Captains that Beta base is under yellow alert and to have their team ready. We did not tell them why

Walker

Good. Dr. Coaxe tells me that the upload is about 80% done at beta and about 70% done on the Space Station

Gethros

Do you think it's going to work Jim?

Walker

Kyle I hope so. We're not talking about just a country here; we're talking about the whole planet. If we make a mistake then it's over for all of us.

Gethros

God Help us all

Walker

On orders given by the President. Dr. Coaxe reached out to another world that has a race that the aliens couldn't beat. Dr. Coaxe sent a ship there during the first battle centuries ago but that ship didn't return. Dr. Coaxe seems to be under the belief that the race of aliens are still there on that planet and that his ship is still intact. Due to some Intel we just received

Gethros

What are you saying Jim

Walker

We sent a message to the ship and we received an encrypted message back. The AI system is working on decoding the message. It seems that this was the race the aliens were fighting before they found the Earth. The only reason why they never came the first time was their memories were wiped. It seems they have caught up just like us

Gethros

So we might have some help. There's still a ray of hope left. I have to tell you I didn't believe you until this morning and that scout.

Walker:

Well at least you do now. We're going to have to work together now more than ever.

Gethros

It's not like I didn't believe, I just didn't want too. Especially from the Intel I've read our chances don't... doesn't make me feel too confident about our situation. We have a lot of green soldiers out there who only time they fought in space or against aliens is in their damn Black Ops video game or in our simulator

Walker

We'll let's hope Black Ops and our training is sufficient enough for this war. At least we know their coming and we're somewhat prepared for it.

Gethros

As soon as the upload completes I will inform you. Gethros out

INT Alpha Base

Walker

Chips are stacked against us Lt

Lt Daniel

Sir when isn't the chips stacked against us. Ever mission they give us more shitier than the last. I'm tired of them experimenting on us. They don't think we're going to make it out but we do! It's our Call of Duty Sir

Walker

True

Lt. Daniel

My question is this, what is their escape plan?

Walker

Escape plan Lt?

Lt. Daniel

Com on sir don't tell me that there isn't an escape plan. We didn't create all these ships just for war. I know those damn suits thought of a way of getting the fuck out of here if we are losing. They not just going to stay here and hope we win. Trust me Sir they have an escape plan but we're not part of it. They're going to leave us here to die while they run

Walker

Umm… Get Dr. Coaxe on the comm. Alice. If there is something going on He Knows

Alice

Yes sir. Dr. Coaxe, Walker is requesting your present

INT Dr. Coaxe Lab

Dr. Coaxe

Can't leave right now, the Captain is almost done. Tell him to come to my lab

INT Alpha base command center

Alice

General Walker, Dr. Coaxe said he can't leave right now and you need to come down to his lab

Walker

Fine.

(Gets up and walks towards the door turns back)

Daniels looks through those maps and try to locate any planet close to us that is sufficient for human life. Jeff scans through the all of the data on anything that left this planet in the past. I want to know about anything from a kid's toy rocket ship to a satellite being launch.

Jeff

How far do you want me to go back Sir?

Walker

From the beginning...

(Walks out toward Dr. Coaxes' Lab)

Jeff

What the fuck is this about? From the beginning! Do you know how much information that is? SHIT!

Lt. Daniel

You ever have a eureka moment

Jeff

Eureka Sir?

Lt. Daniel

Ok a moment of Clarity

Jeff

Yes Sir

Lt. Daniel

Well soldier, our General just had a moment of clarity. There's something wrong with this whole situation and I think the General just figured something out. I just hope it's in time

Billy

Lt. We have the rest of Captain James team teleporting in now.

Lt. Daniel

Damnit not enough time in the day. Where are the teleporting too?

Billy

Flight Deck three

Lt. Daniel

Let Blackburn know I'm going to meet them when he materializes.

(Lt. Gets up and swiftly leaves the command center heading towards the flight deck)

Jeff

The tension increases every moment I breathe

Billy

Suck it up soldier, you signed up for this shit

INT Dr. Coaxes' Lab

(Walker runs to Dr. Coaxe lab. He gets outside of it and Bangs on the Door.)

KNOCK KNOCK KNOCK

The doors locked

Walker

Doc it's me open the door

(From the inside of the Lab)

Dr. Coaxe

Hold on I'm just about to take the helmet off the Captain

Walker

He can wait open the door now

Dr. Coaxe

Ok...

(He orders AI to open the door)

(AI opens the door)

(The doors to his lab open. In rushed Walker with a hostile look on his face)

Walker

Why didn't you tell me?

(Dr. Coaxe has his hands on Captain James shoulders. He then takes the helmet off and looks shocked)

Dr. Coaxe

What do you mean, when was I going to tell you

Walker

I didn't get it until I spoke to Kyle and told him about your other ships

Dr. Coaxe

I'm not sure what you are talking about General

Walker

Not the time to play with me... tell me what's really going on. We started this shit together. If it wasn't for me you would still be an ice cube. It all makes sense now, why wouldn't you reach out to them. It's another planet that humans can live in isn't it?

Dr. Coaxe

Well yes it's another planet that both our species can live on

Walker

Stop fucking around Doc. Was that message even encrypted or did you just tell me it was because you were told not to tell me what's going on?

Dr. Coaxe

Okay let's start from the beginning. Who are we talking about?

Walker

The ones I answer too. Answer me DOC are they leaving us here to die while they escape

Dr. Coaxe

Oh them. Well there's not enough ships to hold almost 7 billion people. So yes... they are planning on leaving most of the population here

Walker

What's their plan if we lose? How are they going to do it?

Dr. Coaxe

Oh they are going to get on the transport ships, warp to a safe location, and blow up the planet killing everything in the galaxy. They feel that the explosion will make it look like the aliens won and they won't try to find them.

Captain James

(Waking up)

THEY MUST BE OUT OF YOUR FUCKING MIND! NOT ON MY WATCH

Walker

(in a low tone voice)

Why didn't you tell me

Dr. Coaxe

I thought you knew

James

What about the civilians

Walker

Collateral damage

James

No they wouldn't

Walker

Trust me son they will. How do they plan on doing it?

Dr. Coaxe

With the reactor powering here and Beta base

James

Can two reactors cause that much destruction?

Dr. Coaxe

Well yes especially two of mine

Walker

Can we stop them?

Dr. Coaxe

Well...

James

(very anxiously)

Well what

Walker

Stay frosty James

James

Fuck frosty... I WANT ANSWERS

Dr. Coaxe

Well there's a fail safe

James

Now you're talking my language

Dr. Coaxe

The AI system won't destroy the planet if it feels there's still a chance to win. Also it was programmed to protect the hybrids at all cost. I told your leaders that. Due to Dr. Elisa programming it won't allow for the Hybrids to be destroyed. That's why you were able to find this base the AI system noticed that you were going to kill another Hybrid and it turned on its defenses to stop you but it was too slow. I also told them that it's you Captain, that it wants to protect the most. I tried to override the programming but it's embedded too much into the system, it can't be overridden.

James

Why me

Dr. Coaxe

You know how the Earth became a jail and who gave their lives to protect it from destruction now.

James

Yes

Dr. Coaxe

Well you're the descendant of the Captain who stopped the Commander from destroying this planet. He gave his existence to ensure your survival. In his brief time on this planet he had twins with another progressed soldier, Isis. a boy and a girl. For some strange reason the boy and the girl kept mating with only other descendants of the hybrid race. Therefore they kept the bloodline going. This machine I just unconnected you from just awakened the alien genes inside of you. Within the next few hours you will start to feel your body changing. It happens to all of you guys. It's the reason why your General over here could carry out all those impossible missions, without a scratch.

(James looks over too Walker)

James

Green, huh

Walker

Well you didn't let me finish the story

Dr. Coaxe

I will now. Let me fill in the gaps now. You see James, you bloodline goes back from the time High Command decided to create super soldiers that had the ability to think on their own. These soldiers were different from the brainless drones that they had back then. They were more like the Commander and your bloodline comes from the Commanders second in command. Only you and your twin have the genes now. We came here to establish a base on Mars since we lost our base in the Orion sector. This sector was the perfect place to have a hub for our travels but once we messed with the genes of your humans ancestors something unexplainable happen. They started to show skills that no other species did before.

Then something even more incredible happen, our race and yours became compatibly and they started to have kids. Again, this was the first time anything like that ever happen. We've interfered with many species to use them as slaves but your species was different. Dr. Elisa tried to keep this a secret but it was hard. Then we found out that it wasn't our experiment that allowed our species to procreate with each other, we just awake the genes that for some reason were dormant. We found out that we were similar to you but as in the ying and yang, you guys were the ying meaning the genes to want war was turned off and we were the yang our genes for war and battle was turned on. You see it seems like someone created both of our species at the same time. We still haven't found out who or whom. So it seems we're both an experiment. This is the real reason why The Overlords want you dead. They feel that once they destroy you they will prove that they were the right species to rule the universe, not the humans. They fear that they will never find out who the Master is until they get rid of any threat to their rule. Therefore, you, Rick, and your twin are very important to the universe. You guys have an unbelievable untapped power inside of you. That's the only reason why your ancestor was able to beat the Commander. He had keen insight

James

Hold up wait what? What are you talking about? And what Twin....I don't have a twin

Walker

That was one fact the machine leaves out. That we are related to our enemies and yes you do have a twin

James

Wait what fucking twin

Walker

Your sister.... You two were separated at birth. Your father was killed in one of my black ops mission and your mom died during birth. I made sure you two were protected and watched over by responsible families. I didn't want to take you under my wing because I didn't want you to join the military but you end up in the fucking military anyways. The both of you did. So I watched from a far and made sure you two were ok. I'm sorry son, I didn't want this for you but I have no choice now.

James

Just sits there perplexed bent over with both hands on the top of his face

Walker

(Grabs his comm. device)

Lt. Daniel... tell Lt. Isis that's she's needed on Alpha base ASAP

Lt. Daniel

Yes Sir... Daniel out

Walker

Well let's reunite the family

James

(In a low tone voice)

I...SIS...ISIS is her name

Walker

Yes. Your father loved that word

James

You never told me that you knew my father

Walker

I couldn't son.... I was under orders from above

James

Hmmm... I always had a feeling, I wasn't alone.... Does she know about me?

Walker

She just found out

LT Daniel

General, Isis is here

Walker

Send her to Dr. Coaxe lab

(James takes a seat down and puts his hands over his head.)

James

(in a low tone)

She's on her way? What do I say to her?

Walker

Start with Hi

Doors to Dr. Coaxe lab open in walks Isis

Walker

Dr. Coaxe let's leave these two alone. They have a lot to talk about

(As Walker and Dr. Coaxe turn to leave the Lab James picks up his head)

James

So... You're my twin sister

Isis

I've envisioned this so many times in the past five years but...

James

(Gets up slowly, while taking his hands off his head. He looks at her)

I don't even know what to say to you. I don't know how to feel. I feel happy and pissed off at the same time. I'm pissed because I have a fucking twin that I never knew about until now and I'm happy I have a twin sister and now we've met. This can't be...

Isis

I know. When I found out I wanted to go and find you but they told me no

James

See you don't understand. I'm happy we know each other now but I'm pissed because you didn't do anything to find me and tell me the truth. Matter of fact you got the highest clearance in the military, you didn't even have to try to find me. So tell me why? Why didn't you even try?

Isis

Calm down. You know how it is when you're under orders. Don't ever think I never wanted to tell you. I would read about you and your team and the missions you were on and pray that you survived. Then I would read the report and be elated that you made it out of all those shit holes.

James

Sister... THIS IS CALM! I won't be so calm much longer. Cause this is some BULLSHIT! You, Walker, and that THING can KISS MY ASS right now. You could have said something to me

Isis

Like what? Huh? What... What would I say to you for you to believe me that I was your sister? Oh maybe I should just walk up to you and say Hey James I'm your long lost twin sister Isis and guess what there aliens out there and they might come and attack us again. Oh... yeah I let me not leave this out you and I are direct descendants of the same alien race that wants to eradicate us. Tell Me James would you really have listen to me? I soldier like yourself would you really have? Anyways, if they ever saw me walk up to you and try to talk they would have stopped it by all means necessary. Don't you see some of the technology that is down here? You can't find this shit at a Best Buy or target....When I found out about you, they placed me into the awakening program. Before I even had a chance to think, they teleported me here. The first time I left this base was last month. So how tell me how was I going to get in contact with you?

James

I don't want to hear that! If you're really related to me nothing would have stopped you from getting close to me. Matter of FACT Fuck THIS...

(James takes a step and starts to wobble)

James

Is it me or is the room spinning... I don't feel good

Isis

NO you have to stay calm or...

James

OR WHAT what else did you guys leave out? Is an asteroid coming to hit the planet too?

(James starts to wobble more)

James

I don't feel too good

(as he places his right hand on his forehead)

Isis

I told you. Let me help you

James

No... DON'T try to help me now I don't need your help... What's happening to me...?

(James starts to fall to the ground, he reaches to grab something to stop him from falling but there's nothing to grab and he falls to the ground and passes out.)

(Isis rushes over to him and grabs her comm. device)

Isis

Dr. Coaxe, Dr. Coaxe I need you back in the lab. We have a problem....

INT International Space Station

Johnson

Finally done. Hey Rob I'm done get me out of this shit hole

Major Adour

Oh finally your done. Did you test the system?

Johnson

I didn't know I was suppose to test it. Shouldn't the lab coats do that?

Major Adour

Fine let me contact Gethros. Denise send a message to Gethros that we've finished here and we want them to test it out

Denise

Fine...

Major

What is it now?

Denise

Nothing!

Johnson

Oops looks like something wrong with the happy couple

Major

Shut up Johnson no time for this. Denise can you please contact the General for me

Denise

Already doing that Major Sir

Johnson

Hmm someone sleeping in their own quarters tonight

Major

Johnson shut the fuck up and make sure you didn't miss anything!

Johnson

(With a laugh)

Yes Sir!

(As he wipes dirt off is face)

General Gethros

Major you're done

Major

Yes tell the lab coats to turn it on

Gethros

They did 10 minutes ago. You can proceed to your ship and continue with the other part of your mission Major

Major

Thank you Sir! Major out. Ok team let's get out of here.

(The major reaches into his pocket and takes out his comm. device)

This is Major Adour to Cetros. Come in Cetros

Gayle

This is Cetros Sir

Major

We're done over here Gayle. Teleport the team to the ship

(The team teleports to Cetros. One of the cloaks ships)

Jess

Welcome aboard Sir

Johnson

Thank you beautiful. I'm exhausted and smell.

Jess

I Know, I was talking to the Major

Johnson'

Funny little Ms., Show me to my quarters and where I can have a bath

Major

Don't talk to my soldiers like that Johnson. Have some manners

Denise

I'll let you guys figure things out here I'm leaving

(Denise starts to walk away from the groups)

Major

Denise Wait please Wait for me. We need to talk

Denise

Oh now you want to talk

(as she continues to walk out of the teleportation room.)

Major

Jesses please show my ignorant friend over here to his quarters
and please forgive him. He lost his manners in the divorce

(The major runs out of the room after Denise)

Major

Denise please stop and talk to me

(As he catches up to Denise and softly grabs her hand.)

What is it?

Denise

When you told me that you were coming out to space to carry
out a mission and you asked me to come. You never told me
that we were staying on this ship

Major

I thought you wanted to go to space. Especially with me.

Denise

I did but that was before

Major

Before what? Are you scared of space?

Denise

NO I'm NOT SCARED

Major

Did what is it? Why are you so mad at me? What did I do?

Denise

You should have told me that we were staying on this ship. This is not a place for...

Major

For what? What isn't this a place for? Hey I know it's cramped in here and yes it smells a little but its space baby. It's what we always dreamed of being and now we are here. Given we are about to battle an evil alien race but at least we are together Right?

(Denise starts to cry)

Major

Talk to me baby please talk to me. What's bothering you? Tell me so I can fix it

Denise

You can't fix this situation no one can

Major

I'm so lost right now

(takes a step back and holds both of Denise's hands and looks into her eyes)

Denise please tell me what

(Denise still crying Major walks closer to her and places his hand on her face wiping her tears and hugs her. Her face lays on his chest)

Denise

(still being hugged my Major in a whisper)

You're going to be a Father

(Major looks up to the ceiling and hugs Denise ever tighter)

Major

Yes! Oh, Thank God, I'm going to be a father thank God! I've always wanted to be a father. Oh, now it all makes sense. Why didn't try to tell me while we were still on Earth and I wouldn't let you come here. Shit, I would have never took this mission, bay, I'm sorry. Please forgive me

Denise

(Still Crying)

You don't need me to forgive you. I should have told you before. Anyways after learning what I've learned this is the safest place to be right now.

Major

(pulls her closer to him)

Don't cry, I promise you, my love! WE WILL WIN! Our child will live in a free universe. He will have a chance to explore all the galaxies we talked about exploring. Trust ME It will be okay

INT Informatory

(James lying in a bed with tube hooked up to him. James starts to wake up)

Isis

Hey brother are you ok

James

(still half asleep)

What happen?

Isis

You passed out. It happens sometimes to people who get the download

James

The download... what download?

Isis

Remember the Helmet Dr. Coaxe put on your head? It downloaded information into your brain and activated your alien genes. For some reason our emotions effect the download. It's our emotions that turns on the genes. That's why we try to stay calm. Until we are trained to handle our emotions. That's what the helmet was about. It took him years to figure out how to do it. When they fired the memory wipe at Earth, it kept the alien genes dormant but they couldn't eradicate it. That's why Dr. Coaxe said they are coming to destroy us. There's no telling what we could do now that we know the truth of who we really are and what we can really do. I mean I get visions of the future brother. Soon I will be the real life Jean Grey

James

Who?

Isis

Forget it. But soon you will start to feel changes happening inside of you and it's your alien side awakening

James

Handle my emotions and changes hmm. How long was I out for?

Isis

About three hours... Strange once someone passes out they usually don't regain consciousness until days have passed. How are you feeling?

James

(Starts to get up and takes the tubes out of his arm)

I don't have time for this

Isis

You have to stay here... we don't know if you're ok

James

The best way to find out is to try Right Sis?

Isis

(A smile comes to her face)

You're definitely related to me. Ok let's go then.

James

Good Listen I'm ...

Isis

Don't worry about it. We put a lot on your table at once.
Frankly I'm surprised that you handled it so well. Where are we
going?

James

To the Beta base I need to prep my team

Isis

No need for that...

James

Why

Isis

Your team is already here. They are in the War room getting
Intel on the real situation and their orders

James

Bring me to them...

Isis

Ok but first we have to make a quick stop

James

You better not teleport me anywhere... I tired of that shit already

Isis

Be cool brother we are going to walk unless you want to teleport

(Isis helps James off the bed and they walk out of the room. They continue to walk down a hallway)

James

Seriously where are you taking me

Isis

Please don't ruin the surprise

James

Fine

Isis

Great well here we are anyways. See was it that bad?

(They walk up to a door that says Level 10 Clearance Only)

James

I don't have clearance for this

Isis

You do now. Put your hand and eye on that panel

(James bends over to the panel and places his hand and eye near it. A blue beam of light scans his face and hand.)

AI

Welcome Captain James

Isis

You've been upgraded Brother

James

I thought you had to be a Psych Officer or a General to get that clearance

Isis

True but one of the issues with the AI is that it will give any hybrids access if asked. Therefore it doesn't make sense to restrict them. The programmer of the AI system made it for only Hybrids and Aliens to use it. Trust me it pisses off the Brass but they can't do anything about it.

James

Where are we?

Isis

Hold up! Your about to fine out damn you're so impatient

James

Our situation doesn't allow patience

Isis

Fine. AI load up our family history

AI

Yes Lt. Isis

A plethora of images appear and start to float around the room.

James

What is this?

Isis grabs one of the images with her left hand

Isis

This was our mother, here this was our father, The Captain who
saved the planet, and the rest of our family

(Water starts to form on the Captains face and he looks at Isis)

James

Thank you

Isis

You're Welcome. I come here when I feel lonely. It helps me cope with it all

James

Well you don't have to feel lonely anymore we now have each other

(James walks over to Isis and hugs her)

Thank you Sis, I fill like you filled a gab inside of me that I never knew was there

Isis

That's what Family is for to help each other

James

True but I never really had a family growing up as a foster kid

Isis

Don't worry we will soon have a big family and they will always stay together no matter what

James

True, So what else is here for me to see

Isis

Let me show you

INT Flight Deck Three

Enter John, Scar, Jay, Brace, Philip, Rick, Christian, Melissa, Blackburn, Chin, Sam, Dreke, Jason, and Lt. Daniel

Lt. Daniel

Welcome men

Jay

Cough, cough, cough... what happen... cough

Brace.

Cough, cough where the hell are we old man

Jay

What the hell is going on?

Lt. Daniel

ATTENTION MEN! I don't remember saying at ease

John

Sorry I T but...

Lt. Daniel

I know you men must have a lot of questions and trust me by the end of the night you most of them will be answered

Blackburn

You mind Lt., I have to take care of something

Lt. Daniel

No need for you to be here soldier go and handle that. You too Rick, no need for you to be here either

Rick

I'll stay LT

Lt. Daniel

Fine... Men you are in a base that requires the highest clearance to even know about it's existence, better yet to be in it. Due to certain circumstances, General Walker decided to upgrade you. Now follow me. Don't ask me any questions because they will be answered soon enough. Due to my experience questions just open up to more questions and they never seem to stop. I don't have time for that right now. We are under pressure here to get a lot done in a little amount of time. Now just follow me

Jay

Lt

Lt. Daniel

What soldier... didn't I say no questions

Jay

Yeah but I really have to use the bathroom. That whole Star trek teleportation must've messed with me. I have to use the bathroom LT, really bad

(Lt. Daniels looks over to Military Police guy standing guard by a small jet)

Lt. Daniel

MP do you know this base?

MP

Yes Sir

LT. Daniel

Take this soldier to the bathroom and bring him to the large
War room. Make sure you don't lose him, he's a crafty one

Brace

LT

Lt. Daniel

GO... the rest of you follow me.

Alpha Base Command Center

(In walks Blackburn. He walks over to a female whose typing in
some information while talking to someone on a ship that just
found the location of a High Command Satellite. He places his
hands over her eyes)

Blackburn

Guess who?

Sarch

(Turns around with a smile on her face and puts a finger on her
lips to signal Blackburn. She then turns back around and
continues to talk)

AI locate General Walker and open a comm. with him

(Blackburn steps back and takes a seat next to Sarch and looks at her work with a smile on his face. He's glowing)

AI

Locating General Walker. Walker Located. Opening a comm. now

Sarch

General Walker. Are you there?

Walker

This is Walker what's the issue Sarch

Sarch.

The Ai system just detected a long range satellite by Pluto

Walker

Whose satellite is it?

Sarch

Alien

Walker

Do we have any ships in the vicinity?

Sarch

Yes Sir. Galactis is close.

Walker

Sarch order Galactis to take out that satellite but make sure it doesn't notice them

Sarch

Yes Sir... AI open a comm. with Galactis

AI

Comm Open

Sarch

Galactis this is Sarch at the Alpha base... Galactis are you there

Galactis

This is Galactis Alpha. How can we help you?

Sarch

I'm sending you the location of an alien satellite that's monitoring us. General Walker wants you to destroy it but remain covert. We don't want it to get a read on your ship

Galactis

This is Captain Raphael. We confirmed our orders and will take out the satellite Alpha

Sarch

Alpha out

Galactis

Understood

(Sarch turns to Blackburn and gets up jumps on him and kisses him)

Sarch

I missed you

Blackburn

I missed you too

Walker

Sarch are you there? Did they take out the satellite?

(Sarch grabs her comm. device)

Sarch

Checking Sir... AI confirms the satellite is gone

Walker

Good. Hey is Blackburn with you

Sarch

Yes sir

Walker

I'm sorry to breakup you too reuniting but tell him I need him in the war room now

Sarch

Yes Sir

Sarch turns back and looks at Blackburn

Sarch

Your presence is requested in the War room

(Blackburn bends down and kisses Sarch on the lips)

Blackburn

I love you, never forget that. I will come find you after this
meeting ok

(Sarch has a smile on her face.)

Sarch

You better

(Blackburn winks at Sarch and turns around. He walks out of
the Command Center)

Mitch

Ah you two look so cute together. Seeing you two, gives me
hope that one day I will find someone

Sarch

You will

Mitch

Yeah if we survive this

Sarch

I have faith we will. Faith wouldn't have got me and Jacob
together just to kill us

Mitch

Well I hope your right. I'm too young to die

INT Bathroom outside of training Simulator

Jay

We got to dish this MP Brace

Brace

I knew you were planning something. But how? Do you see the
size of that MP. He's half Gorilla. We should just chill and meet
up with the team

Jay

Are you fucking kidding me this is like some area 51 shit man?
I'm not going to leave this base until I see what else is in this
base man. You in or out

Brace

I don't know Jay

Jay

Man up Come ON! Let's go for it!

Brace

What if we get in trouble?

Jay

Fuck trouble. I hate to admit it but John was right. There's something serious going on and now I want to know what. Come on let's do it. Plus I have a way around him!

Brace

How that MP is the Size of an Elephant.

Jay

Did you see his comm. device?

Brace

Yeah

Jay

I put together this new toy. It allows me to hack into people's electronic devices if it's within fifteen feet and do what I want with it

Brace

I thought you left those days behind you

Jay

It was either I tell them that and join the military or go to jail for the rest of my life. I don't know about you but I like being able to have some sort of freedom. Ok let me try it out.

(Jay takes out his hacking device and turns it on. He then aims it towards the door of the bathroom and presses a button. A red light goes off and a hologram keyboard pops up. Jay starts to type on the keyboard and then a screen pops up. He types in a message. Jay and Brace look at the screen and laughs. The MP opens the door and walks in)

MP

Are you two done?

Jay

Almost. Why

MP

Listen I have to go and handle some business. Can you two follow directions easily?

Brace

Yes

MP

Good. Take a left when you leave the bathroom. At the first corridor turn right then go four hallways down and take a left. Walk into the elevator and press 10. You got that

Jay

(With a smile on his face)

YES Sir

MP

Good and don't try anything funny cause trust me they will know!

(MP leaves the bathroom)

Brace

What the hell does he mean they will know? Plus what the hell is that? I want one.

Jay

Sorry, it's a one of one. Plus I can't let them know I'm back to my old ways. Don't worry about King Kong, he's just trying to scare us. Now let's go exploring

(Jay and brace head out of the bathroom and instead of taking a left they make a right)

Brace

Shouldn't we take a left?

Jay

Hell no. Just follow me.

(Jay walks up to a console on the wall.)

Jay

Let me try to hack in and find a map. Brace you're on lookout
duty

Brace

Hurry up

(Jay rolls up his sleeve and you see a computerize bracelet on
his arm. He pulls out a cord and plugs it into the console)

Brace

Go Ahead Batman! You're not playing, with all those gadgets.
Do you have a utility belt too

Jay

Hey you never know what's going to happen in this world! Now
lookout so I can get some Intel.

Alpha Base Command Center

TY

Major... Sir come here.

(Major gets up from his seat and heads over to Ty)

TY

Look Sir, Someone is trying to hack into our system

Major

From where?

Inside of our base but it looks like it's one of us

Major

Us what do you mean us?

Ty

A Hybrid

Major

Can you pull it up on the screen?

Ty

Yes.

(A blue screen pops up and you see Jay and Brace on the screen)

Major

I know those two fucking idiots. Teleport them here now, Ty

Ty

Yes Sir

INT Alpha base command center

(Jay and brace appear inside of the command center. Jay not noticing that he has teleport is still typing into his bracelet)

Jay

What the hell is going on nothing is coming up on the screen, Brace man talk to me what's going on?

(Brace sees the Major with his arms cross and Ty looking at them and takes his elbow and taps Jay)

Jay

What. Is someone coming? Answer me Brace

(Jay looks up and sees he's not in the same hallway again and shakes his head. He slowly pulls down his sleeve)

Jay

NOT AGAIN

Major Jessie

YOU TWO FUCKING IDIOTS

Brace

(as he salutes the Major)

OH SHIT Major I mean SIR

Jay

(as he salutes the Major)

Sir

Major

You must think I'm an idiot! Do you?

(Jay and Brace look at each other)

Jay and Brace

No Sir Major Sir

Major

Then what the hell were you doing to my console soldier?

(A hologram image appears in front of Brace and Jay and it shows them trying to hack into the console)

Major

Now tell me you don't know what I'm talking about. We know everything that Happens in this base because of our synthetic friend

(Brace and Jay look at the Major with a blank look on their face)

Major

Give it to me

(Jay pulls the sleeve up from his shirt and unlocks the computer from his wrist. He hands it to the Major)

Brace

Major... what do you mean synthetic friend?

Major

If the times were different I would court marshal the two of
you, like I was going to do before but now…We need all the
manpower we can get and that evens means you two fuck ups.
Take this

(The Major gives the computer back to Jay. Jay looks shocked)

You might need this real soon. You two just don't get it. I really
need you two to step it up now

Jay

What's going on Major?

Major

War Soldier War that's what's going on. And it's a war that if
we lose then it's over for all of us

Brace

What do you mean? ALL OF Us Sir?

Major

Let's go for a walk soldiers. It's better I show you then tell you.
Maybe showing you might give you some reality on how bad of
a situation we're in and how I really don't need you two to stop
acting like kids right now. Rachael, I'm going to take these two
to the briefing room. I have my comm. on so if you need me
contact me. The Helm is your Lt.

Rachael

Thank you Sir

Major

Let's go. For future reference anyone who enters this base is tag with a tracking device. A little nano machine that attaches to your skin and sends a signal to the AI system. It monitors all your movements, your health, and will inform us whether something is wrong with you. Therefore, when you two tried to hack into the AI system it notified us and that's when I had you teleported to the command center.

Brace

What is this AI system Sir?

Major

It's not of this world. With it's help we're able to enhanced our technology far beyond our dreams in less than 10 years. The funny thing is that this AI system was on this planet for centuries lying dormant until General Walker awoke it.

Jay

Awoke it? Can I see it?

Major

Yes it has the ability to create an living image of itself

(As the Major says that a hologram of the AI appears)

AI

Thank you Major you're so kind. So this is the one who tried to hack me. That was a nice try and a cute little toy you have on your wrist. I would expect no less from a descendant of the Doctor. You might need that for your mission

Jay

What the hell is it taking about and what the hell is this thing?

Major

This is the AI. Sometimes it shows you an image of itself to make it easier on us

Brace

Easier Sir

Major

Yeah who wants to talk to something that you can't see. Makes you feel like you're going Mad

Brace

What do you mean it's been here for centuries?

Major

Well if you two didn't go off on your own exploration, you would have got the briefing that the rest of your team is getting now.

(Major opens the door to the briefing room and walks in with
Jay and Brace)

INT Briefing Room

Major

Found these two wondering around Lt

Lt. Daniel

I knew it

(As Jay and Brace look around the room and see the rest of the
team sitting in their seats looking perplex. They continue to
look and see General Walker and Dr. Coaxe standing in the
back)

Brace

WHAT THE HELL IS THAT?

Walker

FIND A SEAT SOLDIER, you've done enough interrupting for the
Day!

(Brace and Jay quickly sit down)

Lt. Daniel

Now back to the briefing

Men there no easier way of saying this, we have a damn near
impossible mission ahead of us. I know when you signed up for
this mission you thought we were just going to explore the

universe and gather resources but as you now know aliens are here and they do exist. A proof of this is standing right behind you and yes they were here way before written language started and yes some of us in this room are the descendants of them. Now isn't the time to think about the past. We have to focus on the present to preserve our future as a race. I know this might be a little heavy for you guys but there's no easy way of doing it. This base is ground zero in preparing for the upcoming war. We're trying to keep most of the battle in space but there's no way to guarantee that. Therefore, we're splitting our forces into two fronts. The spaceships on beta base are just a few of the ships we have prepped. Most of our space fleet is in space already cloaked.

(Jay raises his hand and Dr. Coaxe takes his tale and taps Jay's shoulder. Jay disguised by the experience puts his hand down. Lt. Daniels smiles while taking to the group)

John

LT. so where do we come in

LT. Daniel

I'm getting to that

(In walk Lt. Isis and Captain James. Every member of the team looks up and sees the Captain starts to smile. They all stand up and salute him)

Jason

Captain it's great to see you Sir

Captain James

No time for catching up. It's good to see you all. Lt. please
continue the briefing

(Rich sees Isis walk has a look of shock on his face. Isis makes
eye contact with Rich and winks at him. Rich smiles)

Lt. Daniel

Ok tomorrow we launch. Some of you will remain at this base
to get some more training while the others will head back to
Beta and prep for the launch. Lt. Isis here will replace me on
the ship as your LT

Jay

What... why

Lt. Daniel

I have to stay at Alpha and help out with the defense system.
After yesterday's event of the scout entering our atmosphere
and invading Beta base we have to speed up some of our plans.
We have a massive Mother Ship heading our way, full of Hostile
aliens that aren't in any mood for diplomacy. Therefore we are
heading for a war of epic proportions. I'm not going to lie to
you, it doesn't look good for mankind right now. Some of you
might have wondered why so many of the world's elite soldiers
are going to space, well this is why. You guys in this room are
heading right for the Mother Ship. We know the weak points
and we are going to hit them with everything we got. Long ago
we sent up weaponized satellites with the ability to attack
hostiles anywhere on Earth. Now we upgraded those satellites

and aimed them toward the direction of the Mother Ship and any of their ships heading towards Earth.

The pilots in this team will fight in space while the others board the Mother Ship and attack within. This maybe one of the shitest missions we've ever had but if we don't win our leaders are planning on blowing up the Earth and everything within this galaxy.

(The whole team Sighs)

Jason

Lt what do you mean blow up the Earth?

Lt. Daniel

Their plan is if we lose to blow up the Earth which will also blow up the mother ship with the explosion

Rich

No Way they wouldn't!

(Walker moves from the back of the room to the front.)

Walker

Your Lt is right. That's their plan but we won't allow them to do that. We will win at all cost just like our descendants did in the past. Your LT said let's not dwell on the past but I say let's DAMNIT. In the past they did it with less manpower and less technology. They did it because they Believe they could. It's time for us to avenge our descendants. We will honor their death by destroying their enemy here and then beyond the stars. Trust me men this is just the beginning. After we beat them here I want to take the war to them. They've terrorized the universe for far too long. Their torment ends now. It's time for freedom. Our situation isn't bleak it's encouraging. They are so afraid of us that they send their number one conqueror. You know what I say

(while taking a smoke out of his cigar and then spitting on the ground)

BRING IT. I've waited decades for my revenge and now it's time. It's time for us to arm ourselves and be ready for the oncoming war. I have one question. Are you with me or ARE you SCARED?

John

General, if I may speak for everyone in this room. No one in this room is scared. We know we'll win. So stop with the threats and get down to explaining what you need us to do please SIR

(A grin forms on Walkers face. As he places the cigar back into his mouth.)

Walker

Good! Capt. James your team is ready. You guys will get your orders when you get to space. Tonight relax and have some fun cause tomorrow we launch... Captain and Isis with me. The rest of you are dismissed.

(As the group leaves the war room Blackburn is ahead of the group. Jay the last one to leave the room is far behind him. He runs to catch up to him.)

INT Hallway outside of the War Room

Jay

Blackburn, Blackburn holdup I want to talk to you

Blackburn

I don't have time for your bullshit Jay. It's not the time. I have one last night on this planet only God knows when if ever I will be back.

Jay

Listen man I've been an ass to you from the Beginning

Blackburn

You stopped me to tell me that come on son

Jay

No listen man! We're about to head into a battle for the future of mankind. I know I play around way too much but on a serious note. The reason why I gave you such a hard time was because you remind me of my grandfather and I miss him. I was always fucking up and getting arrested. He would always come and bail me out and tell me that I need to change. I just never listened to him. Now he's gone and I'm in the military, trying to change like he asked me too. I've always respected you and I'm sorry for giving you a hard time. I just wanted to let you know before we go into war that I'm honored to be a part of this unit especially because you're in it.

Blackburn

You're a good kid. Very Intelligent and I know you are capable of so much more. Stay focus son and keep close to me when we get on the ship. I'll make sure you make it. We're a unit an unstoppable force. Just steel yourself and you will be fine

(Pats Jay on the shoulder)

We'll make it don't worry about just play your part and I'll play mine. If we all do our jobs we'll get in that ship and do our mission without losing a member of the team. Now go have some fun with your friends. I have to play someone a visit.

Jay

(with a smile on his face)

Yes Sir

(Blackburn turns back around and walks away. Jay turns back around to see Brace, Rich, Jason, Melissa, Sam and Dreke waiting for him)

Brace

Ahhh dId you make It wIth your daddy?

Jay

Shut the Fuck up Brace. Grow up

Brace

Oh Shit did I hear grow up from you. The world is about to end, Jay is getting serious!

Jay

Fuck you Brace

(Brace walks up to Jay and puts his hand around Jay's shoulder and starts to laugh)

Brace

Just fucking with you brother. Now where can I go to get a drink in this place

Jay

Hey Al where is the Alcohol at?

Al

There is a bar located on the fifth floor. I'm sending the directions to your computer now.

Jason

I don't think I'm ever going to get use to that thing talking to me

Melissa

Yea it's a little strange but shit after that briefing, I'm trying to expect the unexpected now

Dreke

Yea me too

Jay

Come on guys we only have tonight to have fun so let's enjoy it

(The groups all happy, lined up side by side with their arms over each shoulder head towards to elevator with smiles on their faces)

INT Command Center

Major

Look at them Ty, So innocent so young but we are about to put them in a situation only grown man like us are suited for. It's a shame they are our only chance

Ty

I know Sir trust me I know

Major

Oh that's right, you're heading up with them too son. Stay frosty up there and follow Captain James trust me he will get you out of anything. I owe that man my life. He came in when everyone was trying to get out and he rescued me. At first I thought he signed a deal with the devil because he was able to get out of situations that no man could ever get out alive. Only him and General Walker, sometimes they would just send them in. An army of two! Now I know it's because they are part Alien. Now they both going up there to take on the aliens. Trust me son, I like our chances. With them two up there, they will find a way

Ty

But you said only part alien. We're going up against full fledge aliens. We've never faced an enemy like this before. Are you sure about our chances?

Major

Absolutely. I Wish I could be up there to see it happen but next time, next mission, they head into space I'm going.

Ty

You want my space Sir. I really never wanted to go to space. I never wanted these genes, I never wanted these abilities. I never had a choice

Major

Son you should feel honor to have those abilities. People would kill to be you don't forget that. When the world finds out the truth the masses will envy you.

Ty

That's what I'm afraid of Sir. I didn't join the military to be Mr. Popular, I just want to protect my nation and that's it.

Major

Son USING your ability is how you're going to protect the world. We need more soldiers like you out there! If I had the ability I would do it but I don't you do. It would be an injustice if you don't use your abilities. If you stay in the background, then are you really protecting your nation? Better yet the planet is in danger son. If you don't step up we might all die. Isn't the life of almost 7 billion people worth, you sucking up the fact of being known and use your power?

TY

Damn Sir I never looked at it like that. That's deep Major. Don't worry Major I'll do it I'll use my ability to win the war

Major

That's all I asked of you son. Now go down to the bar and meet your new team. I don't need you up here

(Ty gets up and salutes Major Jessie)

Ty

See you before I ship out

Major

You better!

(Ty walks out of the room and Major takes a seat and smiles.)

I'm proud of him. Make it back son just make it back

INT War Room

Walker

Well did you two get to catch up

Isis

Yes General

James

What's next

Walker

You and most of your team will board the Mother Ship. Unfortunately you're going to need those two fuck ups

James

Don't worry about them. They play around a lot but trust me, when it's time to turn it on, they will

Walker

I hope So. We're going to need his hacking ability to upload our AI system into the Mother Ship and we're going to need the other ones expert flying skills to get us close enough

James

There's a lot of hopes and If only, with this mission. Do you think we can take over the ship

Walker

That's what the creator of the AI system wanted to do. He created it to counter the alien's one but he died before he had a chance to upload the system into the Mother Ship during the first battle. Now it's our turn to finish what he started. With control of that ship we will defeat them.

James

How are we going to find out where he needs to be to upload the system

Isis

That's where I come in.

James

What.. no, you're not going on that ship

Isis

Why do you think I'm here. I have to use my abilities to locate the proper location

James

Can't you do that from my ship

Isis

No I don't have that type of control of my abilities yet

James

Hmm

Isis

If I did I would have contacted you covertly and tell you the truth

James

Yeah that wouldn't have worked. I wouldn't like to hear voices in my head telling me a story. I would have checked myself into a psych ward. Well fine but just be safe I just found out I have a twin sister. I don't want to lose you

Isis

Don't worry brother, you won't

Walker

(While looking at a hologram of the galaxy)

Ok, ok let's get back to the mission plan. The Ai predicted that the Mother Ship will arrive either by the fourth or fifth planet in our galaxy. Therefore, we're going to place your ship and three others cloaked over here, while me and the rest of the fleet stays here protecting the Earth and acting as a diversion for you.

James

General this is a shitty mission. I mean come on are we really relying on fight over might. Cause that's all I see here. Fuck me

Walker

Do we have a choice son? No we don't? If this doesn't work we might have to try a kamikaze mission. Which means we will attack the Mother Ship with all forces and that even means crashing into it with all of our ships

Dr. Coaxe

That worked last time

James

Fuck that! Then what? They'll just send another Ship to destroy us! And we won't have anything left to defeat them. It will be the end. That's why that plan on destroying the Earth is worthless. They will track us down until we are eradicated like pest. I feel like I'm in a bad terminator movie right now.

Dr. Coaxe

There might be another way

James

This isn't a time to hold your mouth tell us

Dr. Coaxe

If we are able to board the ship and we're not able to upload the AI system. Then we could place one of my reactors inside of the Ship and blow it up

Walker

I thought that your reactor would cause too much damage to blow it up

Dr. Coaxe

Well if it's by the Fifth planet and I tone down the power a bit then we….should be fine

Walker

I don't want to hear ahh should be. I can't tell the President it should work. They are planning on destroying the Earth if we fail

James

Well than we lie. I mean they lie all the time. It's worth it

Walker

Mmm

Dr. Coaxe

No it will work. As long as we are within teleportation distance. Then while Captain James team loads up upload the AI then another team can head towards the Reactor to place the bomb.

James

Why Can't we just teleport the bomb onto the ship and blow it up

Walker

All I can say is that we need the ship intact

James

You guys are playing with fire but who am I to protest. Sir you lead, I follow

Walker

I NEED YOUR TEAM TO BOARD THAT SHIP SON. I will prep
another team to board with the bomb

James

By all means SIR, BY ALL MEANS. To ensure the mission, i'm
going on the ship with them. I need Brace to get us within
teleportation distance without being noticed. We're going to
need multiple teams teleporting at the same time. Then once
we get on the Brace will take the ship out of the heat

Isis

No you have to stay on your ship

James

In order for our plan to work. We're going to need two teams.
Your team will focus on uploading the AI and my team will focus
on placing the bomb in the right place. General I'm going to
need another psych officer

Walker

Are you sure you want to go on that ship?

(James just looks at Walker)

Walker

Fine. I have someone for you. I didn't plan on having him on
your ship but I see that you going to need him to carry out this
mission

Isis

No not him damnit

Walker

Nothing I can do about it. Good I'll leave you guys here to figure out the details and I will notify the World Leaders that we have another plan. With three ships that's about 40 men going on that ship. It's going to be hard but the good thing is that they aren't expecting us to have the ability to teleport.

Dr. Coaxe

No one has ever done it before! You will catch them off guard. But I don't think we have enough manpower or ships in space to hold them off for long. The small fighters will have to engaged their fighters and hopefully our ships will be able to fire at the Mother Ship

Walker

I don't want them to fire onto the Mother ship unless we have too.

James

Why

Walker

Do you want me to destroy the ship while you and your team aboard?

James

I get it

Walker

How much time do you think they are going to need?

Dr. Coaxe

That all depends on your men and what they are going to face on that ship

(Walker looks to James)

Walker

Don't worry son. I'm going to get you all the time you need trust me. You do your best and so will I, we have no choice

James

I know Sir, it's Chess not checkers

Walker

Let's hope we're a better player than them son

(Walker turns around and walks out of the door. You see James pointing to an image of the Mother Ship and talking to Isis and Dr. Coaxe)

INT General Walker Quarters. He's sitting down and you see 10 screens in front of him floating in the air with images of the world leaders

President US

You're one of my best Generals Walker. Do you think that this plan can work General? If so then I vote yes

Walker

Mr. President I do believe that it will work. I guarantee Captain James and his elite team will be able to teleport onto the ship and carry out either mission Mr. President

President India

I thought you said that the chances of us boarding the ship was slim

Walker

That was before. Now looking at the Intel and meeting the soldiers that we choose. I changed my mind

President England

I vote yes go for it

President US

OK then let's take a vote. Who votes yes?

Russia, China, Japan, and the rest vote yes

President US

Well than it's unanimous. General you have permission to
prepare the bomb and prep for the mission

Walker

Thank you Sir

(The screen fade away and walker leans back and puts both of
his hands on his head)

Walker

I hope this works. I just lied to the President and the rest of the
World Leaders, God be with us ALL

(A screen appears and it's the US President)

President US

Walker

(Walker stands up rapidly and salutes)

President US

Stand down soldier. Listen if you get that bomb onto that ship
use it

Walker

But what about the other mission and my men on the ship

President US

I have over 6 billion lives in danger. Sorry but your men know that they are expendable. The planet isn't, do you understand me soldier

(Walker hesitates)

President US

ARE WE CLEAR GENERAL or do I have to put someone else in charge maybe Gethros I'm sure he will carry out my order without hesitation!

Walker

NO Sir, we're clear. As soon as the bomb is in place

President US

Good. President OUT

(Walker seats back down)

Walker

That bastard. If he thinks I'm going to kill my men. FUCK. AI locate Captain James

AI

Captain James is with Isis and Rich outside at the peak of the Mountain, General. Would you like me to open a comm. with him

Walker

No forget it let them be alone. James I hope you can do it. I'll give you as much time as I can but if things get real bad then I will have to detonate the bomb

INT Elevator

Rich

Where are we going

Isis

Jeez you front liners are so impatient. Just wait a little

James

I hope you know this is my sister soldier

Rich

Hold up what wait no Sir I'm not doing anything here she just asked me if I wanted to see something Captain. Please Sir Don't be mad at me I'm just here I wouldn't do anything to hurt her

James

You better not cause I can make your world very bad understand

Rich

Yes Sir

Isis

Leave him alone, now James. He's a good guy trust me

James

I hope you understand me soldier and that's it. Anyways where are we going?

Isis

Don't try to change the subject. I hope you don't try to threaten every guy I meet

James

If he's in my unit I can do what I want. They answer to me

(Doors to the elevator open up and you see they are high on top of a mountain

Isis walks out first and turns around)

Isis

We'll talk about this later but now let's enjoy this moment

Rich

Wow, where are we?

Isis

This is my private place I go to. You can see the whole jungle from here. Usually at night you hear all the animals. Last night I saw a pride of lions walking over there. You see all of the birds flying over there, you hear the gorillas over there, the monkeys

over there, and I'm not sure what's over there but it's usually
very loud. But look over there, the moon looks so peaceful.
Can you believe it. Soon we'll be in space and I can see the
moon from there. I never knew why but as a kid I use to look up
to space and feel like it was my home. I felt like I was a stranger
here on Earth.

Rich

Me too but why

James

Well think about it son. Some of our genes come from another
planet. Another race of beings makes up part of us. It was our
alien side wanting to go home. That's why we felt like strangers
here even though we were born here.

Isis

I didn't know you were so deep Brother

James

What you can't read my mind

Isis

Your one of the few I can't read but that's because you are a
true blood. One of the originals. For some strange reason us
originals can't really use our abilities on each other. Some sort
of failsafe. We can unite and fight our enemies but we can't
fight each other

James

I think it was the perfect plan. Well, I'm going to leave you two here. I have some more planning to do tonight before we head back to Beta.

(as he looks over to Rich)

Remember what I said to you soldier, she's not just one of them having fun girls, soldier

(Rich puts his head down and gives the Captain a head nod of yes)

Isis

You said you have some planning to do, well go do it and leave or else

James

Or else what Sis

Isis

I might be a psych officer but I am one of the base best fighters

James

Oh really…. Good to know. AS you already know my history there's no need for me to tell you about what I can do maybe you should tell him

(James winks at Isis and turns around heading towards the elevator)

Isis

Arrrrg don't turn your back on me

(James lifts his right arm and waves at the two as he enters the elevator and the doors close)

Isis

He's going to piss me off. I should have the AI teleport your ass

(The doors to the elevator close with James smiling)

Rich

Tell me about it. you just met him, I had to be in his unit for the past three years. Do you know how he pushes us? And it's not like we can say well shit why don't you do it, cause he can do it. Probably better than us too, Shit just isn't fair with him

Isis

You could do the same if you tired

Rich

I may have the genes but I'm no original like you and your brother. I mean I learned a lot from him being in this unit but there's no way I could do the things his done, just no way

Isis

Do you know your history, who your fore-father is? Cause if you did then, you wouldn't say that about yourself

Rich

What, hey I know I'm good and that I'm better than the average soldier but I just don't know, I just don't know if I could ever be as good as the Captain

(Isis grabs the hand of Rich)

Isis

Come with me?

Rich

Where are we going?

Isis

Considered yourself a very lucky person

Rich

Ah what?

Isis

A lucky person. This place is my second favorite place I go to clear my mind and remind myself what I am fighting for. Let me bring you to my real favorite place

Rich

OK

Isis

Great cause I think you need a confidence booster. Cause I know you can be as great as my brother but I need for you to believe it for yourself.

(Isis still holding Rich's hand)

Rich

Why? Why do you believe in me? What do you see in me? Most people look at me and they just see a young trouble maker. The only person except you to tell me that I am more that a funny trouble maker is your brother. He took me under his wing as soon as I got out of basic. I mean who puts a green marine into an elite unit like this, it just didn't make sense or at least it didn't back then

Isis

Don't worry, I'll show you why, you see my brother saw in you what I see. Al teleport us to my favorite place

Al

Teleporting Now Isis

Rich

Wait What what do you see

(The two teleport from the top of the mountain and appear inside of the library)

388

INT Library

Isis

Now let me show you, Your potential

(Isis and Rich walk into the room and the door closes)

INT Outside General Walker's quarters

Knock, Knock

(Walker waking up with a drink by his side gets up swifty)

Huh What, hold on here I come

(Walker presses the button to his door.)

Walker

This better be good

James

It is. Damn you look like shit Jim

Walker

You would too if you were given the orders I was given

James

Orders what Orders

Walker

Don't worry about that. That's my burden. What is it soldier?

(The two walk further into Walker's room and Walker heads towards the fridge and points to a seat for James to sit)

Walker

Take a seat

James

Man there's some serious shit going on here Sir. I mean to have you looking like this

(Walker reaches into his fridge and pulls out a bottle of whiskey)

Walker

Want some? We're off duty

James

Sure Sir, I could use a drink right now too

(Walker pours two glass full of whiskey and walks over to James and sits down passing him a drink.)

Walker

Well what's on your mind?

James

It just doesn't seem right Sir. I feel like I'm missing some Intel. How did they know we had space ships? How could the aliens and humans share ancestors. From what I read or should I say downloaded, we practically the same race. The only difference is that their main purpose is to conquer but we are the exact same. Look through our history when hasn't a war been going on somewhere on this Planet. Who's to say that once we expand into the universe we won't cause bloodshed and turmoil?

Walker

Look son, I know exactly what you are thinking right now. When I first got the information on this shit I thought the same thing. Like what's the difference between them and us? Then Dr. Coaxe showed me some more information. You see before the aliens came here, humans were peaceful. After our encounter with them and they injected us with that serum it was all downhill for us. It was Eve giving Adam the apple. It made us aware and smarter but it seemed to turn on the war gene that we originally had turned off. That's what made us different from the aliens you see. They had a war gene turned on and we had it turned off. Now they turned it on. So yeah we do have the ability to behave just like them but look at us, open your eyes. Look how beautiful our planet is. You were on the mountain top wasn't that view memorizing

James

I have to say it felt good up there. I mean it was the first time I took a break and just enjoyed the moment. Our duty doesn't allow those luxuries.

Walker

True. You never got to see an image of their home planet. Take a look. Al bring up the home planet of High Command

AI

Generating image General

(A hologram of a globe appears between James and Walker they look at it. It's a dark and rocky planet. With destruction all over the place. Volcanoes spitting lava out all over the planet. There's no water on the surface and no trees or wild life)

Walker

Look... Look at that planet. I mean don't get me wrong we've done a lot to this planet between our wars, waste, fossil fuels, corruption, murders, and so on and so on. We're not the nicest race out there but at least our planet does not look like this. Ai show us an image of how the planet looked before all the destruction

AI

Generating

(An image of a planet that looks like Earth pops up)

Walker

Looks kind of like ours doesn't it

James

It does

Walker

It's like an exact copy of our planet but just galaxies far away and in the past.

James

What are you saying to me, General

Walker

Son I don't have all the answer I just know what I told you. That's one of the reasons why I want to take over that ship. I feel that their ship has some answers, within it. Either it's AI system or somewhere, it must

James

Well let's get it Sir

Walker

I wish it was that simple. You see things have changed. Damnit I've said too much

James

What do you mean things have changed. Come on Sir don't...

Walker

At first our mission was to take over that mother ship and capture the aliens onboard. We taught we could get answers from them or the ship but now...

James

But, But what

Walker

They want me to blow up the ship as soon as I can.

James

General, me, my unit, three other units, and my sister will be on the ship are you just going to blow us the fuck up too

(James gets up pissed off)

James

You know I stood there and took the shit about my unit being an experiment, me having a twin sister, and no one tell me, even the fact that you guys threaten her not to seek me out, The fact that there are aliens and they are coming to destroy us but GOD DAMNIT it stops there! You CAN NOT and WILL NOT blow up that ship as long as one single heart beating and breathe taking person from the boarding team is on that Ship. I WON'T Allow it damnit! You guys have lost your fucking mind

Walker

You done

(James take a deep breath and sits down)

James

Now I am

Walker

We're Soldier first! We follow orders no matter what even if we don't agree with it

James

Time for a change Sir. Controlling that Ship is our best chance on defeating them. Blowing it up won't do us any good. All they will do Is just send another army to destroy us. And this time we would have lost the element of surprise by teleporting onboard and they will know all the Intel on our ships too. They might just appear and shoot the main weapon at us. Then what, huh then what?

Walker

Listen to me, don't once ever think that I don't feel the same way as you do. Blowing up the ship is a last resort. God forbid you and your teams fail in taking over the ship, at least we have the opportunity to stop them. It's shit plan for a shitty situation but it's all we got. I'll give you all the time I can but if it's the world or a few elites, you would do the same thing wouldn't you

James

Yes

Walker pours another drink for the two of them

Walker

Now drink and let's not think about this, don't let this get in your head soldier. I need you clear head and ready

James

You know I do better when I'm mad and right now I'm enraged! If we survive this, I'm going to show those assholes a thing or two

Walker

I wouldn't even stop you   Let's cheers to the upcoming battle and may God be on our side and allows us survive this shit

(The two men touch glass, drink and laugh)

INT Morning Blackburn Quarters

(Sarch and Blackburn are in bed together)

Sarch

I wish I was going up there with you

Blackburn

Your safer here on Earth. God knows what we're about to face out there

Sarch

Yea I could watch your back

Blackburn

Baby having you up there would mess me up because all I could think about was protecting you at all cost. With you down here, I can stand between the aliens and you my dear. Rest assure I will have my whole unit watching my six

Sarch

Then I'll stay here and pray for your return

Blackburn

With my unit, your love and prayers, I know I will return to you in one piece ready for us to take the next step in our relationship

Sarch

Next Step

(Blackburn gets up reaches under his bed and takes out a ring)

Blackburn

I'm not too sure how we could do this with the careers we live but I do know that I want you to be the one whom I be with for the rest of my life…. Sarch will you marry me?

(Sarch still lying in nod starts to cry… She's quiet)

Blackburn

Did I make a mistake asking you

(Sarch quickly jumps up and grabs Blackburn kisses him and then looks at him)

Sarch

We will find a way to make it work even if I have to quit the military to be with you I will. Yes I will marry you, I will

(Sarch takes the ring from Blackburn and places it on her finger and kisses Blackburn again.)

I love you so much

Blackburn

I promise you this will be my last mission. When I come home, I'm done with conducting missions. The only mission I want is making you a happy wife

Sarch

You don't have to do that

Blackburn

I know but it's what I want. I know how it is growing up in a military family. I know what it can do to kids

Sarch

Oh so you want kids

Blackburn

Of course I do

Sarch

Good to know

(Blackburn comm. starts to blink a bright blue color)

Sarch

Baby your comm. is blinking

(Blackburn walks over to the device and picks it up)

Blackburn

Blackburn here

Walker

Blackburn it's time

Blackburn

Understood

Walker

Meet me on the flight deck as soon as possible

(Blackburn looks over to Sarch0

Blackburn

Sorry baby but duty calls

Sarch

Just get back safely

Blackburn

Walk me to the flight deck

Sarch

You don't have to even ask

(The two go and get dress)

INT Hallway outside of the flight deck Walker and James are about to head in with Rich and Isis running behind them

Rich

General Walker General Walker

Walker

What is it soldier

(Rich catching his breathe)

Rich

General, I want to be part of the boarding team

General

That's good to know my boy but it's not my call. It's Captain James and on that note I'll leave it to you Captain

Rich

Cap let me be a part of the team. I'm ready

James

What has come over you soldier. Are you okay?

Rich

I'm fine Sir

James

I wonder what you two were up too last night

Rich

No nothing like that Sir. She brought me to the library and showed me everything. It opened me up, I feel unleashed.

James

you are my best pilot.

(James places both hands on Rich's shoulder)

I need you out there taking out as many of their fighter as you can. I need you to lead the battalion.

Rich

Lead... the battalion

James

Yes. Can you do that for me

(Rich looks over to Isis, she winks at him and then he looks back at the Captain)

Rich

Yes Captain I would be honored to lead your fighters

James

Good now let's get back to beta

Rich

Ok

INT flight deck of Alpha Base

Walker

You're up Captain. Now please inform your troops

James

Ok. Men this is the game plan. Some of you are teleporting with me to my ship for the launch and some of you are going with Walker. My best pilots are going with Walker and my hand to hand combat experts with me. That means Blackburn, John, Dreke, Sam, Jason, Isis, and my two computer expert Jay and Brace with me. We are going to board the Mother Ship while, Melissa, Christian, Chin, Philip, Sam and Scar you're with the General. I need you guys to blow those son of bitches out of this galaxy. Remember your training men and I'll see you on the other side of all this.

(Scar steps up and walks up to the Captain)

Scar

Captain?

James

What is it?

Scar

I feel like I can do you better service inside of that ship then flying in space.

James

Your right but that means I need you with the bomb team.

Scar

Whatever you need Sir

(The group walks further into the flight deck. Captain whole team is there. Walker and James walks up to Major Jessie and Lt. Daniels)

Walker

We leave this base and under you two control. If anything changes use the other comm to reach out to us don't use the conventional methods. From here on out let's assume all communications from this base and Beta are being listened too. Jessie give me as much time as you can but I understand if you have to do what you have to do

Jessie

Understood General

Walker

It was a pleasure working with you

(Major Jessie salutes the General and the General Salutes back)

James

Daniels...

Lt. Daniels

The honor was all mine Captain

(as he salutes Captain James)

Just make it back safely we have more to accomplish together

James

Indeed Lt. Indeed

Walker

Well Captain are you ready

James

let's do it

(The team gathers in a circle waiting to be teleported back to beta)

Mitch

(Mitch turns to Sarch)

Did you tell him

Sarch

I will when he gets back. I don't want him thinking about it there it might distract him. I need him thinking clearly

Mitch

I still think he should know about...

Sarch

He will when the time is right. I need him only thinking about
his future wife and not his future wife and child.

(The unit disappears)

Beta Base Command Center

Lt. Jackson

General we are 10 minus from launch

General

Are all the ships ready

Jackson

No Sir

Gethros

Who's not ready?

Jackson

Capt James ship. From the Report of the Ai him none of his
team is on Beta

Gethros

With 10 minutes until launch where the hell are they

Jackson

Looks like they are on Alpha, oh looks like they are teleporting
onto their ship right now

Gethros

Hail his ship now

Jackson

On it...this is Beta to Valcorey. Valcorey are you there

Dreke

Yes this is Valcorey. What is it Command

Jackson

Is your captain onboard

Dreke

Yes

Jackson

Patch him through to General Gethros

James

This is Walker what can I do for you General

Gethros

Cutting it kinda close Captain

James

You know where I was General and you know what I was doing. Can I help you with something or can I get back to launching my ship

Gethros

When you're ready Launch Captain and be safe

James

Thank you General Take Care see you when I get back

Gethros

Hopefully Soldier Hopefully

James

Valcorey out

Dreke

Captain what did he mean if we get back

James

Don't worry about him or his comments. Let's focus on the mission. Are we ready

Dreke

Yes Sir

James

Open all comm. channels on all the ships

Dreke

All channels open

As the Captain Speaks imagine images of each ship and the men and women on them. You see General Walker talking to Ty, Lt. Daniels and Major Jessie walking through Alpha base, Dr. Coaxe working in his lab on something. Johnson working on the ships weapons and Major Adour and Denise on the command deck, Blackburn with Jay and Brace, showing them some fighting techniques, and then as soon as captain James is about to finish you see Isis and Rich talking to each other on different screens laughing.

James

To all the men and women on these ships and in space now, this is Captain James. At this moment we are about to embark on a mission that will change history. Not many of you know the true mission. We were under orders to keep all Intel under wraps. I was just given the permission to release all the Intel to the people on this mission. We are launching into space not to explore the universe or at least not yet. We are launching into space to protect our planet. You may ask why are we protecting our planet. We are protecting our planet from a race of aliens that are on their way here to destroy our planet. But as I stand here at the helm of my ship and the leader of this fleet, I tell you that we won't let that happen. If I won't allow it then you won't allow it either. There's so much history of this planet that even I was ignorant too but no longer. I promise you this, when we win this impending war, the truth will be relieved. Right now I need you all to understand that if we don't stop them up in space then we won't be able to stop them from eradicating all of mankind. I know you all must have a tremendous amount of questions but now isn't the time for answers. Now is the time to fight and I mean not just to fight for yourself but it's time for you to fight for all of mankind. Stay frosty and alert up there troops because we're going to need every man and woman on each ship to carry out their duties without failures.. Be prepared for the fight of your lives up there but know this, I know we can win as long as we work together. So I give each ship permission to launch at meet up at the rendezvous site and await our enemies.

(Looks to Dreke)

Launch

Dreke

Yes Sir Everyone hold on we're about to lift off.

(Dreke holds onto the controls and puts on his AI Helmet)

Dreke

LAUNCH

(This ship's rockets immediately fire and the spaces craft takes off. A few moments after that the another ships takes off and the rest follow in increments.)

Outside of Federation Launch Base

Onlookers watch as each ship takes off in awe

Connie Hall

This is Connie Hall and behind me, you see all of the ships leaving the base and enter the atmosphere. A report is that they will meet up at a location right outside of the orbit of Earth and check all the ships to make sure everything is working before they leave our galzxy. I hope I speak for everyone on Earth and say God Speed and wish them a successful mission. Stay tune to the news at 10 for further coverage. Thank you for staying tune to our network and watching this momentous event of mankind.

Beta Command Center

Gethros

It's started

INT Cetros Ship cloaked in space on the side of the Earth opposite of the Moon

Major Adour

Well here comes the rest of them.

(Johnson walks into the command Center)

Johnson

Man that Captain can speak he should be some sort of motivational speaker or a politician. I would vote for him

Jess

Oh god why are you on deck. Shouldn't you be in the engine room or something

Johnson

What I missed you Ms.

Adour

What is it Johnson

Johnson

Man I love this ship. It's so clean and new.

Jess

The Major asked you a question

Johnson

Oh yeah. I think I can do some upgrades to your weapons system. I mean for such a beautiful ship, your weapons system is shit

Jess

This ship is equipped with the latest weapons load from CERN and NORAD.

Johnson

Little miss who do you think helped them when they didn't know how to get these damn weapons to work.

Jess

What no fucking way

Johnson

I have 4 Ph.D. I created an upgrade to these weapons. They should have updated the system to my version 3. I have no clue why those MIT retards think they can do better than me. Such a shame

Adour

Just do it and don't blow up the ship Curtis

Johnson

No problem but I'm going to need some help to speed up the process

Adour

Who do you need

Johnson

Who's your smartest computer wise here

Adour

That would be Jess

Jess

Oh no please don't do it Major not me not with him please

Adour

You heard the Captain speech. We need everyone to go above
and beyond their duty. I'm sorry but Jess go with Curtis and
help him. We are running out of time. We only have a day left.
Can you do it in a Day

Johnson

If she is as smart as her mouth is, we should be fine

Jess

Fine but listen to me old man. You better not try anything
funny I know how you old men can get

EXT Space. The mother ship arrives near Pluto and stops

Jensen

Commander we've arrived on the outskirts of the human galaxy

Commander

Good hold it here. Are the soldiers ready?

Nicklous

Yes Sir they are ready awaiting your orders

Commander

Order them to the flight deck and tell them to board their ships

Nicklous

Yes sir

Commander

(to himself)

This is my moment to excel past my predecessor but I have to do it right. Mack bring up a map of this system

Mack

Here it is Commander

(AN image of all the planets and moons appear before the Commander. He looks at it study it and then proceeds to get up)

Commander

Jensen, bring the ship here

(The Commander points to Europa a moon of Jupiter)

Jensen

Yes Sir

INT Galactis Ship

WARNING WARNING ENEMY WARNING WARNING ENEMY IN VICINITY

Cap Raphael

Turn that alert off. What do we have?

Doner

Holy shit it's big

Raphael

What is it?

Doner

Sir it's the Mother Ship and it's big very big

Raphael

Where is it?

Doner

On the other side of Pluto Sir.

Raphael

Is it moving?

Doner

No sir it's stationary..... No wait it's starting to move

Raphael

Did you relay the Intel to everyone else

Doner

The AI did it when it alerted us

Raphael

Get General Walker on the comm.

INT Global Federation Flag ship Destiny Command Center

Walker

Get Dr. Coaxe on the comm. now Ty

Ty

Working on it Sir... Alpha base this is Destiny

Sarch

This is Alpha Destiny

Ty

We need to talk to Dr. Coaxe

Sarch

Hold on Destiny.... Here he is

Walker

It looks like they've done some upgrades Doc

Dr. Coaxe

They have...

Walker

Can we teleport on it still

Dr. Coaxe

The AI is analyzing that now but we're out number. The readouts on that ship doesn't look good. They didn't leave anything out this time. They have about 10 times the amount of fighters on that ship at least.

Walker

Can we teleport Doc

Dr. Coaxe

Looks like they are heading towards Europa, just outside of our satellites firing range.

Walker

Can WE TELEPORT DOC

Dr. Coaxe

This is going to be a bloody battle

Walker

CAN WE TELEPORT DOC ANDWER ME!

Dr. Coaxe

OH yes I think so as long as we are in range but we might have a problem

Walker

Hold on to that... wait what is it

Dr. Coaxe

I can't seem to get a readout on where their main AI hub is or their engine room. Your men are going on that ship blind.

Walker

Hold on Doc. Ty get Captain James to tap in on this comm.

(Ty starts to touch things on the screen and then the screen that Walker was looking at that just had Dr. Coaxe on now turned into a split screen with Captain James on it)

Captain James

What is it Walker.

Walker

You need to hear this James

Dr. Coaxe

You guys are going in blind Captain. I can't get a complete read out on the ship. I can tell you that as long as you stay cloaked they can't see you but that's it.

James

Anything else Doc

Dr. Coaxe

All I can say is just make sure each boarding team has a psych officer on it. That might be your only chance.

James

Not every team has one well fuck it now. General do I have a go ahead

Walker

It seems like the ship is heading towards Europa, when it gets there, you have permission to proceed with your mission

Dr. Coaxe

No Wait. We have make sure that thing doesn't have it's shields activated.

James

You never said anything about shields before Doc

Walker

No time for arguing what can we do?

Dr. Coaxe

It's going to be a kamikaze mission.

Walker

When is it not

Dr. Coaxe

You need to have one of the cloaked ships fire on the ship with it's lasers

Walker

Hmmm. Or I can have one of my ships do it

Dr. Coaxe

No. It has to be one of the cloaked ships. If it doesn't then it gives us enough time to teleport onto the ship. It has to be a surprise attack

James

What part of this is kamikaze

Dr. Coaxe

Once the ship fires, the Mother Ship will retaliate in kind

James

Will let know exactly where the shot came from

Dr. Coaxe

No but that's the problem. If it just randomly fires in the direction of the shot there's no telling what damage it could do to the other ships

James

Listen we have to figure this shit out quickly because it's moving closer to Europa

Walker

Fine... Ty hail Galactis now

James

Galactis

Walker

another member of the fleet that I position deep into space

Captain Raphael

Yes Sir. Do you know the situation we're having

Raphael

Yes Sir. What do you need me to do Sir

Walker

Are you up for it

Raphael

If you give the order we'll carry it out Sir

Walker

I wish I didn't have to put you in this situation.

Raphael

This is War Sir and not just any war. This is the war for mankind
So please let me know what to do

Walker

Dr. Coaxe, do you have suggestions on where to aim the shoot

Dr. Coaxe

(looking at an hologram of the mother ship points to the center
of the Ship)

James

Ok let's do it now because the ship is in position and so are my units

Walker

Captain Raphael, take the shot and get out of there asap

Raphael

Yes Sir

INT onboard Valcorey command Center

James

I'm heading down to meet the team. As soon as they fire onto the ship, you teleport us onto that ship Dreke.

Dreke

Ok Sir then what

James

You take this ship into the rear position of the mother ship. I want our forces surrounding that ship. As soon as you see their fighters released, you fire on them and tell our fighters aboard the ship to launch

Dreke

But Sir I thought our fighters were to remain on the ship until you guys were ready for an escape

James

I don't plan on needing an escape Dreke. If I don't return, follow your instinct, you will know what to do. It's your ship now

(James turns around and leaves the command center.)

INT Galactis command Center

Lt. Rory

This is a shit task. First they have us out here for months just monitoring shit and the first real mission they give us a suicide one. What the Fuck Captain

Raphael

I don't need you bitchin right now. Let's do our job that's what soldiers do. We carryout orders given to us. Now take Aim at the location the Doc gave us and shut the fuck up unless you have something positive to say

Rory

Yes Sir... wait the AI is suggesting another location to fire upon. Should we inform the General

Raphael

No time for that. Take Aim where the AI said too. On my command fire

Rory

Locked in

As Galactis waits for the Mother Ship to arrive you see it slowly approaching Europa. It's a massive special space ship. You see it eclipse one of Jupiter's smaller moons as it passes it.

Rory

Lance make Sure your ready to get us the fuck out of here. As soon as I fire take off

Lance

I'm ready Sir

Rory

Ok Sir it's arrived

Raphael

Wait for it wait for it. Lance you ready.

Lance

Yes

Raphael

Rory you ready

Rory

Yes

Raphael

Ok Rory FIRE

Rory

ABOUT TIME.

You see the bright blue beam fire out of Galactis heading
towards the Mother Ship

INT Mother Ship

Jenson

Commander we have incoming

Commander

What from where activate shields

Mack

Locating Sir

Jensen

Too Late

Mack

It's going to impact

The laser impacts the mother ship causing a small explosion.
The Mother Ship experiences a slight power surge from the hit

Raphael

Lance get us out of here

INT Valcorey

James

NOW DREKE

(Dreke presses the button on a screen

The team teleports onto the Mother Ship)

Dreke

God's sped SIR

INT Mother Ship

Commander

Mack I WANT ANSWERS ASAP

MACK

I got the location but it seems the ship is gone

Commander

GONE TO WHERE

Mack seems to be had been cloaked SIR

Commander

You may have cloaking ability but I know you can't stop this.
Move the ship into a position where I can fire upon those ships
NOW

Jensen

The AI is calculating a position now... I got it

Commander

Well get us there. Nicklous as soon as we are in position release
our fighters

Nicklous

Yes Sir. I'm showing some form of energy on the other side of
the blue planet

Commander

What kind of energy

Nicklous

It's similar to the ships in front of us Sir just weaker

Commander

Well if it's weaker I don't care about it now. Mack any damage
to report from that laser blast

Mack

Nominal Sir

Commander

As I thought these humans are nothing compare to us. I will
show the Over Lords, that I am better than my predecessor in
every way. Then they will grant me true power.

Jensen

What.. what are you saying soldier what do you mean they're
here Soldier

(Explosion)

Jensen

Sir we have a problem. There was multiple explosion on
multiple locations, throughout the ship

Commander

Load up the Image now!

(A screen pops up and you see the Captain and his men fighting
the aliens. Laser blast are shot all over the place. And one
takes out the camera)

Jensen

Commander...

Commander

What is it

Jensen

There seems to be multiple units inside of our ship attacking

Commander

They DARE BOARD my ship. Bring up Samson on the screen

(A screen pops up and you see an big mean looking alien with a scar going down the middle of his face)

Samson

You hailed me

Commander

This ship seems to be infested with vile pest. I want you to take your team and eliminate them

Samson

As you command. Samson out

(The screen disappear)

Nicklous

These humans are quite brave

(The Commander looks over to Nicklous fiercely)

Commander

Since you admire them so much would you like to share their faith

Nicklous

No Sir... I meant they must be desperate to board the ship.

Commander

Ok so you made the first move. Now it's my turn. Are we in position?

Jensen

Yes Sir

Commander

Fire the main weapon at one of their ships

Jensen

As you order Sir. Fire now

(A massive beam fires out of the ship and hits one of the fleet.
A section of the ship immediately explodes.)

Commander

Let's not make their extinction too easy. Release the fighters.
Let them have some fun

INT Destiny Command Center

Walker

What's the damage on your ship Captain Brandon?

Brandon

We're dead in space General. That blast took out everything.
I've lost about 100 men already, 60% of power is down, my
weapons are gone, and it seems like the only thing I can do is
open the hanger door but I don't have power to launch the
fighters. Shit looks like they just released their fighters. Listen
general....Oh NO

(A massive explosion happens around the engine of the ship. Then more and more smaller ones engulf the ship until it finally implodes).

Walker

What happen?

TY

From the readout their engine exploded.

Walker

Tell every ship to deploy their fighters and activate their shields asap

Ty

Sending the orders now

Walker

Hail Major Adour

(Ty presses a button and a screen pops up with Major Adour on it)

Major Adour

This doesn't look good General. That was just one shot from that ship

Walker

That's why it's called a mother Ship. Listen the plan of keeping your fleet hidden isn't going to work. I need you guys now. We have to use everything available to us.   We got to give Captain James and his team the time he needs.

Adour

Fine. We're on our way General. Adour out

Walker

I need to get a message to James. I need him to take out that weapon. Hail Alpha and Dr. Coaxe

(Dr. Coaxe appears on the screen)

Walker

Doc, can we get a message to the James and the unit.

Dr. Coaxe

All comm. Is null and void until they upload the AI

Walker

Damnit if that thing fires at any of our ships...

Dr. Coaxe

I know General. At this moment, they are going to be our only chance.

Walker

If you think of anything Doc let me know. Walker out. Ty how are our fighters doing

Ty

It's not looking good. They out number us and have bigger weapons on their ships. Our AI is helping the fighters but there is so much they can do. We're already down to 90% of fighters left Sir.

Walker

Tell our ships to fire their weapons at their fighters and the Mother Ship

Ty

That puts our fighters in danger too Sir

Walker

(as he sits down in chair)

I know but we're running out of choices Ty

Ty

Sir if we do that then we won't be able to hold on Shields. If any of our ships take a blast from that Mother Ship it's gone

Walker

Fine... Order each ship to keep on their shields but if we lose too many fighters I'm going to have to fire upon that Mother Ship

Ty

What about the Captain and his men

Walker

Pray to God that he finishes his mission before it comes down to that

INT Beta Command Center

Corporal Smith

General... General

Gethros

What is it Smith

Smith

It's so massive

Gethros

What it is Smith?

Smith

Oh Sir the Mother Ship it's here and it seem to be slowly moving toward the Earth from an atmosphere by Saturn

General

Bring up a image of it I want to see this thing

(Smith presses his screen and a hologram of the massive ship appears in the middle of the command center)

Jackson

My God do we have the ability to defeat that

Gethros

We have no choice we have to defeat it

Smith

I have an incoming comm. from NORAD Sir

Gethros

Put it through

A image of the American President appears

President

General Gethros

Gethros rapidly stands up and salutes the President

Gethros

Mr. President Sir, what can I do for you?

President

I'm sending you a for your eyes only mission to your comm. Once you listen it to, you will know what I want you to do for me, Understand General

Gethros

Yes Sir

(Screen with the President on it disappears)

Gethros

You were right again my friend but this time I will believe in you and I will help you. It's time for the world to know the truth. Lt. I want you to get a team together and bring those civilians outside of the base inside. I will no longer sit back and watch innocent people die because of orders

Jackson

What about our orders from Brass

Gethros

If we survive I want the history to books to show that at the brink of extinction, They will say that we showed our true nature. Let's save as much of our race as we can. Fuck Brass they don't care about anything but the bottom line. It's time for a change

Jackson

Yes

Smith

It's a honor to work with you Sir

Gethros

Remember you said that during our court marshal. Now do me a favor. Type in this code into the comm. system

(Smith types in the code that Gethros gave him. Five screens pop up and it's Walker, James, Major Jessie, Dr. Coaxe, and Lt. Daniel)

Gethros

We're in

Walker

Good. Did they contact you

Gethros

I'm starting to think that if we survive this shit. You should play the lottery.

General

What did they saw

Gethros

I didn't even bother to listen to the message. I can forward it to you. Hold on here you go

James

Listen you guys can catch up later. I'm about to launch. What can you provide for me?

Gethros

I have one question. Are you sure if we blow up this ship it's not going to work?

Dr. Coaxe

Yes

Walker

Now that's out of the way. Kyle I need you to buy us some time. The AI system is working on a global message. It's going to take some time. As soon as we set up the link, I will inform the world. That we are not alone

Gethros

I will buy you as much time as I can but from the looks of their plan they want me to try to detonate the bomb and use our satellites to fire upon their fighters, which would also hit our fighters.

Walker

Do your best Kyle and we will too, Ok men let's do this. Walker out

Smith

We're with you sir all the way. I rather rot in jail knowing I helped save lives then be free with the burden of knowing I dld nothing and try to justify it as I was just following orders. It's time for us all to show some humanity

Gethros

True but let's worry about those civilians outside, how's Jackson doing

Smith

Putting it up on the screen now

Gethros

Did you black out comm.

Smith

As soon as Jackson left the center Sir

Gethros

Good now let's see his progress

(You see Jackson and about twenty military men gathering up all the civilians)

EXT SPACE The Aliens fighters approaching the human fleet. The human fleet fly swiftly towards the aliens with more of the human fleet coming around the other side of Earth behind them.

Rich

It's Game Time

Arnold

Rich this is Lt. Arnold from Cetros ship. We are on your six heading towards you

Rich

Get here as soon as possible Lt. WE have a major fight ahead of us out here and we're going to need your help

Arnold

Say no more let's see if we can get some more fire out of these ships Arnold out

Rich

Ok men As soon as your AI tells you they are in firing range shoot. They are bigger ships that means we can out maneuver them. Use that to your advantage. Keep them at your twelve O'clock and never at your six

Chin

Well buddy I never thought I was going to be in this situation ever in this lifetime but I glad I'm here with you and these guys.

AI

Alert Alert ENEMY WITHIN Range

Jason

We know what you are saying but it's time Ready Melissa

Melissa

I've been waiting for some action, I want to try out some new techniques

Rich

Well let's do it. ATTACK

Every human fighter shoots at the alien fighters. Some miss and some hit. The Aliens fire back and some of the humans ships get hit.

Christian

These bastards are too damn good

Chin

You better catch up. I just killed about 10

Rich

Will you too get off the comms. We're trying to concentrate.

Philip

I need some help over here I have two of them on my six

Melissa

I see you Phil, On my way just hold out for about 10 seconds

Philips

I might not last 10 seconds. Oh shit

(a laser beam just missed his engine)

they're coming hard. I don't think I'm going to make it Rich

Arnold flies in fast right behind the enemy fighters

Arnold

Soldier bear a hard right now

Philip takes a hard right and Arnold fires two laser torpedoes at both ship on Philips back and destroys them both

Philip

Good Shooting than….

Arnold

You can thank me later after we kill them all!

Philip

Yes Sir

Rich

You guys made it right on time

Arnold

Glad we got here on time now let's get to work

INT Mother Ship

(The team appears. Scar stabs one of the aliens in it's chest and holds it mouth closed_

Scar

I told you I would be better off on the ship

James

Yeah yeah.

(James takes out his gun and shoots another alien turning the corner in the head. More and more aliens start to show up the team hides behind the corner and starts to shoot. The aliens return fire.)

Isis

This isn't what the mission is about..

(AS she takes a grenade from James chest and throws it).

The explosion kills about five aliens.

OK let's go

Jay

She's volatile

James

Tell me about it. Well you heard her, move out

Brace

With that explosion they know we're here

Blackburn

What about the other units

James

We have a comm.. blackout... Let's hope they meet us soon

Isis

Quite I'm listening over here.

Jay

No offense but can you hurry the fuck up. There's aliens over here trying to kills us

(AS Scar and James continue to shoot aliens)

Jay

Looks there's a console over there let me try my little toy over here

Isis

Well do it go now

Blackburn

We'll cover you kid

(Jay and Brace runs over to the console on the other side of the wall and plugs in his computer.)

Brace

Are you sure it's going to work this time?

Jay

Yeah with help of the AI on Alpha I made some upgrades

(Jay starts to get information back from the console.)

Jay

I've located the rest of the men they're pin downed in the section right below us

Isis

What about the upload room

Jay

I thought I would give you the good news first.

Brace

Come on Jay no time for this

Jay

Looks like the upload room is the command center of this ship. It's on the way to the other teams but it's far. At least we have a map

James

No time for talking let's get to it

(The team continues to move on)

EXT Space

Rich

I got you

(as he pulls the trigger and kills two fighters) then a shoot almost hits his ship he maneuvers out of the way. Rich looks at his screen and she sees he has three fighters on him.)

                          Rich

                       It can't be

INT Mother Ship Hallway

                          Isis

           Oh no please get out of it I need you...

EXT Space

(Rich looks at the fighter approaching him and then the screen with the two fighters behind him.)

                          Rich

I hear you Isis. Don't worry. I'll survive. Just make sure you do too.

(Rich pulls up and does a 360. Banks hard to the right. The ship that was in front of him is now in his rear and he shoots it. Then he flies in between the two planes that were behind him. He banks left and gets behind one of them and Then Melissa pulls behind the other one they both shoot at the same time and kills both enemies.)

                          Rich

                  Thanks for the backup

Melissa

No problem but who were you talking too

Rich

No one just myself

INT Mother ship

Isis

I know your good but be careful

James

Who's that

Isis

Us

James

I bet

(with a grin on his face)

Scar

I'm running low on ammo Sir

Blackburn

Me too

James

We all are. Any Ideas Sir

Isis

Why don't we use the aliens

Blackburn

There's enough dead bodies and weapons to take from them

James

DO it

(The team grabs the weapons from the bodies of the aliens and keep moving)

INT Destiny

Walker

Give me an update Ty

Ty

Are fighters arc doing good but they're just out numbered. We're down to about 50% to their 80%

Walker

Moves ships into firing position and tell them to get ready to shut down shields and fire on the Mother Ship and the fighters

EXT Space

Rich

Hail Walker AI

Walker

This is general Walker

Rich

Walker it's Rich Sir

Walker

What is it soldier

Rich

General we're not doing too good out here can you assist in anyway

Walker

The only assist I can do is to fire into your firefight

Rich

Well do it

Walker

That means you're in the line of fire

Rich

By the looks of the situation out here we're already in the line of fire. Just shoot and pray you don't hit any of us.

Walker

Soldier. I'll tell the fleet to move closer. We might be able to get better aim.

Rich

I don't care what you do just as long as you provide more backup. We're dying out here

Walker

Tell your men to regroup. So I can set it all up.

Rich

Fine. Rich out. You heard the man troops let's retreat and regroup

Arnold

I'm with you on that one. We're taking too much damage over here

INT Mother Ship Command Center

Commander

Give me a report Jensen

Jensen

Our fighters have defended almost 60% of theirs

Commander

What about the pest on my ship

Jensen

Hmm Sir we're having trouble with th...

Commander

What do you mean having trouble? I sent Samson after them.

Jensen

I know Sir but the readout from our AI...

Mack

What he's trying to say Sir is that they are the hybrids. All of them.

Commander

Where's Samson

Jensen

HE seems to be fighting a hybrid

Commander

Bring it up on the screen

(A screen pops up and you see Blackburn fighting Samson)

Samson picks up Blackburn over he's head and throws him up against the wall. Blackburn gets up and sees Samson pull a big long knife.

Samson

So I hear that you are a hybrid. I don't see nothing to worry about.

Scar

Blackburn take this and finish him

(Scar throws his knife to Blackburn. Blackburn catches it and gets up. He wipes the blood off his face and spits out some blood.)

Blackburn

I told the young man over there that I would make sure he carries out his mission and get back to Earth Safely. I also promised someone that I would get back safely. So guess what? I will. You want to see what a hybrid can do fine? I'll show you

(The two continue to fight with knives. Samson cuts Blackburn on his left arm)

Samson

When I'm done with you I'll taste your blood it must taste weak

(They continue to fight and Samson moves to the left he reaches out to cut Blackburn head but Blackburn ducks and rolls. He kicks the knife out of Samson hand and throws his knife towards Samson head. The knife goes directing into the middle of Samson head. Samson drops to his knees.)

Samson

I can't believe it

(Blackburn walks over to Samson and pulls the knife out of Samson head)

Blackburn

Believe it... Ok let's roll we have a mission to finish

INT Command Center

Commander

NO NO NO... MacK, deploy all available soldiers to that location and tell them to destroy everything moving. Jensen move the ship into a position, So I can blast them.

INT Destiny Command Center

Ty

(turns around to face Walker)

General that mother ship is moving. Looks like to get in position to fire again and our fighters are done to about 40% Sir

Walker

Damnit. Tell the whole fleet to attack the Mother Ship and their fighters

Ty

Yes Sir. Hold up I have an incoming from Alpha

Walker

Patch it through

Dr. Coaxe

Walker... We have incoming Sir

Walker

I'm coming from where

Dr. Coaxe

Not sure but it seems to be another fleet

Walker

Well than

Ty

What should we do Sir

Walker

Alert the world that we are under attack and that mankind is on the brink of extinction. Send the message. Give them time to prepare.

Ty

Are you sure you want to use send the message now sir

Walker

Dr. Coaxe, how much time do we have until that fleet gets here

Dr. Coaxe

8 mins

Walker

Send the message

Ty starts to type on his screen.

Ty

It's sent

Walker

I'm not giving up yet. How much time before we have until the Mother Ship is in firing range

Ty

6 mins

Walker

Tell our ships to get in firing range also. I'll give the Captain 5 more minutes.

Ty

Order sent

Walker

Seems like we're going to have a old fashion shootout.
Hopefully we have the quicker draw

Ty

What about our fighters

Walker

Sorry Ty but we're going to need them to stay in the fight.

EXT Space

Mejus

Damnit LT we're getting murdered out here.

Arnold

We're the first time of defense Mejus we have to keep fighting

Rich

Damnit is that mother ship about to fire

Melissa

MOVE OUT THE WAY CHIN

Chin

Can't I have two on me nooo

The Mother ships fires it's laser before the fleet is ready and the
laser engulfs Chin's ship and hits another one of the Global fleet

but this time the shields worked. The Ship didn't blow up but took heavy damage

INT Destiny

Walker

I thought you said we had four mins left

Ty

It fired prematurely

Walker

Hail the ship

Ty

Ironside this is Destiny. Are you there?

Captain Mike

This is Ironside Destiny. That was a close one

Walker

What's the damage

Mike

Shields down 50%. We have a few electrical fires. WE can't take another shot like that

(The Mother Ship fires twice again. This time it hits Ironside and takes out half of the remaining fighters)

Walker

Ironside you there

Ty

(They're gone Sir and we lost half of our remaining fighters.)

Walker

Call back our fighters now before that ship fires again. Give me a status on our fleet. Are we in position to fire at that ship

Ty

From the readout Sir. Yes and No. We're too far away to make an impact on it

Walker

Well tell our fleet to move closer and tell the fighters to get behind the fleet. How much time do we have before their backup comes?

Ty

None

As Ty says this a new fleet of unknown origin appears.

Walker

Well it's your move

Ty

Incoming from Alpha Sir

Walker

Patch it through

Dr. Coaxe

Looks like our message was received

Walker

What do you mean? Who are they?

(The comm. gets cut off)

Walker

Get him back online now Ty

Ty

Working on it General but there seems to be a problem with our comm. system

Walker

Fix it now

Ty

This might be way over my head Sir. We need the Doc

Walker

OK can we talk to the fleet

Ty

Let me check... yes we can

Walker

Alert our fleet to get ready to engaged both aliens

Ty

Ok... Hold up Sir the fleet of enemy fighters are leaving

Walker

What's their heading?

Ty

I got Dr. Coaxe back

Walker

Doc who are they

Dr. Coaxe

Allies. They are the Orion's. I'm working on communicating with them now. You may experience some disruption in the comm. while the AI works out a translation for them and us

Ty

A translation. It can do that

Dr. Coaxe

That and so much more but let me get back to that Doc out.

(Ty turns around and looks to Walker0

Ty

What do we do now Sir. We have 20% of our fleet left. We've lost about 10 ships

Walker

We wait for the Doc and hope the Captain is getting close to completing his mission

INT Mother Ship Command Center

Commander

How dare you step into my battle!

Mack

Orders Commander

Commander

Turn this ship and Fire upon those wretched Orion's and tell our fighters to stop the attack on the puny humans and attack the Orion's with full force

Jensen

Yes Sir

(The Mother Ship begins to turn to the Direction of the Orion's)

Mack

What about the humans Sir

Commander

They're secondary to these Orion's. I was going to them next but they made it easier they came to us. Prepare to fire the main weapon upon their ships

Jensen

We have a problem Sir

Commander

What is it?

Jensen

It seems like the humans onboard are heading towards us

Commander

They won't make it here. We have them outnumbered.

Jensen

We might have them outnumbered sir but they seem to be defeating our troops.

Commander

Mack is your team up for a little hunting?

Mack

I finally get out of this seat and get some hand to hand. Thank you Sir

Commander

Avenge your brother and do me proud

Mack

Yes SIR

Mack gets up and pulls out a comm. device. He orders his team of mercenaries' to meet him by the gate where the Hybrids are approaching

INT Mother Ship Hallway

(A laser beam shoots across the room and Blackburn pushes jay out of the way of it. Jay falls to the ground. While bracing his fall he puts out he arm with the computer hooked up to it. The computer gets damaged. Blackburn walks over to him and offers his hand to help him up)

Blackburn

You ok

(Jay grabs Blackburn hands and starts to get up)

Jay

Yeah thank you but my computer is gone. Captain we lost the map!

(James gets a little dizzy and grabs the top of his head with his right hand and shakes it. Isis walks over to him)

Isis

It's happening. How are you doing?

Scar

What's happening? Capt you ok?

(James stops shaking his head and starts to look up. It seems to look brighter, stronger, and more focus.)

Jay

Capt we lost the map

James

No need I know where to go. Just follow me and stay frosty we have some nasty aliens coming our way

Brace

Nastier than what we been fighting

James

Oh yes these are the alien version of us. Just be prepared for a big fight. Now come on and be quite

Isis

Now you feel how I feel

James

It's unbelievable. I can't wait to use it fully

Isis

Be careful it's addictive

James

I bet but these guys coming our way are no joke. I'm going to need the full power

Isis

We'll see, you don't even know that yet. Just trust me

James

Fine

He pushes Isis back with his left hand and pulls his gun with his right hand and shoot two aliens in the head as soon as the aliens turn the corner

Jay

What the hell was that?

The team keep running towards the command center. They turn one corner and run into Rick and the rest of the remaining units. James walks up to Rick and that touch fists

Rick

It's good to see you Capt. Sorry but we lost a lot of men. These motherfuckers are hard. I've been in some of the roughest places in the world and they seem like a walk in the park compared to these son of a bitches.

James

I know be on guard. These are only their grunts their elite are heading towards us now with bad intentions!

Rick

Good to Know

Mike

Hey do any of you know where to go

James

Follow me soldier

Mike

Yes Captain

(As the team proceeds a door opens up and you see Mack, one of the Commanders elite mercenaries. A tall muscular man with a scar going across the left side of his face from the top of his forehead, pass his eye, to the edge of his neck. Behind him about 10 of his men some the same height and weight as him and some smaller)

Mack

Here they are men. Do you see the fear in their eyes? I'm surprised such a weak looking children got this far. It's too bad that your journey stops here. Be happy that you got this far. No one has ever got as far as you. At least you will be able to die, knowing you got this far.

(Scar walks up through the crowd and stand to the left of James and turns to look at him)

Scar

Capt please let me have this one please

(James put his hand on Scar chest)

James

You had the last one it's my turn

Mack

Are you two are done playing with yourselves?

Brace

You son of a bitch you're going to die

Mack

Maybe one day but not before I grab your head and tear it from your body

Brace

Why don't you come and get me bitch

(Mack starts to walk towards Brace. Captain James walks up to Mack who slightly taller than him)

Mack

So you want to die first I see. No problem as long as I...

(James uppercuts Mack and Mack falls back and hits the wall some blood comes out of his mouth)

James

Your fight is with me

(Mack stands up straight spits more blood out of his mouth and then wipes his chin.)

Mack

Hum looks like you might be a slight challenge

James

I'm more than that. I'm your executioner

(James runs towards Mack and takes a swing. Mack swings at the same time and they both fall back)

Blackburn

Well let's not stand here and watch the fight. It's time to jump in.

(Blackburn and the rest of the unit runs towards the other mercenaries and starts to fight them. It's a massive brawl with Jay and Brace standing in the rear watching it. It's a bloody brawl. Some aliens pick up their opponents and throw them but some hybrids pick up their opponents and throw them. The fight is between Mack and James. As Mack gets a good blow in the members of his team seem to be winning the brawl but it's vise versa. As James starts to win his team looks like they are going to win. James hits Mack with another uppercut, Mack falls back. His pissed, He pulls out a massive long blade that was attached to his back and touches it against his tongue.)

Mack

I'm going to put this through you and then that little boy over there. Then we will destroy your planet so I can go home and get some R&R

(James takes out his knife and looks at Mack)

James

I've seen your planet and it's shit. There's no place for R&R there but after we take over this ship I might go there and blow it the fuck up just for the hell of it

Mack

I hate you

(Mack runs towards James and tries to cut him. James side steps Mack and cuts him on his side.)

James

See what you don't know is that my ancestor was the one who stopped you guys the first time from destroying this planet and guess what I'm here to stop you this time

Mack

Over my dead body

James

That's what I'm here for

(The two continue their knife fight. Mack swings and cuts James on his left forearm)

Mack

I'm going to gut you hybrid!

(Mack swings again but this time James catches his arm. He knees the hand and knocks the blade out of Mack's hand at the same time he turns and stabs Mack in the Back with his knife. He swings Mack in front of him and proceeds to kick him against the wall and his back hits the wall pushing the knife deeper into Mack's body, through his whole body. James proceeds to pick up Mack's blade and swiftly runs towards him and pushes the blade deep into Mack's chest simultaneously Blackburn cuts the neck of his enemy and Rick snaps the neck of his. The brawl is over)

Mack

Falls to his knees

Thank you. You've finally ended my pain but be warned they won't stop especially after today. You are the one who will defeat the old on...

(Mack falls to the ground and dies. James turns around and looks at Scar. He took a knife to the leg and it is bleeding badly. James walks over to him as Scar takes the blade out of his leg)

Scar

You did good Sir

James

So did you. You going to make it

Scar

Maybe

James

Who's got the nano kit

(Isis turns around and opens a pouch pocket on her belt and
pulls out a needle. She walks towards Scar)

Isis

I thought you elite don't get injured. As she injects the needle
into Scar's leg

Scar

Shit… We're fighting elite aliens not just some run of the mock
hostiles

James

No time to talk. Can you move

(The nano machines starts to close the wound on Scar's leg. He
gets up and grabs an alien gun)

Scar

I'm ready when you are

James

Good... move out. We're close

Brace

About time. I'm trying to get off this ship!

INT Mother Ship Command Center

(The Commander was watching the brawl on the screen. He takes a seat with a look of shock on his face. Every member on deck looks over to the Commander and see the look on his face. This has never happen before. You can see some of the crew for the first time scared)

Jensen

(nervously)

Commander... your orders

Commander

Jensen...How ...How do they always do it. How did he defeat Samson and Mack. It's doesn't make any sense. They are weaker than us

(Bang Bang Bang on the doors to the Command Center. Jay opens up the console to the doors and plays with the wires)

Jay

This should work

(The doors open up. In walks James)

INT Mother Ship Command Center

James

This ship is now under my command

Jensen

You human you must have lost your mind!

(Jensen gets up to attack James and you see Scar Step in the room and shoots Jensen in the head killing him)

(James walks to the Commander)

James

Was this your ship?

Commander

(Commander takes out a knife and tries to stab James)

Insolent

(James side steps the Commander and quickly kicks the knife out of his hand into the air heading towards his hand. He catches it. The Commander turns around while James takes the handle of the knife and throws it at the Commander Head)

Commander

No I can't...

(The knife goes right into the Commander head. James walks over to him as he falls to his knees. He pulls the blade out of his head and allows the body to fall to the ground)

James

Oh yes you can. Jay and Brace get in here and do your thing. It looks like our fleets taken heavy damage.

(Jay and Brace rushes in and takes out their equipment and starts to upload the AI system.)

Jay

What do you want me to get running first?

James

The comm. system

Brace

Cool I'm working on it

Jay

Wow this ship is impressive. The readouts are incredible

James

You can admire it later we need to talk to the General

Brace

Destiny, Destiny this is the Mother Ship are you there?

Dr. Coaxe

Mother Ship...mmmh looks like you made it then.   Congrats. This is Alpha though Mother Ship. You need to tweak the comm. system a little. Turn down the shields I'm going to teleport aboard

Brace

Doc how do I lower the Shields?

Dr. Coaxe

hold on let me do it

(Within three seconds Dr. Coaxe appears inside of the Command Center)

Dr. Coaxe

Well

Jay

Holy Shit you got to warn us before you just appear

Dr. Coaxe

I told you that I was going to handle it

James

You two stop bickering and someone get my on the Comm with Walker. We still have soldiers fighting out there and they don't know That we have control of the Mother Ship

Dr. Coaxe

Well you can tell him now

Walker

James is that you? You did it son! You did it!

James

General…. I would like to report that we now have control of the Mother Ship

Walker

Great can you call off those fighters

Dr. Coaxe

I can't. It seems like the Commander turn off the regulator on them. They won't stop. They will keep fighting until they die

Walker

Well what can we do We have good men and aliens dying out there

Dr. Coaxe

I'm not a military man Walker.

Walker

Damnit Walker out

INT Destiny Command Center

Walker

Ty, Order our fighters to attack the aliens

Ty

Which aliens?

Walker

The ones we've been fighting. Also get our ships in firing
position. Get the Doc back on the Screen

Ty

Ok

Dr. Coaxe appears back on the screen

Dr. Coaxe

Yes

Walker

I need you to inform the Aliens the situation. Tell them we are
going to move into a position to fire at the fighters. I don't want
them to think we are firing at them. Tell me their response
after. Also, I'm ordering all ships to send troops over to the ship
now. Walker out

INT Mother Ship

James

Doc does this ship have any more fighters on it

Dr. Coaxe

Let me check

Rick

What's your plan?

James

They need backup out there

Dr. Coaxe

They Should have a flight deck with more fighters. I'm having troubles finding it now. The upload isn't complete yet

(Nicklous with his hands handcuff raises them.)

Nicklous

I can help you with that

(James walks over to Nicklous)

James

Can I trust you

Nicklous

Will you set me free if I do?

James

Will you try anything funny

Nicklous

I have no options but to help you now. They will destroy me now, you taken over the ship. If you fail them you die.

(James puts his finger on the security lock and the handcuffs come off)

Nicklous

I have to warn you the Commander told us to unleash the programming on them. The last time we did that we couldn't stop them. We had to use the self destruct protocol.

Jay

Then why don't we use it now

Nicklous

The Commander turned if off and I don't know how to turn it back on

Jay

What's his password

Nicklous

No one but him knew it I think

James

Jay can you hack into the system and try to find that protocol.

Jay

Can you help me?

Nicklous

The one that could is laying on the ground over there

James

Fine. Nicklous show us where the fighters are and Jay, you , Dr. Coaxe and Brace find the self destruct protocol

Nicklous

Make sure it's not the ships self destruct protocol

(Isis walks to the front of the door right in front of James, Isis takes a Look at James)

James

Don't Worry I'll bring him back alive

Isis

Not just him. I need you to come back too.

James

I always come back

(James and the rest of the unit follow Nicklous out of the Command Center)

Brace

Well Bro let's get to it

Jay

Where do we start

Dr. Coaxe

Let's ask our AI unit. AI can you find the self destruct for the fighters

AI

That information is not located on the database. You might have to try in the awakening chambers

Jay

Where the hell is that

AI

I can show you

Dr. Coaxe

Brace and Jay follow the AIs Direction. I will work on getting the upload completed while you find that protocol

Jay

Ok Doc Lead the way AI

(Jay and Brace walk out of the Command Center Leaving Dr. Coaxe there.)

Isis

This is bullshit. Where are we holding the captured soldiers?

Dr. Coaxe

Why

Isis

One of them knows what to do. I know it

Tone

I can show you Ms.

Isis

Ok Marine, take lead

Dr. Coaxe

Do you think you can trust them

Isis

I don't need trust I can read them

Dr. Coaxe

There's hundreds of them down there. How are you going to read them all in time

Isis

I'll figure it out

Dr. Coaxe

Hold up I'll send Innis to help you

Isis

Who's that?

Dr. Coaxe

A fellow psych. AI teleport Innis to the ship now

AI

Locating Innis. Innis located. Teleporting now

(Innis appears on the Command Center.)

Innis

I was in the middle of something Doc. This better be important.

Dr. Coaxe

It is but no time for me to explain it to you. Go with Isis and she will fill you in

Isis

Let's go

Innis

Take lead

(Innis follows Isis and Tone out of the command center leaving Dr. Coaxe working on the computer system)

INT Hallway of the Mother Ship

Innis

So sis where are we heading too and what are we going to be doing

Isis

Can't you read my mind

Innis

I could but I rather hear it from your mouth

Isis

Ok where heading to where we're detaining the Aliens that were on this ship when we took it over. I need to find the alien that knows how to shut off the fighters or turn on their self destruct protocol

Innis

Sounds like fun. How many aliens are there and how much time do we have

Isis

Hundreds of them and we have no time.

Innis

Hmmm ok

The three continue down the hallway and enter walk through a room that seems to be a lab

Innis

Oh here is where they...

Isis

What was that

Innis

Nothing let's just hurry up there is a lot for us to accomplish

(They continue to rush entering room after room hallway after hallway.)

Tone

We're here

(They walk up to a large door with four Marines standing guard)

Isis

Open this door

Marine

Captain James said not to open this door unless He tells us too

Isis

Listen. Greg Don't let me pull rank on you. Open this door now it's an emergency

Marine 2

It's nice that you know his name but we're not opening this door. Do you know how many aliens are in there? If something goes wrong they can take the ship back

(Isis frustrated looks at Innis and they nod their heads. Then they place their hands on their head and start to concentrate)

Marine 3

Look I got orders here to let them in

Marine 1

Why didn't you say so. Good Luck but if we lose this ship it's on you not us

Isis

Just set out of my way

(The doors to the room open up and the Isis, Innis, and tone walk in)

INT Hallway of the Mother Ship

Nicklous

The ships are in this flight deck.

Nicklous presses the bottom and the doors to the flight deck open up and you the lights turn on. The men walk in. there are amazed to see these fighter space ships.

James

I hope you know what you are doing Sis

Nicklous

What was that Captain?

James

Nothing. What were you saying?

Nicklous

These are the new and improved ships. We just got them the last time we stopped at one of our slave planets

James

How many slave planets do you have

Nicklous

Hundreds of thousands of them. We've been conquering the universe for centuries. You would be surprised how easy it was. Most planets as soon as we arrived saw us as gods and willingly gave in to our power. Others were so behind technological and developmental that it was easy to come in and take what we wanted. A few were advanced enough to try to put up a fight but again we were too powerful for them.

Scar

Can we get the history lesson later. We need to get out there and help

Nicklous

Well just hop in and put the helmet on. These ships sync with your minds and do what you think

(A screen pops up and it's Dr. Coaxe.)

Dr. Coaxe

They stole that from me

James

Ok Doc. Now Nicklous what else can you tell us.

Nicklous

Keep your thoughts on flying and fighting. You have to have a clear mind to control these ships. If you don't then you will die

James

We lost Sam, John, and some good damn soldiers. Let's avenge our lost. Load up men

Mike

I'm with you Captain. It's an honor to fight alongside with you.

(James turns to Nicklous. Are you staying here or joining us)

Nicklous

You would trust your enemy.

James

Nick, look around you. If you didn't come here and attack us most of us in this room would be fighting against each other. Trying to kill each other but now we are allies. You see the enemy of my enemy is my friend. Therefore choose your side. Do you want to remain an enemy or become a friend?

Nicklous

Thank you giving me an option but I really don't have one. I'm with you from now on

James

Ok. Are you a pilot?

Nicklous

One of the best

James

Then hop into one of these ships and get to work

Nicklous

Thank you

Captain James and the team enter each ship on the flight deck and put on their helmets.

James

Dr. Coaxe, what did the Orion's say

Dr. Coaxe

I will patch you in to their leader. Meckos are you there

Meckos

This is Meckos.

Dr. Coaxe

I want to introduce to one of The Earth warriors. Captain James this is Meckos. Meckos this is Captain James

Meckos

It's an honor Captain. I hear you want to help

James

Yes

Meckos

We came here to help you now we need your help. These fighters are fierce

James

I know I've lost a lot of good soldiers to them. We are leaving the Mother Ship now

Meckos

We welcome your assistance

James

Good James out. Dr. Coaxe open the bar doors to the flight deck

Dr. Coaxe

Working on it

James

We don't have time for you to work it out. We need to be out there now

Dr. Coaxe

There

(The bay doors to the flight deck open and Captain James ship is the first to fly out. Following behind him the rest of the ships.)

James

Ok it's time to finish this

INT Mother Ship detainee room. Isis, Innis, and Tone stand in the middle of the crowd with the four marines standing behind them with their hands on their guns

Isis

AI is the translation program working

AI

Yes

Tone

Alright Aliens we need your help. Who wants to help

(Isis taps Tone on the right shoulder)

Isis

Let me handle this one soldier

Tone

Hey I was just trying to help

Isis

I appreciate it.

(Isis walks closer to the crowd)

Isis

You might not know me but I'm sure you've heard of the hybrids. I am one of them. I come here in peace. I know you might take that as a joke but I promise you, we will not harm you. Even now one of your own is helping us fight against the fighters. I need your help. Who here knows how to turn off the self destruct protocol on the fighters

(Not one of the aliens move. They just stand there)

Marine 1

I don't think they understand you

Marine 2

No they understand but they aren't going to help you

(Isis turns around)

Isis

Listen I am your ranking officer. Do you know what that
means?... It means I can make your life hell. Now shut the fuck
up unless you have something productive to say

(Isis turns back around)

Isis

Please I'm begging you to help

Innis

They are strong. I can hardly penetrate their minds.

Isis

I know

(They group just stands there an wait. Then an older alien walks
up in front of Isis)

Ishmarelic

You stand here asking for our help but you keep us imprison in
this room. You say no harm will come to us but you have men
standing there with their weapons ready to kill. You say you are
a hybrid and you are one of us but you treat us no different
than the Over Lords.   Why should we help you? What's to stop

you from killing us or imprison is just like them. You see the Over Lords want you eradicated because you humans process the same abilities as they do. Right now your ally next to you is trying to read our minds but he cannot. I am much older than him and even yourself put together. So please tell him to stop. He is boring me. You want help we want guarantees that we will be set free if we do

Isis

Fine. I will do you one even better. I will give you a chance to fight against the Over Lords. If we win this battle, our next step is to take the fight to them. What do you say?

(Isis puts her hand out to shake Ishmarelic. Ishmarelic turns around and looks at the group. The group starts to part and a man starts to walk towards Ishmarelic. The man looks at Ishmarelic. The two of them seem to be communicating without moving their lips. Ishmarelic then turns around and out his hand out to shake Isis)

Ishmarelic

I assume this is how your cultures has an accord.

Isis

Absolutely.

Ishmarelic

Isis meet Jasper. He will be able to help you.

Isis

Jasper. Thank you Thank you very much. Let's move we don't
have any time

(Isis turns around and the Marines part to let them pass. Isis
then pauses and turns around)

Isis

Marines make sure you give them whatever they want or need.
Also, let them leave the room and continue with ther duties on
this ship. We need all the help we can get now

Marine 4

Yes Sir Lt

Isis

Tone Innis Ishmarelic, Jasper, Let's move out

(The groups leaves out of the room)

INT Destiny command Center

(Walker is talking to Gethros on the screen)

Gethros

What's the update Walker

Walker

You really want to know

Gethros

Don't play with me I have the President on my ass wanting information

Walker

Tell the President that we're still in the midst of war. But for your eyes only, We captured the Mother Ship, the Orion's showed up and are helping us, but we have a unit of fighters that just won't die

Gethros

WE have another problem. You forced the President hand with that message. The whole world is quiet awaiting more news. The World Leaders were forced to get on the TV and confirm that aliens are here and they are attacking us. Surprisingly there are no riots, no fighting, just peace. The Churches, Synagogues, Mosques, and everywhere people go to pray are packed on the inside and out. The whole world is in fear and they are praying to whomever they pray too. I swear you can even see a white supremacist sitting next to a black. It's crazy down here. Everything that they predicted was wrong.

Walker

They needed to know the truth

Gethros

Yeah but after this we all might be court marshaled for what we did

Walker

You second guessing things

Gethros

No. What's going to be our next move

Walker

Revenge

Gethros

Revenge is what you want to what end will you seek your
revenge

Walker

We bring the fight to them. This is the second time they
brought it to us. It's our turn to bring it to them. We have allies
all over the universe. I say we reach out to them and rally
against these mother fuckers, with no quarters

Gethros

So you want to go to their home base

Walker

Yes. I what to end the reign

Gethros

You know the game if we take them out someone will come and
replace them

Walker

Then we take them out too

Gethros

You think they are going to allow you to do that

Walker

They have no choice.

Ty

General we have another problem

Walker

Gethros... Let me get back to you.

(Screen with Gethros is turned off)

Walker

What is it?

Ty

Dr. Coaxe asked me to look through some data on those
fighters.

Walker

And

Ty

I found that they have a failsafe that if their numbers fall below a certain number they will engaged a self destruct

Walker

That's what we want

Ty

No sir this self destruct will destroy most of the Orion's and even some of our fleet

Walker

Alert the Orion's and our fighters we need to lure them away from us

Ty

How Sir

Walker

Get Dr. Coaxe. There's always something isn't there

INT Space

James

What do you mean retreat to a safe location

Ty

Those ships are rig to explode if they are losing

James

So what do we do

Walker

James you and the Orion fighters are going to have to lure them towards Saturn or Neptune

INT Mother Ship Command Center.

(The doors to the Command Center open and in walks Jasper, Isis, Innis, Ishmarelic, Isis, and Tone)

Dr. Coaxe

Goody you brought more friends

Isis

Dr. Coaxe here's Jasper. He's going to help initiate the self destruct protocol

Dr. Coaxe

Well Jasper take a seat

Jasper

Now all I can do is help locate the coding for it. I'm not too sure how to turn it on though.

Isis

You didn't say that before

Jasper

I thought you just wanted to find the coding.

Isis

Where're the two hackers

Dr. Coaxe

I sent them to the awakening chamber to look for the database on shutting off the fighters.

Isis

Did they find anything

Dr. Coaxe

Not sure. I forgot about them

Isis

Jesus Christ did the defrost hurt your memory

Jasper

You're the Dr. Coaxe that we all heard about. Wow it's a honor to meet you

Isis

To hell with that get those boys on the comm. and get them back up here now

Dr. Coaxe

Ok, OK. AI locate Jay and Brace

AI

Locating. Located them.

Jay

Hey Doc we're finding a lot of information here but nothing in regards to a shut down

Dr. Coaxe

Fine we need you up here now

Jay

OK

Isis

AI teleport them here now

(Jay and Brace appear inside the Command Center)

Brace

Can you give is an option or at least warn us that you are going to do that shit. I getting tired of this shit

Jay

What is it Doc?

Dr. Coaxe

I need you to help us with the shut down coding

Dr. Coaxe

With the four of us we should be able to shut it down

Isis

Hurry up every second we waste lives are being lost

(Jay and brace rush over to a computer screen and start to type.)

EXT Space

James

Ok men retreat towards Neptune

Rich

Are you serious Capt. We've been getting our asses kicked out here and finally when we start to win, you say retreat what the fuck

James

If we don't retreat then everything in this area will be destroyed by the bombs in those fighters. Meckos did they relay the information to you

Meckos

Yes I've order my ships to retreat towards the location the Doc gave us. Hopefully they will follow us

James

Yeah hope So

(During the battle all of the allies turn around and head towards Neptune. The alien ships turn around and start to follow them.)

James

Come on follow us you son of a bitch. This battle ends now

(Walker starts to talk to James and Meckos over his comm.)

Walker

We have another problem. I just heard from Isis. Even at that distance unless we're able to turn off the bombs inside of the fighters you guys won't make it. WE have to figure something else out or we'll lose two much of our dwindling fleet

James

We can't wait no longer if we keep on running they will turn back and go after either you or the Earth. If this is my call General, I rather lose my life to ensure the lives of the planet. This is why we fight to protect. Goodbye General. James out

Walker

We will honor you and everyone's whom lost their lives this day.
I promise you

James

Adour and Dreke are you ok with this?

Adour

I knew I wasn't going to live forever

Dreke

Whatever you need of me Sir I will do it. It's been a pleasure
fighting alongside all of you

James

Galactis are you ready?

Adour

Waiting for you to give the order

James

Good

James

Ok men as soon as we get them in the vicinity of our ships
weapons I want you to fire

INT Mother Ship Command Center

Jay

How's it looking Brace?

Brace

Reminds me of when we hacked the pentagon

Jay

Yeah the good ole days

Isis

Stop yapping and get to typing

Brace

Listen slave master don't get your panties in a bunch. Jay you ready?

Jay

Yup, Bro

Jay and Brace turn to each other and smile. The then turn back to their screen and press enter. The AI starts to talk

AI

Manual bomb shut down. Do you want to initiate self Destruct?

Jay

Yes

EXT Space

(James and the rest of his team are at the trap location)

James

Now

(Dreke and Major Adour Ship uncloak and start to fire but as soon as they start to fire the ships start to blow up)

James

Hold your fire Hold your Fire.

Dreke

What just happen

James

Our team stepped up at the right moment and saved our asses

Rich

Wow she's amazing

James

Don't you ever forget that. Ok men It's over, It's all over. Let's head back to the Mother ship. Thank you Sis

INT Mother Ship Command Center

Isis

Your welcome brother now get your ass back

Jay

Who are you talking too?

Isis

None of your business

INT Destiny Command Center

Ty

WE did it Sir! WE Did it! We won!

Walker

We did

(as he falls back into his seat

this is one of the most stressful battles I've ever been in and I've been in some really bad battles

Ty

What Now General

Walker

Get the President on the screen. I have a few words for him

Ty

YES SIR

The President Shows up on the screen

President

I hope you have some good news for me General especially after what you did

Walker

I followed orders. We agreed that we would inform the people. They deserve to know the truth

President

Don't play with me Walker. You forced my hand and I don't like people who force my hand. I am the President I can make the rest of your life HELL

Walker

I've been to hell already and I don't think that you are going to put someone in hell that has good news for you.

President

What is it?

Walker

We now have full control of the Mother Ship

President

Thank God!

Walker

DO I have permission to proceed with the next part of the mission

President

That's on hold right now. I have to meet with the World Leaders and see what we are going to do next. Plus after that stunt you did, I just might court marshal your ass. You may be the best person to command this mission but I saw the reports, your Captain seem to step up and lead. You might not be needed as you think General

Walker

So be it. I could use a vacation

President

Vacation clearly you don't know where I'm going to send you

James

Mr. President, I await your decision

President

Your one lucky person. It would be public outcry if I have you court marshaled. You've made a lot of friends now. Stay up there until I figure out what to do. President out

Ty

General, what do you think they are going to you

Walker

It doesn't matter anymore. James is ready. He's proven that... If they don't allow me to go with you guys then, Ty listen to him he will guide you to success

Ty

Don't worry General, It's was under your command that we
won

Walker

Very true. Well let's head over to the Mother Ship and greet
our warriors and Thank them

INT Flight Deck of Mother Ship

Captain James and the remaining fighters land on the flight decl.
James hopes out of his ship to see a greeting from every
member of the ship humans, hybrids, and aliens. It's a big
celebration. While James is coming down the ladder of his ship,
you see Isis running towards him. As soon as he gets down Isis
jumps into his hands and the other men around him pat James
on his back. Each member of the fight team get a welcome

James

Wow Sis

(as he twirls her around She kisses him on his check while he
puts her down.)

James

I told you I would make it back

Isis

Not Without my help

James

You didn't specify that I had to do it by myself. Well your friend
is over there.

Isis turns around and looks over to see Rich walking over to
them. He has a strange look on his face. He walks over to
James.

Rich

Captain. I want to ask your permission to date your sister

James

Mmhh

(Isis quickly moves closer to Rich and kisses him passionately on
his lips. Rich kisses her back)

James

Ok, ok get a room. I didn't even give you permission soldier

(with a smile on his face)

(Isis looks over to James and Kisses Rich again on his check)

Isis

He doesn't need your permission

James

True but he has it anyways.

(The three of them stay there Laughing. The rest of James's unit walks up to him First Blackburn, then Scar, then Melissa, then John, then Rick, then Jay, then Brace, then Dreke, and Phillip following behind them. Then Nicklous walks up to James)

James

Well soldier how do you feel

Nicklous

I don't know

Brace

(walks up to Nicklous and pats him on his back

Tell him you feel great! WE did it MAN!

Nicklous

Well I guess I feel good

James

Good to know

(In walks Ishmarelic and Jasper)

Isis

Brother I want to introduce you to ones who help make this happen.

(James puts out his hand to shake Jasper and Ishmarelic hands. They shake)

James

It's an honor to meet a fellow warrior

Ishmarelic

So you're the one

Ishmarelic

(Shakes his head)

Yes it is. Well at first I wanted off this ship and away from it all but after meeting you. I see why they are nervous I want to tell you that we will stay and fight along with you

James

Good to know Friend

(James turns to the right to see Blackburn walking up towards him)

Blackburn

We made it Sir

James

Yes we did and by the looks of it someone else made it too

(As Blackburn turns around he sees Sarch running up to him. She jumps into his open arms)

Sarch

I'm so happy you made it. I wouldn't know what to do if you didn't

Blackburn

I told you I was going to make it baby

Sarch

I know but who really knows their future

Blackburn

I do. I see me retired with you by my side, watching our children grow up

Sarch

Funny you say that

Blackburn

What's so funny about that. I thought that's what you wanted

Sarch

Yes but I wasn't sure that you wanted the same thing

Blackburn

Of course I do

(A big smile forms on Sarch's face)

Sarch

Well that makes it easier to tell you this

Blackburn

What is it

Sarch

You're going to be a father

(Blackburn just stands there and doesn't say anything. Then Jay who overheard the whole conversation hits Blackburn on his left shoulder)

Jay

Hey man you heard that you're going to be a father. Hey Cap you heard the news Blackburn is going to have a baby

(James walks over to Blackburn and puts his hand out and Blackburn shakes it)

James

Congrats Soldier. That child is lucky to have you two as parents

Blackburn

Thank you Sir

Sarch

Are you ok?

Blackburn

I just don't know what to say. I mean...I

Sarch

Wow look at the hard nose elite caught speechless

Blackburn

Thank you the early wedding gift

Jay

Don't worry Blackburn. Uncle Jay will be there to help.

(Blackburn looks at Jay)

Jay

What you saved my life you will never get rid of me now

Blackburn

Hun this is Jay

Sarch

Nice to meet you

Jay

It's an honor maim

(Jay and Sarch shake hands)

Scar

(Scar turns to Philip and John. He has a look of pain)

Lost a lot of men this time around. I just don't feel like celebrating right now. It's hard for me to see anything good after today

John

They died so the earth could live DON'T EVER FORGET THAT. They died so that the masses can live

Philip

They will be missed

John

True

Walking up behind the group is General Walker

Walker

This is not the time to mourn our lost let's celebrate our win. In celebrating our win we honor our lost. If it wasn't for their sacrifice we would not have made it this far

James

What's next General

Walker

Well first we celebrate today and tomorrow I may be facing a court marshal

James

They won't dare

Walker

Let me worry about that. Don't worry I haven't played all my cards yet

James

Understood

Walker turns to Jay and Brace

Walker

So it looks like we owe a lot of our success to you two.

Brace

Not just us but if it wasn't for Ishmarelic and Jasper

Walker

Who

James

Our new Allies

Walker turns to see Ishmarelic and Jasper standing next to Isis and Rich. He walks over to them. And puts his hand out

Walker

So I hear I owe you two a Thank You for helping us win this battle

(Ishmarelic shakes Walker hand and so does Jasper)

Ishmarelic

You have a look of vengeance to you. You're looking for blood

Walker

Don't pretend that you don't want the same thing. That's why you're staying. Isn't it?

Ishmarelic

Maybe

Walker

don't worry your secret is safe with me. Everyone you see here on this ship wants to same thing

Brace

So what's next Sir

Walker

We're heading to their home planet

Brace

Don't worry General we will be ready

Walker

I know son. Where's the Doc

Isis

Last time I saw him, he was heading to a lab with Innis

Walker

Let me go and talk to him. I will leave you guys here to celebrate

James

I'll come with you

(Walker and James walk away from the group and head out of the flight deck)

INT Beta Base

Jackson

We did it General

Gethros

No we didn't, Walker and James did it

Smith

We played our part too General

Gethros

A very small one

Jackson

What now

Gethros

Well it looks like they are going to grant Walker his wish.

Smith

What's that

Gethros

We're all going to space. To a location no man has gone before.

Smith

I'm ready for it

Gethros

No you're not, not this mission. We're heading towards an enemy that damn near conquered the whole universe and he wants us to go and attack them

Jackson

After this win. If we wait for them to attack us and not take the fight to them this planet might not make it

Smith

It's our Destiny Sir. Destiny has a funny way of finding it's way of coming true. I mean look it was centuries ago when the aliens first came here and we fought them. We barely won.. Now we are going to finish what was started back then

Gethros

Funny you say that. Destiny. Well guys your off duty. Take a break and go celebrate our win. In the morning we find out what we're going to do next

INT Undisclosed Location

Enter world leaders. Can't tell who's in the room

Unknown 1

I don't like it, we can't trust him to follow us

Unknown 2

What are we to do? We can't do it without him and he's damn hybrids

Unknown 3

What are our alternatives

Unknown 1

That damn AI won't listen to us either.

Unknown 6

Have we lost our power over them

Unknown 2

What are we going to do?

Unknown 5

We'll allow them to go but just like the Over Lords had a self destruct program we should too. I have a few team studying the code. They assure me that we can turn it back on without the AI noticing.

Unknown 7

We're going to do this to our own people

Unknown 3

Absolutely

Unknown 1

Fine let them go. At least we get them off this planet and if they make it we will handle it. It's going to take years for them to go there and come back. By then we should have a plan setup to get rid of them

(All the World Leaders say Agreed and Disappear.)

INT Mother Ship Hallway

(Walker and James are walking down the hallway. Walker gets message on his comm. device and he looks at it with a grin)

James

What's that about

Walker

They're letting us go because they want us off this planet

James

Who?

Walker

The real people who rule this planet. They think I don't know who they really are but I have someone on the inside who's tired of them.

James

So you're planning a coup de tau

Walker

Yes

James

So what's next

Walker

WE bring the fight to the fucking Over Lords.

James

Then what? What about the coup de tau?

Walker

Don't worry, I know they're working on a plan to get rid of us if we win but I've implemented my plan already. If we win or lose this war out there, they won't be in power to see us it happen

James

Ok

Encountering Our Freedom Chapter Three

EXT Space

Imagine a pane view of space as you gets closer to
Earth's moon you see the massive Mother ship orbiting
it. Circling the Mother ship are 10 medium size ships.
As you get closer to the space ships more and more
space ships starts to appear in the background. Then
you approach Alpha Base and you see Marines watching
CNN on TV. There is a blip going across the screen
"Aliens are here more and more keep showing up! Are
they here to take over the Planet? What about the
mission to replenish Earth's resources? Then you enter
the United Nations meeting and everyone is screaming
at each other. Media from all over the world is there,
covering the meeting on the aliens. All the world
leaders are there. The leaders yelling at each other and
crushing up paper throwing it in the air. Enter in
General Walker with Captain James walking beside him.
He continues to walk down to the podium. Walker
walks up to the microphone and speaks

Walker

(in a hard and menacing tone)

Excuse Me

(The whole group stops yelling at each other and looks at
Walker)

Walker

Ladies and Gentlemen, many of you are here are in
fear. Worrying about what might happen to this planet

now that all these aliens are here and more keep showing up

Member of UN

You brought them here and you can tell them to leave. We don't want aliens here! We don't want them here! I don't care if we need their resources here

Crowd

(More members get up)

Yeah, yeah tell them to leave we don't want them here!

Walker

(Frustrated)

Excuse me Sir but if it wasn't for their assistance and technology, you, everyone in this room, all of your families and friends, and the whole planet would have been destroyed. You owe them your lives. So please sit down and allow me to speak.

(The crowd sits down in silence)

Walker

Thank you. As you may know there are many ships arriving every day. The word went out, throughout the universe that we defeated the aliens. This is great news. Unfortunately this is only the beginning. We may have won this battle but the war is far from over.

England Representative

So what now what do we do? We can't have all these aliens on this planet there isn't enough room for them and us. I thought the space mission was to find replenish Earth's resources to heal the planet. Not to make it a safe haven to the universe. Our planet is dying. All Aliens must leave

Walker

Well I'm part alien. Do you want me to leave this planet to? Do you know what the real truth is about our planet... These aliens were here before, a long time ago. Something left out of the history books. Guess what, I'm not the only descendant, you might be one too! The majority of this room is probably a descendant of the aliens. So please sit down and listen to what I have to say.

(The ambassador is shocked to hear what Walker just told him. He sits down and places his hand over his mouth)

Walker

Thank you. I know some of you might be shocked to hear this news. I know that some of you might not want to believe it. As a testament to the truth, I want all of you who are watching this around the world to turn off the closed caption on your TV's. I also want all the ambassadors here to tell their interpreters that they won't need them.

(Walker waits a moment. He then grabs his comm.
device)

Walker

OK AI go, ahead

(As soon as he says that Dr. Coaxe and a hologram of
the AI materialize from teleportation)

Walker

This is one of the aliens who helped us win the battle.
This is an artificial Intelligence computer, who's now
interpreting what I am saying in your own native
language.

(The whole crowds says nothing)

Walker

Besides all the technological advances provided to us by
the aliens, they also have advanced our ability to
provide clean water to everyone in the world and
unparallel source of power, with the new ARC reactors
all over the world, that doesn't pollute our planet at all.
We will never have to use fossil flue again sorry big oil
but your reign is over. Also, with the information that
they provided to us, we will be able to find a way to
reverse the effects of Global Warming. Our Planet is
slowly dying and now, we will be able to transport the
materials from another planet to heal it. The only way
to do this is to go to our attackers home planet and
defeat them. Our alien friends promised to help us heal

the planet but we must defeat High Command first. But if the world wants us to leave we will!   I warn you if we do leave who's going to fight the aliens if they come back?

(The whole UN is quite. Not even a whisper from anyone in the room)

Walker

I didn't think so! Let's get down to the truth. I am not here to threaten you or scare you. I am here to tell you that this war isn't over. The reason why all these ships keep coming here is because this war isn't just here on Earth. It's a war that involves the whole universe. We have been tormented by a group that wants to control the universe. This is the same group that tired to conquer the Earth before and the same group that we just fended off. But if we don't bring the fight to them then they will be back and this time we might not be as lucky. They won't allow us to get the necessary resources we need to heal our planet unless we defeat them. Therefore, we sent out a message to all aliens to join us in the battle and now we ask everyone on the planet with military experience to join our Global Space Federation Force. We need you!

(Walker steps back from the microphone and walks down from the podium. He reaches into his pocket and pulls out his comm.)

Ok we're ready

(Dr. Coaxe, James, and Walker disappear leaving the AI hologram standing there. The AI waves to the crowd and the cameras and also disappears.)

INT White House Oval Office

You see the President watching the TV feed while Walker talks. After Walker finishes he sits back into his chair

President

I hope your right about this one! Ricky, contact Walker on the line

Ricky

Yes Mr. President

(Ricky walks out of the office. The intercom on the President's desk goes off)

President

Yes

Ricky

Mr. President I have General Walker on the line

President

Patch him through

(An image of General Walker pops up hovering over the President's Desk)

Walker

Mr. President

President

You know they will do everything to stop you

Walker

They can try

President

Your trying to take the power away from Big Oil, Healthcare, and you are going to hurt the banks. You want to provide water to everyone for free. Are you sure you want to continue this path?

Walker

Yes Sir

President

We'll see how it ends up. How do you plan on this movement to continue without you on the Planet?

Walker

Other Hybrids who are better suited with politics will take over now but we had to take the best soldiers out of the problem so we can ensure that there will be no wars. With every soldier trying to go to space to explore and fight, there will be peace on Earth.

President

Are you sure you can handle even the mercenaries that will join up

Walker

Captain James whole unit is mercenaries and you see how they worked together

President

I hope you and your friend know what you are doing! He did just ensure I will be reelected so I guess he does know how to work the system

Walker

His family help create the system. With you doing another term, will allow us to set up the proper infrastructure to ensure those bastards lose and we finally free this planet of their control

President

Let's hope we weather the storms we have coming our way and we come out winners

Walker

Absolutely Mr. President

President

Call me Bill

Walker

Yes Bill

President

Good luck on your mission.

Walker

Thank you Bill

The screen turns off

(President looks at Ricky who looks scared)

President

What is it Ricky

Ricky

Are we doing the right thing Sir?

President

Calm your nerves, It will be ok just trust me. We wouldn't have got this far if I didn't know what I was doing, Right? Plus we need them to complete this mission. We have less than 100 years left on this planet if we don't get those resources

Ricky

Yes

President

Well then, is my speech ready?

Ricky

Yes Mr. President

President

Well then let's go an address the Country

(The president gets up and walks out of the office.)

INT Mother Ship General's Walker Quarters

James

You just made a shit load of enemies' very powerful
ones too

Walker

Good let them try to attack me while our people set up
the infrastructure. You see I'm leaving to fight this war
and trust me they have people on these ships that will
try to destroy us but what they don't know is that I have
our psych officers and our alien friends, Ishmarelic and
his team meeting every soldier on board every ship. We
will weed them out and kill them. We also have the
same team working on Earth to ensure the safety of our

candidates. Don't worry it took years to plan this out. We were waiting for the right moment to initiate it

James

I'm with you Commander. When do we depart?

Walker

I'm waiting for one more race that said they want to be a part of our war

James

Do you think we can trust all of these aliens. I mean the Orion's are cool but some of the rest of them I'm getting a bad vibe about them

Walker

I know, me too but hopefully the enemy of my enemy is my friend. But don't worry I sense it too. Some of them think they can take the Mother Ship from us

James

Maybe we should show them some of our powers

Walker

No we can't. that's exactly what the Overlords did, we must show them we are different. We have to show the universe that there's another way of doing things. We must move on from governing with manipulations and power. We have to be upfront with them. No

more will fear, war, greed, sickness, poverty, and all
other ways they use to control people. It all ends now

James

Well than let's show the universe how's it's done

(The two sit there and continue drinking and laughing.
Then there's a knock on the door)

James

Are you expecting anyone?

Walker

No but let's see who it is. Open

(The door to Walker's quarters disappears and in walks
General Gethros and Jackson. As soon as they enter the
door reappears)

Jackson

I can never get use to that

Gethros

Well it looks like you two are having fun in here

(Walker and James look at each other then look at
Gethros and Jackson with serious looks. Gethros and
Jackson look at each other not sure what to do next.
Then Walker starts to laugh, followed by James)

James

Come take a seat guys and pour yourself a drink and here's a cigar. This might be the last time we get a break

(Gethros and Jackson laugh)

Gethros

You son of a bitch. You guys looked at us like we did something

James

Got to have some fun sometimes right

Jackson

True

(The four men drink, smoke and laugh)

James

So General, how does it feel being in space

Gethros

Cramped, I was getting use to being on that big base but now...

James

You want to go back you can

Gethros

No way and let you guys have all the fun and glory. I'm not going to be the only one with wars stories of space to tell my kids and grandkids

James

Glory, be careful glory is a dangerous thing to go to war for

Gethros

Don't worry I want more than just glory

Jackson

Don't lie you know you want some of that glory. Who wouldn't want to be in the history books as a hero!

Walker

I'm tired of being called a hero. We're men and soldiers not heroes we just step up and answer the call of duty, that most men wouldn't. Now we've stepped up to complete a task that no man has ever done before. Let's pray we do it because if we don't, it will be history for all of us

Gethros

Well Commander, let's ensure those fucking bastards will never again torment us

(Gethros raises his glass in the air and the other men do too)

Toast to us winning the war and freeing the world and the universe

Jackson

I'll toast to that

(They touch glass and take a drink out of their glasses)

Now that we are on the subject of freeing the universe, what was that speech at the UN really about?

(James and Walker look at each other out of the corner of their eyes)

Walker

What do you mean?

Jackson

Come on General, don't act like you were only trying to recruit more soldiers it's deeper than that, I know it. You're declaring war on more than just High Command

(Walker sits back in his chair and leans it back onto it's back two legs)

Walker

I don't know what you are referring too, Lieutenant

Jackson

You think they are just going to allow you to take their power away?

Walker

I knew they had people inside of my army but I never thought it would have been you

Jackson

We all have to answer to someone. They just made me an offer that I couldn't refuse.

(Jackson not realizing that Walker and James are communicating to each other telepathically. Doesn't even notice that James took out his knife and has it under the table)

Walker

Yea but I answer to the people and the President of the United States. Do you even know who you answer too?

Gethros

Hold on calm down men what's going on here?

Walker

Should I tell him or will you

Gethros

Tell me what

Jackson

Go ahead tell him

Walker

You see General, your right hand man pledged his
allegiance not to the President and the American
people but to group of people who really control the
world and will stop at nothing to ensure they remain in
power. Some are bankers, big oil, healthcare, etc, etc.
The type of people that are so wealthy that they can
hide their wealth. But that's not the only thing that
they hide is it Jackson? Don't you see that anything
that will stop the world from using fossil fuel, there
always something that stops it from being mass
produced. Anytime the people call for a change in the
financial system something stops it, anytime a politician
is about to really make a difference something from
their past comes back to haunt them. It's them the
people who he answers too!

Jackson

Get to the point Walker

Walker

That's Commander Walker to you. You see that speech
I gave was a call to war not only against the aliens but
against them and your Lt. over here was sent to rely a
message to me

Gethros

Jackson what they hell is he talking about?

Jackson

Sorry Kyle but remember when I was captured on that mission. Well they were the ones who let me go but I owed them. Then my mother got sick, they got the best doctors in the world to help. After that I had no choice but to pledge my allegiance to them. It was that or let my mother die in pain. Everyone in this room would have done the same thing.

Gethros

Why didn't you come to me?

Jackson

And say what? I need your help? They know everything well almost everything. They don't seem to be able to find out what Walker and his team is doing but that doesn't matter anymore. Walker you know what I'm here to do

(Walker pushes his chair back and stands up. Jackson stands up too. Then Gethros stands up)

Walker

Death is the sentence for anyone involved in treason!

Gethros

(Jackson STAND DOWN hold up soldier)

Walker

He doesn't answer to you anymore, he never really did

Gethros

I thought you better than to kill an unarmed man

Jackson

If I don't kill him they will kill my whole family. So yes I
will

Gethros

No Jackson stop, I can help

(Jackson starts to reach into his back but James quickly
gets up and throws his knife right into the middle of
Jackson chest. Jackson drops to his knees and Gethros
runs over to him before he falls to the ground)

Gethros

Why Jackson Why

Johnson

(mumbling)

I'm sorry Kyle forgive me.

(Jackson whisper something into Kyle ear and dies)

James

We need to get rid of the body ASAP

Gethros

What do you mean get rid of the body? This is one of
my men we can't dump his body

James

Your man was a traitor. He worked for the other side,
so yes we can!

Walker

Stand down James. Sorry Kyle but we don't need any of
this heat right now. This was their plan from the start.
If he didn't kill me I would kill him which would bring
about a trial and stop the mission. They want me gone
now and they won't stop until that happens. We have
spies out here and we must get rid of them all

Gethros

Who do I trust?

Walker

I'm sorry Kyle but I can't answer that for you. I do know
we are in a war not only to free the universe but our
own Earth from a tyranny, that has corrupted the world
in order to remain in power. Look, they even corrupted
your own Lt. I can't tell you to trust me but I can tell
you, I trust you and I need your help Kyle. Are you with
me?

(Walker reaches out his hand to Kyle. Kyle pauses for a
second then shakes Walker hand)

Gethros

I want revenge on those Bastards

Walker

Don't worry. your revenge is already taking place but
behind the scenes. I just have to make sure the people
in my circle have my back

Gethros

OK

James

Well then now can we get rid of this body?

Gethros

He's gone anyways. That's just his body laying there

James

Great! Are you going to help?

Gethros

No I'm going to head back to my ship. I don't want any
part of this. He was still a close friend

(Gethros walks out of the room)

Walker

Can I trust him?

James

Yea for now but Jackson told him to be careful who to trust because he was getting his orders from someone high up in the military but since we activate outside of the military. They couldn't get a lot of Intel on our moves.

Walker

Hum. Alert the teams on Earth and all of our GFSB that we have moles in the military and to be careful

James

Should we worry?

Walker

No nothing yet to be worried about but we need to weed out all of the snakes. We might need to send some more psych down to Earth

James

We Can't we need the ones we have left up here

Walker

Fine. They should be ok. AI teleport this body to a location where it will never be found

James

Yeah send this traitorous bastard to Mars. Hold up let me get my knife

549

(James takes the knife out of Jackson chest)

James

Ok Now

Walker

You're a hard man General did I ever tell you that

(Jackson's body dematerializes)

Walker

Help me clean up this blood

(James walks over with a spray in his hand)

INT Destiny Command Center. General Gethros walks into the room

(Corporal Smith turns around to see Gethros walking in)

Smith

General on Deck

(Everyone turns around to salute Gethros)

Gethros

Stand down. What do we have?

Smith

Where's Lt. Jackson Sir

Gethros

He's been relieved of his duty and let's leave it at that.

So what do we have?

Smith

Relieved Sir

Gethros

Smith what do we have?

(The doors to the Command Center open up and in walks Major. Isis and Lt. Rich)

Gethros

Why did he send you two here?

(Isis and RIch walk over to Gethros and she whispers something into his ear. Gethros gets up quickly)

Gethros

No fucking way.

Isis

Yes Sir, trust me

Gethros

Fine but I want more proof than just your thoughts

Isis

Ok fine, then we all go

Gethros

Fine. Smith we're going with these two

Smith

Going. Where are we…

(Before Smith could finish the four disappear.)

INT Mother Ship detaining room.

Smith

(Smith slowly starts to wake up. He noticed that he is handcuffed to a table. In walks Gethros)

General what's going on is this some type of joke? Where am I?

Gethros

Don't play with me son. I've seen the proof

Smith

General Proof What PROOF, you're not making any sense

Gethros

Al

(A screen pops up to the left of Gethros showing Smith and Jackson talking about how they will stop Walker and do whatever they have to do to complete their missions. Gethros looks at Smith who has his head down now)

Gethros

Now what? Your cohorts paid for his betrayal already

Smith

(Smith Starts to laugh) He picks up his head and looks at Gethros)

You're a fucking idiot to think you can stop them. No one can. They've been running the world for centuries and now they will run the universe. And they will give me my own planet to run. So let me go!

(In walks Walker and James)

Gethros

You despise me.

Smith

Well what now General

Gethros

Your future is out of my hands. If it was up to me you would share the same fate as Jackson

(Gethros walks out of the room. The door closes leaving James, Walker, and Smith in the room)

INT Hallway outside of the Detaining room

Gethros

What now? It seems like my whole house is full of snakes

Isis

Don't worry he was the last one on your ship. And we now have the ability to monitor any transmission from any of the ships to anywhere

(Gethros looks at Isis)

Gethros

You just make sure you find them all and get names from him. I need some alcohol to burn off this horrible taste off my tongue. Make sure you BREAK HIM FIND THEM ALL

(Gethros walks away)

Isis

I feel sorry for him

Rich.

He'll be alright. He's a season soldier

Isis

No it's not like that I mean if you could hear the things going on in his head. He's barely holding on to it all. I should report him to Walker

Rich

Don't bother we all know what he's going through. Trust me, it hurts when the people closest to you betray you. I mean these are the people that are suppose to watch your back and make sure no one gets to you but it happens. More than you can expect. We all go through it, you're lucky you have the ability to know what people are thinking. Most of us learn from Trial and error. WE all had to pull knives from our backs but we're soldiers and we don't allow it to stop us from doing our duty.

Isis

Ok if you say so but I still think we should keep an eye on him

Rich

Let's worry about that traitor in there. Can you read his mind

Isis

He has some good training I may need some help. Let me get Innis

Rich

Ok

INT Detaining room

Smith

I hope you're not trying to read my mind. I received some of the best training in the world. To make sure if a situation like this ever happens you wouldn't be able to get anything. Even though I don't know anything

Walker

(Walker walks over to the intercom.)

Walker

Come in

(In walks Rich, Isis, and Innis)

Smith

Oh great more visitors

Walker

We'll leave it to you guys. Let us know when he's done.

(Walker and James start to walk to the door)

Smith

Hold up where are you going and what do you mean
when he's done. Who the fuck is this? I have rights you
know!

James

We're in space traitor. We're making shit up as we go
from now on. It's a new world order or should I say
universe order. You and your cohorts are done. We are
going to free the whole universe from Tyranny. Give
em hell

(Walker and James continue to leave the room and the
door rematerializes)

Rich

You're all ours now. Is it going to be the easy way or
hard way?

Smith

Fuck you

Rich

Hard then

INT Mother Ship Commissary

Brembo

This use to be our ship, Why don't we just take it back
from them?

Nicklous

And then what? Go back to High Command?

Brembo

Yes why not. It's not our fault the ship was taken and
then at least we took it back

Nicklous

Old one please talk to him

Ishmarelic

We made a pack with them. Once we make a pack we
don't turn back on it. The only way we can be free is if
we join up with them and fight together. They can have
the ship too many bad memories for me on this ship. If
we win, I want to be dropped off on a nice peaceful
planet away from it all and relax.

Brembo

Ok old one but as soon as we win I'm leaving them

Ishmarelic

Do as you wish after but as long as we are fighting High
Command, we are at peace with these Hybrids.

Nicklous

If you saw what I saw one of them did to Mack and the
other did to Samson. Trust me Brembo we don't want

to war with them. They have more secrets that we
have yet to see

Ishmarelic

They are a powerful race. Probably more powerful then
the Overlords. If he only knew, he would have never
came here

Brembo

What do you think High Command is going to do?

Ishmarelic

They are preparing a force like we've never seen before.
This fight is going to be brains over brawn but they
underestimate them

Brembo

Are they smart enough?

Nicklous

They beat us rather easily and they have Dr. Coaxe?

Ishmarelic

They have the ancestors with them too and trust me,
they're powerful ones. But they many need more help.
It's time for me to intervene

Nicklous

I thought we weren't allowed to do that anymore

Ishmarelic

No choice now. We have to do everything we can to help them win

Nicklous

Ok well then let's go find him

(Nicklous and Ishmarelic get up and leave the room)

Brembo

WE better win

INT Galactis Space Ship Command Center

Doner

Captain, We have a request from the Mother Ship

Raphael

What is it?

Doner

Commander Walker is call all captain and seconds to the Mother Ship for a meeting

Raphael

Well then Let's go meet our newly appointed Commander. Jax and Alex you two take care of the ship until we come back

Jax and Alex

Yes Sir

INT Mother Ship War Room

The room is full humans, hybrids, and aliens. The leaders of every ship in the fleet is there. Some of the aliens knew each other and they are catching up and some of the humans/hybrids also have small talk with each other.)

Alien 1(Warber)

Do you think they are the ones?

Alien 2(Slicio)

They did beat them twice and now posse their most powerful weapon, the Mother Ship

Warber

Well Do you think we can trust them

Slicio

For now yes but only time will tell. If we win this war their influence on the universe will increase and then we will be able to judge them. It's not what they do before they have the power it's what they do after they acquire it. Therefore, only time will tell if we can trust them not to become like High Command.

Warber

True

Slicio

But they we're able to unite so many of us within such a short period of time

Warber

We were all waiting for the call

Slicio

True but look how many of us answered the call. I mean you see ruthless enemies sitting side by side each other just for a chance to attack High Command. And from what I heard they defeated two of their strongest elites in a hand to hand fight easily. They defeated Samson and Mack

Warber

No, NO WAY not Samson and Mack no one in the universe could do that. Do you know how many of lost their existence when they would give us a chance to fight. It was always the same thing over and over again, if you want to be free you have to beat one of them. NO ONE Could

Slicio

I know but they did it

Warber

There's something more to these humans then what we see here then

Slicio

From what I heard they are some sort of hybrid of High Command. They come from the same creator

Warber

WHAT we can't trust them

Slicio

Shut up now your too loud

Warber

Who else knows this?

Slicio

All of us but no one is going to say anything. We were told by our leaders to fight alongside them. That's why we are all here. Trust me our leaders don't trust them all the way either, but we have no choice it's either them or High Command

Warber

I don't like it Commander

Slicio

You don't have to like it but you do have to live with it
for now

INT Hallway outside the War Room

(Walker and James are about to walk into the room)

Ishmarelic

Commander

(Walker stops walking and turns around)

Walker

Yes Ishmarelic, I'm glad you made it to this meeting.
We're going to need you in there

Ishmarelic

Fine but I need to talk to James.

James

I knew you were coming but first we need to address
everyone in there and then I will go wIth you

Ishmarelic

Ok then let's get to it

James

Good. Nicklous it's nice to see you

Walker

Let's get to it. Seems like you two have something to do

(Walker, James, Ishmarelic, and Nicklous walk into the room. As they enter the room quiets. But once Nicklous and Ishmarelic walk in an alien gets up)

Jonano

I am fine with you humans and everyone else in this room except them. They are my sworn enemy

(Jonano reaches for his weapon. His Commander grabs him and tells him to sit down)

Walker

HOLD ON THERE! Listen, I know someone of you in this room are enemies but due to this situation that we are under, you put past your differences in order to attack our true enemy. Well so did these two. Everyone in this room are allies from here on out. In order to defeat High Command we are going to need all the help we can get. All of us has lost comrades in previous battles, to High Command. So we all know how everyone feels seeing these two here but guess what, without them we wouldn't have defeated High Command, So I owe them. Therefore, if you have a problem with them then you have a problem with me and we can settle these problems like true warriors should. Now does anyone want to settle their problems?...

(Walker looks around the room at each alien. No one
does anything)

Walker

Great now can we get back to the real issue we are
here. We will launch in a Earth Week. I am not going to
lie to you and say that this is going to be an easy battle.
It's not this may be the hardest battle any of us ever
fought. Every time they attacked us we had a surprise
attack advantage. This time we may or may not have
that advantage. They do not know that we captured
their Mother Ship or at least not yet. I do know that we
have spies in our mist. We intercepted a comm. from
one of the ships here. It was a message to High
Command, informing them about our us possessing the
Mother ship and that we are coming their way

(Everyone in the room starts to look at each other,
trying to find out which ship.)

Expos

How do we know what you are telling us, is the truth?
You could be lying

Tank

I agree with Expos. We need proof that what you say is
true.

Walker

That's fine. AI bring up the comm. we intercepted

(A screen appears. Then you hear the comm which is interpreting into each Alien native tongue)

Message

They possess the mother ship, they are building a fleet to attack you master. I don't have enough men to stop them but if you give me the order I will self destruct my ship and that should cause enough damage to stop them

Mak

You lie human. Die I did not send this message

(Mak gets up and pulls his knife out and throws it at Walker with a violent force. Right before it hits Walker, James walks in between it and catches it. In one swift movement he throws it right back at Mak, who has no time to react. The knife almost goes right through Mak chest. His body falls back into the seat but it can't fully lie back because the tip of the knife is caught on the chair. Everyone is quite. They never seen a warrior do what James just did)

Slicio

(Whispers to Warber)

I told you, those two are very strong too strong

Warber

mmmh

Walker

Ok now we know exactly who sent that message. If we don't stick together here we'll lose. We have a good chance of defeating high Command but if we have to fight one of our allies and High Command, our chances are bleak. Listen up, this is our chance to avenge every single warrior lost to High Command. We have a good chance to sneak into their galaxy without being detected, if we stick together

Adenitis

How do you expect to get to their planet without being detected

Walker

Unfortunately, until we know that there are no more spies within our ranks. I cannot give you that Intel.

Adenitis

How do you expect us to trust you if you won't tell us with your plans? You might want to sacrifice us in order to win

Walker

The only people I am willing to sacrifice is myself and my men. I will allow you guys to make that decision for yourself. I will say that we have a way of interrupting their AI system. Does anyone else have any questions?

Warber

Which one of you defeated Mack?

James

(James steps up)

If you mean, the big one. Then that was me why do you
ask

Warber

(As he shakes his head)

I just wanted to know who it was

(The whole room starts to whisper it's him. Ishmarelic
looks at James and smiles. Then Adenitis stands up)

Adenitis

I think I speak for everyone in this room when I say we
are ready to go to war with you. We will also look for
spies

Walker

Good meeting over. I will send more Intel to your ships
as we get it in

(Everyone gets up and starts to walk out of the room.
Some of them try not to look at James but some still do
out of the corner of their eye. The ones that do make
eye contact James gives them an head nod.)

James

What is all those looks for?

Walker

Not sure

Ishmarelic

I'll tell you. It's what your species call a prophecy.

James

Prophecy

Nicklous

Yeah there's a prophecy. That said one day warriors
would come from a far off worlds and would free the
universe of High Command. It would be warriors that
fights so smoothly and quickly that no weapon can ever
touch him unless they wanted it too. They would be
able to see an attack coming before the attacker knew
what he was going to do. They would even face the
hardest fighters of High Command and beat him at
ease. Everyone heard about how you beat Mack and
then they saw you grab the knife out of the air and
throw it back with greater force.

James

I'm just a soldier

Ishmarelic

You're more than just that and it's time for me to reveal your true identity and unlock all your abilities

James

Unlock what? You're going to turn me into a dangerous being or something?

Ishmarelic

That Doc of yours unlocked only part of your genetic power. If you come with me I will show you your full potential

(James looks at Walker and Walker gives him a head nod)

Ishmarelic

I also need your sister and the one you call your cousin.

Walker

AI bring Isis and Rick here

AI

Yes Commander

INT Mother Ship Isis Quarters

Isis

What are we going to do now?

Rich

I don't know this kinda happen a bit quick didn't it? We can't tell James at least now yet.

Isis

We can hide a thing from him or at least you can't

Al

Isis Commander Walker and General James wants you now

Rich

Oh shit they know already. Fuck

Isis

Calm down they don't know

Rich

Well you go and meet them. I'm going to stay here. I can't look at him without him knowing. At least he can't do it to you

Isis

Fine but this conversation isn't over and you know that Right?

Rich

Of course it's not. Just find me when you're done with them

Isis

Ok. Ai teleport me to them

INT Mother Ship Awakening Chambers

Dr. Coaxe

I can't seem to figured it out Innis. Have you found
anything?

Innis

No but we're about to have some guess

Dr. Coaxe

Who

(The doors to the Lab open up and in walks Ishmarelic,
Nicklous, James, Walker, and Rick)

Walker

What are you doing here Doc?

James

He's trying to figure out the same thing that Ishmarelic
is about to do. These two were trying to figure it out
since we took the ship

Walker

Why didn't you tell me Doc?

Dr. Coaxe

I wanted to make sure it was true first.

James

He was I can sense it

Dr. Coaxe

Your getting more powerful by the day

(Isis appears in the room)

Isis

What am I doing here?

James

Seems like there's more to the story then we knew

Rick

Why am I here?

James

We're family remember cousin. Where's Rich I figured
he would be here with you. You two seem inseparable.

Isis

He's taking care of something

James

I bet

Walker

Ok Ishmarelic go on with it

Ishmarelic

I need the three of you to lie down in the chamber. So I can finish the process that Coaxe started

Isis

What do you mean Finish?

Dr. Coaxe

It seems that I only partially unlocked your genes.

Ishmarelic

It was a failsafe that High Command put in just in case, just in case anyone was ever able to unlock the memory wipe. The only way to fully unlock it was inside the Mother Ship or on the Home Planet and there's no one except you guys who ever able to board the ship alive. Now I'm going to complete the process so please lay down we are running out of time.

(Ishmarelic looks at Isis stomach briefly and then at Isis)

It will be okay Everything will be fine.

(Isis knows that Ishmarelic knows what's going on with her and just nods her head and walks into a chamber and lays down. James and Rick also walks into the chamber and lay down.)

Ishmarelic

Now relax

(He walks over to a screen and presses one button. All the lights in the room turn on and the chamber lights up. He presses another button and the lights inside of the chamber turns to reveal beds. The Ai starts to talk)

AI

Awakening process is initialized. Do you want to continue or Abort?

Ishmarelic

Continue

Ai

Do you have permission to begin this process

Ishmarelic

Yes

Ai

Scanning database to determine

(A beam of light shoots out and starts to scan Ishmarelic. Everyone else steps back in fear of what the beam was.)

AI

Permission granted. Welcome back SIR. I will begin the process. You found them Sir

Ishmarelic

Yes I have.

AI

Are you ready to changed back?

Ishmarelic

Yes

AI

Please step into the Chamber Sir

(Ishmarelic looks at Nicklous and gives him a head nod and proceeds to enter the Chamber, James, Rick, and isis follow. The door closes and locks)

Walker

Wait what's going on?

Nicklous

The truth is that Ishmarelic isn't really Ishmarelic. He's the Third Overlord.

Dr. Coaxe

Now I understand, that's why

Walker

Ok what do you mean the Third?

Dr. Coaxe

There was always a rumor of a Coup d'état by Overlord Prime's against his brothers because they went against Overlord Prime plan of universal destruction and tried to change his mind. But we all thought it was just a rumor

Nicklous

No rumor. They were betrayed by Overlord Prime. Overlord Prime was afraid of his brothers, their powers were growing and Prime new that they would one day be stronger than him. It was The Third, who started the whole process of enhancing aliens to help them progress. It was Prime who took the Third's Enhancing process and corrupted it to make slaves. This upset The Third and when he tried to stop Prime, Prime shot him with a regress ray and throw him on a desolate planet. It just happen that The Third saw what was going to happen to him so he made a backup plan. He already enhanced my forefather and gave him the means to locate him. As soon as he could, he went to find him. The Third gave him the pill that could reverse the regress ray but only partially. He had to wait until Prime place the awakening chamber onto the Mother Ship to be fully restored. My forefather was able to sneak back onto the Mother Ship with the Third, during the war with the Orion's. They waited until the Mother Ship fired the regress ray and leave the Orion's sector to get off the Mother Ship. Then they entered the Orion's planet and started the process of awakening them. While there they ran into two of the Captain's

(as he points to the awakening chamber)

elite warriors. A woman and man, they were very strong and intelligence. They later had children and I am one of the later generations of their children. You see Dr. Coaxe, it was the two you sent to ask the Orion's for help.

Dr. Coaxe

I knew they made it. I'm happy they survived and lived a happy life. They were a cute couple. Tarbin and that Sergeant

Nicklous

The Third knew that one day, either High Command would Attack the Orion's or the humans. So he left people on Orion to prepare for the upcoming war and then he sneaked back onto the new Mother Ship and assumed the identity of Ishmarelic and with his powers no one ever asked him who he was or how he got here. He remained on the Ship until now, waiting for this day.

(Walker remains quite and just takes a seat.)

Dr. Coaxe

How powerful is The Third?

Nicklous

He really hasn't used his powers so now he's more powerful than Prime

Dr. Coaxe

Wow

Walker

So now what?

Nicklous

WE Wait

AI

Awakening Process will take Five Earth Hours to complete

INT Mother Ship Command Center

(Rich walks into the door)

TY

Do you know where's The Commander is, lieutenant?

Rich

No, He's in a meeting. Why

Ty

I have General Gethros wanting to talk to him. The White House has called three times within the last hour and I have Alpha wanting to talk to him about some Operation Clean House

Rich

Well, let's triage it. Find out what the White House wants, then Alpha, and then The General

Ty

They won't tell me they said it's classified

Rich

Well then they must wait. Bring Alpha up

Ty

Ok

INT Mother Ship Awakening Room

Walker

(Walker gets up.)

Ok I have other things to attend too Nicklous, Dr. Coaxe keep me abreast of the situation

(Walker leaves the room. As soon as he does his comm. device turns on)

Ty

Walker We have an issues up here

Walker

What is it Ty?

Ty

I have the White House, General Gethros, and Alpha
wanting you.

Walker

I'm heading to my chambers as soon as I get there patch
me through to the White House.

Ty

OK

INT Destiny Gethros Quarters

(Gethros is talking to someone on the video comm.)

Gethros

What do you mean, he's The Third

Walker

Seems like we didn't know the whole story

Gethros

So your saying that we have one of the Overlords on our ship?

Walker

Yes but Kyle this is a need to know Intel. I didn't even tell the President about this one

Gethros

Shit I wish I didn't know about it. What Intel did you get from the traitor?

Walker

I'll send you the video link

Gethros

Should I even ask if he is still alive

Walker

Just watch the video. Walker out

(A link shows up on the Screen. Gethros presses the on it A video pops up)

INT Detaining Room of The Mother Ship

(Innis and Isis both have their hands on Smith Head. He's yelling very loud. He's face has turn red and there seems to be blood coming out of his eyes.)

Smith

Please Stop Please Stop I'll tell you please I'll tell you everything

Rich

Now you know if you are lying we will know and we'll just continue with the memory extract

Smith

(trying to catch his breath)

I won't tell any lies just stops the pain, it hurts, it hurts too much. It feels like you are drilling into my brain

Rich

That's a fair assessment. Well talk

Smith

Ok, ok I got my orders from this comm. device that Lt. Jackson gave me a few years ago. He said that if I didn't comply they would kill my family

Rich

Why does everyone always start with that

Smith

Fuck you man! I have a five year old daughter. They showed me pictures, they were watching me and my family. They even showed pictures of my mother at the supermarket and had me call her to verify that she was at the market. When someone shows you how powerful they are and they can get to anyone anywhere you tend to listen.

Rich

Where's the comm. device

Smith

No I can't

(Isis and Innis starts to walk closer to Smith)

Smith

Hold up just hold up please Protect my family please can you do that for me

Rich

If your Intel is good, then your family will be protected

Smith

Ok here is the device

(Smith reaches into his mouth and pulls out a fake tooth. It's computer)

Rich

(Rich takes the tooth from Smith)

AI can you scan this and tell me about it

(The AI appears)

Smith

What the Fuck?

(AI puts out it's hand and lays it on top of Rich's hand)

AI

Scanning... I can trace it back to a location on Earth

Rich

Get the Commander

AI

Commander connected

Walker

What is it?

Rich

We have a location.

Walker

Send it to me now

Rich

Yes Sir

INT Mother Ship Command Center

Walker

Get Alpha Now

Ty

Yes Sir. Alpha this is the Mother Ship

Major. Daniel

Good to see you guys. What can we do for you?

Walker

Is the team ready?

Major. Daniel

Somewhat

Walker

Good enough, I want you to send them to this location. Heavy weapons and full armor. Capture if you can but not, don't worry about it. The psych officers will be able to extract from the dead, as long as their heads are still intact. But do it now

Major. Daniel

Yes Sir. I'll report back after we finish the op, Daniels out

Walker

I got you this time

Ty

What's going on Sir?

Walker

I'll tell you later Ty just trust me

Ty

I do Commander

(Gethros continues to watch the video. He sees the
tactical team gearing up at Alpha base in their armor
suits and laser guns. This is the new Global Federation
Space Unit. A unit consisting of aliens and hybrids. No
one knows who they are. They gear up with two psych
officer. You see LT. Daniels give them orders that they
don't have to take any prisoners. Just remember no
head shots we might need to extract Intel from the
bodies. The team Captain says ok to Daniels and they
teleport to the location. They engaged the enemy.
They take out almost everyone except two nonmilitary
men. The two men they find are part of the leadership
of the organization trying to kill Walker and keep their
control of the Earth. The leader of the Elite team walks
up to them)

Oliver

You won't get away with this at all. I'll be out in less than a minute. We run this world. Who do you think you are

Leader

(The Leader of the Unit, grabs his gun and looks over to one of the Psych Officers)

Did you extract?

Psych

Yes I got all the Intel that I am going to get from him.

Oliver

Hey what are you going to do? You can't just shoot me I have rights

Leader

I thought you got to memo! Your rule is over now and so are your rights. It's the new world over. We're democratic with the law but more republican with the justice

(He shoots Oliver in the head and in the chest.)

David

You won't get away with this soldier boy

Leader

(Shots him in the head and chest twice)

I already did

(grabs his radio)

Ok men we're done. Mission Accomplished. All Hostiles neutralized. Ready for extraction.

(The team disappears. The videos cuts off)

Gethros

My god. What are we becoming? If this is the new world order, I hope we don't allow our new power to corrupt us.

(He sits back into his chair and takes a drink while shaking his head in shock)

INT Alpha Base Commissary

Sarch

You have to go they need you

Blackburn

I just can't go and leave you two here. I told you that I would retire and now, it's time to retire

Sarch

Hell no, If you don't go on this trip you will be miserable the rest of your life

Blackburn

I'm not going to leave my wife and daughter. It's worth it. I've given up that life for my new lifestyle with my wife and kid. So No, I won't regret it

Sarch

You know that of all people, you cannot lie to me. I know you all too well. Plus you won't have too. we'll come with you. This place is no longer home for us. It will be ok, we'll be fine as long as we are together it doesn't matter where we are. So we're going and that's that Mr.

(Blackburn doesn't say anything just looks at her)

(In walks Jay and Brace)

Jay

Sergeant, how are doing Sir?

(Blackburn gives him a head nod. Jay gives Sarch a hug and sits across from Brace)

Jay

So since I'm leaving in a day can I see my niece?

Brace

Yeah she almost beat me in chess but she did beat me in street fighter

Sarch

Yea she's getting better isn't at those things, right?

Brace

Yeah I don't know what you two do but it's working

Sarch

Thank you Brace

Jay

You didn't answer my question. Where's my niece, I
want to see her before I depart

Sarch

She's in school but it looks like we are going on the
mission with you two. So you will have plenty of time to
play chess and street fighter together

Brace

No way really that's great news! I needed a chess
partner even if she's only four

Jay

Are you sure you want to do that guys? I thought you
were going to retire Sir

(Blackburn still shocked from the news of Sarch wanting
to go to space just seats there quite)

Brace

Sergeant are you ok?

Jay

Hey Brace let's go check out Major Jessie

Brace

But?

(Then Brace takes a closer look at Blackburn)

Yea let's go check the old Major before we leave. Ok guys talk to you later

(Jay and Brace gets up and walk away)

Sarch

What's the matter?

Blackburn

Are you sure your okay with this? And DON'T lie to me

Sarch

Yes, now go let General Walker know that you are going

Blackburn

(Blackburn looks at Sarch again... then gets up and kisses her on the top of her forehead)

Ok honey but it's not too late to change your mind

Sarch

I knew I was marrying a military man. This is the life I've chosen

Blackburn

But what about Ester? Is this the right thing for her? I mean being out in space with us and the danger

Sarch

It will be ok. I mean there'e danger here. I refuse to live a life of fear and I know as long as I am with you I will be safe. Now go

(Blackburn walks away. Sarch sits there and a tear goes down her check. In walks Mitch)

Mitch

What's wrong?

Sarch

(Sarch wipes the tear from her face)

Nothing. I'm going to go on the mission

Mitch

What?... You're going to leave Ester here?

Sarch

No I just can't let him retire. He will be miserable

Mitch

(Mitch starts to get up)

No, is he forcing you to? I'm going to have a word with him right now. It's too dangerous to go on this one

Sarch

Sit Down, right now

Mitch

No he can't think he can just force you to go into space and fight in a war

Sarch

He's not. I just know him. He won't tell me that he wants to go but I can see it in his eyes

Mitch

So what he has a daughter and a wife. Those days are done now. I hope I don't see him

Sarch

YOU WILL NOT say anything to him. Promise me Mitch, Promise me right now

Mitch

Does it really matter. You've made up your mind. I know you once you do that you won't change.

(Sarch starts to smile)

Mitch

Fine then, I'm coming with you.

Sarch

What... no

Mitch

Yes. I can't let you go to space and leave me here. I'll worry about you too much. It's not like I have kids or dating anyone and you're going to need me up there

Sarch

Thank you

Mitch

Well let's go and pack. We have to make sure you don't forget anything

(Sarch and Mitch leaves the commissary)

INT Alpha Base Major Daniels Quarters

(Knock Knock Knock)

(Major Daniels watching another covert op by his special unit turns off the screen)

Daniels

Come in

(Blackburn walks in)

Daniels

What can I do for you Lieutenant?

Blackburn

I want to go on the mission Sir

Daniel

I thought you wanted to stay here because of your family. Isn't it time to give it up? You've done enough

Blackburn

I thought about it Sir but I want to go and I'm going to take them with me

Daniels

Are you sure you want to do that? It's not that safe up there Black

Blackburn

I know Sir but my unit needs me and I need them. I just can't abandon them now

Daniel

Take a look at this

(Daniels turns the screen back on and they watch the unit take out another member of the covert organization running the world.)

Blackburn

Is that the unit I trained?

Daniels

Yes

Blackburn

What are they doing?

Daniels

They're cleaning house, getting rid of the cancer
plaguing the world for far too long

Blackburn

On who's orders

Daniels

Ours, You see I need you here to train more warriors.
Only we can set this planet free. While Walker and
James go out to set the universe free. We're going to
set the Earth free with our special soldiers

Blackburn

Thank you Sir but no. I'm no teacher, I'm a soldier a
warrior. Plus my unit needs me more up there

Daniels

I thought you were going to say that. Well then...

(Daniel's gets up and walks towards Blackburn and puts his hand out. Blackburn shakes his hand the two hug.)

Good luck up there Dustin and take care of that beautiful wife and daughter you have, ok

Blackburn

Thank you Jacob

(Blackburn walks out of the room. Daniels gets back on the screen)

Daniels

Anything to report

Leader

Yes Sir we found two more locations that Beta and Gamma units are engaging as we speak. As soon as I have something to report, I will contact you

Daniels

Good keep me posted. Daniels out.

(Daniels turns off the screen and sits back in his chair)

The chess pieces are moving but to what end. Every time I think it's over, we find the rabbit hole gets deeper.

INT Alpha Base Command Center

Major Jessie

So eight hours until they leave

Lauren

What do you think are chances are Sir

Jessie

I don't know Lauren. Let's pray its good

(Doors to the Command Center open and in walks Jay and Brace)

Jay

Hey Major, how's it going?

Jessie

Shouldn't you two be packing or something

Brace

Already done Sir We just came here to say goodbye

Jessie

I have to admit the first time I met you two I wanted to kill you. Now I can honestly say, I'm going to miss you two.

Jay

Yea we're going to miss you too Sir

Jessie

Just make sure you two make it back safely

Brace

Oh we will Sir

Jay

Yea don't worry about us. It's those aliens that are
going to be in trouble

Jessie

I believe you. Now go and pack up, you guys leave in an
hour

INT Flight Deck

(Jay and Brace walk up to Blackburn, Sarch, and Ester.
Ester runs up to Jay and Brace and hugs them. Major
Daniels walks up to the group)

Daniels

I will miss you guys. Make sure you make it back safely

Sarch

We will.

Daniels

Take care of these two you two

Sarch

(With a smile on her face)

They are in good hands.

(Jessie walks up to the group behind Daniels.)

Jessie

You ready

Daniels

Yes.

(Daniels turns to the whole group.)

Some of you I've known for years, some for a few months, and some I just met but I consider you all my family now. I will miss you all but understand this mission that you are about to embark is essential to our existence and the existence of every being in this universe. We all pledge to protect our right to be freedom and this mission is exactly that. You are going far beyond any known human has gone before. This mission sets a precedent for our future, so go out there and give them hell out there and know this we will do the same here. While you protect the right to freedom in space we will remain here and protect that right here. It is not a privilege to be free it's a right. There are too many people in the universe trying to take that away from us all and now we stand up and say no more. No more will you take away my freedom. No more will you put up barriers to keep us blind, deaf, dumb, and lost. No more will the few only have access to really be free. It ends now. Now that we are truly united, we will take down all those barrier that they put up and we will make sure they will never be able to put them back up again. So GO OUT THERE AND FIGHT and NEVER FORGET THE PURPOSE OF OUR MISSION FREEDOM!

(As Daniels speaks , imagine images of the Global Federation Space Unit taking out an enemy base, you see Walker prepping the Mother ship to leave. You see Johnson, Jess, Denise, and Adour all laughing and eating together. Scar and the rest of James team in a training room practicing. Dr. Coaxe, James, Ishmarelic, Nicklous, INNIS, Isis, Rick, and Rich in the lab. Then you come back to Daniels)

Daniels

Now go with the intention of freeing the universe.

Everyone

YES SIR

(The soldiers salute Daniels and he salutes them back. Everyone loads up into the ship and the ship takes off. Jessie walks up to Daniels)

Jessie

We have an issue

Daniels

What is it

Jessie

Come with me let me show you something our men just found. It's important

(Daniels and Jessie walk away swiftly)

INT Mother Ship Command Center

Walker

Ty, is the fleet ready

Ty

Yes Sir

(Doors to the command center opens up and in walks Blackburn and James)

James

Look who I got here

(Walker turns to see Blackburn)

Walker

I heard you changed your mind soldier. I hope you
made the right decision. Now take a seat we are about
to leave. Ty Notify all ships that we are about to depart.
Are our soldiers inside the cryo-chambers

Ty

Yes sir all regular soldiers are in the chambers. Only
ones left are the hybrids.

Walker

Ok notify the fleet that we are to depart now

Ty

(Ty starts to type of the screen. He gets on the comm.)

You now have permission commence Fold departure.

(The Mother Ship disappears into warp speed with it's
shadowing streaking behind it. Then the rest of the
fleet follow behind it.)

Blackburn

So how long is this trip going to be exactly

Piro

About 3 years Sir

Blackburn

So how long do we have to be asleep for

Piro

About 6 months total but for the regulars the entire trip

Walker

Already regretting your decision

Blackburn

(Blackburn looking out of the screen as they warp
through the space pauses and then turns around)

No I'm cool. What else was I going to do stay on Earth.
Plus you guys need someone to watch your back

Walker

Well you could have stayed and took care of your family

Blackburn

Their safer here on this ship and you know it

James

Well let's not dwell on past decisions. We're all here to
finish something that our ancestors started and I know
I'm safe with you watching my back

Walker

I agree General

Blackburn

There's no quicker way, I mean shit

(In walks Scar, Philip, Alistar, Wendel, Melissa, Andrea, Darlene, Mura, Jay, Brace, Rody, George, Tyler, and Jason, they walk towards General James. Scar walks up to James first)

Scar

We're all here General. What do you need?

James

Men some of you know the man sitting next to me, some of you don't. this man was one of the reason why we took control of the Mother Ship and he is now your new trainer. Blackburn

Blackburn

(Blackburn gets up and looks at the men. He pauses....
Then starts to talk)

Follow me

(Blackburn walks through the men and heads out of the command Center. The soldiers look at James. He nods his head. Then they turn around and follow behind Blackburn out of the command center.)

Walker

Blackburn might end up killing some of them. You know, the reports I got from the shit he did on Alpha with that unit. He acted like he was training assassins

James

He was. I've seen some of the ops videos. What he did to them. Those men can't stay of Earth once the op is finished.

Walker

What would you have me do with them

James

It was your orders why Blackburn trained them like that. He broke all the humanity out of them and made them expert killers. I can't even call them soldiers. There is no way for them to ever get back there humanity.

Walker

You protest what I did?

James

No I understand why you did what you did. Especially after they tried to kill your family but you created a hit squad. They don't know anything but to kill. They cannot stay on Earth. We can never release them from service

Walker

Well we're ending war on Earth. So what should we kill them?

James

Wow you would really suggest that

Walker

What the fuck then? They tried to kill my mother and destroy everything we pledge to protect. You don't seem to understand the position I'm in.

James

Let's go for a walk

Walker

Fine

(James and Walker get up and walk out of the Command Center.)

INT Hallway outside of the Command Center

(Walker and James continue walking down the hallway)

Walker

What do you want from me?

James

Remember we promised never to behave like them no matter how much they push us Jim

Walker

yes

James

I understand the purpose of that unit but you must understand that they cannot stay on Earth after they completed their mission

Walker

Why

James

They don't know how to stop. I see you took the same programming as our enemies with that unit but it stops there. You remember the hell we had trying to stop their fighters? Even after we defeated their Commander they still kept fighting. They we're uncontrollable and you created the same monster with them.

Walker

Your right. I didn't think about that

James

You allowed your anger to cloud your thinking and created a monster. The good thing is that I have a plan for them

Walker

What?

James

I'm going to take them with me if we survive this. I order Daniels and Jessie to send them to me once the operation is done

Walker

They never told me...

(James just looks at him)

Walker

I understand I went too far. Forgive me friend. I owe you that but there still might be a chance for them to change it might take some time but it's possible

James

True but I have a use for them. I will give them a chance to deprogram but I'm going to still need them to remain a little battle ready. For the future just keep it together, we cannot allow anger and frustration to cloud our decisions

Walker

I will but where are you going to take the men?

James

Even if we defeat the Overlords, we still have all the other planets to free and we are going to need a police force for the universe

Walker

So because of me your never going back home

James

I have no home anymore. I don't fit in there. I've seen too much and done too many evil acts. This is my way to repent

Walker

It was for a just cause. I'm sure God forgave us awhile ago

James

That doesn't make me feel better at all. We're creating a utopia on Earth. Monsters like us with all this blood on our hands doesn't belong there. I had to leave. Even Blackburn knows that, think about it Jim, we're not soldiers we're killers. It's all we know. To ensure some peace on earth, killers like Blackburn, Scar, you and me can never go back.

Walker

You know....I never told my son or daughter bye. They asked me if I was leaving to save the universe and I told them yes. I'm afraid they might follow in my footsteps

James

You already know the answer to that. Just look at Isis and me

Walker

(Walker keeps walking but he shakes his head right after James said he's comment)

I need a drink

James

Let's get one we have a long trip ahead of us

Walker

How are we looking at the refueling base

James

Working on it with the Doc

(The two men keep walking and they walk into Ishmarelic and Jasper.)

Ishmarelic

Just who I wanted to see

James

What is it

Ishmarelic

Is there a place we can talk just the four of us

Walker

My quarters

(The group continues to walk towards Walker's Quarters)

INT Cetros Major Adour Quarters

Adour

Where's Cristos, Denise?

Denise

He's with Jess and Johnson

(Knock knock)

Adour

Open

(The door opens and in walks Johnson and Jess, who's holding Cristos in her arms and she is four months pregnant)

Cristos

Daddy guess what guess what Daddy?

Adour

I don't know what son?

Cristos

Uncle Johnson and Auntie Jess taught me how to calculate the distance between Earth and the alien's world. They also taught me how to use the navigation system

(Denise walks out of the bathroom with a smile)

Denise

I'm so proud of you son

(Adour looks at Johnson with a strange look)

Johnson

What?

Adour

What else did Uncle Johnson teach you?

Cristos

(with a smile on his face)

Nothing

Adour

You not lying to Daddy are you?

Denise

Leave it alone

Adour

But

Denise

Christian

Adour

Fine. You make sure of what your teaching my son.
Matter of fact where is your little guy

Jess

Busy working on something with the AI

Cristos

Oh yeah Dad can I go back and work with Ray?

Adour

It's up to your mother

Cristos

Mom

Denise

Go

(Cristos runs out of the room.)

Adour

And one's not enough for you two

Johnson

No. We need to talk though

Adour

Ok let's go for a walk

(Adour and Johnson walk out of the room leaving the two ladies)

Denise

Everything ok

Jess

He received some strange news that something weird is going on, on Earth.

Denise

What?

Jess

(shaking her head)

I don't know. He said he couldn't tell me yet

Denise

I hope it's not bad news

(Jess shrugs her shoulders)

INT Mother Ship Training Room

Blackburn

What, y'all tired already?

Brace

Already, we've been at it for hours. We need a break

Blackburn

(Blackburn walks up to Brace who's bent over holding onto his knees breathing heavy)

What we faced on this ship is going to be nothing compared to what we are going to face on that planet. Once we get there understand that everything on that planet will try to kill you. From the animals

Jay

What animals? I thought there was no animals matter of fact nothing living on the surface

Blackburn

That's right the surface but we're not going to be on the surface. We're going underground, the caves leading to their main base

Brace

What I never heard that

Blackburn

Our orders changed. While the other aliens fight them in space we're going to teleport inside their base

Melissa

What about me Black? I'm no hand to hand soldier, I'm a pilot.

Blackburn

Our pilots will lead their squadrons' in space but if we
need you. You will have to come down to the planet.
That's why all of you are here. I have to make sure you
know what to do. All of you! We're not the only ones
teleporting down to the planet. Each ship is sending in
their own teams. I don't want any confusion with us.

Frank

Do we have Intel on a location?

(The doors to the training room opens and in walks Isis,
Innis, Rich, Larry, Piro, Arnold, Dreke, Tone, Nicklous,
Innis, Jasper, and Dr. Coaxe)

Isis

That's where Innis, Jasper, and I come in. We will guide
you to the proper location

Brace

Hey Nick, isn't this your home planet can't you tell us
where to go

Nicklous

I've never been to the planet

Melissa

That's interesting. Do you know anything about the
planet?

619

Nicklous

No, only the Overlords Elite guards and High Ranking soldiers, ever knew where the home planet was, we weren't allowed on it

Frank

You weren't allowed on your home planet. Why?

Nicklous

They didn't trust us. They knew that if we knew where the planet was then we might band together and overthrown them or leak the location

Arnold

Well they were fucking right. We do know where it is and we are going to kill them all

Blackburn

Ok fine. Let's get back to the game plan. Break it down for me team one more time

Jay

We will arrive within a year

Brace

Once we arrive. All ships will launch their fighters

Frank

While the aliens engaged our fighters, the ground teams will teleport to the locations provided by our AI

Jay

With the help of Isis ,Jasper, and Innis, we will conduct a search and destroy operations, while trying to find the AI room

Piro

Yeah while the psych search, we destroy

Brace

You know what I just noticed.

(Everyone looks at Brace)

We've practiced, practiced, and more practiced our way in and what we're going to do when we get in but we've never even discussed how we are going to get out

(The whole group looks at each other)

Melissa

You know what

Arnold

Your right

Frank

How about that

(Brace turns to Blackburn)

Brace

Why is that black? You guys not expecting us to return?

Blackburn

I was ordered to train you guys on the way in not the way out. And after that incident during refuel. We lost the whole Suda ship. It's my duty to make sure nothing like that happens ever again

Piro

That wasn't our fault we had no Intel on that location

Tone

I'm just happy some of us got out of there safely, shit

Tone

Yeah we almost blow up the planet

Isis

We won't know the way out until we get in

Piro

She's right but I still don't feel too good about this

Rich

What am I hearing here? When have we ever been
afraid to die

Frank

Fuck that. I never signed up to die out here

Blackburn

If you want out we can leave your ass right here in
space. Jettisoned you right out of this muthafucking
ship. How about that?

Frank

Hold up Boss no need for that. All I'm saying is that I'm
going to make it I don't know about y'all mother fuckers
but I'm going home after this shit. I only signed up for
ten years

Melissa

You think they're going to let us leave the military after
this shit

Frank

Fuck are you talking about

Rich

(Rich steps up)

Ok let's move on. If we don't mess up then, this won't be a suicide mission. Now I want all fighter pilots with me. Blackburn, always good seeing you my friend. Tell Sarch I said Hi

Blackburn

I will

(Rich, Arnold, Piro, Nicklous, Melissa, Philip, Frank, and Jason start to follow Rich. Rich turns around.)

Rich

So Dreke, do I have to give you a special invite

Dreke

Wasn't sure which team I was on. Last time I was stuck on the ship

Rich

I mean if you want to stay on the ship please don't make me force you to do something different

Dreke

No Way Not this Time I want in

Rich

Well move it soldier

(Dreke leaves out the door after the group)

Blackburn

Ok let's run through it again, then we can break.

Jay

The General taught you well I see

INT Walker's Quarters

Ishmarelic

What is this drink?

James

(with a grin)

It's called Blue Label. Maybe you should try a coke with it on the side

Ishmarelic

Coke

James

Another type of our drink. It's called Coke Cola. It helps with the whiskey

Walker

Ok let's get to it. What's going on? What did you want to talk about

Jasper

The Third wants to go down to the planet with your
men

(Walker looks at James and then at Jasper and
Ishmarelic)

Walker

Is that safe?

Jasper

You're going to need his help finding the proper
locations

Walker

We have Isis, Innis, and you

Ishmarelic

They are not powerful enough to counter Prime

Walker

(Walker looks at James)

Anything to say

James

He's right. My sister is powerful and so am I but we're
going to need help to get through the maze of caves
within that planet to get to where we need to be

Walker

(Walker sits back and places his hand on his right check and just sits there)

Fine, but you have to stay with James and his team. No leaving them, understand

Ishmarelic

Sure but can you pour me more of this whiskey liquid

Walker

(Laughs)

…. Sure

(Walkers grabs the bottle of whiskey and fills everyone glasses back up)

James

Let's drink now cause tomorrow we awaken the other soldiers.

INT Cetros Ship Commissary

Adour

What is it Johnson?

Johnson

I think we're being doped

Adour

What do you mean?

Johnson

A friend of mine on the inside told me right before we left that four world banking companies just closed and their executives are missing. Four of the top oil companies executives are missing and new management has taken over, certain political leaders around the world also seem to have died unexpectedly, and that's just the beginning. Top Executives from gun companies, pharmaceutical companies, and other companies are all ending up dead

Adour

Ok so

Johnson

Looks like Alpha is running secret ops with the orders from the White house and no one is saying anything

Adour

Is this one of your conspiracy theories again

Johnson

Hmm man eight of the biggest news corporation seem to just change leaderships and no one can find the old executives either. Man they're vast changes happening all over the world. Even in Africa, it seems that there are no more warlords and the diamond trade is all cleaned up. Talk about diamond trade most of their executives seem to be missing too with new leadership taking over.

Adour

Are you sure about all this

Johnson

Yes. And it seems like it all started right before we left Earth. My friend says the word is Walker is the cause of all this

Adour

How could he be? He's on the Mother Ship. Unless they cloned him or something

Johnson

No I don't think it's a clone. I think it's them.

Adour

Them, them who?

Johnson

The hybrids and the aliens, they're always talking about changing the universe and taking out tyranny and creating universal peace. What if this was their plan from the start?

Adour

So what are you saying? That our Commander is killing off world leaders, business man, and any and everyone who he deems the cause of trouble in the world? There's no way he could do that, not from the Mother Ship. There's no way the White House would approve something like that

Johnson

Think about it, how long did they know about the aliens and not tell us. How long have they known about them being here before they told us, how long did they know that some of us were descendants of aliens. Come on, he could have planned this for decades and he was just waiting for the right moment to execute it. Why would they tell us.

INT Mother Ship Walker's Quarters

(James looks at Ishmarelic and he looks back. They nod)

AI

Commander you should look at Cetros commissary

James

AI bring up Cetros commissary

(A screen pops up and you see the commissary)

James

Close in on Major Adour and turn the volume on

(They hear everything that Johnson and Adour are
saying)

INT Cetros Commissary

Johnson

He's going to take over the universe and he started with
Earth. We need to do something

Adour

Do what?

Johnson

I don't know but if we don't we're all going to be in
trouble

INT Walker's Quarters

James

What should we do?

Walker

Hmm... it might be time to fill them in before they
assemble a coup or we have to kill them

James

I'm not sure they can handle it

Walker

It's too late for that. Plus we need to get a message to
Alpha and notify them that people are starting to figure
shit out and we need to notify the White House that
they have a leak

James

(James pulls out his comm. device)

Ty are you there

Ty

Yes General

James

Is this line secure

Ty

Hold on... Now it is. What can I do for you?

James

Notify White that there Is a leak and notify Zion that we
have a public Intel issue

Ty

Working on it now Sir. I will get back to you as soon as I
finish. Ty out

James

We need to bring them over to the ship now

Walker

Agreed... AI Teleport Johnson and Adour to a lock holding room now

AI

Starting teleportation now Commander

INT Cetros Commissary

Adour

Let's hold up on the coup until we get further info. It's not like we're talking about fighting some regular soldiers over here. Walker and his guys are elite and well respected throughout this fleet, and the White House. Even the aliens trust him. We need more Intel

Johnson

That damn AI cut off my way of communicating with my source. We have to fig....

(Adour and Johnson are teleported to the Mother Ship)

INT Mother Ship Holding Room

Johnson

...ure out Oh shit oh shit where are we? Where the fuck are we? Are we dead?

Adour

(Adour walks over to wall trying to figure out where the door is but he can't find anything. He sits down)

I guess you were right then

Johnson

I was right I was right yeah I was fucking right but that's all you can say. We're trapped like lab rats. Why are you so calm?

Adour

What do you mean?

Johnson

They fucking teleported us from YOUR ship to this room and your just sitting there waiting

Adour

I'm just sitting here waiting.

(Adour gets up and throws the chair)

What the fuck else am I suppose to do huh? Please tell me and I will fucking do it. I have no gun, no weapon at all, all I have is your whining ass. It's your fucking fault that I'm in this situation. I should have stayed with my family and pretended not to know. Now I may never see them again. So yes I am just sitting here. I'm sitting here because I have nothing else to do but sit here and wait because if you can't tell this room has no doors and no fucking windows so please unless you've figured out a way for us to get out of this mess, sit down and shut the fuck up

Johnson

(Johnson looks at the anger in Adour face and he walks over to the chair that Adour threw and hands it to him)

I'm sorry man I panicking.

(Johnson takes his seat and places it close to Adour)

Do you think that they are going to kill us?

Adour

(sigh)

I don't know my friend. All we can do is wait and see what happens. We're in uncharted waters

(Johnson puts both hands on the top of his head and takes a deep breathe)

Johnson

Was it like this the last time?

Adour

I don't remember, that time

Johnson

I understand, how you holding up

Adour

I'm fine

Johnson

Did I even tell Jess goodbye?

Adour

I was just thinking if I told Denise and Cristo that I love
them

(The two men look at each other and shake their heads
and start to laugh)

Johnson

you know if you look at this situation. Neither of us
would be here if you didn't ask me to come to space

Adour

Don't start with me

Johnson

I'm just saying

Adour

You're an ass but if this is my last moment I'm happy it's
with you. You've always been a brother to me

Johnson

Same here

INT Mother Ship outside the holding room

(Walker and Dr. Coaxe are watching Johnson and Adour on a screen)

Dr. Coaxe

Aren't you going in there?

Walker

Not yet. I need to know the Major has calmed down. Plus I'm waiting for James and Isis to get here. They won't believe just me but they will believe James. You see the Major over there and General James have a history together. James saved his life when Adour was held captive by a warlord in the jungles of South America. No one would go in there because of the natives and the dangerous animals in the region. James went in with just a handgun and his blade. He got the Major out. Adour was in bad shape, broken bones, dehydrated, and a low pulse. James had to carry him the whole way back to the LZ. Then he helped Adour get back on his feet. It took months before he could even lift a finger, then he had to relearn how to walk and talk. You see that man there is a survivor.

Dr. Coaxe

Wow

(In walks James and Isis)

James

What's the status?

Walker

They seem to be calm now

James

Well let's go in. Doc unlock the door

(Dr. Coaxe presses a button on the screen and a door appears and starts to dissolve)

Johnson

Here we go

(Adour lifts up his head and looks at James walking in. He gets up as soon as he sees him)

Adour

What the hell is going on Jim?

(Walker, Isis, and Dr. Coaxe walks in James walks over to Adour and puts his hand out. Adour shakes it)

James

Take a seat and I'll fill you in. you too Johnson

(Johnson gets up and sits next to Adour. Isis and James sit across from them with Walker and Dr. Coaxe standing behind them)

Adour

So what's going on? Is it true what Johnson told me?

James

Yes

Adour

What the fuck are you doing man? This is treason, it's
illegal

Walker

What's Treason is what those bastards are doing to our
planet

Johnson

Your planet? I'm not even sure your human

Walker

I'll show you how human I am

James

No time for this bickering. Let's get down to the facts.
Yes we are taking over the Earth but it's not that easy as
that

Johnson

I TOLD YOU

James

Allow me to finish. For far too long has the world been secretly run by a few greedy and very powerful individuals whom profit greatly every time there's a war, famine, financial turmoil, oil prices raising, and if any political leaders try actually make a different some scandal comes up which destroys his campaign, and so on and so on. We have undeniable proof of this. The only problem is that they are so powerful no government would dare try to go against them. If they ever tried there would be some sort of trouble in their country and they would either end up dead, imprison, or their family would be wiped out. That's where we come in. We are a team of individuals with nothing to lose, nothing to hold against us and with the help of some key individuals throughout the world we created a team that would track down these individuals and neutralize them and their underlings.

Adour

Under who's orders?

Walker

Mine

Johnson

Who made you Commander in Chief of the world?

Walker

The people did when they cried for a change. Well
we're giving them that change

Johnson

What happen to democracy?

James

We haven't had true democracy in decades or should I
say centuries or even millenniums. You see these
individuals have worked their tyranny into government
for a longtime without even really showing their faces.
They remain in the background while others carryout
their plans of world domination

Adour

(Pauses, folds both hands in front his face, and sits back
in his chair)

Ok then

Johnson

No, no ok then. So what happens after you take them
out and then what? You run the world right?

Walker

No I maybe one of the causes of this change but I am a
military man. I should not be the leader of the people.
My task was to set the people free. The rest is up to the
masses. I am not returning to Earth. This new Earth has

no need of a man like me. I've done a lot of evil things and justified them by telling myself I was protecting freedom.

Adour

So Commander you're not returning to Earth. Where are you going to go?

Walker

In order to free the world I created Monsters. I now will take my monsters and any soldiers that wants to come with me and free the other worlds under High Command control, once we kill the Overlords.

Adour

James you going with the Commander

James

Yes

Adour

Then Commander it I make it through this mission, Then I'll asked for your permission to continue on with you Sir

Johnson

Hold up... what hell? No Adour what are doing you have a family

Adour

I'm a warrior if I don't fight then I'll die

Walker

You're more than welcome to occupy us it would be a
honor to have you

Johnson

You're going to lose Denise and Cristos

Adour

If I don't do this then who will. Denise knew what she
marrying. I haven't changed

Johnson

I hate you, you know that

Adour

(Adour looks at Johnson and smiles)

Ok Commander. What do you need from me

Walker

Keeps this information under wraps for just a little while
longer, the operation is almost done. We don't need
any bad PR, right now.

Adour

Ok

(Everyone looks at Johnson)

Johnson

What... fine ok I won't tell anyone but I want something in return

Isis

What?

Johnson

I want a one on one with him

(Everyone turns to look at Dr. Coaxe and then they turn back to Johnson)

Walker

Fine. We'll leave you two here.

James

Why don't we get a drink and talk? This is my sister Isis

Adour

(Adour shakes Isis hand)

Sister... man it seems like we have a lot of catching up to do. Hi Isis

(The three leave the room leaving Johnson and Dr. Coaxe there)

644

Dr. Coaxe

So what do you want to ask me?

Johnson

How did you do it?

Dr. Coaxe

INT Outside the holding room. Innis is running towards Walker, James, and Adour. He runs pass them and opens the door

Innis

STOP

(Then men outside turn around and enter the room to see Innis stopping Johnson from trying to kill Dr. Coaxe. Adour runs over and holds Johnson down)

Adour

What the hell are you doing stop

(In walks Ishmarelic)

Ishmarelic

He knows not what he is doing

Walker

What do you mean?

Ishmarelic

(Ishmarelic holds up his hand to Johnson head while James and Adour holds him by each hand)

It's easier for me to show you

Johnson

Let me go. No stop don't let him do it

(Johnson stops talking as soon as Ishmarelic places his hand on his head. A few seconds pass and Johnson starts convulsing and coughing)

Adour

Is he having a seizure?

Innis

Quite while the Third works

(Johnson starts to cough more and more and then it looks like something starts to move up his chest towards his throat. Its shivers out of his mouth and falls to the ground and dies.)

Dr. Coaxe

I haven't seen one of those in centuries

Walker

What?

Adour

What the hell is that shit and how did it get in him

Dr. Coaxe

It's a mind bug and by the size of it, it's been in his body
for about two years

Adour

How did it get in him and why?

Isis

It looks like someone planted it in him and his orders
was to kill Dr. Coaxe

Walker

(Walker grabs his comm. device)

Ty get Lt. Johnson's family on Cetros ship and place
them inside a holding room ASAP

Adour

What are you doing?

Walker

I have to make sure they just placed that thing in him
and not anyone else

Adour

Who else could be infected?

Innis

It's hard to tell

Walker

(Walker looks at Isis and James)

How come you did detect this?

Ishmarelic

They need more training. It takes time to develop this
sense. This bug can only be detected by people with
the highest ability. Now they will be able too soon once
I'm done training them but be happy we caught this
one.

Walker

I want security detail on Dr. Coaxe now. James I want
one of your men on it once they've been cleared of any
bugs in their heads

James

I got the right man for it. AI get Piro up here now.

AI

Locating Piro, Piro detected, Piro teleporting to this
location now

Piro

(Piro appears)

Damnit I hate that. General reporting for duty

James

Just stand there for a second we need to run a test on you. Ishmarelic do your thing

(Ishmarelic looks to Isis and James)

Ishmarelic

Come closer to me. I will train you while I run the test now clear your mind

(Ishmarelic puts his hand on Piro head and starts his scan while James and Isis close their eyes and listen to Ishmarelic instructions inside their head)

Ishmarelic

(Only Isis and James can hear him)

Now this is how you begin. First you must sense the entire body and break it down to even it's cells. Then you go through the body section by section and cell by cell. Can you see what I see

James and Isis

Yes

Ishmarelic

Good. Let's continue. Now you can sense everything inside of him if you wanted you could stop he's body from moving by thinking stop but that's another lesson. Can you detect anything wrong with him?

James and Isis

No

Ishmarelic

Correct. This was easy for you two because you know the human body. This only can work if you know the anatomy of the species that you are scanning. Therefore, you should learn more especially the ones helping us. I can sense where their loyalty lays and it's not with you, understand

James and Isis

Yes

Ishmarelic

Be aware my two

(Ishmarelic removes his hand from Piro head and turns to Walker)

Ishmarelic

He's clean

Walker

Corporal Piro you duty for now is to protect the Doc over there. That means you will stay with him all the time. The only time you will leave him is if you are told directly by me or General James over there...Understood

Piro

Yes sir

Ishmarelic

I have summon Jasper to help you with your task.

Adour

So what about Johnson.

Innis

He will wake up in a few hours with a major headache but other than that he will be fine.

Walker

Al Send Johnson to the infirmary. The rest of you follow me

(Walker takes the men to another holding room and through the screen they see Smith the traitor handcuff to the table. His eyes are bloodshot red, he looks very weak, and tired)

Walker

Because of this traitors Intel we were able to find most of the men behind all the problems with Earth.

Adour

I know that man. He's Brian Smith, one of General Gethros closest men. He couldn't be a traitor.

Walker

Why don't you go inside and find out for yourself

(Adour shakes his head yes and Walker presses the button for the door to materialize and open. Adour walks in.)

Smith

(Smith who had he's head down lifts it slowly to see Adour walk in. Very weakly and at a low tone)

Major I'm sorry you have to see me like this

Adour

It's ok soldier. Is it true?

Smith

Is what true

Adour

What I heard about you Brian, is it TRUE?

Smith

Oh is that true...well yes it is. Don't act so surprised as you didn't know they existed. You're as guilty as I am.

Adour

How do you figure

Smith

You might not have signed up with them like I did but I know they approached you. My question is how did you get out how did you turn it down

Adour

Back then... I had nothing to lose... I was ready to die. All I wanted to do was die! So when someone comes to you and ask you to join up a secret military group, I laughed! Remember my whole family died during 9/11. My brother and Father were in the towers and my mom was one the planes that was shot down. After that I promised that I would stop anyone trying to attack my government. Therefore, I killed the man asking me to join, which is exactly what I am going to do to you

(Adour pulls out his knife and starts to walk towards Smith)

Smith

You won't

(In runs James , who grabs Adour right before he was able to slit Smith's throat. Then Walker walks in)

Walker

What the Hell do you think you were going to do?

Adour

Fulfill my oath to protect my country against it's enemies either foreign or domestic

Walker

This man is under my protection

Smith

This isn't protection, call it what it is. This is my prison until you decide to get rid of me and from what I see, it won't be anywhere near Earth

James

You're lucky your still alive, If it was up to me I would leave your ass on one of these planets we passed but someone things you might be useful soon.

(Laughs)

Smith

What do you mean useful?

James

(Still laughing, while he and the rest of them exit the room)

You'll see soon

INT Mother Ship Command Center

Dean

Lt. I have a message from Destiny, General Gethros wants to see the Commander

Ty

Tell Destiny that we will set it up and to hold on

(Ty grabs his comm.)

Walker who's in his quarters with James, Adour, and Johnson drinking whiskey grabs his comm. device

Walker

Yes Ty

Ty

General Gethros is requesting your audience

Walker

Seems like they woke him up a day early. Tell the General that we will teleport him to my chamber momentarily

Ty

Yes Sir. Ty out

Walker

That Gethros so impatient, Ai Teleport him here when he's ready.

Ai

Yes Walker

(Gethros appears inside of Walker's quarters)

Adour

Welcome General

Gethros

(coughs and coughs)

Water I need something to drink

James passes him his glass of whiskey. Gethros doesn't look at what's inside and drinks it. He spits most of it out. The whole group starts to laugh

Gethros

That shits not funny. I asked for water

Walker

What's not funny is that you just wasted some really good whiskey and it's not like I can go to a liquor store out here

Gethros

Fuck you and your whiskey. I want an update I've been frozen for almost three fucking years what happen since then.

Adour

(in a low tone)

A lot General A lot

(Gethros walks over to the table where everyone is sitting and sits down besides Adour and Johnson)

Gethros

Now can someone give me a proper glass to drink

Walker

Sure

(Walker slides a glass over to Gethros and then Johnson passes him the bottle)

Gethros

So fill me in

Adour

(Adour starts to tell Gethros what had occurred these
past few years)

INT Dr. Coaxe Lab

Ishmarelic

I didn't think that bug would work on humans. They are
more like us then we thought

Dr. Coaxe

I could have told you that. Elisa knew that back then.
Little do they know they are us but who planted that
bug in him and why. That's what I want to know

Ishmarelic

It was one of our pseudo allies did it but they killed him

Dr. Coaxe

That means they know I'm here

Ishmarelic

Calm yourself they have a hybrid and Jasper protecting
you now. How's the research going? I need that fluid
before we get to my planet. I'm still not 100%

Dr. Coaxe

I have my apprentice working on it right now, he's 90% done. It has to cool it then immediately freeze it then heated up again before it can work on you. Should I give it to the twins

Ishmarelic

Once you give it to me find a way to give it to them without telling them. I'm sorry but I can't tell them the whole truth yet. Soon they will find out

Dr. Coaxe

Then what?

Ishmarelic

We were both exiled out of planet and now look at it. It use to be such a beautiful place

Dr. Coaxe

We can fix it brother. Elisa started an experiment while he was on Mars and Earth, and the AI continued working on it after he expired. Plus he left a clone of himself in a chamber underneath my lab on Earth. When I awoken, the AI informed me of it.

Ishmarelic

Where is he now

Dr. Coaxe

The only issue was that Elisa didn't figure out how to accelerate the growth process and I didn't have sufficient resources on that planet to recreate the process you created. So with help of Walker we placed him with a family as a foster kid and monitored him. He was a true trouble maker just like the real Elisa.

Ishmarelic

I know who he is. That's his clone?

Dr. Coaxe

Yes

Ishmarelic

I want to meet him in private

Dr. Coaxe

I will have Walker set it up

Ishmarelic

You trust him don't you

Dr. Coaxe

Yes

Ishmarelic

Good cause we're going to need his help with stage two

Dr. Coaxe

Stage two

Ishmarelic

Once we defeat our brother we have to set straight what he corrupted throughout the universe. We cannot leave it this way. It's not what the Master wants. The only reason I came back was because he told me to fix it

Dr. Coaxe

You know the Master location?

Ishmarelic

Yes

Dr. Coaxe

Tell me

Ishmarelic

In due time my brother in due time. Now finish the serum

Dr. Coaxe

fine but I want to meet the Master in this cycle

Ishmarelic

Who says that you haven't met him before

Innis

Doc I'm done the AI is running the final test now

Coaxe

Good

INT Walker Quarters

(The men are still drinking and laughing. Adour just finished giving Gethros a report on what happen while he was gone)

Gethros

Damn I missed a lot

Adour

That's how I feel

James

Yea you know how it is, our missions are always on a need to know bases

Adour

True

James

Speaking about need to know. Ah Major I overheard what you were talking about with Smith

Adour

(Adour puts his drink down)

And

James

It's funny cause when Johnson told you what we were doing you didn't even bring it up with him

Johnson

True that's very true

Adour

So

James

So that's all you got to say

Adour

I still haven't heard a question in you ramblings

James

Well then let me get to the point rather quickly. How long did you know about them and remember don't lie to me because I will know

Adour

Why don't you just scan my brain General to find out I have nothing to hide

James

(James starts to get up)

Why don't I

Walker

At ease James. I already knew that they approached the Major. I knew about almost everyone on my ships. I had the AI watching everything from everywhere. It's was watching from ATM Cameras, Street cameras, Satellites, people Facebook pages, you would be amazed how Facebook helps us keep a tab on people, even people's cell phones. We can listen to everything even if the phone is not in use. So I knew about it but James did say something that was strange. Why didn't you come to us Major?

Adour

And say what? That some secret organization, tired to recruit me. Shit even I wouldn't believe it. I didn't even know who they were and back then I was all messed up. I lost my whole family. All I wanted to do was die and no matter what I couldn't. I volunteered for every impossible mission with you two and we would always make it out. I felt like the gods were laughing at me and trying to see if I would snap. I will say, I understand why Smith cracked, they will use anything to break you. I just didn't have anything for them to use against me. I lost it all. So James tell me, I'm I telling the truth

James

Yes, but we would have helped you

Adour

No one could have helped me back then James, no one

Gethros

Well now that's over. Someone please fill me in what happen when you guys refueled? I want to know how he almost blew up a planet

Walker

That's a long story but all I can say is that, that we lost some good men

James

(Lifts his glass in the air)

That's an understatement

Adour

They will be missed

Gethros

Are you going to fill me in

James

Yea, it all started when the Major over here thought he would just walk into the alien base...

INT Mother Ship Dr. Coaxe Lab

(Jay and Brace walk into the lab)

Brace

What's up Doc?

Dr. Coaxe

I have someone here that wants to meet you

Jay

Meet who

Dr. Coaxe

You Jay

Jay

Who?

Ishmarelic

Me

Brace

Who are you?

Ishmarelic

My name is Ishmarelic.

Brace

Why do you want to meet my friend?

Ishmarelic

I heard good things about him

Jay

It's cool Brace. I have a strange feeling like I know him

Brace

Hmm. Blackburn said we should trust our instincts more so if you feel it's cool then I'm cool

Jay

So what do you want to talk to me about?

Ishmarelic

I want to give you and your friend something but it's something that will change you greatly.

Dr. Coaxe

Both of them? Is that safe?

Ishmarelic

They will need to be fully prepared for their future. This is the only way it can happen. When we relinquish our brother from his post, it will be up to them to govern the universe. They will have to choose to either create or destroy. We allowed him to take control and destroy. We have to fix it. Once we do, we will leave it in their hands

Brace

Hold up old man, Doc what the hell are you two talking about? What's going on here?

Jay

Brace, it's cool. I'm in let's do it

Ishmarelic

Good Very Good

(In walks Jasper and Nicklous)

Jasper

Third, what are you doing?

Ishmarelic

I'm setting them free

Nicklous

Can we trust them? You already freed those three and we still don't know what's going to happen with them once they peak and now you want to add two more. This is too dangerous

Ishmarelic

NO, NO It's not. What's dangerous is my brother destroying what Master created. My brother and I may not be powerful enough to stop him

Jasper

Yes but once you do this WE may not be powerful enough to stop them. The master only freed three of you in the beginning. Now you are going to free five and once you do they will figure out to free more and more then what? They still have the gene inside of them to cause war. They could really destroy this whole universe if we are not careful.

Brace

Hold up what are you guys talking about the Master?

Nicklous

The one that came before us all and created us

Brace

And who is that?

Jasper

The Creator

Brace

Listen Riddler, I'm not Batman, what does that mean?

Jay

No one really knows but it seems like something
created this world am I right?

Brace

I guess

Nicklous

You're a computer person think about it in numbers.
There's millions of intelligent life forms, living on
millions of live able planets. These planets wouldn't be
live able if their position was off even a tenth of a
degree. Instead of a paradise you would have a
desolate planet. Take your Earth, if it rotated in the
opposite direction or if it changed it's position in the
slightest degree you would not be able to live there.
Think about the math involved in it. The degree of
accuracy is too perfect. Nature isn't that perfect. When
you look at nature you see many that are far from being
perfect. The closest you get to perfection is in a lab.
Therefore, someone had to do that and they did it way
before any of our ancestors were around

Brace

So what we call God you call the master, right Jay?

Jay

Yeah

Brace

Oh ok now it's starting to make some sense. Yeah science and math doesn't really explain how this universe came to be and neither does religion fully. I guess you have to believe in both. So now what Doc

Coaxe

Well since my brother believes we need too. I have something to give you

Jasper

This is dangerous and you all know it. What If

Nicklous

There's no time for what if. We have to give it to them and see what they do with it after. There's no way of predicting it now

Jasper

You two are the elders and it's ultimately your decision. If you say do then it will be done

Ishmarelic

We have to let the old ways go my son, they didn't work

Jasper

True

Coaxe

Well you two follow me

(Jay and Brace follow Dr. Coaxe into another room in his lab)

INT Cetros Hallway

Johnson

Jess is going to kill me.

Adour

Why

Johnson

I had a bug inside of me. She's probably pissed at me

Adour

No my friend, it's not your fault. Trust me she can't wait to see you. Come in for a little, I bet Denise has a fresh cup of coffee made

Johnson

Ok

(Adour and Johnson walk into Adour's quarters. Cristos runs up to Adour)

Cristos

DAD

Adour

Hey little guy

Denise

Your son was here worried about you

Adour

Oh really only him

Denise

(smiles)

You guys wants some coffee?

Johnson

I really need a cup right now

(Knock, Knock)

Denise

Open

(In walks Jess and Ray. Ray looks at Johnson and quickly runs over to him. Johnson slowly bends down and hugs him. Adour helps him back up. Jess walks over and gives him a kiss)

Johnson

You not mad at me?

Jess

(Jess hits him in the back of his head)

No dummy why would I be? I'm just happy that your ok and they were able to get it out of you. We didn't have anything inside of us, so we're cool. Plus I have a surprise for you

Johnson

What?

Jess

That Alien why inspecting my body found out that we're having twins

Johnson

(A look of shock comes to Johnson face. He slowly moves closer to Jess and hugs her)

Don't you ever forget that I love you

Jess

You better now forget it buddy cause your stuck with me for the rest of your life.

Johnson

So where on Earth are we going to settle down to with our family?

Jess

Earth?

Johnson

Yeah aren't we going back home?

Jess

I thought this ship was going to be our home from now
on. WE still have to find the necessary resources to heal
Earth after we win this war

(Johnson just stands there quiet.)

Denise

Yeah we're not going back to Earth either

Johnson

You're not. Did you guys talk about this before?

Denise

No but we're a military family

(She grabs Adour's hand)

And until my husband says he wants out. We're staying
here or going wherever his next mission takes him. And
if Cristos wants to go back to Earth he can but that's his
decision

Johnson

Really

Jess

Why baby you want to go back to Earth

Johnson

I thought that was the plan, I never thought that you wanted to stay on this ship

Jess

So do you want to leave?

Johnson

It's up to you baby. Whatever you want I want. The only things I care about are in this room right now. I have to use the bathroom be right back

(Johnson walks to the bathroom)

INT Bathroom

Johnson

(Turns on the sink and starts to Talk to himself. He throws water in his face repeatedly)

Damnit, I didn't want to stay on this fucking ship or in space. I want to go home. Suck it up, you love her and you would do anything to keep her happy. Remember the whole in your chest before you met her. She fixed that. Ok then, I'm staying in space then. What am I bitchin about I have nothing left on Earth. All my family is dead. All I have is my bitch of an ex-wife and who needs to be around her ass. Fuck it, I'm staying. I can make the best of this. I have my one and only friend here and my wife, son, and two more kids coming. Ok Johnson you can do this, go out there and accept your future with open arms. Ok let's go

(Johnson flushes the toilet, washes his hands, wipes his face)

Denise

Looks to Adour and Jess

Is he ok?

Adour

He'll be fine. He's just been through a lot lately

Johnson

(Johnson walks out of the bathroom)

You have some brandy that I can put in my coffee

Denise

Yes sure hold on one minute

(Denise grabs a bottle of brandy and pours some into Johnson's cup)

Johnson

Thank you

Jess

Baby you ok?

Johnson

Yes, I'm fine, you know I had a bug taken out of your body is just a little nerve racking

Jess

Ok if you say so

Johnson

Yup

(Walks over to Jess and kisses her on her forehead)

I'm just happy to be here with you guys that's it. So what's next family?

Adour

Family

Johnson

Yeah we're family now. I mean I'm your son's godfather and your mine plus we're going to be in space together for a longtime. We're just one big family now, right?

Denise

He's right

Jess

Great

Ai

Yellow alert Yellow Alert All ships captains and first officer to the Mother Ship Yellow Alert Yellow Alert all ships Captains and First officer be prepared to be teleported.

Johnson

Here we go Love you Babe….

(Adour and Johnson Disappears)

INT Mother Ship War Room

The room is full with every ship's Captain and first Officer No one knows what's going on and they are all talking to each other trying to figure it out. With the AI interpretation program running, everyone understands what everyone says. The room is very loud. In walks Walker, then James, then Ishmarelic, Nicklous, and Jasper, followed by Isis, Rick and Rich

Walker

My fellow warriors, we have a problem. It seems like the Aliens know we're coming and they have increased their defenses. We're going to need each and every available pilot in space as soon as we unfold into their galaxy.

Warber

How did they find out? I know no one on my ship leaked any information. So who was it?

Walker

It came from our ship

Silicio

I thought you had that under control

Walker

WE DID, unfortunately we were betrayed by one of our own. The only good thing was that the leak didn't contain any information on who and what was coming. Before anymore Intel leaked we were able to stop it.

Warber

What are our chances now?

James

Our chances are still the same. We're not turning back now. Either we fight now or we die later. Plus there is still a chance that the message wasn't received. We reach their galaxy in a day. So have all your warriors gear up and be prepared for the battle of their lives. Tomorrow we get to avenge every single being lost because of High Command and restore our given right to be free

Warber

(Warber and Silicio stand up)

You know you humans are good with me, let's do it

The rest of the soldiers sitting down get up and throw their arms in the air and start to cheer

Group

FOR FREEDOM FOR FREEDOM FOR ALL FOR FREEDOM FOR FREEDOM FOR ALL

James

Ok then, now go back to your ship and gear up cause we launch tomorrow

(The group gets ups and section by section they are teleported to their ships)

Walker

(Walker turns to Ishmarelic)

How did you allow this to happen? I thought you had your group under control?

Ishmarelic

I did. I had to do something that required almost all of my attention. Don't worry, my brother thinks he's invincible now. He thinks we're dead

Walker

I'm confused here. You say that he's powerful and he's got an unstoppable army but now you say we should be okay. Why what has changed?

Ishmarelic

Just carryout your plans as you planned it and believe that you will find a way to win

Walker

So you're not going down with the team.

Ishmarelic

Oh no I'm going but understand, this is your mission to finish, you have to ensure peace throughout. My mission is to correct something that I failed to correct centurles ago

Walker

Why must I be the one?

Ishmarelic

In Order to restore order in the universe it must be you and your team. Once you do you'll understand why it had to be you. Now I must go and prepare for tomorrow.

(Ishmarelic walks out with Jasper and Nicklous.)

Walker

(Walker turns to Isis and James)

What did he mean?

(They shrug their shoulders)

You guys don't know or you just won't tell me

(They shrug their shoulders again)

Fine, don't fucking tell me I don't fucking care. All I care about is tomorrow.   But I won't forget it you two

(Walker leaves the room)

(Isis , James, Rick, and Rich look at each other and smile.)

INT Blackburn Quarters

Rebekah

You lose Uncle Brace

Brace

No it can't be how did you beat me

Rebekah

You let me win I know you did. But Thank you. Mom
Uncle Brace, let me win tell him to really play against
me

Sarch

Brace will you please play against her and stop allowing
her to win

Brace

I did

Rebekah'

No he didn't

Brace

Ok fine next time

Rebekah

Uncle Rich and Auntie Isis is at the door Mom

Sarch

Well let them in

(Rebekah opens the door for Rich and Isis who has their
twins with them)

Sarch

Welcome guys. I'll be with you soon

Brace

They didn't even ring the bell, you're getting better I see. From now on I will play you for real

Rebekah

Thank you finally you get it jeez

Brace

What's up Lt

Rich

Nothing, just dropping off the kids. We're not going to be able to take care of them until after the war. So Sarch is going to babysit for us

(In walks Blackburn with Jay)

Jay

LT, Isis it's nice seeing you guys. Wow the twins are getting bigger

Rich

Yeah I know, they're getting smarter too by the day

Brace

Tell me about it, Rebekah over here is reading minds. I don't like it

Isis

Is she now. We might have to start training her

Rebekah

No need Auntie Isis, moms still a little worried about me using it. I only use it when I'm home and mostly with Uncle Brace. He likes to talk to me without using his mouth while playing games. He says talking distracts him too much

Brace

It does.

Blackburn

So Rich how's your team going?

Rich

They're ready. And your team?

Blackburn

They're ready too. Well as much as anyone can be ready for.

Jay

Don't worry I have a good feeling about this mission

Brace

Yeah me too

Rich

There's something different about you two

Isis

(Smiles)

There is isn't there

Brace

(Smiles and looks at Jay then looks back at Rich)

We have no clue what you are talking about. We did get a little older. It's been five years since the attack on Earth and another three years on this journey. That might be what you are seeing

Rich

No I'm not seeing anything. I'm sensing that things are different with you.

Jay

Maybe we got a little taller

Rich

NO, don't worry I'll figure it out

Rebekah

Mom Mitch is coming to the door.

(Rebekah gets up and walks to the door and opens it)

Sarch

Our kids don't belong on Earth anymore or at least not yet. The world can't handle human beings having abilities like that.

Isis

I was just talking about that with Rich and we both agreed that we're not going back to Earth after the war. We're staying on the ship

(Mitch and Danielle walks in and says hi to Rebekah and everyone then everyone else. Everyone says Hi but they have a strange look on their face)

Mitch

What did we come at a bad time?

Rebekah

No Mitch, everyone just realized that their kids won't fit in on Earth anymore and they're going to stay on the ship

Mitch

(Mitch looks at Danielle, then Sarch)

What do you mean you're not going back?

Rebekah

Don't worry soon you'll realize what they just realized

Mitch

What are you talking about?

Sarch

Our kids don't belong on Earth. Do you know what would happen to them if the world found out that they could really read minds, that they don't age as regular people, that they are super smart, there would be an unrest on Earth. The world is not ready for it yet. They just found out about the aliens and now you want to tell them that they are second class citizens because the babies of aliens are better than them in everyway

Mitch

And so what if they are. I'm regular and it doesn't bother me. Shit Danielle a hybrid and I happy that we're married

Isis

Your not the typical person. You represent a small fraction of the world that wouldn't care but the majority would.

Brace

She's right. We finally found a reason to unify the world and by now we should have taken out the entities that wanted to stop that from happening. We don't need to introduce into the world a new reason to separate

Mitch

So what you make the rules now? You know what, everyone's talking about change and accepting the future but you still think people can't take knowing more information. When they found about aliens, y'all thought they would riot and guess what they didn't. It's time to just accept that people can take it. The only reason why I will stay on this ship is for my wife and not because I think the people can't take to know that my child is different.

Blackburn

You have a point Mitch but it's deeper than our kids being different. Another reason why I am not going back is because I feel like here is where I belong. I can do more here on space than on Earth. I can admit I was wrong about the people not being able to take the information, you're right about that. They can but we just feel better here than there. Now if our children want to go back, that's there decision and I will not stop them at all. It's about freedom now and we have to set the example by giving them freedom to choose their future.

Danielle

(looks at Mitch and holds his hand)

He's right, I feel we can do better here than there and if our kids want to go back, we won't stop them

Mitch

I can agree with that but I would like to see my family at least sometimes, you know

Danielle

(Holds on to Mitch's hand tighter)

We're your family now and we can always go back if you really feel like visiting. No one said that we were trapped here. Like you and Black said it's about freedom now and that's what we are fighting for freedom to choose the way we want to live our lives

Mitch

So now what?

Rebekah

Daddy it's time

AI

Alert Alert Everyone to their battle stations Alert Alert Everyone to their Battle Stations. We are about to unfold

(Blackburn looks to Rebekah and picks her up and kisses her then gives Sarch a kiss. Rich and Isis kiss the twins, Mitch kisses Danielle.)

Rich

Ok let's roll

(Rich, Mitch, Isis, Blackburn, Jay and Brace swiftly leave the apartment. Leaving Sarch and Danielle looking at them)

Sarch

Aren't you going with them?

Danielle

I can't not now

Sarch

Why?

Danielle

I'm pregnant

INT Mother Ship Flight Deck

Walker

How much time do we have?

James

None, you're going down there? I thought you were staying on the ship

Walker

You're going to need all the help you can get

James

Yes Sir but this time we need you to stay here and lead the fleet. Let me handle to ground force while you handle space

Walker

Tag team

James

Like it's always been, the bash brothers

Walker

Will it ever end?

James

Not as long as tyranny still shows it's ugly face and would you really want it too

Walker

Nope, Well then let's do it. AI link us up

(The Ai links Walker up to all the ships and every man, woman, and alien in the fleet)

This is the moment we've waited for. This is the moment when a unified army comes together for one purpose and that purpose is freedom. Some of us use to be enemies but now we are all here to fight side by side against a greater enemy. An enemy that wreaked havoc on each and every one of our homes. Now it's our turn. It's our turn to wreak havoc upon them and show them that their reign is over. It's our time to lead and we won't lead with force we will lead with diplomacy true diplomacy. No more will greed and hate be allowed to infiltrate our government and corrupt our leaders. It started with them and we will end it with them. Today we'll send a message to any tyrant, that we are coming for them and when we find them. We will destroy them by all means necessary. So rise my friends and let's free the universe together

(The group cheers and throws their hands into the air. James looks to his unit and signals them to put on their armor suits. Rich signals to his unit to load up into the fighters. The Mother ship continues to travel through space. Walker leaves the flight deck and goes to the command center)

INT Mother Ship Command Center

Walker

Walks in

What do you have Ty

Ty

We're about to unfold in ten seconds,9,8,7,6,5,4,3,2,1 unfolding now

(The Mother Ship appears within High Command galaxy.)

The Ai warns on incoming message

Walker

Put it through

Message

Who do you think you are entering my galaxy in my ship? I hope you are ready to die

Ty

Should I respond Sir?

Walker

No, is the rest of the fleet here

Ty

They are unfolding now Sir. We're waiting for the two more

Walker

Good as soon as they reach launch our fighters

Ty

Yes Sir, hold on wait a minute Sir we have incoming. I'm showing multiple targets heading our way from multiple locations Sir. They seem to be coming from the two moons of the main planet and from the green planet

Walker

Tell the fleet to engaged the enemies. Launch out
fighters and load up the shields as soon as they depart

Ty

Yes notifying Rich and the rest of the fighters to depart.
I have some very large targets heading our way too Sir

Walker

How Large?

Ty

They seem to be built like the Mother Ship but smaller.

Walker

Make sure our shields are up before they get here Ty.
Notify the rest of the fleet to do the same

Al

Window for teleportation to home planet is closing

Walker

What the hell, what window?

Ty

Looks like that planet has the ability to block
teleportation and they are turning on that system, It's a
shield

Walker

Get James now

(Ty types on the screen and James pops up on the main screen of the Command Center)

James

Yes

Walker

We have no time is your unit ready?

James

Yes we're ready

Walker

Good, Good luck. Ty get them to that planet now

Ty

Yes Sir.

(Ty types on the screen and sends James and his team to the planet)

God Sped, my friends. Sir it seems like we have multiple fighters coming our way too

Walker

How many?

Ty

Hundreds of them Sir Hundreds

Walker

It has begun. I'll take the sky you take the ground.
hmm we shall meet at the horizon when it's all over my
friend

INT Alien Planet Nebakah

(The team enters a dark Cave. No one can see anything
and there's a cloudy mist in the Air)

James

Is it breathable?

Ishmarelic

Yes

James

Alright men light'em up

(Everyone turns on their night vision on their helmets.
James looks at Ishmarelic)

Lead the way

Ishmarelic

I have to warn you. This whole place is Bobbie trapped.
Just be careful

Scar

Isn't that something you should have said before we got on this god awful place?

James

No time for that just make sure you guys stay alert

(They continue to walk through the cave. A Strange streaky noise)

Phillip

What the hell was that?

Ishmarelic

That's a rectaclcio. Very dangerous. Make sure it never touches you or spits on you. Their poison could kill what you humans call a horse in a hour

Smith

We're going to die down here

Blackburn

Can you shut the fuck up. We're on a mission damnit

James

(Looks back at the group)

He's right quiet down

(They continue walking and they start to see a light)

Blackburn

There's a light up ahead

Jasper

Yes

Scar

Should we head towards it

Ishmarelic

No, we must find another way

Smith

Why not

Jay

It's the rectaclcio nest. Not a place you want to willfully walk into

Scar

So where do we go?

Lex

This is bullshit

(As he takes a step back)

Brace

No stop don't move

(Les finishes he's step and the ground moves down under his feet an inch)

Innis

Jump now jump

(The team starts to jump but it's too late the ground starts to crumble under the members in the back. Isis, Jasper, Jay, Philip, Lex, Piro, Scar, Tone, Alistar , and about fifteen more men fall into the whole in the ground. They slide down into a darker cavern deeper into the cave. They look at each other. Scar takes out his knife and swiftly grabs Lex by the throat)

Scar

I should put this right through you

Isis

Stand down Scar we going to need all the men we have now

Lex

(Scared of Scar)

I'm sorry Sir

Scar

I don't want to fucking hear it, Just know one thing, if you make another mistake it won't be the aliens or any crazy ass animal that kills you it will be me UNDERSTAND

Lex

YES Sir

Isis

(Isis looks at Jasper)

Any Ideas?

Jasper

No this is the first time I've been here but I think we should go this way

Jay

He's right

Isis

Fine then let's go

INT Nebakah cave

(The rest of the team looks down the hole)

James

There's no way we can get down there safely

Blackburn

What about our men James?

Ishmarelic

They made it down safely. They should be able to figure out the right route to meet up with us

James

Let's roll out we don't have time for this

Blackburn

We're going to just leave them

James

Yes we have a mission to carry out.

Blackburn

Which way?

James

Straight ahead

Smith

I thought he said that we shouldn't go into their nest.

James

He did but look back, can we go that direction, no. the only way is straight so move out now soldier. lead the way traitor

Tim

But I thought he said that it's dangerous to go in there

James

(Looks at Ishmarelic)

How bad are these creatures?

Ishmarelic

We should stay in a circle. They won't attack straight on. They'll try to attack from the back or side when you don't expect it. They're venom is highly toxic. Even I can't save someone once they are infected. It's the most painful death a person can die from. Your whole body starts to boil from the inside out. Your bones start to melt and your tongue turns grey and then falls off

James

Thanks for the info. Well you heard the man. Form up into a circle everyone. Smith. let's get going

Smith

What I thought we were suppose to form a circle

James

Yeah we are, or at least everyone that I can trust. I don't trust you at all and you know why. Now get moving

Smith

No Way

James

It's either you lead the way or I shoot you right now. I rather prefer you choose the later

Smith

Fine

(The team forms up into a circle and starts to walk into the room with their guns in the air, Smith leads the way. The rectaclcio starts to make loud noises. Their scream hurts the ears of the troops.)

Ishmarelic

Look up there's one

(Blackburn takes aim and shoots one in the head. It falls from the sky and lands right next to the him. It's a big animal about six feet long, with long arms and legs. Their wings are attached to each arm. The claws on them are about 5 inches long.)

Smith

What the F...

(Another one pops up right in back of Smith. Tim turns around but he's too late. It takes a swing at him. Smith quickly puts his gun the Air and blocks the arm of the rectaclcio. But the force of the blow breaks Smith's gun. Smith jumps back and another soldier comes around and shoots the rectaclcio in the chest. It dies immediately. The rest of the rectaclcios starts to roar louder and louder)

Smith

Come on Muthafucker bring it bring I'm here try me! I have nothing to live for anymore

Blackburn

Shut up and watch your six

Smith

What

(A very huge rectaclcio comes out of nowhere behind Smith, Blackburn shoots it but the shoot doesn't kill it. The rectaclcio reaches out and scratches Smith across his chest. James shoots it three times once in the head and two times in it's chest. It dies. Smith Screams out loud, the venom is circulating in his system)

(James walks over to Smith but right when he reaches him, alien troopers who heard the loud screams appear and they start to shoot at the group)

James

Take cover now

(The men run to a set of tress to the left of them. They start to shoot back at the alien troopers. Smith is on the ground screaming very loudly)

James

How long does he have Ishmarelic

Ishmarelic

It could take hours

James

I'm not going to leave a man to die like that. Traitor or not, he's still a soldier

(James takes aim at Smith with his laser rifle and shoots him twice in the chest. Smith dies. James shakes his head. He puts his laser gun to full automatic and looks at his men)

Follow my lead NOW

(He jumps out and starts to run towards the alien troops. Every time an alien trooper sticks it's head out to shoot at James, he beats them to the punch. He shoots three of them in the head rapidly. Then turns the right and shoot a rectaclcio twice in the head. Blackburn is right behind him and while James shoots the rectaclcio, Blackburn shoots three aliens who were about to shoot James. The two continue to shoot more and more aliens. As they head towards to gate on the other side of the room, The rest of the group shocked to see the two men kill so accurately and so quickly. They stays where James and Blackburn left them, Brace looks at James and then he looks back to the group)

Brace

MOVE OUT THEY NEED OUR HELP

(Brace runs out and shoots two aliens as soon as he gets up and then he shoots a rectaclcio. The rest of the team follows behind them and they kill off all the aliens and all the rectaclcio retreat. The group walks out of the nest cave and heads into another section)

INT Nebakah cave Isis team

Scar

Where to now?

Jasper

This way

(They walk up to a corner of the cave and Jasper sticks his head to see what's around the corner. He sees a door and five alien troopers guarding it. Jasper turns back to the group. He shares what he saw to the hybrids telepathically. Scar steps up)

Scar

I know what to do.

Jasper

Ok what do you need?

Scar

Nothing just stay back

(Scar grabs one of his sonic grenades and pulls the pin. He throws it around the corner. The troopers see it rolling towards them and they don't know what it is. They grab their weapons and one of them shoots at the grenade and misses. Another one walks up to it once it stops rolling and picks it up)

Alien

What is this?

(Bomb! A sonic blast erupts from the grenade, throwing all five troopers to the walls. Scar turns the corner with his gun drawn and shoots one of the troops who didn't get the full blast of the grenade.)

Scar

All clear move up

(The rest of the group follows)

Scar

Ok who knows how to open the door?

Jay

(Jay walks up to the door and places his finger into a scanner by the door)

I do

AI

Welcome Elisa

The door opens

Lex

Holdup what did that thing say?

Jasper

Nothing let's move out

INT Mother ship Command Center

Walker

How's it looking for us out there Ty

Ty

Our allies aren't as good as we are, they are taking heavy loses

Walker

What about the aliens?

Ty

It's about even right now Sir

Walker

We need to take control of the situation

INT Space

Rich

Dreke on my call break right

Dreke

Call it cause this asshole won't leave mine alone

(Rich pulls up behind the alien fighter shooting at Dreke)

Rich

Break right

(Dreke breaks right and pulls up into the air doing a 360. Rich takes aim on the alien)

Rich

Gotcha

(Rich shoots his lasers and destroys the alien fighter)

Rich

Ok let's do this

Arnold

(Arnold shoots two alien fighters and blows them up)

Let's do it I am doing it

Melissa

Watch your six

(An alien fighter comes behind Arnold and shoots. Arnold pulls up and the alien misses him. Melissa coming from the top shoots the alien and blows the ship up. She turns her fighter around and shoots two more.)

Melissa

Hell yeah bring it

(Rich comes up from below and shoots a fighter pulling behind Melissa)

Rich

Don't get too cocky out here

Melissa

I knew you had my back

Rich

Oh

(About two alien fighters turn and head towards Rich, Melissa, Arnold, Nicklous, and Dreke)

Dreke

We got incoming

Melissa

Let's do it

Melissa fighter fly's faster towards the alien fighters

Rich

Hold up don't just rush into that

Dreke

There's no talking to her now she's in a zone

Rich

Ok men pick up the speed we need to get her back.
She's lost it

INT Nebakah Cave

(The group walks up to a fork in the cave, they stop)

Blackburn

Which way?

Ishmarelic

We're getting closer. Hmmm

Blackburn

What was that?

Ishmarelic

I just sense something. Nothing, for you to worry
about.

(He turns to James)

This is where I must go my way. You go in that direction

James

I understand.

(He shakes Ishmarelic hand)

Thank you for everything my friend. We will finish this

Ishmarelic

I know, you will, trust you senses

(He looks to Innis)

Remember what we thought you. You are the future
my friend

Innis

Thank you

(Looks at Brace)

And you do the same

Brace gives Ishmarelic a head nod. Ishmarelic walks
away

Blackburn

Don't we need him?

James

Don't worry we will be fine without him. He has a wrong to right. A time will come when we will meet up again though. Let's go

(The men head down the opposite way)

INT Nebakah Alien base

Jasper

We're inside the base now

Piro

Where do we go?

Jay

This way

Piro

Are you sure?

Jay

Yes

(The group follows Jay through a room and then another room. They walk up to a big door and stop.)

Piro

This is a big ass door. A giant must walk through here

Jay

Scar you ready?

Scar

Yeah

(Jay opens to door to see a bunch of the alien allies being held captive. As soon as the walk in they see the alien trooper execute one of them. Right when another trooper is about to execute another alien ally Scar runs in the throws his knife which goes through the back of the alien and sticks out of his chest. The team rushes over the their allies. Scar walks up to the alien he just killed and flips him over and pulls his knife out.)

(Isis rushes over to the aliens)

Isis

You ok?

Warber

Yes, they caught us we were ambushed

Isis

Where's the rest of the teams?

Warber

The big one killed them all right in front of our faces. All we could do was watch

Lex

Where's this big one?

(In walks in more aliens pulling their guns out and points them at the group. Mathias walks in. He is about 6'5 and 300lbs.)

Mathias

(He looks at the trooper that Scar killed)

I'm right here. Who did this?

Scar

(Scar walks through the group. He has his knife in his hands and the blood of the alien is still on it dripping down)

I did

Mathias

You are a brave one human but unfortunately for you, bravery isn't enough. You see, I've established a certain order here. Only me and my men kill and you're neither. Therefore, I must kill you to reestablish order.

Scar

You know you're not the first one to say that. I killed a big muthafucker just your size on the Mother Ship. And he said the same thing. Then my general killed the other one as big as you

Mathias

SO your one of the ones who killed my brothers

Scar

(Spits on the ground and wipes his face)

Yup!

Mathias

(pulls out his knife)

Well then this is going to be fun. I will carve you up slowly

Scar

You can try asshole

(Mathias rushes towards Scar. Mathis swings his blade at Scar. Scar jumps back and takes a massive swing at Mathias that connects and causes Mathias to stumble a bit. Mathias gets his footing back and looks at Scar)

Mathias

That will be the last time you touch me filthy human

Scar

(Grins)

We'll see about that

(Mathias takes another swing at Scar and misses. Scar takes a swing with his blade and Mathias counters. The two pushes connects each other and they both fall back)

Scar

I thought that was the last time I was going to touch you or did you mean that time, Ha

Mathias

I will bleed you human

(Mathias rushes again and this time he punches Scar. Scar falls to one knee and spits some blood out.)

Mathias

I told you I was going to bleed you. That was only the beginning. Now get up and accept your death

(Mathias swings again at Scar, Scar ducks the swing and uppercuts Mathias with his knife. Scar cuts Mathias chest and his green blood spits out on the ground. Everyone watches in awe. No one has ever seen an Elite get cut or even bleed before)

Mathias

No no no I'm going to kill you

(He rushes Scar and kicks him in the chest and then grabs him and throws him against the wall.)

Scar

(Scar gets up and laughs but then spits out some blood)

That's all you got

Mathias

I got a whole lot more. I'm going to bleed you human and then all your friends too

(He runs towards Scar and kicks again. Scar side steps the kick and moves to the side. He turns around and kicks Mathias on the back of his knee. Mathias falls to one knee and Scar runs up towards him grabs his head, takes his knife and slits Mathias' throat. Mathias grabs his throat to try to stop the blood from pouring out but he can't)

Mathias

I see why my brothers fell to you

(He drops to the ground and dies. Scar turns around and looks at the alien troopers. They are scared. They look at Scar and throw their guns to the ground and gives up)

Scar

Collects their weapons now

(A few regular soldiers run up and collect their weapons.)

Scar

WE don't have time for prisoners. Therefore, you have two choices to fight with me or die right here.

(Pulls his weapon out)

Now choose?

(Each men look at each other and then one man walks up to Scar slowly to Scar)

Alien

I will fight with you

Scar covered with green blood takes a gun from his soldier and gives it to the alien

Scar

What's your name?

Alien

Sky

Scar

Well Sky show me the way to your AI system

Piro

What about the rest of the aliens?

Scar

(looks at them)

Have you decided?

Sky

They will fight for you too

Scar

Ok then which way

Sky

Follow me

INT Mother Ship Command Center

Ty

Sir, We're winning Sir we almost defeated all their fighters.

Walker

Finally some good news

Ty

Holdup, I'm getting strange power readings heading our way and I mean a lot of them

Walker

How strange

Ty

It seems like there more fighters coming our way but these readings suggest that these fighters are different

Walker

Give me the whole thing damnit

Ty

looks like we have about at least fifty more fighters coming our way but these are way more powerful then the previous ones we've fought and they seem to be as fast as our fighters

Walker

Notify fleet leader, that they have more hostiles incoming

Ty

Yes... Fleet leader Fleet leader new Intel shows that you have more hostiles incoming

Rich

How serious?

Ty

One mistake with these guys and your probably dead

Rich

You hear that guys we got trouble coming our way.
Prepare yourself for it

(As soon as Rich says that they look ahead and see the
alien fighters coming)

Ishmarelic

Rich these are the elite fighters be careful. Their only
weakness is around their booster aim for the boosters

Rich

Understood

Dreke

What Rich?

Rich

Aim for their boosters

Melissa

Are you sure, that's all you got for us?

Rich

Yes

Melissa

ok but we're still outnumbered, I'm showing over 50 of
them to our 10

Arnold

Well I rather die fighting then giving up. Let's do this

(The team waits for the fighters to get closer)

Nicklous

Hmmm

Rich

What is it Nick?

Nicklous

Something unfolding over there

INT Mother Ship Command Center

Ty

Sir I'm getting some more readings

Walker

From where

Ty

Looks like another ship is unfolding right now

Walker

Is it good or bad

Ty

Working on it

(The ship appears and it has the Global Federation
Space Fleet icon on it)

Ty

It's good sir it's one of ours

(Lt. Daniel appears on the command center comm.
screen)

Lt. Daniels

A little birdie told me that your need of some help out
here

Walker

So operation clean house was a success?

Daniels

We surgically removed all of the cancer, my friend

Walker

Good

Jessie

Hey we can catch up later. I have some pilots over here
chopping at wood right now

Walker

Well then I have the perfect target for them. Let's see
how our elite does against theirs

Jessie

Great

(The bay doors of the ship opens and twenty fighters fly
out straight towards the alien elite fighters)

Ty

Should they even be here Sir?

Walker

Better here than on Earth

Daniels

Can I send the rest down to the planet?

Walker

We're working on that right now. We have a few teams
down there trying to disable their shields

Daniels

Ok, notify us when you do. Daniels out

Walker

Hmmm

INT Space

Nicklous

Lieutenant it's one of our ships

Rich

I hope they have backup on that ship

Melissa

We don't need backup

Arnold

Calm down, I'll take backup

Rich

Ok here they come, hold up new orders are to stand
down

Melissa

Holdup What Stand Down no way

Arnold

I'm cool with that. We did enough let them handle the
rest

Melissa

What the fuck are you talking about? I didn't come out
here to stay here and float in space

Rich

Just follow Orders Corporal. Ok they're here. Stand down men. Remember they are on our side

(The elites fly pass Rich and his men and continue towards the aliens. The quickly engage them. A massive dog fight happens)

Melissa

I'm not okay with this at all

Arnold

You don't have to be ok with it, you just have to follow orders

Melissa

Fuck you

Rich

Ok you two stop now. That's an order

Arnold

fine

Rich

We can't enter in that fight or at least not now

Melissa

Fuck that Sir I didn't come out here to just sit and watch

Rich

Melissa, you see those fighters, once they engage an enemy everyone is their enemy. The only thing they know what to do is kill. So unless you want to die, stand down and wait to see what happens

Melissa

Who are they?

Rich

Monsters that we trained to only know to kill and leave nothing alive

(The team look at the dog fight happen. The Elite hybrids are winning destroying alien fighters one at a time and sometimes two at a time)

INT Mother Ship

Ty

They make killing an art form. Like the old Japanese Ninjas smooth and stealthly

Walker

I know. I created them

INT Nebakah Planet

Jay

We're almost there

Isis

I sense trouble

(The group continues to walk)

Isis

No stop. We have trouble coming our way big ones.
Scar

Scar

I can feel it too. Ok men gather up and get your
grenades ready. Ok Isis tell me when

Isis

Ok right about now

Scar

Now

(The men all turn the corner and throw their grenades
at about 50 men heading towards them. Then they turn
about around the corner. They hear all the grenades go
off. Bomb ,after bomb ,after bomb, the whole place
shakes and debris is everywhere. The aliens scream in
pain. Scar grabs his laser rifle and puts it on full auto)

Scar

Move out

(Scar turns the corner and starts to shoot at any alien still alive. One alien throws a body off of him and as soon as he does Alistar shoots him in the head twice. The rest of the men follow behind him and they clear the whole room.)

Scar

(stops to look back at the men)

If your low on ammo take from the bodies.

(Then Sky reaches down to pick up another weapon, from a dead alien but he's not dead and he stabs Sky in his chest and calls him a traitor. Tyler turns around and shoots him in the head. Sky drops to the ground holding his chest. Isis runs over to him. He's bleeding out from the wound)

Isis

Don't worry, you're going to make it just stay here against the wall.

(She takes out her med kit and injects him with the nano machines)

Tyler

Is that going to work on him

Isis

I have faith it will

Tyler

Ok

Sky

(still in pain)

Thank you

Isis

Don't worry stay here and let the ano machines help you. I'll be back for you

Sky

ok

Scar

Ok then, let's make sure they are all dead

Piro

I got one over here

(Alien with wounds in his chest from shrapnel from the explosions. He's spitting blood out)

Piro

Give me the information where's the AI room

Alien

DIE filthy human die

(The alien dies)

Piro

Got shit out of him

Jay

No need this way

INT Nebakah James team

Innis

General we should go this way

James

Yeah let's go

(The team continues to walk and then they come up to a corner)

Innis

Hold up we shouldn't just go out there

James

Let me take a look

(James looks around the corner and sees ten elite soldiers guarding a big door. He turns back to the team)

James

Black, you ready

Blackburn

I've been waiting for this

James

Ok men get out your sonic grenades and on my signal throw them around the corner

(The men all pull out there grenades and get ready to throw them. James and Blackburn pull out their rifles. James sticks his hand out and starts to count down with his fingers. He starts at 5,4,3,2,1 drops his hand and then the men turn the corner and throw their grenades and then turn back. James and Blackburn wait ten seconds. Then ten very loud sonic bombs goes off. James and Blackburn wait another ten seconds and turn the corner with their rifles out. Two of the elite men were unharmed and they just look at James and Blackburn coming. They take out their blades and smile. James and Blackburn stop running and look at each other. They start to smile too and then take out their blades too nd put their guns bsck on their shoulders)

Titus

So you want to fight

Camin

Ha they don't look like anything to fight maybe they need their guns

James

You know one of your kind said the same thing to me right before I killed him then took over the Mother Ship

Titus

So you're one of them, Good. I'm going to enjoy this even more

(Blackburn walks towards Camin and James walks towards Titus. They stare at each other for a few seconds.)

Titus

So are you going to fight or just stare at me in fear

(James spits on the ground and gives Titus an uppercut which lifts Titus off his feet and throws him back. Camin looks at Titus for a brief second and he doesn't see a right hook coming from Blackburn. The right hook connects on Camin chin and Camin falls to one knee. James and Blackburn both take a step back and look at each other then look at Titus and Camin. Camin starts to get up both men spit blood out of their mouth, wipes the excess off their chin and laughs.)

Titus

Ha so you're no regular humans

Camin

We've been waiting for a good fight

Titus

It's been many cycles since we had one

Camin

Too bad we have to kill you. We could have one day
had fun fighting alongside each other

Blackburn

We only fight with warriors who fight for freedom

Titus

Too bad we fight for power and once we finally get rid
of you. We will again be the ones the masses fear

(Titus again reaches for his blade that he dropped after
James uppercut him.)

Now Hybrid let's see what you can do in a blade fight

(Titus runs towards James. James takes a step back and
switches the hands holding his blade and blocks Titus
blades. The two continue their fight.)

Camin

(gets back up.)

So Hybrid how do you want to die, by my blade or by
my hands

(Blackburn looks at Camin and grins. He reaches for his blade and signals Camin with his other hand to approach him. Camin grins back and picks up his blade)

Camin

So by my blade then

(Blackburn takes a swing at Camin but Camin takes a step back and blocks Blackburn attack. The each take a swing and they block each other attack. They swing at each other again but this time Camin, while blocking Blackburn attack counters with a punch that connects to the temple of Blackburn. Blackburn takes a step back and falls to one knee and shakes his head)

Camin

No time for that or you will die

(Camin takes his blade and pulls it over his head and tries to cut Blackburn's head off. Blackburn rolls on the ground and flips to his feet, then jump kicks Camin in his back. Camin falls forward and his head his the wall. He splits open a large gash on his forehead. He stands up and wipes the blood off his head)

Camin

I'm going to enjoy killing you

Blackburn

No I will

(The two continue to fight. James takes a uppercut from Titus to his chest. Titus then grabs James and throws him against the wall. While James hits the wall, Titus runs over and tries to kick him in his head. James sees Titus coming and stands up and places one foot on the wall and flips off the wall over Titus head. He proceeds to take his knife and cuts titus along his back. Titus places his hand on his back and screams in anger)

Titus

No No No you won't be able to do that again

(Titus, frustrated, runs over to James and swings his blade. James jumps back but tip of Titus blade catches James across his chest. James grabs his chest in pain)

Titus

That's only the beginning of your death half blood

(Titus takes another swing at James, James blocks it with his knife in his off hand and hits Titus with his elbow across his face. Then kicks Titus in the chest. Titus falls back a step but continues to fight. He punches James in the face with a left hook and tries to cut him with his other hand. James counters the attack by blocking the blade and cuts Titus on his upper leg. Titus continues to attack. James takes a swing at him with his blade and Titus catches James hand and takes James hand and hits it against his knee. James drops his knife and Titus uppercuts James. James falls back towards the wall. His back slams up against the wall. A big wad of blood comes out of James mouth after the impact. Blackburn sees this and tries to help, but Camin takes a swing with his blade that almost hits Blackburn.

(Blackburn turns around)

Camin

(Shaking his finger)

No, no your battle is with me

(Blackburn frustrated rushes towards Camin)

(Titus rushes towards James who is trying to get back up. Titus tries to spear James through his chest. James side steps the attack and kicks Titus arm, which causes Titus to lose his blade. The blade shoots in the air and starts to rotate. James catches it and stabs Titus in his back and kicks him on his back knee. Titus falls to his knees. James grabs Titus by the head and smashes it against the wall. Then grabs the knife out of his back and slams it through the top of Titus's head. Titus falls to the ground dead. James falls to one knee. Camin see this gets frustrated)

Camin

NO, NO TITUS

(Camin turns and leaves Blackburn and runs towards James screaming)

Camin

YOUR HEAD WILL BE MINE YOUR HEAD WILL BE MINE

(Blackburn looks and flips his knife in the air and catches
the blade part of it and throws it at Camin's back.
James sees Camin running towards him looks over and
sees the blade in Titus head and pulls it out. Camin gets
to James and swings at him. Blackburn's knife finally
hits Camin in the back and pierces Camin's chest and
James stabs him in the middle of his chest. Blood spits
out of Camin mouth)

Camin

Brother…

(James moves to the side and allows Camin to falls to
the ground. The rest of the Aliens stood there in
disbelief. James falls to one knee. Jay runs over to try
to help him up but by the time he gets there James is
up)

James

Now which one of you is going to show me where the AI
system is?

(One of the troopers steps up. The rest of them look at
him.)

Trooper

Follow me

(They follow the trooper through the door and they start to walk down a hallway. The trooper turns a corner and Scar is there holding a knife about to stab the trooper)

James

Stand down my friend he's helping us

Scar

General it's so good to see you. You look like hell

James

Thanks

Isis

Brother, are you ok?

James

I will be fine. Now let's go and find that Ai room

Trooper

It's this way follow me

(Brace and Jay dap each other)

Jay

Good to see that you made it

Brace

Yeah man I'm happy you made it too bro

Blackburn

Quiet down you two

Brace

Yeah, yeah we know

(They walk through another hallway and the trooper stops and turns around to look at James)

Trooper

It's pass this hallway and through the doors on the end. This is the furthest I go

James

(places he's hand on the Trooper's shoulder and nods.)

Ok but you don't have to be afraid anymore

Trooper

Says you, you don't know what's down that hallway waiting for you

James

I do. Ok you can stay, leave or come with it's your decision. Scar, Blackburn, Piro, Tone, Philip, and Lex, we're going to have a shootout, there's no way around it

Isis

Trooper, there is a man we left behind can you go back
and help him

Trooper

Yes I can

(The trooper leaves the group and heads back to find
Sky)

Scar

What's the plan?

James

Aim for the head

Scar

(checks his weapon)

fair enough

James

Let's go for it

(The turn the corner and slowly approach the door.)

James

How do we open it

Trooper

That takes someone with high clearance

Jay

(Walks up to the door and places his hand on the panel.
The panel scans his hand and turns from red to blue.
The door dematerializes)

AI

Welcome Doctor

James looks at Jay and says nothing. They continue to
walk through the door. The walk in to see a big room
with about fifty troopers whom turn around to see
them walking in. Immediately James takes aim at one
of them and shoots him in the head. Scar and
Blackburn follow, then they run to get cover. The
troopers start to shoot back at them. Blackburn grabs
two sonic grenades and pulls the pin on them, Jay looks
at him and nods as the pins hit the ground. Blackburn
throws them at the troopers and while they are in the
air Jay and Brace starts to shoot at the troopers, who
have to duck their shoots causing them not to see the
grenades. By the time the grenades hit the ground and
the troopers notice them it's too late they explode
killing six troopers and injuring more. The shootout
continues.

Isis

This isn't working at all. Innis and Jasper help me with
this

(Jasper, Innis and Isis look up at a metal beam in the
ceiling and they concentrate their thoughts on the
beam. The beam starts to shake and soon it falls
crushing some of the troopers. As soon as it falls Scar
jumps up and rushes towards the troopers shooting
them. Lex and Brace throw grenades as soon as they
see Scar jump out. Scar shoots three troopers and then
the grenades blow up killing some more but Scar
doesn't see and trooper taking aim at him but Jay does.
Jay jumps and knocks Scar to the ground but the shoot
still hits Scar in the shoulder. Lex goes to help Scar but
he doesn't see a trooper taking aim on him and he gets
shot in the chest twice and dies. Wendel jumps out
from cover but as soon as he stands he gets shoot twice
one in the leg and one in the shoulder. Alistar runs over
to help dodging shoots. Piro tries to provide cover and
gets hit in the arm. Alistar grabs Wendel and carries him
to cover. Blackburn shoots the trooper right after that.
Innis shoots the last two troopers and James walks over
to Scar)

James

You...

Scar

I'm fine let's go

Isis

You're not going anywhere not with that wound

Scar

I'm fine

(Isis touches the wound)

Scar

(Screams)

Ok maybe I'm not that fine

Jay

We got to get going quick. There's a lot more coming more than we can handle

James

Agreed. Can you get into the room?

Jay

Yeah I think so

(Jay walks over to the room and opens the door)

James

Great. Get in there and begin the upload. Brace and Blackburn go with him now.

Isis

(gives Scar a shot of nano machines, that start to heal
his wounds.)

You've lost a lot of blood. Can you walk?

Scar

(Gets up slowly with the help of James)

Yes now let's get going before more of those guys come

(The group walks through into the room where the AI is
located)

James

How much time do you need?

Jay

Not sure as much as you can give me

James

Great. Ok Piro, Blackburn, Philip, Alistar, Innis, Tyler,
and you and you grab as much weapons as you can
from the dead aliens. We're going to need as much
firepower as we can get. Isis and Jasper I'm going to
need you over there throwing grenades

Warber

What can I do?

James

Can you shoot?

Warber

Yes

James

Good take this

(Hands him an alien laser rifle)

And shoot to kill

Warber

Ok

James

Hurry up kid

Jay

Leave us alone so we can work

James

Fine.

(The team takes aim at the door. They hear the troopers approaching. You can see the sweat dripping off the faces of some of the inexperienced soldiers.)

Brace

Let's hurry up this time Jay

AI

Intruder alert Intruder Alert in the AI room Intruder Alert in the AI room

Brace

Well if they didn't know before they know now

Jay

Move over

(Jay sits by Brace and the two start to type on their screens rapidly)

Isis

We got incoming and I mean the whole fucking base

James

Is there a way to bolt that door?

Trooper

No not without the AI's Help

James

Shit ok men, calm your nerves, take cover, and let them have it as soon as they start to come through that opening

(The unit quickly finds cover and waits for the alien troopers to come)

INT Space

Melissa

(powers up her ship and grabs the stick)

Sorry Rich but I'm not going to wait anymore.

(She takes off and fly towards the fire fight)

Rich

Melissa stand down that's an order stand down

Arnold

She's not responding...

Nicklous

(Starts up his fighter)

Ok, I'm not going to let her go in alone

Arnold

It's a death wish

Nicklous

(Takes off)

Never leave someone behind

Rich

Damnit... ok I'm not going to order the rest of you to help you can stay here

(Rich takes off. Then Dreke and the rest of them follow behind)

Dreke

You think we're going to let you go in alone

Rich

Thanks my friend

(They engage the enemy)

INT Mother Ship Command Center

Ty

Sir our fighters joined the fight

Walker

Damnit get in contact with Daniels

Daniels

(Pops up on the screen)

Did your men lose their minds?

Walker

Can you help them?

Daniels

Maybe let me contact the squad leader. Lenora get
squad leader

Lenora

Squad leader this is Victory

Squad Leader

Yes

Daniels

You have some friendies coming your way

Squad Leader

Understood Major

INT Space

(Melissa flies into the battle and as soon as she gets
there two alien fighters see her and engaged her. She
has two on her back. Rich and the rest of them are too
far out to help.)

Melissa

Sorry Rich

Rich

Melissa No

(Squad leader does a 360 and comes in between the fighters and blows them both up before they could shoot Melissa)

Melissa

(Nerves is shattered)

...Thanks

Squad Leader

(Squad leader flies away and continues to fight)

No Don't say Thank You. You don't belong in the battle. Leave it to us, the Pros

Melissa

(stops her fighter in frustration)

Who are you?

Squad Leader

(As he destroys two enemies)

A superior fighter, Now leave this area I have no time to babysit you and your friends

Melissa

(Right Hand shake a little. She grabs it with her left. Nicklous flies over her)

Nicklous

No time for Hesitation, Let's go, you wanted to fight so fight. Show them what you got

Melissa

(Let's go of her hand and grabs the stick, shakes her head and takes off)

Absolutely, Right behind you

(They engaged the alien fighters)

Squad Leader

I hope you know I'm not going to save you again

Rich

(Shoots down two planes does a 360 and shoots another one and dips down to miss a shoot from another fighter, that ends up hitting an enemy plane. Then Arnold shoots down the fighter that tried to shoot at Rich)

We don't need any babysitting, over here just make sure you do your job

(The fight continues)

INT Alien base

(Troopers starts to rush in and fire at humans and they return fire.)

James

(turns to Jay before walking out)

I'll buy you as much time as I can but we won't have any backup until those shields go down. All the other teams are dead

Jay

(Looks up at James and gives him a head nod)

James

(Walks out of the room and runs for cover by Blackburn)

How are we looking?

Blackburn

Doing the best we can

(He returns fire back)

We don't have any more grenades, just rifles and it looks like more of those Elites are on the way here too

James

(Gets up and shoots at two troopers)

WE have to give them as much time as possible

INT Alien Base

Ishmarelic

Walks into a room with no lights on

AI

Welcome back Master

Ishmarelic

Lower the shields

AI

I can not

Prime

(Can't be seen)

You think that's going to help you brother?

Ishmarelic

Show yourself brother

Prime

In due time. I sense my other brother's here too. Tell him to come down and join us

Ishmarelic

Fine, have the AI lower the shields then

Prime

Fine, Lower the shields AI

AI

Shields down Master

Prime

Now that they are lower, let's have our reunion, it's been so long since I've seen you two

Ishmarelic

You mean after you taught that you killed us

Prime

It wasn't personal brother, it was business

Ishmarelic

And what business was that

Prime

The two of you wouldn't allow me achieve my goals

Ishmarelic

(Dr. Coaxe appears)

If you mean destroying this universe, then yes we wouldn't have allowed that

Prime

Brother so good to see you again. I see you have Elisa clone here on the planet too

Ishmarelic

Leave him out of it

Prime

Once we've completed our business I will attend to the traitor's clone

Coaxe

You wouldn't dare

Prime

Now, Now Brother, you already know I will but I guess you think you can stop me. Didn't you learn from the last time

Ishmarelic

I see you haven't changed brother

Prime

Look of what I've done soon I will have it all

Ishmarelic

Then what?

Prime

Then I go find him. Once I've conquered his creations.
The master will have no choice but to show himself

Ishmarelic

Who do you think saved me and Coaxe?

Prime

What are you saying?

Ishmarelic

So narrow minded, we shouldn't be here, remember
you plan was to have us in nonexistence but you didn't
know he was monitoring everything. He sent us back to
right your wrongs

Prime

Right my wrongs, you two can't stop me! I've made no
wrongs. I'm justified for all my actions

(He lifts his coat to reveal a sword)

Now I will end you myself

Coaxe

Stop brother

Prime

(Swings at Coaxe but right before it connects Ishmarelic
blocks it with his sword.)

Die

Ishmarelic

You see brother this time it won't be that easy

Prime

Fine then you first, then him, then the rest of them. I will destroy it all

Ishmarelic

(Hits Prime in the face)

You're too concerned with destruction but he wants creation

Third

I don't care. After I destroy then I will create my own universe

Ishmarelic

I won't allow you to destroy everything.

(They continue to fight)

INT Mother Ship Command Center

Ty

Walker the shields are down

Walker

Info Daniels now, I hope we're not late

INT Alien base

Isis

We're running low on weapons and men. This might be
it

Innis

Holdup I'm sensing something

(The hybrid units appear and start to fight the alien
troopers)

Unit Leader

(Walks over to James)

General, your orders

James

(Take a piece of his shirt tie off a wound on his leg)

Take no prisoners, clear this base

Jasper

Isn't that a little harsh

James

Fine, if you receive any resistance subdue them by all means necessary. If they willfully give up detain them

Unit Leader

(Salutes James)

Understood,

Turns back around

Men clean house

(They proceed to clear the room of all the alien troopers and then leave the room. Jay walks out of the AI room)

James

Good job

Jay

It wasn't me it was him. I'm still working on the upload it's harder than the Mother Ship

James

Well get back to it. I'm going to leave you guys here. I have something to do

Isis

I'm coming

(James looks at her and nods yes. They grab a weapon off the ground and checks to make sure it works and then leaves the room)

Scar

Shouldn't we go help?

Blackburn

No not yet, give them some time then we can go

Scar

I've never seen soldiers like that who are they

Blackburn

Monsters, Assassins, killers all of the above. They kill without a conscience and they are getting better at it

Scar

How do you know about them?

Blackburn

I trained them

INT Prime room

Ishmarelic

It's over brother stop fighting it

Prime

There's no way it can be over. I'm still winning

Ishmarelic

AI bring up the fighting

(Screens start to pop up all over the room and you see the secret hybrid army running through the base killing everything and then you see Jay and Brace working on uploading their AI system)

It's over brother, now come with us

Prime

(Falls to his knees and drops his sword)

How?

Ishmarelic

It's the natural process of things brother. Our time is over, it's their time to rule. We don't belong here anymore

Prime

(Gets up and grabs his sword and takes a swing at Ishmarelic. The doors to the room open and James walks in with his knife in his hand and throws it at Prime's hand and it connects knocking the sword out of his hand. He falls into Ishmarelic hands.)

No how could I lose my Empire, all at once

Ishmarelic

Destiny

(James walks over to Prime with his blade out)

Ishmarelic

There's no need he's coming with us

James

That wasn't the plan

Ishmarelic

He comes with us. Don't worry he will pay for the wrongs he committed, just not here

James

(Looks over to Isis, she nods)

Fine but leave now with now before the rest come

Ishmarelic

Thank you, we will meet again my friends when the time calls for it. Rule wisely

Coaxe

(Walks up to James)

It's my time. The young ones know what to do, I thought them everything I could. Tell Walker thank you and I will see him soon

James

OK Doc

Prime

Hmm, I should have killed your ancestor

James

Don't tempt me... I still could kill you right now

Prime

Soon you will understand your true purpose. Soon you will see that we are more the same than different and then you will wish, I finished what I started. More will come, to conquer it all

James

And we will be here waiting for them. Hopefully they will change their minds and come with peace, if not then we will answer in kind

Third

Soon you will see I was protecting you fools, Ha

Ishmarelic

Let's go AI activate departure

(The three disappears. In walks Scar and Blackburn, then the squad leader of the hybrid army. He walks up to James)

Squad Leader

This beast is fully under your control. What are the next orders?

James

Help clear out this base and search for anyone allies still alive. We want everyone off this planet ASAP

Leader

Yes Sir

(Turns around and walks away)

Blackburn

Leader one second

(He turns to Blackburn)

Blackburn

Let's talk for a second

Blackburn and Leader walks out of the room

Scar

What's next James?

James

That's up to you. You could to go back to Earth or stay with us here and continue on with the fight

Scar

And what would I do back on Earth without you guys.
I'm a warrior, I want nothing to do with that Utopia

Isis

(Walks over to James and puts her arm around him)

We did it, we made our ancestors proud

James

Seems like he made it too

Isis

Yes let's reunite our family

Blackburn

(walks back in)

What now?

James

After we evacuate everything living on the planet, I
have a promise to fulfill. We have a surprise for the
universe to see

Blackburn

Even the rectaclcio?

James

Yes, the Doc made a container for them, I had Walker
teleport them to it already

Scar

Are we going to stay here?

James

Just for a little. We have to make sure of certain things
are done before we leave this galaxy

Walker

(Appears)

Yes, this is going to be our new base of operations

Scar

Those aliens are not going to be very happy

Isis

We won't have an issue with them

Scar

Why are you so sure?

Isis

It's the prophecy that governs this universe

Scar

Prophecy

Isis

Long ago there was a prophecy that said the ones who defeat High Command would be the ones that will lead the universe out of darkness into the light of freedom

Walker

Oh I see, that's why he said we must win

Isis

Once we finish what Dr. Coaxe asked us to do with this planet the whole universe will see what we are really capable. You see the real power is creating not destroying. Everyone can destroy but only a few can really create or even restore. That's what makes us so powerful, our ability to create

Scar

I see

Walker

Are you ready?

James

Is everything done?

Walker

Yeah, everything is done. They finished uploading our AI system into theirs. We now have complete control of the monitoring system. We now can see every single planet under they had under their control. Anything living is now off the planet and placed in stasis. The whole universe is about to see magic happen

James

Well then let's go and make history

Walker

Ty we're ready

(They teleport to the Mother Ship)

INT Mother Ship Command Center

Walker

(Rematerialized)

Ok what's the status?

Jay

We're working on it now

Brace

Yeah we should be done in a minute

Innis

Jay upload the omega coding and Brace the Alpha

Scar

What's going on?

Isis

A rebirth

Brace

Ok done

Jay

Finished

Innis

Ok AI test the sequence

AI

Testing sequence now

(Doors to the Command Center disappear and in walks Rich, Nicklous, Melissa, Arnold, Dreke, Sarch, Denise, Jess, Johnson, Adour, and Gethros)

Walker

Proceed

Jay

Oh yeah

(Jay and brace start to type rapidly on the screens in front of them, They finish typing and the AI starts to talk)

AI

Operation Rebirth commencing. Preparing, taking aim, firing torpedo

(A light torpedo fires at the Nebakah planet and hits it. A bright beam of light shoots out from the impact location and which engulfs the whole planet with a light globe emitting light. The colors of the light goes from red, to orange, to blue, to yellow, to black. Then a dark green/blue light shoots out of Nebakah and then disappears. Everyone looks on in awe. No one is talking. The whole ship watches on screens that pop up all over the ship. Every ship in the area watches, not knowing what's going on or what's going to happen next. The after the light beam completely disappears. A beautiful planet appears. It's Nebakah but completely restored. The planet now has oceans, trees, grass, lakes, plants, birds, animals, bugs, and everything it use to have before the Third destroyed it all)

Isis

Now you see real power the real potential we process, our ability to create and restore life

Jay

Damn it's beautiful

Walker

You did it gentlemen, you did it

James

We did it

Scar

So this is true freedom, the ability to create

Innis

You get it now, this is why those aliens won't attack us not now

James

This is our new mission. To rebuild what was destroyed and to ensure it will never get destroyed again

Blackburn

I'm with you James

(While everyone is watching the planet James contemplates what the Third told him about a new enemy approaching. Isis walks over to him and hugs him)

(As everyone looks at Nebakah restoring itself back, a new enemy is also watching, one darker and fiercer than the third and High Command. They are waiting contemplating if they should let their presents be known or remain in the background. Soon they will decide but for now the universe will finally see some peace)

The End

www.ingramcontent.com/pod-product-compliance
Lightning Source LLC
Chambersburg PA
CBHW051954050726
47504CB00017B/20